Voices Whisper

Linda Lee Graham

Voices Whisper is a work of fiction. Names, characters, places, and incidents either are the product of the author's imagination or are used fictitiously. Apart from those clearly in the public domain, any resemblance to actual persons, living or dead, events, or locales is entirely coincidental.

Copyright © 2012 by Linda Lee Graham

All rights reserved.
No part of this book may be reproduced in any form or by any electronic or mechanical means including information storage and retrieval systems— except in the case of brief quotations embodied in critical articles or review— without permission in writing from its publisher, Repository Press, LLC.

ISBN (Kindle E-book) 978-0-9832175-4-1
Print Book 978-0-9864170-0-9

Published by Repository Press LLC

www.LindaLeeGraham.com

Editorial Services provided by Jennifer Quinlan, Historical Editorial

Cover design by Razzle Dazzle Design
Cover image: © Jeff Wickham

Books by Linda Lee Graham:

Voices Beckon
Voices Whisper
Voices Echo

To my husband, for providing love and sustenance throughout

1 Charleston, SC, August 1790

"I HAVE MEAT for the pot, Ma." Poised on the cottage threshold, Liam held the hare so that it was silhouetted in the fading twilight. Then he noted the fire had died.

His shoulders sagging, he tossed the game aside and crossed the gloomy room to kneel at the hearth, poking and prodding until he raised a spark. He'd left fuel close before he'd gone, couldn't she have . . .

Nurse the fire, not the frustration.

"Ma? Did ye hear? I got supper."

She was ailing worse than she'd let on; this was one of her hard days. He couldn't fault her for it. And God's truth, he didn't. Life had thrown so many hardships her way, and each one conquered brought two more calling. She couldn't keep up, not with having the care of him as well as herself. He was more trouble than not, Reverend always said.

The hearth fed, he glanced toward the far corner to see if she had wakened, the pile of bedding now visible in the fire's glow. "Ma? Ma, ye've let loose your blanket." He went to her, chastising her mildly. "Ye'll only be getting worse if ye let the chill in, aye?" He tucked the blanket under her chin, then stroked the hair back from her cheek and bent to kiss her forehead.

Cold. So cold she was, so still . . . as cold and still as death. "No . . . no . . . Ma . . . no . . ." He backed away, one foot stumbling behind the other, over and over until he reached the far wall, shaking his head from side to side, blinded as the tears fell freely. "Please, Ma . . . no . . ."

She wouldn't have left him alone.

She couldn't have. With nothing? With no one?

He fled, fled before watching eyes could mock his grief. He fled from the knowledge that, aye, she had. She had left him alone, with nothing, with no one.

"LIAM."

Liam woke instantly at the urgent whisper, tensed for flight. Rob stood over him, a finger on his lips. "Outside," Rob whispered, canting his head to silently indicate his wife's sister, Becky, who stood over a mewling baby cradled in the corner. Liam felt, rather than saw, the force of the scowl she directed his way. He needed no light for that.

With Rob's aid he stood, his senses still reeling, and let himself be led outside. The flame from the street lamp tossed uneasy shadows about the porch steps, adding to his befuddlement. Resting against the outside wall of the house, he bent with his hands to his knees and sucked in the warm and muggy air.

Rob held a flask to his mouth. "Drink."

He took a sip, then followed Rob's lead and dropped to the dirt, his back against the dwelling. Closing his eyes, he willed the trembling to stop and himself into the present. Not so hard, given the overwhelming stink of the slave trade plaguing Charleston harbor.

Within minutes the shaking stilled and his breathing slowed. Dragging a forearm across his brow, he mopped the sweat and took another swallow of the whisky, this one longer, before capping the flask and handing it back.

"I'll go. I've a bit of blunt stashed. I'll find lodging elsewhere." Rob had enough on his hands without his adding to it. Becky had a right to be fashed; it would be hours before she'd get that baby to sleep again.

"The hell you will," Rob answered mildly. "You're my brother, and I pay more than my share of the rent on this place.

Ye'll stay until Mrs. Hale is ready to leave."

Not true. The brother part. He and Rob were both orphans. He nodded, however, because Rob was the closest he had to a brother, save Davey.

"Right, then. At least I'll get ye some decent whisky, Rob. Don't think I've ever tasted worse than that."

Rob snorted. "Tell me that when ye're newly married with a bairn on the way."

"Willna happen. No' if forfeiting good whisky's the price." He felt Rob studying him and resisted the urge to squirm.

"What brought it on, Liam, the dream?"

He shook his head and a corner of his mouth quirked in a grimace. He didn't know; he had never known. It had stopped for awhile, Rob was no doubt thinking. It had stopped for years.

He reached for the flask again. He'd soon as not talk of the dream. "Fine lad it'll be. Your brains, Jane's sweet nature."

"Might be a girl."

"Ye'll be a good father, whichever. It'll be a lucky bairn."

"Hmmph." Rob stretched out a hand and gripped Liam's shoulder in a rare gesture of affection. "As were we, Liam."

Lucky in Mr. Oliver. He'd been their master, true, but he'd seen well to their care over the years. "Aye, I expect we were at that." Liam nodded, placing his hand briefly over Rob's. "Will ye come back? On a visit?"

"Not soon. I can't manage it."

"Tell Becky it'll be two days more. Mrs. Hale wants to be back in Philly no later than Sunday." She'd only traveled to give Davey and her granddaughter Elisabeth time to settle in on their own.

"And then what?"

He knew what Rob was asking; the worry had been brewing in his gut for days now. He shrugged, having no answer.

Aye, and then what?

He was on his own now. What were his plans for the future?

Philadelphia, PA, August 1790

"Well, well. Look what the tide's done brung in." John glanced up, the knife he held never pausing as he chopped the greens laid out on the table. His mouth widened in a grin, and his teeth shone bright white against the coal black of his skin.

"Did you bring Mrs. Hale?" he asked, scooping up the pieces and dropping them into the iron pot waiting on the tidy brick hearth behind him. "What you thinking, boy, robbing her thataways?"

"Lisbeth doesna have a sister. Thought I'd land me the next best thing. It's good to see you, John." He grabbed the man, gripping his hand hard before taking a seat at the scarred wooden table. John sat opposite him, setting a jug of small beer between them, and Liam reached for it, downing several large swallows gratefully.

"Hellish hot," he said, swinging halfheartedly at the fly circling the lip of the jug. "Dinna ken how ye can think of cooking in this heat."

"People still gotta eat," John answered. Never one to just sit, he reached for a nearby knife and set to cleaning his nails. "How's Rob getting along?"

"Well enough. Did I tell ye Jane's expecting?"

"You don't say." John shook his head, frowning. "Him and Jane shouldn't have gone so far south then. Not with Mr.

Oliver's grandbaby."

Huh. Mr. Oliver's grandbaby. Wonder if that's how Mr. O thought of it.

Rob had cleaned Mr. O's chimney when he'd been a lad of five. Somehow, in the midst of the grime and the havoc, Mr. O had discerned his potential immediately and had convinced the sweep to sell Rob's indenture. To hear Mr. O tell it, it'd been an act of sheer genius on his part. And it had. Rob had repaid the favor tenfold. He was a good lad: intelligent, steady, and honest.

But grandbaby? John was stretching with talk of blood kin.

"Well, Jane's family is down there. I expect they thought Philly too far north." He hoped John would offer up something to eat with the drink. He hadn't eaten since supper last night. "So, is David eating ye out of house and home, then?"

"Ain't seen much of that boy. You think that what's done happened to the victuals?" he asked, a gleam in his eye. "I tells you what, I make something for supper, no one shows. But sure enough, it's done gone the next morning, and I gots to start again."

That answered that, then. There were no victuals to offer up. He grinned. "Something's more enticing than food, aye?"

"Mornin', noon, and night?" John snorted, then took a long draw from the jug before passing it back. "Don't know how long the boy can keep it up."

Liam choked, his fist flying to his mouth as he struggled to swallow. Slamming the jug down, he stomped his feet in turn as he chortled. "John, ye old dog."

John laughed as well, his head bobbing in time with his snickers.

"May I intrude? What's so amusing?"

Ah, hell. Elisabeth.

He turned, his face a friendly mask as he rose to greet her. She wore a simple blue gown, one he hadn't seen before, one that might be deemed modest by eyes other than his own. The lightweight fabric draped enticingly, and his eyes swiftly traced the lovely curves of her petite frame.

Well, if he'd expected her to age into a crone, he'd have

done well to be absent years, not weeks.

"Nothin', lass," he said, "John here's just filling my head with his yarns. Ye're no' intruding. I was hoping to see ye. Ye'll sit with us a spell?"

John stood and checked the water level in the kettle, then swung the iron arm that held it over the fire. "You'll want some tea, Miss Liss?"

"Yes, please." She went to Liam, kissing his cheek in greeting, and he did his best not to stiffen as her fragrance surrounded him. "We've missed you, Liam. Haven't we, John?"

"That we have, missy."

"Ye look wonderful, Lisbeth. Marriage agrees with ye, then?" he asked as he sat. "John here's been telling me he doesna ken how long Davey can keep the pace he's been keeping."

"He works very hard. Did you realize tomorrow's the last day? He'll receive his papers; his indenture will be complete."

David served as apprentice to the *Gazette*, had been for nigh on six years. He sighed, his belly churning. With David a free man, there would be nothing to keep him in Philadelphia. He'd been itching to get to Baltimore for some time now, anxious to start his newspaper.

David had a plan. Of course he did. He always did. He'd planned years ago to make the most of his timed served. So he had. He'd been promoted foreman of the shop in record time and was now known and respected as one of the fastest compositors in the city.

Then, he'd planned to wed Elisabeth when any eijit could have told him it was impossible. The lass was well outside his class and a Catholic to boot. Yet, here he was, married to her—in spite of her father, in spite of his uncle.

David always knew the direction he was headed. It would be nice if it were a gift he could share.

"I knew it to be close, lass. Have ye made plans, then?"

"No . . . no, not yet. There hasn't been time, what with one thing or another."

Liam caught the grin on John's face before the man ducked his head, ostensibly to retrieve the kettle. "Hmmph, well then."

His fingers drummed rhythmically on the table while his mind sought an image other than the "one thing or another."

"John, you and the boys still be fishin' the same spot come Sunday?"

"Sure will, Mr. Liam. We'll be watching for you, now that you be back." John carefully poured hot water into Elisabeth's teacup. "Let's get some food in you, Miss Liss. You done eat nothing this morning."

"Thank you, John," she said, stirring the tea. "Will you come to dinner on Sunday, Liam? I'll stop by tomorrow and invite Mr. Oliver personally, but if I miss him, will you do so?"

"Sunday? John jus' said—"

"Miss Liss does the cooking on Sundays now, and she be getting right good at it."

"Well, then, I wouldna miss it. Listen, Lisbeth, I've a few things now, need looking after, and I should let Mr. O know I'm back. Would it be all right if I came by later, d'ye think, to see David?" He paused, reconsidering, not sure of his reception. He likely should wait a day or two, give the family time to be a family, now that Mrs. Hale had returned. "Ne'er mind. I'll jus' stop by the shop tomorrow."

"Don't be absurd. You're always welcome in this house. Though, would you mind spending time out with him tonight? I'd like to talk to Grandmother about some things, and I haven't—"

He bolted from his seat, planting a quick kiss atop her head.

"Liam? Don't go! For mercy's sake, I didn't mean to rush you off. You've barely said hello."

"Ye're a gem, lass," he said, raising his hand in parting as he hurried to the door. "We'll talk again soon."

"I 'spect he's just anxious to visit with young David, Miss. Liss."

Aye, he was that. Though it wouldn't be the same.

Nothing would ever be the same

August 1790

"David, the watch just called the hour."

He grunted. He'd only just closed his eyes, hadn't he? Hell, he'd be paying all day for the late night with Liam. He reached for her, muttering an incoherent protest when she rolled away.

"It's your last day; you shouldn't be late. I'll wait downstairs, and we'll have breakfast."

Groaning, he opened his eyes. "Nay. Stay in bed, lass." He moved his feet to the floor, gingerly, then rose slowly as he tested his balance. "No sense the both of us up," he said, knocking the candle off its holder with a clatter as he groped for the flint box at the nightstand.

"Shh, remember Grandmother's home." She reached across the bed and took over the task, lighting the wick in several deft moves. He grunted his thanks.

Pulling on his breeches, he went to the washstand. Empty. He eyed the fragile porcelain pitcher with apprehension. Fine things were a burden, you ask him. He hadn't harmed anything in the house as yet, and best the first time wasn't when he was still half-lushed and Mrs. Hale newly home. Cautiously, he lifted it, handling it with care as he slowly filled the basin with water. Splashing water on his face, he held a cool, damp cloth to his eyes until the fog cleared some, then turned to Elisabeth.

"Bring me something midday? If ye're out?" he asked, pulling his shirt over his head.

"Of course. Grandmother will want to go to market and to see you as well. She missed you last night." She came and straightened his neckcloth, then smoothed it flat. "I've invited Liam and Mr. Oliver to dinner tomorrow," she announced, tiptoeing to plant a kiss on his brow. "I'm going to cook."

He picked her up and carried her to the bed, dropping her. "Stay in bed." Sitting beside her, he reached for his boots. "Dinner, aye? Well, they're good friends; they willna mind."

She took hold of a pillow and swung it at him. "Ha."

He pulled on his boots and stood. "I'll be late again, Lisbeth. After quitting time, I'm expected to host my own sendoff. It can be brutal. Less ye come to rescue me."

"No, I'm not going to spoil tradition and give a bad name to wives. I'll drop off food, though, so as the main course isn't spirits." She lay back suddenly, an odd look crossing her face, her hand going to her belly.

"Elisabeth?"

"I'm a little tired. I think I will sleep some more. Go now, and hurry home after your celebration. I'll wait up for you, all right? We'll celebrate on our own."

He grinned. "I'll do my verra best, lass." He gave her a last quick kiss. "Ye're sure ye're feeling well enough, then?"

"I am, and Grandmother is here, if suddenly I'm not. Now hurry, don't be late."

"I'm asking John to see to your breakfast. You eat; promise me, lass?" She wouldn't admit it, but he knew she hadn't been feeling herself the last few days. It worried him.

She nodded, her blue eyes wide, without guile, and he left, though not without pausing on the landing, uncertain if she'd reach for the chamber pot soon as he'd turned his back. He closed his eyes in a brief prayer of thanks at the silence, then trotted down the steps.

DINNER GUESTS. He truly was married. Maybe John would show mercy, leave something substantial for Sunday's meal before he took off tonight. Just as a precaution, in the event Lisbeth's turn at the fire didn't go well.

The morning was quiet, the air hot and heavy. One of the vendors rewarded his slow amble through the Market Street stalls, offering him a sweetbread she deemed unworthy of sale, and he stopped for a moment to chat while she finished her setup. Not because he particularly wanted to, but because he'd learned years ago a smile and honeyed words paid back in spades on this street. By the time he rounded the corner and unlocked the darkened *Gazette* office, he'd licked his fingers clean and filled his belly full.

The shop was empty. Where the hell was Samuel? He circled the room, lighting several candles. That boy should have been in before him. He'd had to leave the comfort of his wife's bed three blocks away, on three hours sleep and a gut still full of whisky. Yet, he'd made it on time. The lad only had to haul his lazy—no, not his concern, starting today. Leave it be.

David pulled the leather apron over his head and moved a candle to his case. He'd finished setting the treaty with the Creeks the day before; the only copy he'd left to complete was Schill's bid for his wife to return to his bed. The man had come in twice this week already, to remind them of it. The way he saw it, the man had wasted his money. Mrs. Schill had taken the five bairns with her; there was no way could she mind them all, not on her own. She'd be back soon enough.

He picked up his composing stick, swiftly setting the first line, then ran his fingers across the row of type. He hadn't had any luck finding a set of metal he could afford. This one was sweet. He'd been fortunate with the press, finding several within his budget to choose from. It didn't worry him that all were in a bad state. He was fair handy; he'd fixed the one here often enough. Maybe he'd choose one Monday, so he could get started on the repairs.

Should he still follow through, though, without a set of type? Would he be better off, seeking a journeyman's wage? A thorny question. Being his own master carried so much risk.

"Morning, David."

"Samuel. Ye're late, lad."

"Aye, but you're not in charge after today. And Robert's

over with Sellers, so no worries."

Robert Store was the lead journeyman in the shop, superior to the lot of them.

David grinned, shaking his head. "Plenty of worries, ye ask me, if that's the attitude of the youth today. Start on those pelts in the corner, aye? Blow out the candles as well. It's light enough now; we dinna need to burn the profits."

Samuel nodded, yawning, his hands raised in a futile attempt to tidy the fair hair that wisped about his face as he obediently trudged over to do as asked. "When's your treat, David?"

David sighed. He wanted to part without a fuss. "Noon sounds good, aye?"

Samuel laughed. "No, Mr. Hall won't allow that. No one will be in shape to work after. I 'spect it'll be at quitting time."

"Noon sounds good," he said again, though of course Samuel was right. Mr. Hall, their master, would never allow it.

"Not likely. Robert told me it's to be just after dark," Ian said from the doorway, a full hour late.

"Morning, Ian. Glad ye could make it."

Ian belched, grabbing his apron and sliding it over his head. "Happy to oblige ye."

"Place is going to hell in a hand-basket," David muttered.

Ian, a big, gangly fellow, had served his apprenticeship alongside David. Though he'd finished his service months ago, he often worked the press when they were shorthanded. He didn't seem to have the ambition to seek full-time work elsewhere and, apparently, could afford not to. Although, to be fair, underemployed journeymen printers swarmed Philadelphia.

Which was why he planned to leave. With no more than the prospect of a dilapidated press. And no type.

And a wife to support. A wife used to many luxuries.

Stop. He closed his eyes, drawing in a long breath. Stop now. He could do this. He opened his eyes and watched Ian at the press, the long tail of his red hair swaying with each impression he made, the rhythm of it somehow soothing.

She wouldn't have all she was accustomed to, to be sure; but, he *would* take care of her.

August 1790

"So YOU ENJOYED YOURSELF after all? Are you planning to sleep the whole of your first day free?"

He woke slowly, befuddled and blinking as a soft hand stroked his hair back from his forehead. Focusing on her words, he remembered. Coming in late, finding Elisabeth asleep in the parlor, sitting at her feet, falling asleep with his head in her lap.

Doing a fine job, he was, proving his worth to Mrs. Hale.

"Glad it's over," he said, scowling as he straightened his legs and worked loose the cricks in his neck and shoulders. "Can do without the scrutiny and the questions."

"I'm certain it wasn't like that at all, David; you work with very nice people. It's only you don't care for being the focus of attention." She ran her hands around his collar, fussing at its wrinkled state. "If you're feeling well enough, we should get dressed for church."

Fully awake now, he looked at her, grinning as he reached out and traced a trail along the neckline of her gown, down the slope of her breast to the valley between, then slowly up again, his calloused fingertip raising gooseflesh on her soft creamy skin. It'd been near two days now, since he'd lain with her. "Aye, we should. I'll help ye."

Smiling, she stilled his hand with hers. "I haven't time for your 'help.' I told Grandmother we'd leave early and walk her to her church."

Elisabeth had set aside her Catholic faith and chosen the Presbyterian church upon marrying him. It might have caused him remorse, if she hadn't already alternated attending Mass with the Anglican service her grandmother favored.

"Right, then." Sighing, he stood, grimacing at the ache the action brought. He kissed her, running his tongue round her lips. "Mmm, peaches. I'll meet ye upstairs, aye? I need to eat."

"Hurry, now."

"Lass, less ye're planning on wearing that nightdress, I 'spect I no' only have time to eat my breakfast—I'll have the time to run to the river, catch it, clean it, and cook it. And *still*, I'd be waiting on you. Did ye save me any peaches?"

"Yes. Eat only those on the plate. Don't touch the ones in the bowl; those are for my pie."

Right. Dinner guests. What the hell was a husband's role when one had dinner guests?

"HOLD ON, BESS. Where're ye off to?"

"The cellar. I forgot potatoes for the soup. Open that, will you?"

He opened the hatch and followed her down, closing the panel after him. Sunlight filtered through the cracks, casting a soft, mellow glow over the bins, and a cool, earthy odor surrounded them, isolating them from the oppressive heat of the city above.

"Feels good." He took off his hat, rubbing his forehead with his sleeve.

She merely nodded as she stood before the potatoes, chewing her lip as she worried over choosing the best. He watched her mouth, tensing as her teeth bit at her full bottom lip, coloring it from pink to red as the blood rushed in response. A bead of perspiration traced a path from her brow to her ear, and he changed its course, reaching to trail a fingertip down the line of her cheek.

He knew she was nervous about the meal; it was to be her first for guests. Maybe he'd be doing her a favor to take her mind from it. The choice of one potato over another couldn't matter much. He stood behind her and placed his hands on her hips, his fingertips meeting over her belly, and pulled her close.

God help him, she smelled as heaven must. Her scent alone made him dizzy with need.

"I didna hear a word of the reverend's, lass, so busy was I with dreaming of you," he whispered, nuzzling her neck.

"Mmm." She closed her eyes, and for a brief moment relaxed in his arms, humming her contentment until the rumble of a carriage outside brought her back to the present. Straightening, she pulled away. "Stop tempting me. I have dinner to prepare. I think I should have added potatoes before church." She piled her selection into her apron, no longer as choosy as she'd been moments earlier.

"I'm dying here, Bess." He reached for her again, and his tongue traveled from her ear to where her cotton shift met her neck, the taste of her shooting straight to his groin. His hand fondled her breast, fingers teasing, and she moaned softly before protesting yet again.

"David, there's no time. And Grandmother's resting in the room next to ours." She tied the corners of her apron up tight and turned toward the ladder. Two of the potatoes escaped and fell to the ground.

"I'll get them." He bent, retrieving them easily in one hand while slipping his other under her skirt, running it up the back of her leg as he stood up behind her, his fingers seeking while his mouth found skin once again and nestled in the crook of her neck. Her knees buckled, and he knew he had her consent. Tossing his handful; he emptied her apron into the bin.

"Days it's been, days. Ha' mercy, lass. I need ye." He turned her to face him, kissing her mouth to forestall any reply. "I'll be quick. No one said anything 'bout going upstairs."

Her lips pinned under his, she made a small sound of surrender, and her hands fumbled at his breeches. He backed into the bin of onions and sat, quickly hefting her gown and lifting her to straddle his lap.

Her eyes met his as he entered her, desire darkening the blue to indigo. "David," she said softly, as her arms tightened about his neck.

He could feel her heart pounding against his chest, her need now as urgent as his own. He loosened her cap so her hair fell about in waves, enveloping them, its scent mingling with that of the earth and her own. He dropped a hand between them, caressing her, watching as her eyes flared in response. With a cry, she buried her face in the crook of his neck, her lips warm against his skin, the tip of her tongue cool.

"Jesus, Mary, and Joseph," he breathed, clenching his teeth as she whimpered and tightened her hold on him. "Ye're like heaven, Bess. So help me, ye are."

True to his word, he was quick. He held her close, whispering endearments as she cried out and clung to him, squeezing her tight until their breathing finally slowed and the world about them drifted back into focus.

Minutes later she drew away, a hand going to her hair, a wry look crossing her face as she glanced about their surroundings and swatted at a fly that buzzed between them.

"Sorry," he said with a slow grin.

"You're not the least bit sorry," she said. Her hands stilled at the sound of footsteps and voices from the floor above. "Oh no, they're early!"

"In the kitchen? That'll no' be Mr. O." He listened. "It's Liam and John. I thought John had the day off."

The back of her thighs clung damply to his as she eased up slowly, uncoupling. "How is it you always get what you want?"

He lifted her easily and set her on her feet, caressing her curves as he adjusted her clothing. She was looking especially lush; must be from keeping pace with his meals. On her own she tended to forget to eat. "Ye didna want?" he asked, smoothing her gown.

"Oh, you know I did. You saw to that." She turned from him and ran her fingers though her hair, loosening the heavy damp strands that clung about her face, then quickly coiled it all into a respectable knot.

He chuckled. "And if I hadna, ye would've left. I'm no fool." He stood, adjusted his breeches, then gathered the potatoes.

"David?"

"Hmm?" He turned to face her, waiting.

She brought a hand to his cheek, then tucked a loose curl behind his ear, the gesture slow and tender.

"My need for you overrides my judgment. It worries me some. Do you think that will change, given time?"

"I hope not," he answered with a small laugh. Her somber expression didn't lighten, and her eyes seemed almost sad. "I've been asking myself that question for years now, Bess. I canna answer it." He searched her eyes. "It's no' such a bad thing, though, is it?"

"I'm not sure." She shook her head, her eyes filling. "No. It's not. I mean . . . well . . . as long as I don't lose you, it's not such a bad thing."

Aye, and that was the crux of it, wasn't it? The vulnerability. The knowledge you were but a heartbeat away from mind-numbing loss. The bring-you-to-your-knees, rip-your-heart-out, kick-you-in-the-gut sort of loss. He set the potatoes aside and tied her cap, grunting.

"Dinna ken where ye'd get a damned fool idea like that," he said, the gravel in his voice grating to his own ears. "No' likely, so dinna cry now." He turned her toward the ladder and patted her backside. "Better head up, 'fore we're missed."

"YOU LADS DID well. That's quite a spread ye have there, Liam." He dropped the potatoes on the table, alongside the fish that were laid out. "John, I thought you were off today."

"Tomorrow 'stead. Mrs. Hale don't mind. Figure Miss Elisabeth could use some help, her first dinner party an' all. You mind we add these fish in with those vegetables, Miss Liss?"

"That's what I forgot! A meat. I thought it was missing potatoes. Oh, drat it all. No, I don't mind, John."

"Taters do it good too, miss. Smells right appetizing. This here bread is pretty and fresh as can be. You didn't need me at all."

"But ye're staying, right, John?" David asked.

John smiled, shaking his head at the note in David's voice. "Sure thing, David. Only saying she don't need me none."

"Thank you for the vote of confidence, John," Elisabeth said dryly, eyeing David.

He grinned wide, counting on dimples to soften the plea he'd made to John.

"I'll be right back," he said. "I need to tidy the mess I left outside."

Liam hadn't said a word, and his scrutiny was near making him squirm. The lad was too canny by half. He followed him out the door and stood watching from the step, silent as David gathered up the rotted shingles he'd tossed from the roof. Finally, Liam spoke.

"What's a God-fearing lad like you doing working on the Sabbath?"

"No' working. Just tidying."

"Hmmph. Doubt Reverend John'd see it that way."

He scowled. Liam was right. Uncle John wouldn't. Didn't mean he needed reminding of it.

"Check your breeks, Davey. Pull yourself together, man."

David felt the heat as his cheeks flamed, and his hands flew to his breeches in dismay. Lisbeth would be madder than a wet cat, she thought anyone guessed what they'd been doing. Finding everything in order, he glared back.

Liam grinned, pushing himself from the door frame. "Ha! I knew it!"

"Eijit." Raising a hand in an obscene gesture, he took off to the front of the house, calling out behind him, "Ye know of stews and such. Lisbeth's nervous. Make yourself useful and see to her needs, will ye?"

5

DAMN. DAVEY TOOK a flyer with a gentry lass in the root cellar. On the Sabbath, no less.

He couldn't even share the story over a pint, seeing as how the lass was the man's wife. Still chuckling, he walked back into the kitchen. Best not speculate on swiving and his best mate's wife—not with his traitorous cock already taking an interest in the subject. Especially not after receiving permission from the man to see to her needs.

"Lass, is your Grandmother in the parlor? I'd like to visit some, if so."

"Go see, will you?"

The scent of roses and beeswax filled his nostrils as he stepped into the immaculate hall, welcoming with its fresh display of flowers, gleaming table, and row of upholstered chairs pressed up tight against the wainscoting. A framed sketch of David and Elisabeth, uncanny in its likeness, sat beneath one of the vases.

Davey had come up in the world, for sure. Like as not, he didn't touch much, save Elisabeth.

He walked through to the parlor. Finding it empty, he lingered in front of a painting, a landscape. It reminded him of Scotland. The work wasn't remarkable; the longing it invoked was. He'd thought himself well rid of the place.

"Can I help you . . . sir?"

He started, jolted from his reverie, and turned to face Tom, Mrs. Hale's servant. The word "sir" had come a tad slow, laden with an obvious reluctance.

"No. Thank you, Tom. I can find what I need, well enough. And it's not here." The diversion of Mrs. Hale unavailable, he walked back into the kitchen.

Elisabeth stood at the fire, scowling at the pot. Bursting into tears, she tossed the spoon she held, and it skittered clattering across the tabletop.

"Miss Liss?"

"Why didn't I remember meat, John? You've certainly told me enough times." She sat at the table, her face in her hands.

"Now, Miss Liss, there's no harm done. Nothing whatsoever wrong with vegetable soup."

"There is; you know there is. I can't feed three grown men on a pot of vegetable soup."

"John's right, lass. I'm happy enough with soup. If Mr. O's still hungry, we'll stop and get something to eat after dinner."

John frowned at him as she sobbed afresh. Seeing the remark invoked an effect opposite his intent, he added, "Ahh . . . I'll go see about Mr. O. Make sure he remembers about coming o'er. Ye want me to send David in, to see to ye, lass?"

"No!" She turned on him, glaring through her tears. "Why on earth would you do that? You think I want him to see me like this? Whatever is the matter with you?" She paused, her breath caught on a sob, and then blew her nose. Holding up a hand, she shook her head and dabbed the linen about her eyes.

"Don't go, please," she asked. "I'm sorry, truly. I honestly don't know what's the matter with me these days, Liam. Stay. It's been so long since we've talked." She indicated the spot on the bench next to her. "Please?"

He hesitated, wondering if he shouldn't take the spot opposite her instead of aside her, until he saw the brief flash in her eyes at his delay. Hurt? Well, hell. Sooner he moved past this, the better.

And he *would* move past it. He always did.

He sat beside her and took her hand in his, as he had done

countless times over the years. So far, so good. John nodded his approval.

"Davey gonna whup me for sparking his wife?"

"Don't be absurd." She clutched his hand tighter, one last sob shaking her shoulders. "I'm done now, I promise. Don't look so alarmed." She moved a loose bit of hair from her eyes and managed a weak smile. "Tell me about the classes you'll be taking."

"Havena decided," he said. Her eyes widened at his abrupt response and he offered up another topic, softening his tone. "I hear Washington's passing through soon."

"Will you go with us? To see the fireworks?"

"Aye, I think so." President Washington would arrive later in the week, en route to Mt. Vernon from New York. The town officials were planning fireworks in the man's honor. He'd enjoy standing aside her, watching her face light up at the spectacle.

Maybe he should decline when the time came.

Jesus, she was alluring. Her blue eyes glistened under long fair lashes, and a faint flush stained her cheeks above lips still swollen with . . . well, that wasn't helping. He looked away, searching for a subject that would dampen his ardor.

The back door opened, and David stepped in, Becca trotting behind. "Suppose ye'll be wanting your wife back, Davey." Becca jumped up in his stead, settling in Lisbeth's lap.

David clasped his shoulder, then dropped down on the bench, draping an arm round his wife, pulling her close, while dumping Becca, her cocker spaniel, to the floor.

"David!"

"She'll be fine. She's a dog, aye?"

A dog given her by Rory Smith, a man Davey had once considered a rival for Lisbeth's affections.

"I thought I heard your voice, Liam. Tom said you were looking for me." Mrs. Hale looked as if she'd recovered some. Though she always held herself erect, not stooped like so many her age, he knew the trip had sapped her strength. He had seen it in her eyes, the silver buried within the gray not so quick to sparkle those last few days, and in her step, slowed by the arthritis that sometimes plagued her.

John pulled a cushioned chair to the table, and Liam held it steady as she lowered herself into it. "I was seeking ye, ma'am. How are ye feeling today?" he asked, taking a seat beside her.

"Splendidly, Liam. I've a letter for you, from Charleston. It arrived before we did, can you imagine? From Miss Jenners."

"Have ye, now?" He shifted in his seat, wishing she hadn't thought to mention that at this moment. Mrs. Hale had set herself on seeing him married, and no amount of talk would dissuade her from it.

He'd have expected she'd be more concerned with his lack of prospects than with his matrimonial status.

Elisabeth smiled and leaned toward David, whispering so as Liam could hear, "She's tasked herself with finding him a suitable wife!" David grinned, his brown eyes twinkling as they met Liam's.

"Now, Elisabeth, you stop that, or you'll embarrass the young man. He's hard enough to help without David's interference," Mrs. Hale said. "Besides, Miss Jenners isn't even one of my candidates. That acquaintance was entirely Liam's doing, and I daresay it won't last longer than any of his others. What you truly need, Liam, is someone who can match that quick tongue of yours."

He risked another glance at David, who, still grinning, made a rapid hand gesture behind Lisbeth's back, in case he needed reminding of the merits of a lass with a quick tongue. He cleared his throat, choking back a laugh, then turned so David was out of his line of sight.

"Ma'am, I appreciate your effort, truly I do. But, like I told ye before, I hate to have ye trouble yourself."

"It's no trouble at all, Liam. Now, Miss Harbinger interested you as well, I suspect." She nodded thanks to John as he set a cup before her.

She had thrown Hannah Harbinger his way the last week of their Charleston visit. He had to admit, she did interest him some. He might not mind discussing it with her further, only not with the audience gathered.

"Yes, ma'am, I'd agree with ye there." He rolled his shoulders and glanced again at David.

David took the cue. "Mrs. Hale, can we delay this jus' a bit? I told Liam I'd help him with a matter this afternoon. We should leave, so as we'll be finished by dinner."

"Good gracious, yes. I'm only thinking out loud."

Liam stood and leaned over to kiss her cheek, whispering, "We'll talk later, aye?" She squeezed his hand, nodding.

THEY WALKED TO the end of the block in silence. Only once they were out of earshot did David start in with his chuckling.

"Dinna ken what ye're laughing at, Davey." Liam grinned, picturing the potential lassie. "She's spot on. Never could resist a lass wi' a quick tongue."

The man howled, slapping his back with a force that had him missing a step or two. "Sounds like ye left a good part of your visit untold."

"Oh, aye, it was a fine time." Though now, with thoughts of Mr. O fresh in his mind, he was thinking his time might have been better spent sorting his future, instead of gallivanting about Charleston. "I'll tell ye more of it later."

"Where are we going?"

"Home." He and Mr. Oliver didn't live far. Just a world and some blocks away. "I've something to show you. Your wedding present."

"I don't need a wedding present, Liam. Get a trinket for Lisbeth."

"Nay, this is for ye. I wanted to, so dinna be ungrateful."

"How is Mr. Oliver?"

"Loose ends, seems. College doesna start for a week, ken? That nosy Mrs. Holmes, the one next door, remember her?"

"The widow?"

"Aye, one of them. Jesus, the street's fair littered with them. I think she's set her cap for him. She came up twice yesterday."

"Well, he may have been lonely, what with you and Rob gone, and his academy disassembled."

Rob had only recently married and moved to Charleston.

And Mr. Oliver's Academy, a successful venture for the last six years, had shut up tight in June when Mr. O opted to take a position with the college.

"Mayhap, but I'm back now. I hope he doesna do anything rash, like marry the woman. I'm no' even sure she can read."

David snorted. "That's no' what one needs in a wife."

"Oh?" He looked at David, wrinkling his nose at the thought of what else Mr. O might need in a wife. Though he'd been his master and guardian, he was also the closest he had to a father. "Seems he might like to have a conversation with a wife now and then," he said. "And have her add to it."

"Be quiet, will ye? Ye know what I mean."

Liam studied him. Lisbeth had a quick and lively mind about her; surely the man appreciated it.

"No' sure tha' I do," he answered slowly.

He opened the door to the strong smell of Mrs. Nailor's boiled cabbage. Wasn't much of that when he, Rob, and Mr. O were the only occupants. The widow leasing the space had made it her own, leaving no evidence of the academy. She was a good tenant, despite her crop of unruly boys, boys that had caused her to be evicted from the last place. Mr. O had some experience with unruly boys.

A feeling of sadness tugged at him. Things had changed so fast these last months. He climbed the narrow stairs to his quarters, David following.

"Look who I brought back, sir."

Mr. Oliver had dragged his chair from its usual spot over to the window. Sunlight streamed in, its harsh light illuminating not only the pages he read, but his features as well. His sandy hair, gone white in the sunbeam, was wild about his face, framing jowls that hadn't been visible two years past. The sadness stopped its tugging and settled squarely about Liam's heart as the man looked up, startled, his smile growing wide as his watery blue gaze landed on the two of them.

Mr. O thought the sun rose and set on Davey, and it wasn't only due to David pulling him and Sean from the sea. No, Mr. O had latched on tight to the lad, thinking he'd finally found the answer to keeping Liam on a straight and narrow path. He'd been right. For the most part.

"David! Good day, lad. I haven't seen you in weeks."

"Sorry, sir. I meant to stop in and check on you."

"Don't be absurd. I don't need checking on. Elisabeth has told me how busy you are."

"Ye've been verra generous, allowing her use of the place. I can see quarters are getting snug."

Elisabeth taught an adult reading class one night a week. At first, she'd held it in the rooms reserved for Mr. Oliver's Academy; now, she held upstairs in the living quarters.

"I'm glad to do so. She's very generous with her time, and the print shop's been very generous with supplies."

"Mr. Hall claims it's self-interest," David said. "The more Philadelphians who read, the more who have reason to buy the *Gazette*." David, with Mr. Hall's blessing, sent all the cracked slates unsuitable for sale her way, as well as slate pencils, both free of charge.

"I expect he's right." Mr. Oliver rose from his chair, placing his book on the table. "I'm stepping out now, Liam. Have you seen where I laid my hat?"

Plucking it from the rack he'd placed by the staircase, just so Mr. O *couldn't* misplace his hat and coat, Liam set it atop the man's head. "Where're ye off to, sir? Dinna forget dinner, now, aye?"

"That's not for some time. I told several of my students I'd join them for coffee." He pulled his hat over his head, then patted the top of it soundly. "It seems Liam thinks I've become a doddering old man in his absence, David."

"Naw, Mr. O, never."

"I'm honored Liam and I are among your first guests, David. I don't believe I've experienced one of Elisabeth's forays in the kitchen as yet. I trust it will be as excellent as everything else she undertakes."

"Aye, sir," David said. "She does well enough. She's just learning, ken?"

"Of course."

"Later then, Mr. O," Liam said as the man lumbered his way down the steps. "Thirsty, Davey?"

"Aye." David sat at the table, his knees dancing a rhythm underneath. "Liam, what do you think my role is this afternoon?"

"Huh?" He brought over the jug of ale, offering it to David first.

"It's no' my house. It's Mrs. Hale's. Yet it's my wife offering up supper."

Liam bit the inside of his cheek, considering. "Mayhap ye carve the meat."

"It's soup."

"Well . . . the bread, then."

"The bread."

"Aye, the bread," he said, warming to the subject. "Then after, ye bring out the whisky."

"Hmm."

"For me and Mr. O."

David sat quietly, seeming uncertain, and Liam pressed his advantage.

"The good stuff, mind." He knew the Hales kept good whisky in the cellar, as John had set him to fetching it once when he had his hands full with other tasks.

"Huh." David took a long draw off the jug. "I think I'll ask Mrs. Hale. She'll know."

Liam sighed as the prospect of a livelier dinner faded. "I suspected as much. Marriage has ruined ye, mate; turned ye to mush."

"I'll remember that, next ye need my help with some lassie's brother."

"Oh, I'm thankful, mind." David *had* got him out of a tight spot last night, no two ways about it. Just having the lad at his back averted all sorts of trouble. "Come o'er here. I'll show ye your gift."

David followed him the few steps to the corner of the room where he pulled aside a piece of canvas.

"Holy hell," David whispered, his jaw dropping, He looked

at the mound of metal, then at Liam, his wonder evident.

"And before ye speak of refusing a gift, ken I won it in a card game in Charleston. Didna pay a dime. Could give it to Ian if ye dinna want it. I know I've no use for such."

David stooped to get a better look at the type case, reaching a hand to touch a corner as if he were caressing a lass.

"How?"

"He was going back to England, bang-up cove. I think it was a lark. Or mayhap his father thought to set him up in a trade, and he didna care for it . . . I don't know."

David didn't respond as he picked up a piece. "Caslon, like new," he said quietly. He crossed his legs and sat on the floor facing it, running his hand over the metal, his expert eye quickly cataloging the components.

"All here. Why? Why would one risk this in a game of cards?"

Liam dropped down next to him. "Dinna ken."

David took his eyes from the type and studied him.

"I don't," he said, spreading his hands, palms up in puzzlement. "I do know he didna look at it the way you are. He didna give it a second glance when he handed it o'er to me."

He'd know there was more to it. But one of the best things about David was that he didn't pry. Liam watched as a corner of the man's mouth lifted in wry acceptance of the explanation.

"I don't have the will to refuse, Liam."

"Ye're no' to refuse. Remember? It goes to Ian, should ye refuse."

"I'll never forget it. Never. Thank you."

Liam grinned and stood. "You're welcome. I'm going to change out of this shirt now, smells like fish."

David nodded, turning back to the metal, absorbed once again as he pulled the tiny pieces out one by one, checking the state of the letters.

Liam watched him a minute before he took to his tasks. Like as not, he'd not only have time to wash and change, he'd have time to finish the book he'd been reading, and all before Davey'd be finished reading the alphabet.

6 September 1790

DAVID LEFT THE SHOP grinning, flexing his fists as he sauntered down the street. Though the man had offered only an afternoon of work, it was worth it to wrap his hands round a set of type. Hadn't lost his touch, not an error in the piece.

Between that and the few hours he had snagged on the wharves this morning, covering for Liam while he went to class, he had more than enough blunt in his pocket to spell John in the marketing tomorrow, plus he could stop for a pint. Liam should be finishing up about now.

He paused at the corner, glancing down the street as something caught his eye. Was that Mr. Hale standing aside that coach? It had been years since he'd last seen him, but he thought the man familiar. He stopped a small boy plodding up the hill. "That carriage, lad—you know where it's from?"

"New York," the boy said.

New York. It likely *was* Hale. Elisabeth hadn't mentioned she expected him. He wondered if she'd even written the man that they'd married. They never talked of her father; she stubbornly refused to speak of the subject. Well, now what?

He sighed, resigned, then walked down the hill to the coach. They'd be sharing quarters, best start on a civil footing.

"Mr. Hale," he said, greeting the man as soon as he turned from retrieving his bag.

Hale looked at him, quizzically, clearly not recognizing him.

"David Graham, sir. Your son-in-law."

The man's face turned white, his lips quivering while his eyes blazed and darted about as if he were struggling for control. David remained calm while the coachman looked on, alert for a morsel of gossip to feed his waiting wife, no doubt. The horses stood placid and motionless amidst the commotion, save for the constant twitch of their tails and ears against the merciless flies.

"Might I walk back with you, sir? I believe we've things to discuss."

Hale pointedly ignored the hand he'd extended, turning from him as he spoke in clipped tones to the station master. David stood, waiting, until the man took off in the direction of the Hale household. He followed.

"Sir, I apologize if I took you off guard. I expected Elisabeth would have written you." Hell, he felt the eijit, carrying on a one-sided conversation. At least his stride easily outmatched the man's; he didn't need struggle to keep abreast. "We were married earlier this summer."

Stopping abruptly, Hale turned toward him, his face inches from David's. "Guttersnipe, you think you're married? She's not of age. All you've done is ruin her."

Had the man gone daft? "I've no idea what you're talking of, sir. Mrs. Hale gave her consent; I believe she's Elisabeth's guardian, is she not? Although Elisabeth is of age, should she need be, she had her birthday this summer, ken?" A look he couldn't define flickered across Hale's face.

"You'll not get a penny from me, not one penny."

Sweet Jesus. They were attracting attention now. He cast a quick glance about to see those within earshot. He wouldn't put it past Hale to call out "thief." He kept his voice low, though full of steel, lest the man doubt his resolve.

"Ye listen to me, Mr. Hale. Listen well." He took hold of his elbow and pulled him along forcibly. "I don't know your reasons for taking a dislike to me. Ye've never said more than three words directly to my face, never cared to know a thing of me. I'll hold no grudge for that, none, for Lisbeth's sake." They were on a side street now, and he slowed his pace, though he didn't loosen his grip.

"I don't want her dowry, and I'll no' take her dowry. That may be hard for ye to understand, but know it to be God's own truth. Elisabeth is my wife now, and there's not a damn thing you can do to change that. Know that I'll cherish her, protect her, and provide for her until the last breath I take." They rounded the corner. Hale, ever conscious of his dignity, hadn't struggled to free himself from David's iron grip on his elbow.

"We've ten steps left for ye to make up your mind, so be quick about it, sir. Elisabeth and I have been staying with Mrs. Hale until we leave for Baltimore, but I can change that fast enough, should ye find the prospect of living near your daughter distasteful. I'll no' give ye a second chance. Time for tha's long past." He released his grip on the man and bounded up the steps.

"I want you out within the hour, boy."

David didn't turn as he opened the door. "Lisbeth? Come, quick. Your da's seen fit to surprise us with a visit," he called into the house. "We'll need to make room, lass, so pack a bag."

But would she? He could mask confidence well enough for the sake of Hale.

But would she, when faced with the choice yet again?

7

"BIT SHORT THERE, Mr. Cross," Liam said, counting his pay as the merchant doled it out, coin by slow coin. "Tha's sixty barrels in yon wagon, no' fifty."

The man frowned, recounting. "Ahh, so it is, Mr. Brock, so it is. There," he said, depositing another coin into Liam's waiting palm. "Ye'll be here tomorrow?"

"I will. For three hours. I've a lecture early on." He took his leave and followed the wharves north, wondering where David was. They had planned to meet for a swim and a pint.

"Per-er-ch . . . you wanna buy an-ee per-er-ch?"

Liam winced as the fishwife crossed his path, the piercing pitch of her cry grating as she strove to compete with the bellow of the oysterman, both eager to unload the day's end goods. The only thing still on the wharves was the air. Still and close, so dense it was near a chore to take a satisfying breath. A blessing in a way, as he'd vow the putrid stench from the leavings of the trade was thick enough for the eye to see, hanging heavy, quivering, as it wafted about the quay. Reaching the dock he and David had settled on, he stripped off his shirt and boots and dove in.

Damn, it was wicked hot. Untying his hair, he ducked his head to slick the long, black strands back from his face before he retied it. He'd give David another minute, then he'd leave without him. Pulling himself out, he sat, closing his eyes to shut out the chaos of the quay as he turned his face to the sun.

He heard the clip-clop of hooves at the same time the shot rang out. Then a child's scream. Clutching his shirt, he leapt up and raced through the narrow alleyway to Water Street, sidestepping debris and those standing in his way. The carriage stood at the entrance of the close, skittering to and fro as the horse carting it reared, its front hooves dancing high. A woman knelt by a crying child, cooing comfort while her hands patted her about, presumably searching out harm done.

He reached for the reins, speaking softly to the beast while the driver tended to his coach and righted the baggage. Little by little the horse calmed and the carriage stilled.

He cast a glance down the road and scowled. The Haberdash lads. And, if their swagger was any indication, both were lushed.

Jamie Haberdash carted the fowling piece over his shoulder; his twin Angus carted the string of birds. Thirteen years old, what was their father thinking, giving them a gun and letting them wander about? With a final whisper to the horse, he released the reins and walked to meet the boys.

"Good evening, lads." He reached for Jamie's gun, depositing it over his own shoulder. "Your ma ken ye've been drinking?"

"We have not, Mr. Brock!" Angus said, hiccupping, his face scrunching as he struggled to assume an indignant expression, the shock of red curls, freckles, and easy smile proclaiming anything but. Liam resisted the urge to reach out and tousle his hair. "It's hunting supper, we were."

"Aye, to be sure. And it's good lads ye are, bringing home a passel of birds like that." He reached inside Jamie's shirt, pulling out the flask. He opened it, sniffing, his nostrils flaring as scents of the sea and peat rose and stung his nose. Upending it, he winced as he watched the precious remainder flow out, mingling with the muck that was Water Street.

"Mr. Brock!" Jamie protested, reaching for the flask. Liam pulled his hand back, out of reach, until he'd emptied the flask of the last drop.

"Ye ken ye can get locked up, discharging a firearm on city streets? What would your ma say then, her birds decorating Mrs. Deputy Sheriff's table?" Tucking the empty flask into the boy's pocket, he handed back the gun, indicating the carriage with a nod.

"That woman in yon carriage complains? Ye'll be finding out for yourselves, quick enough. Now get on home, lads, afore she has a mind to."

"She's coming, Angus. Run!" Jamie urged, tugging on his brother's arm. The boys disappeared as they darted up an alleyway, hastily mixing with the market crowd.

"Sir! You let them, go? That little girl could have been killed! What were you thinking? How on earth will they ever learn?"

Ah, hell. The woman was of a mind to complain.

He turned, then grinned, his eyes traveling over her in frank appreciation. The word "luscious" sprang to mind. Her forest green jacket hugged every curve like a well-made glove, and the woman had curves aplenty. She wore her jet black hair swept up high, framing a set of full, red lips and clear green eyes shaded by long, thick lashes. A mosquito hovered above the perspiration pooling at the base of her neck, and his hand rose to brush it aside before he thought the better of it.

Aye, luscious.

"No worries, ma'am. I'll speak to their mother. They'll learn quick enough, trust me. She's a fast hand with the switch. Is the lassie unharmed?"

"Yes, I believe so. No thanks to those hooligans you've let escape."

He took her elbow and led her back to the carriage. "Are ye newly arrived in Philadelphia, then?"

"Unhand me." She yanked her elbow from his grasp. "Tell me, is it customary in America to let children discharge firearms on city streets while men approach women half-dressed?"

Her eyes traveled over him—with nothing akin to appreciation, and he saw himself as she must: barefoot, shirtless, wearing soggy trousers carrying more stains and tears than he cared to count.

"Hmmph. Ye look full enough dressed to me. Is it they're wearing even more layers o'er in England, then?" he asked. He stooped to retrieve his shirt, slapping it hard against his thigh to shake off the dust. "Like as not, ye'll find it too hot here."

She picked up her skirts and climbed into the carriage with neither a word nor backwards glance.

Liam grunted, turning away as well. Striking though she was, he wasn't of a mood to play. He was too weary from the day's labor in the heat and too heartbroken at the thought of the fine whisky that now lay in the dust. Thinking his boots had damn well better be where he'd left them, he walked back toward the wharf.

Haunting green eyes she'd had. Reminded him of the sea.

He'd near lost his soul to the sea, once.

8

"HEY, JOHN. DAVEY HERE? We were to meet for a pint. I had to amuse myself o'er one."

John passed him a jug. "Young David's done busy, I expect."

"He's no' here, then?"

"He's here. Jane," John said, waving the back of his hand at the woman who came in carting the tea tray. "Git on back out there. Tell Mr. David that Mr. Liam's here for him."

The woman rolled her eyes, then released a long suffering sigh as she turned to do as John asked.

"Mr. Hale done showed up."

Interesting. The man had been absent years. Had he come in response to the news of Elisabeth's marriage?

"Is that right? And?"

"House done be too small. They be leaving."

"Too small?" He took another long swallow before setting the jug down. "Listen, is Mrs. Hale home?" he asked, swiping his hand across his mouth as he stood.

"Don't you be going out there, Liam. Now's not a good time."

Jane walked back in. "They done gone, Mr. Liam. Just a minute ago. You can catch 'em outside, if you be quick about it."

Liam shook his head and walked out. Surely the help had this one wrong. But he caught sight of David and Elisabeth as they started up the footpath, and sure enough, David carried a satchel.

"David! Wait up!"

David raised a hand to acknowledge him as a carriage rounded the corner and stopped in front of the house. A woman waved at Davey and Lisbeth.

"Elisabeth! Is that you? Wait!"

"Rhee? Rhee? Oh my word, it truly is! David, look, it's Rhee!" Elisabeth ran to the woman, grabbing her as she stepped down. They held each other, laughing and shouting nonsense, turning round and round in circles like eijits.

Ah, hell. Luscious, green-eyed shrew was Rhee. Lisbeth's childhood friend, fresh off the ship from the mother country.

And taken for a long ride by the coachman. He bit back a grin. He should intervene, given the exorbitant fare the man likely charged for the meandering route he'd taken. But he didn't. He stood back, watching her and Lisbeth. She caught sight of him in the midst of one of her merry whirls and stopped short, her mouth tightening. Taking Elisabeth's hand, she marched back to the driver, and in the heat of an impassioned, though quiet exchange, he could see money change hands. From his to hers.

"Liam, we need a place to stay."

"What?" Surprised, Liam took his eyes off the women and looked at David. David indicated the front door with a curt nod, and Liam glanced back to see Mrs. Hale at the doorway.

"Elisabeth, child. I think perhaps now isn't the best time for a stroll. Your friend must be exhausted from her journey. Wouldn't you agree, Edward?" Mrs. Hale looked up at her son as he filled the doorway beside her. The man drew himself up, hat in hand, his face a study in contradictions as varying emotions flashed across it.

Well, that explained the anger bouncing off Davey. After a long moment, the man sighed and stepped outside, motioning the four of them in. Liam held back, ready with his string of polite excuses, but David stuck his fist in his back, pushing him along, seeming to require his company.

"Of course, Mother. Rhiannon, what a welcome surprise." He went to her, reaching for her hand, bringing it to his lips. "What a lovely young woman you've become. May I introduce Mr. Graham, Elisabeth's husband? And this is their good friend, Mr. Brock. Gentlemen, I invite you to make the acquaintance of Miss Rhiannon Wynne, our dear friend from England." He stepped aside. "Come inside, and we'll see to your baggage. Welcome to Philadelphia."

"Mercy, Mr. Hale. Doesn't Elisabeth ever tell you anything?" Miss Wynne leaned in to kiss Hale's cheek, embracing him. "It's Mrs. Ross. I married last winter."

9

DAWN FOUND ELISABETH in her garden, yanking out the tiny green shoots that had thrust their way through the soil overnight. She looked up as a hand gently touched her shoulder.

"I'm sorry, child. I expect you've guessed I told him about the baby."

"How could you, Grandmother?" Tears filled her eyes, and she wiped an arm angrily across her face before they could spill. "David doesn't even know. Papa doesn't deserve to know."

"Your father is my son, Elisabeth, and I love him dearly. No matter what he's done. I think perhaps you'll understand once this baby is born." She sat on the bench and patted the spot next to her. "Sit with me?"

Elisabeth struggled to her feet and sat, taking the cup of tea her grandmother offered. "I planned to tell David this morning, but he was gone by the time I woke." For the first time since they'd been married, she hadn't awakened with his arms around her. "If Papa tells him first . . ." She stopped, shaking her head as she pulled out her handkerchief to blow her nose.

"Your father is a good man, Elisabeth. Confused, yes, but deep down a good man. Please understand. I was so afraid he'd make a choice he couldn't take back, or say something he couldn't retract. I had to let him know what was at stake before he did so."

"Poor Rhee, do you think—"

"Yes, poor Rhee." The back door slammed as Rhee stepped out. "Do you think you ladies might apprise me on what I walked into yesterday evening? I declare, the tension was thicker than these abominable flies."

"Don't leave, Grandmother," Elisabeth said, as Mrs. Hale rose to offer her seat to Rhiannon.

"No, please don't, Mrs. Hale," Rhiannon said, taking a seat across from the bench. "I'm sure you'll aid immensely in my understanding this drama. I hope you don't mind if I get right to the point, in case we're interrupted." She took off her hat, swinging it back and forth as a fan.

"Let's start with David, shall we? I have to say; I knew darn well you hadn't given up on him, Beth. Now, I can delight in the fact I was correct. But you were never quite clear in your letters on what precipitated the split. I tell you, it's quite maddening when I can't shake the details out of you in person. Am I to ascertain that Mr. Hale had something to do with it?"

Elisabeth smiled wanly, nodding. "He's never felt David was good enough for me. But he is, Rhee! He's too good for me, he's—"

"Yes, yes, we'll get into all that later, but right now, we haven't the time," Rhee said, interrupting. "I'm sure he's a paragon of all the manly virtues. First, though, while it's only us ladies, I need to know some background. I can't help you going forward if I don't, now can I?" She rose and paced the flagstones lining the short path.

"So, shall we begin, say two, two and a half years ago? Back when things were progressing quite nicely between you and David. Perhaps too nicely, given the way the man oozes—umm, pardon me, Mrs. Hale. Let's just say, I do have eyes." She reached down and plucked one of the blood-red blooms from the flowers, weaving it through the thick wave of black hair she had pinned up behind her ear. Rhee was nothing if not flamboyant, and she'd only become more beautiful since Elisabeth had seen her last.

"I love your garden, Beth. You've done a beautiful job. So

now we get to Mr. Hale. Mr. Hale, naturally possessing a father's instinct, doesn't approve of how nicely things are progressing and forbids you to see the man."

Elisabeth nodded, reaching for her grandmother's hand. The pain still too raw, she couldn't share how Papa had threatened to sell Polly, her maid and cherished companion, down South if she didn't comply with his decision. Or, how he'd played a part in David's imprisonment. My God, if David discovered her father's influence in that . . .

She swallowed with difficulty, forcing the fear past the lump in her throat and tightened her grip on her grandmother.

Rhee's gaze dropped to their hands, then rose as she caught sight of Elisabeth's spaniel. "Well look who's here. It's Becca, right? Come on up here, sweetheart." She sat and patted her lap. Becca jumped up, swiping her face with her tongue. "You're a dear, aren't you?" Rhee laughed and pushed her snout away, settling her down as she stroked her.

"Now, I believe Mr. Hale must have had a powerful persuasion on his side, but that's neither here nor there at the moment. A very powerful persuasion, because even once Papa disappears on mysterious business, you and David remain apart. Perhaps David moved on to another woman, but I think not. He strikes me as a very intelligent man."

Elisabeth laughed. "Rhee, for heaven's—"

"No, no, let me continue. I'm doing well so far, aren't I? Now, I last hear from you in the spring, not more than six months ago, I think. Still no mention of David in your letters. Most of which were becoming quite morose, Elisabeth. I daresay I don't know why I traveled across an ocean to visit such a dreary place as Philadelphia."

"You came because you'd been promising to come for ages. But what about Mr. Ross, Rhee? You were so vague in your letter—"

"Never mind me just yet. Next there's the dashing gentleman from the mill, who, by the way, you must introduce me to now that you've relinquished your hold—he sounds quite prosperous. He did elicit a small spark of interest in you, so I suppose he's somewhat intriguing as well as prosperous. Perhaps I'll have need of an intriguing escort while I'm here."

"I'll be happy to introduce you to Mr. Smith, Rhee, but—"

"In a minute, dear, I suspect we're running out of time. Now, besides Mr. Smith, there's the random mention of this and that boy in your letters, though anyone with half a mind can read between the lines and realize they're only a bother. And then there's David, whom you pointedly omitted *any* mention of in your letters. Mrs. Hale, I declare you're looking at me as if I'm a bit of lace you can't quite decide whether to procure."

"Am I? Don't pay any attention to an old woman. Continue on, please."

"Hmm. Well then, where was I? This is the part where I'm dying to know the details." She set Becca down and reached across, grabbing Elisabeth's hands. "How in the world did we go from morose to married in the space of three months?"

"I'd had enough of morose. I asked him if he'd marry me."

"You didn't."

"I did. And he said yes. We plan to move to Baltimore, though I'm not sure when. Until then we are staying with Grandmother."

"Except your Papa isn't happy about any of this, is he? Is it possible he hadn't even known you and David were married until after he arrived?"

"Well, yes. Things had happened so fast, you see." But she would never have written him. She was too angry over the things he'd done to keep her and David apart, things she would never speak of to David, things she'd probably never speak of to Rhee. Rhee still had a fondness for Papa.

"And I believe you and David were seeking lodging elsewhere when I first arrived? That is, until Mrs. Hale intervened. Where were you going? Is this where that Mr. Brock enters the picture?"

"Well, I suppose we would have stayed with Mr. Oliver and Liam. We may still, if David wants to. I won't have him feeling unwelcome."

"Of course not. Then I could have my own room, couldn't

I?" Rhee stood, shaking her skirts of the dirt Becca had left. "My, it's warm already, isn't it?"

"Oh, Rhee. Don't be angry; it's little more than a block away."

"I'll only be angry if you go to Baltimore and ruin my visit. Because I don't think I'd care to travel to Baltimore. Perhaps your grandmother could entertain me well enough if you were only a block away."

"I'd love to have your company, Mrs. Ross. Elisabeth has told me so much about you over the years; I feel you're a member of the family."

"You'll find she's much better at parties and balls than I've ever been, Grandmother."

Her grandmother squeezed her hand, and nodded her head toward the street. "Child, here's David now. Why don't you go to him and talk things through? I'll take Mrs. Ross inside for breakfast."

"I'll be back, Rhee," she called as Rhiannon waved and headed toward the back door. She kissed her grandmother's cheek. "Grandmother, she's married. Even if she weren't, I'll not have Liam breaking her heart, do you hear me?" she whispered.

"Whatever are you talking about, Elisabeth?" her grandmother asked as she returned the kiss and followed Rhee into the house.

"MAY WE WALK? Do you have time? Where did you go?"

He pulled her into his arms, kissing her forehead. "I went to see Mr. O, 'fore he left for the day. And aye, I'd like a walk. I'd only planned on working here today. I'll still do that in an hour, if Mrs. Hale thinks it appropriate." Taking her arm, he guided her toward the market. "Let's get some breakfast. We can take it creekside and sit for a spell."

My word, she'd aver the man knew every food vendor in the market. Each greeted him by name as they walked through the stalls, choosing an assorted jumble of sweets for their meal. Fortunately he'd eat them all, as merely looking at them caused her stomach to turn.

He led her to a path outside of town, and they walked in silence while he ate and she thought. A hawk circled lazily overhead, screeching its contentment from a cloudless, blue sky, while a rabbit darted across the path, wary in their presence, prompting her to think she should have brought Becca. It was a lovely morning, not stifling hot as yet. Little by little, her melancholy lifted.

"Ye're truly not eating?" he asked, before taking the last bite.

"No, I'm truly not. Finish it."

"Och, did I miss it?" He stopped her as he turned to look behind them. "The creek should be close."

"Look! I don't have these." She walked off the path to a cluster of small blue wildflowers and bent to break a few stems.

"Bess! Watch for snakes, aye? Here it is." He grabbed her hand and pulled her after him, following a game trail barely visible in the waist-high grass, stopping when they reached a thick grove of trees shading an area with little groundcover. He reached a hand behind his head, pulled his shirt up and off, and laid it on the ground. "Sit."

She sat, taking care to set her flowers safely aside while he slid on his heels down the small embankment to the creek. He rinsed the sticky sugar residue from his hands and doused his face with water.

"John saved you breakfast, if you still want more," she called after him.

He climbed up the bank and dropped down beside her, managing a small smile. No dimples. Mercy, the position she'd put him in. Would he forgive her? They were quiet for awhile, listening as the trees sang their soft song in the breeze and the creek tumbled over its pile of pebbles. Finally, she spoke.

"David, I'm so sorry I didn't write Papa of our marriage. He wasn't expected to return until after we'd left for Baltimore. Honestly, though, I know it's inexcusable."

"I think ye owe him an apology as well, lass. It was a shock to the man, hearing it first from me."

Apology, her foot. That's the last thing she'd give. "I'll

speak to him; I promise."

"Were ye ashamed, then?" he asked, his fingers stabbing at pebbles lodged in the dirt.

"If I were the least bit ashamed, I'd not have married you, would I?"

His hand went to the nape of his neck, kneading, and he didn't answer for a long time. Finally he turned to her, watching intently as he said, "Ye did say, lass, your need overcomes your reason."

She flinched. "Don't," she said, moving her head slowly from side to side, her eyes locked on his, willing him to see the truth. "Don't." Her stomach fluttered violently, and she took a deliberate breath, bidding the nausea down.

"Don't do this, David. Please. Don't twist my words. Don't let him make you feel things that aren't true. You know, you *must* know, that I've never been ashamed of you. Never. Not once. You *must*." Sunlight sifted through the canopy overhead, and she watched as something in his eyes softened. Her stomach quieted as he reached a hand to her face.

"Aye. I know. But can ye tell me why ye didna tell the man?"

"I was—I *am*—angry at him. I know it's a childish reason. I will speak to him and try to explain.

"Today?"

"Soon."

Sighing, he took her hand in his, rubbing her palm with his rough, calloused hand. "There's more though, aye, Bess?" He looked up at her, his manner seeming uncertain. "Ye havena had your courses since we've wed. Do ye think . . ."

He knew then. He'd shouldered so much already and now this. Blushing, she nodded. Shifting away, she picked up one of the pieces of sycamore bark that cluttered the forest floor and busied herself with peeling slow, meticulous strips from the husk.

"Are you angry?"

He snorted. "The things ye get to thinking when left on your own." He shook his head, as if in wonder. "Nay, no' angry. Worried, aye. But no' angry. I had a hand in it, aye?"

Relief coursed through her as she heard the truth in his words. Thank you, God. Thank you.

"Well, not precisely a *hand*."

His eyes shot to hers, shock plainly written across his face.

"Well, you did once explain how things work, didn't you? I don't believe you mentioned anything about a hand. I would've remembered if you had." She set aside the bark and reached out, fingering the hair he had tied back, twirling a thick brown curl in her fingers. "You were quite specific, and no, a hand most definitely was not culpable."

He laughed then, his shoulders shaking. He laughed until tears fell. "By God, Bess. By God, I love you."

"Good. I wondered, when I woke up alone."

"Ye did no'! Ye are never to wonder o'er that, no' ever." He lay back on the grass, pulling her with him, and she lay an arm across his wide chest, taking comfort in his strength. She'd be content to lie there for hours, doing nothing more than listening to the steady rhythm of his heart, but she knew Rhiannon was waiting.

"Why did you go?" she asked, trailing a finger through the bristly brown hairs on his chest.

He turned to her, rising on an elbow. "We're to stay with Mr. Oliver, and I needed to arrange it. I canna afford more, lass. What with Congress coming, the rents have risen. It's likely only until your da leaves. I know it's no' what ye're used to, and I hate that, truly. But I think the bairn will be better off if you're no' worrying over your da and me clashing. I'm sorry about your friend's visit, but it's no' so far, and she'll still have Mrs. Hale."

He ran his fingers through her hair while he talked, lifting it and watching it as it fell in waves, over and over again. "And remember, Jane had Rob build a wall in the bedroom. Our space will be small, but it will be our own."

She nodded, searching his expression. He hadn't mentioned Baltimore. She had changed everything, turned his life upside down, when she'd asked him to marry her. He'd had his own dreams and plans, and she hadn't been in them. Baltimore had.

"I don't mind. I'd rather be with friends. But what about

your work? What about Baltimore?"

He brought a hand to his temple, his long, strong fingers massaging outside his eyes. "There's piece work enough here, and I know most of the masters in town. We canna go to Baltimore until the bairn's born. We can't. I'll no' take ye in winter. I'll be too worried without Mrs. Hale near; I'll no' risk it. So we'll go to Baltimore next June. Once your da returns to New York, I'll see about returning ye home."

"My home's with you. It is, David," she said, insistent when she detected skepticism in his gaze. "I've already talked to Grandmother and Rhee about leaving. Only I hadn't planned further than the next few weeks."

"I'm sorry, Bess."

"For what precisely? For making me happier than I ever imagined possible? For giving me the hope and promise of a child? For accepting and loving me in spite of my father's small-mindedness? For–"

"Cease, wench!" He rolled on her, covering her, kissing her until the words stopped, his morning whiskers rough against her cheek. "Are ye planning to let me love ye whilst Mr. O is in the next room?" he whispered.

"Absolutely not."

"Thought not. Then ye'll have to deem it proper 'fore noon. Whilst he's at the University, aye?"

"Aye," she answered softly, one hand pulling his head back down to hers, the other reaching for his breeches.

10 September 1790

"Ye should ha' seen the man's face, Mrs. Hale. Near tae weeping, he was, when I uncovered the heap." Tom placed the tea platter between them, alongside a plate filled with tiny bites of food sized for a lady.

"Thank you, Tom. That will be all." She picked up her cup, taking a slow sip of tea.

"Yes, ma'am," Tom said as he left, with nary a glance at Liam. He knew the man would soon as have him thrown out by the scruff of his neck, had not Mrs. Hale told him to consider him a member of the family.

"I'm so glad, Liam, for both our sakes, that he values the gift. I don't mind telling you I had some misgiving capitalizing on another's misfortune. It did soften the guilt, hearing David talk." She shook her head, smiling. "My word, he went on for hours about it. I daresay I know more about type than perhaps I care to. I'm not sure I've heard him speak of Elisabeth in that manner." She picked up a chestnut fritter, taking a delicate bite. "You did splendidly, Liam, besting the gentleman."

Liam snorted, downing one of the fritters in a swallow. "It was your stake and foreknowledge, ma'am." Odds were he wouldn't have run across the man on his own. Not so many gambling away their trade. The cove had had some talent at cards, though, and there'd been a time or two he feared he'd lose her stash. He grinned, recalling the round that had won him the type. "But, aye, I did do well."

"Now he's anxious to find a press. I shouldn't think he'd be in such a hurry, should you?"

"Maybe not in our minds, Mrs. Hale. But the lad is keen to get his start. We're to lose them, and soon I'm guessing."

"I don't want to think about that."

Neither did he. But he did; it was never far from his thoughts.

"Now, about the type. Mind it remains our secret. I can't have my family knowing I condoned gambling for personal gain." The gray in her eyes twinkled silver as she smiled, and the lines about her face deepened. She reached into the drawer beside her, passing him the letter he'd received from Sally, then proceeded to launch a discussion on the virtues of Hannah Harbinger.

He reached for the letter, tucking it inside his waistcoat, recalling the lassie's saucy smile as he did. Sally was a very agreeable sort, and he had cause to regret not meeting her earlier in the Charleston visit. But it was for the best. Catting about with the granddaughters of Mrs. Hale's friends would do her no credit.

He commented, polite-like, that Miss Harbinger was very charming, and indeed, learned as well. But he didn't go so far as to suggest he'd start a correspondence with her, and Mrs. Hale, keen as she was, dropped the matter fast enough.

"I asked my attorney about investing in the certificates, Liam."

"Did he recommend it?" Mrs. Hale had wanted to invest in the public certificates that were all the rage now.

"No. Unfortunately, he agreed with you. Perhaps I should have you look into the road shares you mentioned." She drew another packet from her drawer, placing it on the tabletop between them. "But first, I've a business proposition for you."

"More gambling? I'm no' always so lucky, mind," he said, grinning.

"I expect it's somewhat of a gamble on my part," Mrs. Hale

said. "Although it's one without nearly as much risk." She looked at him, her voice taking on a serious tone as she held up a finger, in the manner of scolding him. "Don't argue, don't talk back, don't move—not until you hear me out."

Wary now, he inched forward in his seat, the toes of his boots shifting slightly, angling for the door.

"Wha's that ye have there, ma'am?"

"It's a contract." She reached again for a fritter, taking another bird-like bite as her sharp eyes watched him closely. "Mr. Donaldson drafted it."

His mind raced, discarding one scenario after another as he contemplated why she'd feel the need to tell him of her legal troubles. Donaldson was one of the best. He'd help her fine. He chewed on a thumbnail as he watched her, waiting for the rest.

"This country will need fine young attorneys as it struggles to its feet, wouldn't you agree? Mr. Donaldson has lamented the lack more than once over the years, and he claims it's one of the reasons it took longer than it should to settle Mr. Hale's affairs. When I saw Mr. Donaldson this week to rearrange a few things, now that Elisabeth has married, he brought it up again. Not that there is a lack of young men, mind you, but a lack of young men with aptitude." She smiled, shaking her head. "It's the prerogative of each generation, it seems, to disparage the talent of the generation following."

She tapped the packet, her hand still graceful in spite of the bends arthritis had bequeathed. "He's willing to take on a student, Liam. And his fee won't exceed the amount you returned to me upon winning that card game. Actually, the amount you returned should cover a year's living expenses as well, should the young man be of a frugal nature. I believe the student would find him a conscientious mentor. Do keep in mind, please, that I was fully prepared to lose that sum."

Liam's heart raced so, he had trouble taking an even breath as he listened. He had told all, including himself, that he had no firm plans of pursuing law, he was merely considering it. The expense, the years wasted while he saved against it, the unlikelihood of a reputable attorney taking on a bastard, orphaned Scot . . .

"Now, he's more than willing to take a young man of my recommendation. He asked, however, that there be a trial period. As a precautionary measure, in the event he and the young man aren't suited to one other. That's only fair, I suppose. It is a big commitment on his part."

He turned his gaze to the hall, feigning interest in her man, Tom, as he doled out duties to the day help who stood waiting, making swift notations in the ledger he carried as he moved. His interest become genuine as he realized the man could read and write. Leave it to Mrs. Hale.

But he need think of the matter at hand. Some classmates from the college complained bitterly they were no more than unpaid clerks for their masters and would know little more coming out of a law apprenticeship than they had going in. Given what he knew of Donaldson, he was bound to be a scrupulous master. A student of his would likely receive the finest of training and not be put to skink. A student of his would garner respect. A student of his would land well on his feet, with clients to spare.

He wiped his palms down his breeches and briefly shut his eyes, watching as the future he hadn't dared hoped for clicked into place. But was it the future he wanted?

Nay, it wasn't.

Aye, it was.

No matter. He couldn't take it. It smacked of charity for he was no relation. Besides, he'd had enough of being tied down. Mr. O had released him months ago, and he'd yet to do anything about it. He might as well still be bound to the man. As he'd be bound if he accepted this offer. He swallowed, then looked at her, shaking his head. "Mrs. Hale, I canna—"

"Can't—or won't, young man?" Her eyes pinned him, flashing a dark gray as she drew her lips tight. "Make sure you understand the difference, before you let someone else take the opportunity." She pulled back the packet, patting it soundly, grace forgotten.

"I fully intend to sponsor a worthy young man, Liam. I'd

hoped it'd be you, as I expected I might receive a complimentary legal service now and again, in the bargain." She finished her tea in one long swallow and placed her cup down clattering on the saucer, pushing it away as she prepared to rise. "I trust you can recommend another, given your associations at the college? Mind he's worthy, now."

Jesus, Mary, and Joseph! He shook his head, blinking.

"Now, hold on there, Mrs. Hale. At times, it's just like a woman ye are." He reached across the table, covering her hand with his own before she could rise and stash the papers back in her drawer. "Pardon, ma'am, but ye didna let me finish, now, did ye? Sit, will ye? I was aiming to say, I canna thank ye enough."

She settled in her seat and her mouth curved for the briefest of instants in satisfaction, then fell as she let her eyes fill. She made a show of dabbing at them with her handkerchief.

"Ma'am?"

"I was so afraid you'd refuse, Liam. I'd appear a foolish old woman, having promised Mr. Donaldson I knew just the man."

He laughed, rolling his eyes. Jesus, she was something. "Let me see the contract, ma'am. So as to assess the deal ye made us."

She did say there'd be a trial period. He wasn't tied to anything, only thinking on it.

11 SEPTEMBER 1790

"Elisabeth?"

"Up here," she called. She trailed her fingers back and forth across her abdomen, a distraction from the queasiness, then steeled herself to rise.

"I've brought bread. Plain, dreary bread. Your John insisted. Where are you?"

"Right here." She stood in the doorway that led to their sleeping quarters, such as they were, and watched Rhee's face as she topped the stairs and looked around the room, taking it in at a glance.

"Hmm, bookish lot, aren't they? There's not much to clean at least. A blessing, as I'm sure that task will now fall to you." She sat at the table and unloaded her basket, then patted the top, indicating Elisabeth should sit as well.

How she'd missed Rhee over the years. Any other friend would have so much more to say regarding her "reduced circumstances." She left the doorway and went to embrace her.

"Oh, for heaven's sake, dear. It's much too hot to be squeezing the breath out of me." Rhee stood and held her, patting her back. "Go ahead and cry; it's only me."

"Rhee . . ." Memories of the past two days assaulted her and she clung, sobbing, to Rhiannon's shoulders until the tears were spent. Pulling back, she offered her friend a shaky smile. "Good morning."

Rhee forced an indelicate sound through her nose and pushed her down on the bench. She picked up a nearby pitcher, sniffed at its contents, then used it to dampen the handkerchief she carried.

"Here, hold this over your eyes. They're a most unbecoming shade of red."

"I declare; I cry at the drop of a hat now with this baby coming."

"You've always cried at the drop of a hat, Beth. I'm glad to find something unchanged." She pulled forward the bread, breaking off a piece. "Here, your grandmother said this would help settle your stomach. I wasn't permitted to cover it with butter and jam."

"Thank you." She took a small bite and held it on her tongue, letting the taste and smell settle in her mouth before she swallowed. "It's not David, Rhee. I don't want you to think that. And it's not living here."

"I didn't think it was. Any fool can see you adore the man. You'd follow him anywhere and not think twice. I expect it is the baby. I hear tell that carrying does upset one's emotions. That, and your two unexpected visitors."

"I'll explain about Papa later, all right? But you, I'm so glad you're here, so very glad."

"And?"

"I know you haven't cast blame that I've left you at Grandmother's, but I feel bad about it nonetheless. As many years as I've waited for you to visit, and now I abandon you?"

"Stuff. You were right, it's barely a block away. Your grandmother is delightful, and I have the best of accommodations. What more could a guest ask?"

"Rhee, what about Mr. Ross? Gracious, you write that you're coming, then add he won't be accompanying you as a mere postscript. You'd barely mentioned the gentleman before. How did you come to marry, and how long *have* you been married?"

"It's a story. Why don't—" She stopped, her eyes going to

the landing. "Mr. Brock."

"Didna mean to interrupt."

"Well then, perhaps you shouldn't sneak up the stairway." She turned back to Elisabeth and said quietly, "Go get dressed, dear."

"My apologies. Is there any water left in that pitcher, Lisbeth?"

Elisabeth nodded and stood, patting Rhee's hand. "You'll become accustomed to it Rhee; the man moves like a cat."

She poured a small amount of water into Liam's waiting hands, and he splashed it over his face, rubbing it down his neck. She reached for the jug of ale the men kept on the side table, handing it to him, and he accepted it greedily.

"Gracious, Liam, you're soaked clear through. I know you've a lecture to attend; you'll want to clean up. We'll get out of your way. It will only take me a minute to get ready."

He snorted, setting down the jug.

She laughed. "It will," she said, insistent. "I had almost finished when Rhee showed up." She tiptoed and kissed his forehead, making a face at the salty taste. "Wait for me, Rhee, and then we'll go for a walk. Liam will entertain you."

"No. No, I'll come help you. The sooner we leave, the sooner Mr. Brock can attend to his needs."

"MERCY, I THINK I can detect steam rising from the roadway. Let's walk toward the river. Perhaps we'll be in luck and catch a breeze while I show you the sights. There's an inn riverside, one with a tea garden. We can enjoy refreshment while we talk."

"All right. Listen, Elisabeth. I think you should take more care now that you're living in a house full of men. I haven't met Mr. Oliver, but if he's anything like that Mr. Brock . . ."

"Rhiannon! Liam is my dearest friend. I daresay he's the brother I never had."

"Hmm. Well, be that as it may, you should take care you're fully dressed before leaving your quarters. That's all I intend to say on the subject, other than I'm not quite sure his eyes follow you the way a brother's should."

Elisabeth laughed. "Between my shift and my robe, I believe I was more fully dressed than you are right now," she said, with a pointed glance at Rhee's less than modest neckline. "If Liam ogled anyone, though I think he was too weary to make the effort, surely it was you."

"That reminds me! Guess what?" Rhee added a small skip to her steps, her green eyes sparkling with anticipation as she smiled and clapped her hands. "We're to go to the dressmaker tomorrow. Mrs. Hale said that we might. I've the authority to outfit you in the latest of fashions. You've several months before your confinement; there's certainly no need to look quite so motherly yet."

"Oh, Rhee . . . I don't know. David—"

"It's her wedding present. She said she hadn't had the opportunity to give you one yet. Please don't argue. Certainly David wouldn't begrudge your *other* dearest friend the delight of spending a few weeks following silly womanly pursuits."

She ignored the jibe. Rhee knew perfectly well where she stood in her affections. The gift, however, worried her. Grandmother's list of "wedding presents" continually grew longer, and David, when he noticed, that is, bristled at the support.

She squeezed Rhee's hand, smiling. "I suppose not, especially now that you're in want of a wedding gift as well."

"Where are all those people traveling, Beth?" Rhiannon asked, pointing at the ferry leaving the shoreline. The small wherry was filled to capacity, and the oarsmen looked as if they were struggling with the load.

"To New Jersey."

"Is there anything for me to see in New Jersey?"

"Of course not. There's nothing in New Jersey. Those people are merely returning home after visiting our markets."

"Oh, of course." Rhee turned back to her, clearly amused. "And New York? I expect there is no reason to visit New York either, while I'm in America?"

"I don't know why you'd care to. Most of that city will be in Philadelphia come winter."

"Elisabeth!"

She turned at the call, surprised to see the young man hurrying after her, his hand held high to gain her attention. As thin and wiry as he'd been as a boy, he wore ill-fitting trousers hanging by a prayer. She wouldn't be surprised to find the grimy red bandana he'd tied about his neck was the same he'd worn years ago, on the *Industry*. Sailors tended to be superstitious about such things—as well as chronically impoverished.

"Why, Alex! I hadn't known you were in town. Alex, this is my good friend, Mrs. Ross. Rhiannon, this is Alex Mannus. I've known him since coming across. He was a crew member on the ship."

"Showing you the sights, is she, ma'am?"

"Soon, I expect. I've only just arrived."

"Well, then, I shant bother you. I was only wanting to offer congratulations on your marriage, Elisabeth. I saw Davey this morning, and he told me of it. Been a long time coming."

"Thank you, Alex. You were in Jamaica, right? Have you been in town long?" She suspected not. He would have been at Mr. Oliver's last night if he had, camped out with his mates in every spare corner.

"Got in this morning."

"Jamaica? Do you sail there often, Mr. Mannus?" Rhee asked.

Elisabeth watched him as he bounced nervously off the balls of his feet, his eyes darting to and from Rhee, or more accurately, her bosom. Lands, it was like watching a moth drawn to a flame.

"Yes, ma'am," he answered, suddenly tongue-tied as he felt the focus of her attention.

"Not with the summer storms, I wouldn't think."

He shrugged, never having been one to pay much heed to his safety. "Yes, ma'am, even with."

"Do you know much of the country?"

"Yes, ma'am. Some."

"We'll visit later, Alex," Elisabeth said. "I'm anxious to hear of your trip."

He recognized the dismissal as they drew abreast the inn and took his leave quickly, a last wistful look back as he ambled on down the road.

"Gracious, Rhee. You had that poor boy tripping over his tongue. He usually talks up a storm; one can barely get a word in edgewise. Tell me, are you truly interested in the West Indies?" she asked, once they were seated and had their tea in place.

"Yes, I am," Rhee said.

"Well, he'll be in port for at least a week, I expect. Perhaps you'll catch him at a more lucid moment. Now, then. What about Mr. Ross?"

"Where shall I begin?"

"With how you met him. You'd never mentioned him before your marriage. I'm assuming it was a whirlwind courtship? And then tell me why you've come without him."

"It was arranged by Papa." Rhee shook her head, her eyes on the cup she held. "It's my fault, I suppose. I had a number of eligible suitors, but I couldn't seem to make up my mind. So Papa decided for me. He was to take another position abroad, you see."

Shrugging, she sighed. "He said I couldn't be left alone, at least not unwed. He had made the acquaintance of Mr. Ross some time ago and knew of his circumstances. He's a widower—childless, thank the Lord. I can't see myself suddenly elevated to the position of stepmother."

"Is he an agreeable sort, your Mr. Ross?"

"He's not entirely disagreeable. He's wealthy, or I believe I should have come running to you before the blessed event."

"Yet?"

"Yet, here I am." She shifted in her seat, avoiding Elisabeth's eyes as she turned to survey the harbor. "He left me last April after we'd been married less than three months. He had matters to attend to in the West Indies. He has various holdings there, sugar plantations and whatnot. He didn't want to explain in detail, and he didn't want me to accompany him. He decreed the risk of summer fever too dangerous for one unaccustomed to the islands. Plus, he'd be busy with 'family' matters, and I mustn't concern myself."

"Though you're family, as well, aren't you?" she asked quietly.

"Apparently not. You see, I hadn't succeeded in giving him an heir."

"In three months' time? Good Lord. What did you do, Rhee, when he left? And he does mean to come back, doesn't he?"

"He deposited me in Bristol at the home he'd shared with his first wife." Rhee's gaze swung back to Elisabeth, her eyes snapping with fury. "I hated it there, Beth. Hated it." Her hands fisted on the tablecloth, drawing it forward as she grasped it, and Elisabeth reached out to steady their cups. "The whispers. You can't imagine. Such nasty friends the man has, to let me hear their whispers concerning the Negro wench he keeps."

"I'm sorry." Elisabeth closed her eyes as sadness overwhelmed her. She had known Rhiannon since they were in the nursery. Vibrant, beautiful, and loving—she had always been the one expected to make a brilliant marriage to a man of her dreams and mother scores of beautiful children. She could do no less, not according to Mr. Wynne, her papa.

Yet, here she was, trapped in a loveless marriage, abandoned, temporarily or not, for another. "I'm so very sorry."

"It's possible there may be a child or two as well," Rhiannon said quietly, her shoulders slumping. "I'm not entirely sure." Her hands slowly released the tablecloth, carefully smoothing the creases she'd left. "So, I went home. Only to discover I had no home. Papa had sold it before going abroad. I suppose there's a letter awaiting me in Bristol apprising me of that fact."

"Oh, Rhee." She moved to the chair beside her and reached for her hand. "I'm so glad you came."

"I had the means; if nothing else, he's left me well provided for in his absence. I'd nowhere else to go as I wasn't returning to Bristol." Rhiannon gave her a shaky smile, her eyes glistening with unshed tears. "I confess it gives me some pleasure, spending his money on whatever pleases me. That's horrid, isn't it?"

"Of course, it gives you pleasure, and it's not the slightest bit horrid. I shall shore up my energy. I daresay a visit to the dressmaker is merely one item on a long list."

David never paid close attention to what she wore. He'd likely never even notice a new gown or two.

12 OCTOBER 1790

"CAN I BE DOING something for ye, sir?" David asked.

As soon as he'd rounded the corner he had spotted Mr. Hale, standing quietly opposite the townhouse. Concern had crashed through him, as he thought maybe something had happened to Elisabeth, though it quickly lessened to chagrin as he realized the thought made no sense.

He viewed the street afresh through the man's eyes: the rubbish heaped aside the dwellings, the market carts parked haphazardly outside vendors' homes, some filled with goods too spoiled to sell, the stream of dirty, impoverished transients heading in for the evening to each of the four boarding homes the Alley housed, and last but not least, Mrs. Harbuckle publicly haranguing her husband from an upstairs window as he headed into the Bull's Head for the evening, his only response the stream of spittle he aimed behind him.

"No, Mr. Graham," Hale answered, not deigning to glance his way. "I think you've done more than enough, wouldn't you agree?" He turned and walked toward Second Street without waiting for a response.

David stood a moment, stock still with his hands fisted, until the urge to beat the man senseless subsided, then he crossed the street, kicking a pile of rubbish on his way, scattering wide the refuse. He dropped to the doorstep, cradled his head in his hands, and focused on stifling the rage until his breathing slowed.

Because the man was right.

And because Elisabeth worried so when he worried.

Finally, with a sigh, he stood and collected the rubbish back into a tidy heap, lest Elisabeth trip on her way to or from the doorstep, then headed inside, climbing the stairs.

"Hello, Liam. Is Lisbeth sleeping?"

"She's no' here," Liam said, pulling a shirt over his head. "She left hours ago with her friend. Dinna ken if they've been back. I've only returned a few moments ago myself."

"Up for a pint and supper, before we go to the meeting?" Elisabeth had her class of ladies coming tonight, and he and Liam had planned to attend the meeting of the Pennsylvania Abolition Society shortly thereafter. If supper wasn't laid out by now, none would be forthcoming.

"Aye."

They left the townhouse and headed two doors up to one of the neighborhood establishments. "Are ye coming, man?" David asked, his hand hovering over the tavern door.

Liam had paused in the footpath, seemingly absorbed in the foot traffic on Second. David joined him, craning his neck to see what had held his interest. "What is it ye're looking at?"

"Tha's Hamilton." He indicated a short man, one dressed in bright green, standing erect with the bearing of a military man, outside the sign of the shoe. Deep in conversation with the cobbler, his hands moved emphatically as he spoke.

"How do ye know, and what's it to do with supper?"

"He's Secretary of the Treasury, Davey. I know what the man looks like. I've seen him a time or two lately, where he shouldna be, down in Southwark."

"Doesna sound like ye, Liam, judging a man for that." He grunted. "Ye were there as well, aye?"

"I'm no' married, ken? He is. Notice I dinna ask for your company any longer."

And that was a good thing. One less vice to weigh on his mind come Sundays. "He looks a bit a skite to me. Mayhap he's other business there."

"Skite or no', he's an eye out for an agreeable lass as well." Liam turned away, and they entered the tavern. "It's only October, ken; none of them have to be here until December. Did ye know he studied well under the required time, 'fore passing the bar? On his own?"

David grinned, thinking he finally might be hearing a goal, or at the very least, an admission of interest, from the lad.

"Mr. Hall did say he was a man to keep an eye on. I wasna sure it meant it as a compliment."

"He doesna dither about. He's pushing hard on his national bank. He gave o'er New York, he's so keen on the idea."

A central issue that summer had been the site of the permanent capital. Hamilton, a prominent New York attorney and strong supporter of that city, had suddenly bargained it away. The President had finally signed the contested Residence Act, and the federal government would be out of New York City by autumn. Philadelphia had been granted the coveted status of temporary capital, to be followed by a move ten years hence to a permanent site on the Potomac.

"That was in exchange for the federal government assuming all the states' debts, Liam, not for the national bank."

"He needs money to pay those debts, doesn't he? The states owe o'er twenty million dollars on top of what the federal government owes. Where's he to get it?"

Taxes? Probably not. He shrugged. Liam didn't actually expect an answer.

"The bank, David. He'll sell shares in the bank. Not only has he bound the states up tight, he's secured his bank in the bargain. The man's a genius."

The War of Independence was an expensive war, no doubt, and the soldiers fighting it had received debt certificates in lieu of pay. The nation had no money for pay, and whether it ever would had been uncertain. So many of the soldiers, prizing cash over a piece of paper that may or may not ever hold any value, had sold their certificates at a steep discount so they could put food on the table. Other soldiers had exchanged their certificates for land in the west, land that was nigh impossible to settle because of its lack of roads and constant danger from Indians.

And now, with the promise of a national bank, there was a chance the certificates would be paid at face value. Many objected, complaining the speculators who had "swindled" the soldiers would be the only ones benefiting.

"I think Mr. Hale might be one of those dealing in certificates, Liam. He's knee deep into something. I recognized one of the men at the house while I was working on the fence last week, a land agent, and not a reputable one, I'm thinking. I heard talk from a few subscribers whilst I was at the *Gazette*."

"Do ye think Hale knows?"

David shook his head. "No. I overheard him telling the man he was interviewing local firms, that given the distance from New York, he was unfamiliar with Philadelphia agents. I had the impression this was their first meeting." He'd like to think Hale wasn't deliberately exchanging worthless land for certificates. He'd like to think the man truly thought the land was everything he represented it to be. He'd be his child's grandfather, if nothing else.

"Ye need to say something."

"Hmmph." He couldn't see a conversation about much of anything in their future. Not while his fist still ached to wipe the man's face clean. He changed the subject.

"What d'ye think of Rhee, then?"

Liam shrugged, taking a slow swallow of ale. David laughed.

"What's funny?"

"That ye willna speak of her." David shrugged as well. "But ye're right, what's there to speak of? Attractive, vivacious, charming, curves that ne'er—"

"Careful there, Davey, or I'll be telling Mrs. Graham your eye is wandering." Liam drummed his fingers on the bar as he turned to look behind him. "'Sides, the lass is married."

"I didna ask, did ye want to bed her. I asked what you thought of her."

Seemed to him Liam had gone out of his way to be decidedly less than charming to the lass. Normally, he didn't pay heed. The man had too many strung along to keep track. It was a wonder Liam himself could keep track. But he couldn't help but like Rhee, and he was curious what Liam might have seen in her that he hadn't.

"If ye know something I don't, tell me, aye? Lisbeth spends hours out and about with her."

Liam shook his head, saying nothing.

"Then best be making your peace, Liam, whatever it be. She's no' leaving soon."

"And why is that? Where's Mr. Ross?"

"Dinna ken; Lisbeth hasna said." He motioned to the barkeep. "Let's get supper now. I missed dinner earlier."

"How long ye think your wife will be setting tongues to wagging with her teaching?"

Turning the tables, was he? David knew well it was past time she stopped. It wasn't seemly, not in her condition. It wasn't seemly period, for one of her class.

"I told her no' past December."

"I know well enough what you told her. I'm asking how long ye think it will be. I wager it'll be well past December. Likely till ye head for Baltimore. Matter of fact, tha's what she told Mrs. Begly last week."

David bit the inside of his mouth, absorbed in the dents that marred his pewter mug. He could reaffirm he'd only allow her to continue through December—that's when she'd likely start showing she was carrying. Or he could let it go. Because, like as not, somehow she'd end up doing exactly as she pleased, and somehow he'd end up thinking he'd given her leave to do so.

"Did she now? Well, mayhap. I'll have to think on it."

"Aye, I 'spose ye will."

"One day, Liam . . ."

"Oh, I dinna think so." The barkeep set a plate of chicken between them and Liam, bent on being contrary, picked up the leg, knowing full well it was David's preference. "Willna catch me trussed up tight in apron strings," he said, fitting the words in between chewing. He canted his head toward the entrance. "Go outside; see if the lassies are arriving."

David grabbed the thigh remaining and walked to the door, looking down the street toward Mr. O's. Two women were walking up the steps, chattering away; one held a small child by the hand. He went back to his seat.

"Aye, they are. Why?"

"Finish up. We should check back with Lisbeth before our meeting."

He stood, wiping his hands down his breeches. "What's the hurry?"

"One of the women showed with bruises on her face next day. I was thinking her man might be of a mind to follow her this time."

"Damn you, Liam. Why in the hell didna ye say something earlier?" David threw some coins on the bar and left the tavern, not waiting for him to follow.

Liam trotted after him. "David, ye can't go storming in there. Ye'll embarrass Lisbeth." He grabbed his arm in an attempt to slow him, then ran in front of him, blocking the doorway. "Seriously, mate. Think. Take a breath."

Think. His temper did him no favors with Lisbeth. Think.

"We'll sit by, natural-like."

"Move, will ye, 'fore I pick ye up and toss ye?"

"We'll sit and read, right? Natural-like."

"Right."

Once upstairs, he made a quick survey of the room. Ten to twelve women all crammed together, chattering like magpies. Rhee stood in the corner with Elisabeth, helping her gather the slates. No worries, then.

He took the book Liam handed him, then followed his lead in sliding down to the floor, seated aside the staircase. Natural-like.

13 October 1790

"What do you mean, 'later?' I thought we were to walk to the falls this afternoon, Liam. You promised! My mum gave me the hours off, special for it."

Liam looked at her, her sweet face rearranged in a pretty pout, her blonde ringlets dancing beneath her cap as she stomped her foot. "Five minutes is all I'm asking of ye, Hannah. Five short minutes." He *had* promised, and this would be the second time he'd left her standing. There'd be no chance for a third.

She set her hands upon her hips. "Five minutes so you can talk to another woman!"

He grinned. "A friend of my mate's. She's no' another woman." He kissed her cheek, his eyes following Rhiannon Ross as she continued north on Third. "If ye find ye canna wait, I'll understand." He didn't wait for a reply as he jogged up the street, weaving through the market crowd, hurrying to reach her before she went much farther.

"Mrs. Ross!"

Hearing her name, she turned. If he didn't know better, he might think he detected a flash of relief in her expression. She waited until he came abreast, ignoring the ongoing foot traffic that had to veer around her.

"Mr. Brock, good afternoon," she said pleasantly, with nary

a trace of disdain.

Damn, she was a sight for dreams. His fingers itched to touch her face, and he turned his head before taking in another breath, lest her scent lead him to do something he'd regret. He'd have done well to stay by Hannah's side.

"Aye, that it is," he said, examining the shops across the street as if he'd never seen them before. "Listen, Elisabeth said ye were to meet her at Eliza's. I left her there a while back. Was she mistaken?"

"If Eliza's her dressmaker, then no, she wasn't mistaken." She thrust a scrap of paper at him. "Is this the right address? The gentleman at the dry goods wrote it down for me, as I'm afraid I didn't remember the location."

He didn't glance at it. "It's south of here, ma'am, so ye're heading in the wrong direction."

"But . . . " She pointed to a doorway, indicating the number atop it, then looked back at her paper. "Are you telling me, Mr. Brock, that these buildings are not numbered properly?"

He reached for her, pulling her back to the safety of the footpath, as she had come close to landing in the gutter when she stepped back to view the shop numbers. "Dinna ken. I do know it's south of here."

"Oh, now I'll be late!" She squared back her shoulders as a side of her mouth stiffened in a grimace. "Hell's bells."

She laughed at the look of shock on his face, and her irritation seemed gone in an instant. "I learned it from the crew, coming across. It has a decidedly nice ring to it, wouldn't you agree?"

"Ahh . . ." He looked back where he'd left Hannah standing and found the spot empty. "Ahh . . . aye. Listen, would ye like to walk with me? The shop is on my way."

"Actually, I would. I hate to keep her waiting."

"It's an easy city to navigate, Mrs. Ross," he explained as they walked. She didn't take his arm, mayhap as he didn't offer it. "Ye'll do well to envision it as a square, with Market Street in the middle, the numbered streets crossing it, beginning with First down by the river. The tree streets ye'll learn in time; they run same as Market, from the Schuylkill to the Delaware. Sassafras, Mulberry, Chestnut, Walnut—"

"Yes, yes," she interrupted, frowning at the sundial on the building across the street. "Are we almost there? I need to arrive before she changes her mind."

"Changes her mind about what?"

"New gowns. Good heavens, why ever else would one schedule an afternoon at the dressmaker?"

She smoothed out her own gown as they walked, straightening out the lace edging and whatnot that adorned it, drawing his eyes to the enticing display of bosom above the lace. Jesus, just one touch he'd like, one accidental brush of his hand so he'd know if her skin was as soft as it appeared.

"Surely, Mr. Brock, you could have reasoned that out on your own. Why, the way Mrs. Hale goes on, you're destined to replace General Washington in twenty years."

"President," he said, tearing his gaze from her chest. "And he'll likely be long passed by then."

Now Lisbeth hadn't mentioned new gowns. He'd have remembered if she had. Davey would be worried about the cost of new gowns, and he'd have heard it thrice over by now. He bit back a grin.

Distracted, she slowed, her eyes darting about the storefronts. He supposed they were now in territory familiar to her.

"Pardon, what did you say?" she asked.

"President Washington. He'll be dead in twenty years."

She sniffed, the topic no longer of consequence. "That's it, right?" she said, pointing a finger at the small house adjoining Bee's Apothecary.

"Aye, it is."

"The gowns are a gift, so don't you dare tattle on her."

"Lisbeth's a—"

"Yes, yes, I know," she said, interrupting once again. "A dear friend. Thank you for going out of your way, Mr. Brock. It was kind, and I appreciate it." She nodded her head in the direction they'd come, toward the bakery owned by Hannah's family. "And I do believe, if you hurry, that is, you might find that adorable young child is still waiting for you."

It meant nothing. Nothing that she had noticed him, had picked him out amongst the scores of people milling about the markets today. Nothing.

Adorable young child, his arse.

"She might forgive you. Perhaps you could say I'm a friend of the family."

"Oh, aye. That I already did. I tol' her ye're my stepmother." He tipped his hat. "Good day, Mrs. Ross."

14

"I DECLARE, I DON'T THINK I've ever seen Eliza so excited, Rhee."

"Maybe so, Beth. But does she have the skill, do you think, to follow through?"

"Oh yes. The skill and the energy. The only thing Eliza lacks is imagination." Which was probably why her fees were so reasonable. "And your drawings certainly make up for that lack. Are you certain you should have left them? You should know she'll use them for others."

"She's welcome to do so. What purpose does it serve to outfit one's self in the latest of fashions if no one is aware it is the latest of fashions?" She took Elisabeth's elbow, steering her in the direction of the Hales'. "Don't despair; I've a few tricks remaining."

Elisabeth laughed. "Oh, I've no doubt of that." She looked about, then shook her arm free, as she realized Rhee was leading her home. No, not home. To her father's. "I'm not going, Rhee. I'm not ready." Her hand went to her midsection as she backed away.

"Truly? Because I am. And Mr. Hale is past ready." She stopped, facing Elisabeth. "Beth, it's time. David agrees with me as well, so don't use his baby as an excuse. The longer this goes on, the harder it becomes."

"I'll talk to him, Rhee—I told you I would. I need time." She recognized the stubborn set of Rhee's shoulders, and added, "Tomorrow. I will tomorrow, all right?"

"No, it's not all right. You will lie awake all night dreading the day to come, and probably make yourself sick in the process. Listen, Elisabeth, whatever it is, wouldn't it be better to have it past? If not for your own state of mind, then for the baby's sake?" She placed a hand under her chin, pushing it up. "For David's sake? That man worries so about you, you know. Do you want him to convince himself he's driven such a wedge between you and your family that it cannot be breached?"

Elisabeth's eyes narrowed. "You're quite ruthless."

"Is that any way to speak to your dearest friend?" She took her elbow again, gently pulling her forward. "And stop mangling that shawl, or I'll regret lending it to you. Now, your papa is waiting for us. As is Mrs. Hale." She glanced at Elisabeth, as if assessing her composure. "Mrs. Hale, or I—or both of us if you wish, can stay."

Elisabeth shook her head, swallowing. "No." She'd manage on her own. Rhee was right, to continue procrastinating was ridiculous. She was a grown woman after all, married, with a baby on the way. "No," she said again, summoning a tad more conviction.

"HELLO, PAPA."

"Elisabeth, I'm glad you've come." He took his seat after she did, his hands resting easily upon his knees. His attire was impeccable as always, his nails clean and groomed. "I've been wanting to talk to you."

Why, he wasn't even apprehensive about this conversation. Of all the nerve.

"Perhaps I'll be the one to begin." She reached for the teapot and poured a cup of tea for each of them, then handed him his. "I'll not defend my choices in this conversation. Other than to express I'm sorry you can't see past your petty prejudices to see the worth of the man I've chosen. And make no mistake, Papa, I have chosen David."

"Against my express orders."

"Hmm," she said, "Well, yes. I suppose it was against your express orders." She set down her cup and smoothed her skirt, wishing she had thought to bring a handkerchief. Deliberately, she clasped her hands in her lap and looked straight at him. "I expect I thought myself able to make reasoned choices on my own. Well, no matter. What I think we need to speak of is Mr. Wallace."

She watched him closely, taking in the look of bewilderment that first crossed his features, then the look of alarm as his eyes widened. He dropped his gaze to the tea tray and added a lump of sugar to his cup, stirring it. Papa detested his tea sweetened.

"He stopped in, you know, several months ago." Her hand went to her cheek as she recalled the blow he'd delivered. "It seems he thought you'd reneged on an agreement."

"That man is despicable. Always one with a hand out. Why in God's name he thinks I'm the one to fill it, I've never known."

"He is despicable; I'll not argue with you there. John and Tom were admirable, though, in their defense of our home. You needn't worry that you left Grandmother and me unattended in the face of his accusations."

"I'll remember to express my gratitude." Hale nodded his head once, and rose. "He's demented, Wallace is. I hope you paid no heed to his ravings. I do apologize that he disturbed the tranquility of our home. I trust you were in no serious danger and I'll speak to the sheriff about the situation."

"Not in too much detail, please. When all's said and done, you're still my father; I'd hate to have you tossed in prison for manipulating the law. It's quite an awful place, given Grandmother's accounts. She supports the Society for Alleviating the Misery of Prisoners. Did you know that? I'll have to trust her assessment, given David's absolute refusal to discuss the conditions."

She watched him as he made his way around the room, lifting and setting one object after another. Finally, with his hands clasped tight behind his back, he turned to face her again.

"I found David has nightmares of the time he spent there.

Nightmares where he'll toss and turn violently, then lie trembling when I awaken him. It may have been only a few days he was incarcerated, but it made quite an impression. Tell me, did you count on that?"

"I've no idea what you're talking about, Elisabeth." He reached for the bell, signaling the end of tea, as well as their conversation. "We'll talk after supper, shall we? When you're feeling more yourself."

Her hand swung out, swatting the bell to the floor. It rolled toward the window, tinkling a weak response until it lay soundless, its brass reflecting the light of the afternoon sun.

"Bloody hell, do you think you can simply deny responsibility? That I'll meekly sweep this under the rug and dutifully return to being your obedient daughter?" She stood, pacing back and forth before him. "*I* was the one who secured his release. *Me*, do you understand?" She jabbed a thumb to her chest, making her point, glaring at him, and he had the good sense to avert his eyes, a hand going to his throat as he loosened his neckcloth.

"No one else seemed able, Papa. I didn't understand why, not at the time. It never occurred to me the reason was my name, 'Hale.' What an utter fool I was." She shook her head, looking at the carpet, then bent to pick up the bell, carefully placing it on the table. "In my naiveté, you see, I simply assumed others didn't have the wits to follow the proper channels."

How angry she'd been. At everyone—including David. The anger had clouded her vision and distorted her reason. It had been a horrid time.

"It's laughable now when I think of it. And embarrassing. That I thought myself more capable than Liam, Mr. Oliver, Rob—even Robert Store and Mr. Hall." She cringed each time she thought of it, wondering if her own family's involvement in David's imprisonment would somehow come to light. Surely someone would eventually come to that conclusion, given it was normally a straightforward procedure to obtain a bond. The thought sometimes kept her awake at night.

"I wonder if it's occurred to anyone else? Do you think it

has? It's fairly obvious in retrospect that the court papers stipulated only a Mr. Hale could approve the credit worthiness of the bond." David's release had been conditioned on that bond.

She looked directly at him, her eyes searching his, her voice softening to a whisper. "It's the custom to keep court records on file for years, isn't it Papa? Do you know my biggest fear? That he'll find out and leave me. How could he possibly stay, knowing what the grandfather of his child is capable of?"

Hale sank to his chair, his forearms resting on his knees, his shoulders sagging in defeat. Pity moved her, he looked so disheartened. Her anger spent, she took the chair opposite, placing a hand on his knee.

"Why, Papa? Why? Why did you do it?"

He raised his head and rubbed his eyes, his fingers lingering at his temples. "I don't know, Beth, I don't. I hadn't intended to. Honestly, I hadn't. You must believe me. But from the very first, Wallace identified my desire to keep you from that . . . from those . . ." His lips tightened as if to keep the words from spilling out, and he sighed, looking to the empty fireplace, unable to meet her eyes.

"He saw an opportunity, and he took it. The man is cunning and tenacious, for all that he's a drunken fool. And he had a daughter, a daughter I believe your Mr. Graham was attracted to at some point in time. I didn't care to hear the details; I paid him a small sum and washed my hands of the matter. Or I thought I had."

And the daughter, Sarah Wallace, had named David the father of her unborn child. Given the Wallaces had no means of supporting the baby, it had been only a matter of time before the Guardians of the Poor tossed David into jail, pending receipt of a bond guaranteeing his payment of child support.

Papa added another lump of sugar to the tea he'd left cooling, and brought it to his lips. Grimacing at the taste, he set it down.

"Elisabeth, I have felt regret. I doubt you'll believe it, but I have. Not that I thought of it often, I confess, but when I did, I did so with a feeling I can't quite explain. A feeling that it was another who made those choices. I'll admit, if you hadn't found out, I'd be content to ignore the regret." He looked at her, his eyes traveling to her belly.

"I don't hate your Mr. Graham. In truth, I haven't given him much thought at all. I do find I dislike what he represents. The naked ambition, the stubborn inability to ascertain and appreciate one's station in life."

She bit her tongue against any response. If this was to be his apology, Rhee, Grandmother, and David were to be sorely disappointed in her refusal to accept reconciliation.

"I'm aware your grandmother sees my actions as approaching unforgivable and that you may see them as completely unforgivable. As it stands, I'm forced to concede you may be right, and I may be wrong. I'll admit the concession is out of fear I'll never see my grandchild and that I'll be viewed as a pariah by those I love. I sincerely hope it will become more, that I'll truly accept your marriage to Mr. Graham. I pray I will. I fear I have many faults, Elisabeth, and without your mother's guidance they seem to have run rampant."

Oh, cunning, bringing up Mama. She kept silent.

"You remind me so much of your mother, Beth," he said, his watery blue eyes beseeching her. "Perhaps you could see it in yourself to provide the guidance I've been lacking without her? You have my apology. I truly am sorry for the weakness I displayed. I'll apologize to your Mr. . . . . to David as well."

"David doesn't know. And he's not to; do you understand? You may apologize for your past disrespect and rudeness, but not for your involvement with Mr. Wallace." Detecting the relief in his eyes, she almost reconsidered. But no good could come of David knowing, none.

"Very well, Beth, as you wish." He stood and reached for her hand, drawing her up and embracing her. Slowly, she returned the gesture. Mama would have expected no less from her.

15 October 1790

"WHAT ARE ALL THESE, Elisabeth?" Rhee asked, thumbing through the notebooks stacked on the table.

"Oh, Rhee, don't touch!" She tried to respect the men's privacy, truly she did, but it was hard in a place this small, especially as they always left things lying about. Except those notebooks. Liam was uncommonly careful with those. She was surprised to see he had left them on the table. "Those are Liam's, and he insists they're in a certain order. He'll know for certain if they've been shifted."

Rhee ignored her, opening one and skimming the pages, then another, her brow furrowed. "Are they to do with the college?"

Elisabeth looked over Rhee's shoulder, curious herself. He'd labeled the first one "Law of Nature," and inside it looked as if he were listing laws under headings of land and civil, criminal, and ecclesiastic. The next one was bare, save for his headings. Four others were filled with what seemed to be legal terms, definitions, and case summaries.

It surprised her, the words written. Liam had stubbornly refused to admit that he had an interest in pursuing law. What he told himself was anyone's guess; he simply refused to speak of the matter and she had finally ceased questioning him.

Any fool could see he'd make the perfect attorney. For

years now, he'd shown an avid interest in the new government—the laws that governed it and the men that presided over it. David went to Liam when he questioned a concept. Liam—not Mr. Hall, not Mr. Oliver. The man had an unerring ability to explain the unexplainable and to argue the unarguable.

He wasn't happy, doing whatever it was he was doing. She knew that, even if he didn't. It puzzled her, worried her, and made her sad, as she'd never before known him to be aimless. She had begun to suspect self-doubt held him back. Why, she couldn't imagine. But what else could it be?

"I don't know, Rhee. I don't believe so, not directly anyway. I thought his courses were Latin and Euclid's Elements. Or perhaps Latin and geography; he's so maddeningly vague when I ask." She left Rhee's side and sat to change her shoes. They were expected at Grandmother's shortly, for supper. "It's my guess they relate to the work he's doing with Mr. Donaldson. Did Grandmother tell you?"

"She's mentioned something about a trial clerkship, but I suppose I didn't think it would require this level of effort. Why, he has notes here on theory as well as what appears to be current cases, all of them quite concise."

Elisabeth laughed, remembering Rhee had an older brother, a stepbrother, who was an attorney. "Mercy, Rhee. I'm not sure why you have such a poor opinion of Liam. He's quite brilliant."

Rhee appeared lost in thought, then she closed the notebook and returned it to the pile, carefully straightening the edges so they'd appear undisturbed.

"I'm not sure where he finds the time to be brilliant, given the activities I've seen him engage in. I've been in Philadelphia . . ." She paused, cocking her head while she thought. "Six weeks. Yes, I've been here all of six weeks, and I'll warrant I've seen him on the streets with five different girls, all young enough to be . . . well, very young, let's leave it at that."

"I didn't mean to imply he was brilliant with his personal affairs, quite the contrary. Will you help me with these buttons? David should be home soon. I want to be ready."

"Shall I set out the ale as well? I made certain it was of a stronger variety than the last we purchased." She reached for the jug, then stopped, her hand poised in midair. "No, perhaps it should be whisky."

"Oh, Rhee, stop!" Elisabeth said, laughing. "It won't be that bad."

"Well, supper last week doesn't rank high on my list of enjoyable evenings." Rhee grabbed her shoulders and spun her around. "Let's get you dressed, then I'll hurry home. Because, on further reflection, I believe it should be Mr. Hale I douse with the whisky."

"IF HE SAYS one word about 'steady work,' we will walk out. One word." She closed the door and skipped down the steps, taking David's hand and swinging it as they walked. "So eat fast, because it won't be but minutes before he does."

"'Steady work' is two words."

"Ahh, so it is. Aren't you in a generous mood? Just two words, then."

"Dinna fash, Bess. I don't take it to heart. He's every right to question."

He squeezed her hand as they walked and gave her a smile—a smile that didn't quite reach his eyes, a smile that didn't flaunt his dimples, a smile that she had come to know as his married-David-with-a-baby-on-the-way smile.

She turned her head as her eyes filled, determined not to add tears to his worry, and tried again.

"Ian stopped by today." Ian's brother had a boat, and had offered it to David and Ian for the day as payment for repairing his wagon. They had been planning the outing for weeks. "He wanted to know if you still planned to fish with him on Saturday."

"Oh, aye. Dinna ken why he'd be asking ye that."

"Actually, I told him no." She shot him a sideways glance from under her lashes. "I told him no, you were much too busy with worry. That you haven't had a second to spare for anything other than worry for weeks, truth be told. It's actually a full time occupation, this worry, and—" He cut off her words with a kiss, picking her up off the footpath to meet his lips, turning her in a slow circle. When he released her he wore a smile, a smile that at last reached his eyes.

"Ye did not."

She reached up and brushed a loose curl from his forehead. "No, I did not." She placed a finger on his mouth, slowly tracing its fullness as she watched his eyes, his pupils flaring at her touch. "But I did ask him to bring you back in time for supper. It seems Liam has plans for Mr. Oliver that will extend straight through supper and beyond. Some event or other at the City Tavern."

He grinned, this time displaying dimples. It was the grin that never failed to turn her knees to pudding. Thankfully, he held her tight as he bent to kiss her again, and she reached her arms around his neck, pulling him close.

Hopefully, Papa wasn't standing at the window. He'd frown on her kissing a man in full view of the neighbors, husband or not. They might be in for more than words of "steady work."

16 October 1790

DAVID HOOTED WITH LAUGHTER, slapping his palm down hard on the table. "I'm thinking she won, Liam."

He hadn't had a hope in hell of winning himself. Not against Liam and Mr. O. An underdog like Rhiannon Ross taking the hand was satisfying indeed.

"Hah!" Rhee rose from the table, twirling round on her toes, her hands outstretched, reveling in her victory. David gestured his approval with a thumb in her direction.

"Don't be foolish," Liam said, squinting as he looked hard at the hand. "Hmmph, well, mayhap."

"Oh, no, there's no 'mayhap' about it, Liam. The lass won. Fair and square, as I see it. Congratulations, Mrs. Ross," Mr. Oliver said, looking at Rhiannon with a new-found respect. Not often did even Liam best Mr. O at whist.

"Why, thank you, Mr. Oliver, for your very gracious concession." She came up behind him, draping her arms around his neck and planting a kiss atop his jumble of sandy white hair. David grinned as he watched the man fumble with his spectacles, his color rising.

With a pointed glance at Liam, Rhee came back to her seat and reached out, scooping the meager stakes to her side of the table.

"I'll walk ye home, Rhee, soon as I check on Bess."

"Liam can do that, David," Mr. Oliver said.

Except for Liam hadn't offered and never had. Besides,

David thought he might take the opportunity to talk to Hale.

"Nay, I need to speak to Mr. Hale about a matter. I willna be gone long."

He walked to their room and knelt by the bed, placing a hand on Elisabeth's forehead. She didn't wake, and her forehead was cool. She looked well enough; it was only she was always weary. Mrs. Hale had said it was to be expected, and he wasn't to worry. But what she hadn't said was how to stop the worry. He kissed her cheek, adjusted the blankets, and went to collect Rhee.

The night was cold, and a bitter wind fresh off the Delaware blasted up the Alley, rattling the chains that held the signs and whistling through the debris that littered the roadway. He closed the door firmly behind him, lest a stray gust tear it open and chill the indoors. One of the Nailor lads had felt the brunt of his tongue last night when he'd gone downstairs after midnight to seek the source of a draft, and had found the door wide open. He'd given the lad cause to think he bore the future of David's kin on his shoulders, until Liam'd run down to fetch him and make peace.

He just didn't know how he was to stop the worry.

With an effort, he turned his attention to Rhee. "Are ye warm enough, then, lass? I can run back up, get something of Lisbeth's." He grinned, thinking the skin Rhee displayed could account for Liam's loss. Rhee suffered no compunction playing up her assets, but she did so with such charm, no one could fault her. She had even the Reverend eating out of her hand, the two times she'd joined them for service.

"No, I'm fine. But walk faster."

"Where'd ye learn to play?"

"My father. The times we were short of other players, he'd deal and take turns moving from empty seat to empty seat, explaining his strategy with each hand. I had no choice but to learn the game well."

"And so ye did. No' often one bests Mr. O at whist. Liam either, for that matter."

She laughed, clapping her hands as her feet danced a wee skip. "I'll have to write Papa. He'll be so proud."

"Does Mr. Ross play?"

The smile disappeared. "Never with me. I received a letter today. Did Beth tell you?"

"Aye. Will he be joining ye, then?" He knew the man wouldn't; Elisabeth had told him as much. But he thought he ought to ask, lest Rhee think he knew all her private business aforehand.

"No. He made no mention of joining me."

"Winter's nigh. He likely wouldna start a journey now."

"Hmm. I expect you're right." She opened the Hales' front door and went inside. "Well, thank you, David. Now, don't forget supper tomorrow night; Mrs. Hale so looks forward to those meals." She pointed down the hall to a dimly lit room. "It looks as if Mr. Hale is still in his study."

"Aye. Good night, Rhee." He fingered the scrap of paper in his pocket and walked down the hallway. Hale sat in an upholstered chair by the fire, staring silently into the flames. He looked up when he heard David's footsteps outside the room, and his gaze seemed wary.

"Good evening, Mr. Hale. Would ye mind if I have a word?"

"No. No, of course not." He rose, going to the decanter on the desk and refreshing his drink, bringing the glass to his mouth. Seemingly as an afterthought, he remembered his manners and poured David a drink as well, then sat, indicating the chair opposite with a nod.

"How is Elisabeth?"

"She's still cool to the touch. But she's weary, most times."

A small smile showed on Hale's face, and he took a sip. "I remember Abigail, her mother, was as well when she carried Beth. She'd drop off shortly after supper." His face clouded. "I know the worry, Mr. Graham. But the chance of fever has abated. For a few months anyway."

"Aye." David toyed with his glass, turning it round and round in his hands, forearms resting on his knees as he leaned toward the fireplace, his eyes on Hale. "Her mother . . . was she petite, then?" Elisabeth's mother had died in childbirth. It was a constant worry for him, even knowing it wasn't a trait necessarily passed down.

Hale nodded, and David watched as the man's eyes filled before he averted them to the fire.

"She's no' eating as she should, Mr. Hale. What she does eat, doesna stay down."

"Bring her home."

"She willna come. I've tried." He held steady as the man looked at him, his gaze assessing as if to determine why he had no hold over his own wife.

"It's surprising, isn't it?" Hale said, a corner of his mouth rising in acknowledgment of David's defeat. "Her mother was the same. Docile to all appearances, yet invariably I'd be caught unawares to find myself doing her bidding, rather than her doing mine." His voice caught at the end of his recollection, and David rose, pacing to give the man time to collect himself.

He'd do anything to keep Bess well. Anything. If he thought bringing her back would benefit, she'd be resting upstairs now. But Mrs. Hale kept insisting she was experiencing nothing out of the ordinary. That he needn't be concerned. That his worry was the only thing worrying Bess.

"A man approached me at the Coffee House the other day, Mr. Hale. I've his information here." He pulled the paper from his pocket. "I knew him from the *Gazette*. He'd come in often, trying to drum up clients for his surveying business. He's an honest man, according to what Mr. Hall says. I'd concur, hearing of his dealings with others this past year." He laid it on Hale's desk, not willing to test the man's pride in taking it from his hand. "I thought ye might be interested; I told him I'd pass it on."

Hale looked at the desk, quiet, and it seemed as if he were considering David's words.

"I best be getting back, lest Bess wakes." He set his empty glass on the desk. "Thank you for the whisky, sir."

"Good night, Mr. Graham," Hale answered, a faraway look still claiming his features.

"Aye. To ye as well, Mr. Hale."

17 October 1790

"Ye know what ye should do, Davey?" Liam said, grunting as he picked up his end of the crate.

"What's that?" he asked, blindly kicking aside a jug the wind had rolled in his path. It was a bonny day to be working dockside. Every flag on every ship was flying large this morning, snapping crisply in the breeze. They heaved the crate over the edge to the waiting barge, then retraced their steps to the wagon to retrieve another.

"Hone your shorthand."

"Why would he want to do that?" Ian asked. He sat lounging atop the crates already loaded, whittling away on a piece of bone while he watched them work.

"Aye, why would I want to do that?"

"Congress is coming. The coves will be here in little more than a month." Liam motioned with a tired wave for him to wait, and bent, forearms to his knees, while he caught his breath.

"Ye get more sleep, ye could keep up. Ye've too many irons in the fire." And he himself had too few. He sat on the wharf, thinking as he waited.

"You still planning on more time at your learning?" Ian asked. "Not getting you anywhere, not from where I'm sitting."

"Not sure, Ian," Liam answered slowly. "Need some help with your ciphering, then?"

"I can figure the coins due me from an honest day's labor. Don't need no college to cipher that."

"Ye're right, Liam!" David jumped up as soon as the reason occurred to him, pacing quick steps in front of Liam. "Holy hell, why didna I think of that?"

"Think of what? What are you two talking of?"

"Work, Ian. Getting ahead. Grabbing opportunities," Liam answered.

"Piss on that." He kicked the crate he sat on with his heel. "The way I see it, the chap that owns this cargo is the only one here with any opportunity. And you lads are the ones guaranteeing it by loading it for him. All while he sits back, cozy-like, counting his coin." He spat his contempt, missing Liam by inches. "Opportunity, my arse. I've been in this country ten years, and I ain't any happier than I was back home. It's the same thing, different name, all over again. A fight for nothing is what it was."

"Aye, well. If ye'd paid any attention at all along those ten years, ye might have caught we've won the right to the *pursuit* of happiness, not the gem itself," Liam said, his palms on his knees as he pushed himself upright. "No one owes you a damn thing, 'cept a fair day's wages for an honest day's work."

"You're so damn smart, why are you the one carting this man's riches? You'll find out for yourself, time it comes to get your own clients. Ain't no one going to see past your burr and your worn out coat."

"Ian," David said. "Leave off, man."

Liam, rested now, indicated with a wave of his hand they should grab another. "No. He's right, Davey. For once."

"Canna we finish without a brawl?"

"Sure we can. Just won't be as entertaining."

"The shorthand, Liam," David said, trying to get the conversation back on track. "You're meaning stepping in on Congress, aye?"

"Aye."

The House of Representatives wasn't closed as the Senate was. Citizens were permitted to watch the proceedings, and there was plenty of interest from citizens who had neither the time nor the patience to attend. The newspapers would be wanting to print a summary of the goings-on.

"I could take the notes, and set them as well, should I find a steady master willing to pay. Or I could sell them, couldna I?"

"Aye, I think ye could," Liam answered. "Ye're fast. Likely ye'll be faster than others at it." Load in hand, they crept toward the barge one step at a time, David taking his turn walking backwards.

"Mr. Hall stocks books on the craft. Remember, Ian?"

Ian, disgruntled, didn't bother to answer as he jumped down. He waved a hand as he took his leave, mumbling something about seeing him Sunday.

"Faster, if ye get tutored, David. Mr. Donaldson's daughter can tutor ye the particulars, I wager, as she does a fair job for Donaldson."

"I can't spare the coin for that. I'm thinking Mr. Hall wouldna mind loaning the book."

"She's been complaining her roof needs fixing, 'fore the winter weather comes. Her husband's a ship captain, mind, ne'er here when she needs him. You could work out an exchange." He jerked his head upwards, indicating David should stop. "Count o' three, Davey."

They counted, then heaved the crate to the top of the waiting stack. Liam jumped on the barge, handling the rope that would secure the load and tossed an end to David.

"Lisbeth take issue, ye think, ye closet yourself with another? She's a beauty, this one."

"Nay, she wouldna." David frowned, wondering if she in fact would. "Will ye speak to Miss Donaldson?" he asked as he knelt and reached below the barge, tying off the rope.

"Mrs. Baylor. Aye, I will." Liam jumped back to the wharf, wiping his hands down his breeches. "There's Mr. Wills now. Let's collect. Can ye spare enough for a pint?"

David nodded, his thoughts on the months ahead. Congress should sit through March. That would be steady employment throughout the winter. He'd been worrying about the winter, given picking up the odd job on the wharves would be nigh to impossible. He knew some of shorthand already, reading it anyway. That put him steps ahead. He flexed his fingers, itching to get started, now that he had a plan.

"Here," Liam said, dumping half the coins he'd collected into David's palm. They walked a block, turning up the alley that led to the Man Full of Trouble Tavern.

"Can we stop by and ask her first?"

Liam looked at him, his eyes traveling head to toes. The heat had abated, but nonetheless they were both grimy and drenched with sweat. "Nay," he said, wrinkling his nose and raising his forearm to wipe the sweat from his forehead. He opened the door of the Man, motioning David in ahead of him. "And I think it best ye speak first with Lisbeth, given your last spell with aiding a lass bereft of a husband."

The barkeep set two mugs in front of them, and David grabbed one as he took a stool, the well-marred pewter cool to his touch. "What're ye . . . oh." He felt the heat creep up his neck as he recalled the summer he aided a widow in need of a full bin of wood.

"Jesus, Liam. Ye're daft, ye think I . . . I . . . I would never . . . hell, Elisabeth's my wife."

"I didna say I thought ye would. Only that ye should clear it with her." He took a swig of his ale, then turned to look over the other patrons in the tavern. "She's been crying at the oddest things, ken? Who knows what she'd think."

"Mrs. Hale says that's normal, the crying."

"Huh. Well, talk to her tonight, aye? I'll talk to Mrs. Baylor this afternoon. Maybe she'll say yes, and maybe she'll be willing to start right away. Ye can be on that roof by Saturday morning if that's your aim."

"Right, then." He'd talk to Elisabeth this afternoon. If he was to be repairing a roof, there wasn't time to waste; the weather could turn any day now. Which reminded him, she wanted to spend a day out and about while it was still fair.

"Are ye free Sunday? I told Lisbeth we could walk up to the Wissahickon. If the weather holds, we can stop at that tea garden she favors. Ye can bring . . ." He paused, trying to remember the girl's name. "Amy. Ye can bring Amy."

"Mayhap. Who's going?"

"Ian and his lass."

"I thought she threw him out."

"She did, but all's forgiven now."

"That's all?"

David looked at him, puzzled.

"Is that all who's coming?"

"Oh, aye." The bartender joined them, idling a few moments exchanging tales with Liam of last Saturday evening's gossip. His own thoughts wandered to the evening he and Bess had shared Saturday, when the others were out of the house, and his fingers curled hard on the mug as the recollection played out.

"What about Rhee?" Liam elbowed him, bringing him back to the present.

"What about her?"

"Will she be joining ye? On Sunday?"

"Oh. No, she won't. She's heading upriver for a few days, with Alice Johnson and that bunch," he said, surprised by the question. Though he'd eased off being contrary, Liam still paid Rhee no heed. "I think to stay with the Collin family, maybe? I'm no' sure."

"God in heaven, Davey, why're ye letting her do that? What do ye know of Collin?"

What the hell? "Ye be thinking I'm the lassie's keeper, then?" he answered, frowning. "I ken nothing amiss of the Collins. No' even sure I could pick them out on a street." He looked at Liam. "And what's it to ye, besides?"

"Nothing."

David watched with a scowl as Liam upended his mug, finished it, then slammed it on the bar.

"Let's go."

Jesus, there was no relaxing with the man these past weeks. Full of knots he'd been, near as bad as Ian.

18 NOVEMBER 1790

SHAD COLLIN. DAMN IT ALL to hell and back.

"Good morning, sir."

"Good morning, Mr. Brock. You're on time, I see. A moment of note." Donaldson stood at the window, leafing hastily through a thick volume. "I read through the analysis you prepared."

"Did ye, sir? Was it . . .?"

Donaldson's chin rose in the manner of giving grudging approval, and he nodded. "I was pleasantly surprised. You raised some valid points."

"Pleasantly surprised" was high praise indeed, coming from this man. Very high praise. It made the nights he'd labored over it worth the loss of sleep. He turned to hide his grin.

"We'll review each of them after dinner. I trust you'll manage to stay awake through the afternoon?"

The urge to grin evaporated in an instant. Whether it be the hours he'd labored at the wharves, or the evenings he'd spent with his mates or his lass, Mr. Donaldson seemed to begrudge them all. At first the disapproval had come as a surprise. The classes he'd missed in order to work took nothing from Donaldson. He needed the labor; he hadn't an income, not unless he took the coins Mrs. Hale had offered.

The late nights? Well, hell, the man didn't own him.

He hadn't lashed back at the censure. Not yet anyway. But he feared the time was coming.

"I'll manage, sir."

"You've a good deal of potential, Mr. Brock. It pains me to see potential wasted."

"Aye, sir." Biting his tongue against further response, he set his notebooks on the side table and stood in front of the bookshelf looking for the volume he'd left off with yesterday afternoon.

"You're looking right at it, Mr. Brock." With a loud sigh to signal his displeasure, Mr. Donaldson reached around him and took the book from the shelf, setting it on the table.

"Keep busy with where we left off while I finish with this matter. I tell you, I spend more time on rascals than their worthless lives warrant." Donaldson returned to his desk, his disgust now settled on another. "Let that be a lesson to you, Mr. Brock. Choose your clients carefully. Wealthy, but not so much they've lost their sense."

"Aye, sir." He sat, opening the book, flipping to the last page he'd read the day before. Mr. Donaldson tended to go on about—that was it. Worthless rascals. Mr. Collin was one of Donaldson's clients. Looking at his mentor, he closed the book. He had been the Hales' attorney since before the Revolution and knew most everyone who was anyone in the county.

"Mr. Donaldson, might I take another minute of your time?"

Donaldson scowled as he glanced up, taking off his spectacles. He had a full, round face, one that tended to stay flushed more often than not, and his bald head, framed here and there by small tufts of white hair, shone bright in the weak afternoon sunlight streaming through the windowpane. The scowl wasn't always one borne of irritation; he'd learned that quick enough. The cove only had trouble switching his eyes from near to far.

"There's a lass, see—" *Now* it was a scowl borne of irritation, and the spectacles went back on as Donaldson refocused on the papers in front of him.

"She's headed out to Shad Collin's for a few days with others, and I'm thinking she may not . . . Mr. Collin's a client, aye? If she were your daughter, would ye let her attend? See, she's a ward of Mrs. Hale." So to speak.

The man's head shot up at the last. He'd have to remember that, the sway her name carried.

"Why didn't you say so, instead of blathering about? Now, what's this?"

"She's been invited to the country. I know some of the bunch attending, and I'm thinking it's not to be the gathering she's expecting. I believe ye've said a word or two about Collin in the past."

"I trust you don't repeat any of the words or two you might hear in this office."

"Of course not, sir. But, I was thinking, if ye agreed there might be a cause for concern, I could perhaps deliver Collin some documents for ye come Saturday." His blood raced as he envisioned the plan. A day on his own. A day in the country, out of this office. He'd like a day on his own to think.

"To see if she need come home, ken? Before any trouble occurs."

Donaldson reached for a blank sheet of paper, writing a few lines with care. "Take this, it authorizes the stable to put the fee on my account. I'll have Nora put together a packet for you to deliver. Bring the girl home, Mr. Brock." He shook his head, his hand reaching to rub his forehead. "Lord knows, I don't need to be on the wrong side of Mrs. Hale."

HE TOOK HIS time, keeping his mount down to a steady trot. The trees above were a riot of dancing color and the sunlight wove a shimmering path through their canopy to the carpet of red and gold beneath the horse's hooves. He pictured Mrs. Ross amidst it all, laughing, her arms outstretched as she did one of her silly twirls in celebration of the beauty.

The Pennsylvania countryside was a show this time of year, no arguing that. Closing his eyes, he took a deep breath, savoring the clean, earthy odor drifting off the forest floor as he listened.

It was soothing—the drone of the insects, the song of the birds.

Maybe he'd keep riding. Forget everything. The docks, school, the law office, obligations and responsibilities . . .

He'd spent an hour after quitting time cajoling information from Nora Baylor, Donaldson's daughter. As he suspected, he'd found out Collin was a client who needed Mr. Donaldson's services often, given the scrapes the cove found himself in. Too much money in his pocket, too much time on his hands, and too little sense in his head.

He'd heard rumors Nora occasionally passed time at the man's estate, whilst her husband was at sea. Something she hadn't wanted her father to catch wind of, and one of the reasons he'd cautioned David to include Lisbeth in his dealings with the woman.

Normally, he wouldn't have given it a second thought. But with Lisbeth feeling peaked, in bed more often than not these past weeks, Hale's subtle but constant disparagement about David's prospects, and David's own worrying over his lack of steady work . . .

Well, a woman like Nora Baylor could do a lot to soothe what might ail a man.

It made him uneasy, thinking of the time David would spend alone with the woman.

He decided he'd forgive him for letting Rhee go off. Davey wouldn't have known of the cove's predilections; seems Mr. Donaldson had done a good job of keeping those that blackmailed and complained, paid off and silent. He himself might not have known, if he hadn't spent time there when he was catting about with Victoria Billings, and he hadn't shared that with David—it was one of those memories he kept pushed to the side, locked in a box.

He sighed. Nay, he would have known regardless, given the whispers he'd heard. It would have been enough for him to put two and two together and come up with more than four. He'd seen it growing up in the estates surrounding, as gents from the south would leave their wives and families behind as they came up north for all manner of sport.

Not David, though. Debauchery wasn't something he would have come across. God-fearing lad had had a ma who kept him close.

He wondered if Rhee had. She didn't strike him as a babe in the woods, though that could be more to the part she'd played in his dreams than anything else. But if she cared for that sort of thing, he'd not interfere. He wasn't one to cast stones.

He came to a clearing and saw the house ahead. It was a large house, two stories high, set back from the road a good ways and framed on two sides by tall trees. The north wing, though built in the same style, didn't quite match, having been rebuilt after the British burned it during the Revolution. He rode up the drive, passing through an extensive lawn, then to the stables kept behind the house. Dismounting, he waited for the stable boy.

"Good afternoon, lad."

The boy nodded, taking his reins. "You be staying overnight as well, sir?"

"Nay. I have some papers for Mr. Collin."

He and Shad were on a nodding basis, no more, but he'd know him when he saw him. He followed the walkway back to the front and climbed the steps to the porch. After satisfying himself the porch was empty, he walked to the front door and let the knocker drop.

A tall, gaunt, black man opened the door, his face an impassive mask.

"Good day to ye, sir. I'm here for Mr. Collin. I know the way, dinna mind seeing me to him." He walked past the man before he could answer. It was an impressive entryway, flanked on either side by a number of doors and crowned by a staircase that flowed to the landing above. He followed the path down the entry hall, heading toward the sound of women chattering. With luck, he'd know one or two of them. Aside from Mrs. Ross, that is.

"Why, I declare! If it isn't Liam Brock."

He entered the room and went to the redhead, taking her extended hand and kissing her cheek. "Susan, it's good to see ye, lass. Is Nate with ye?" No more than five feet tall, Susan was attractive enough in an unassuming way. She'd spent a month on his arm little more than two years ago, and they had parted friendly when the time came. She'd been with Nate much longer, though apparently the bloom had worn off that rose as well, if she was here.

"Nate's a bore. He's always working. I came with Rebecca Higgens. You know Rebecca, don't you? Heavens, I didn't expect to see you, of all people. How fun!"

This lass could chatter incessantly, and he kept his eyes on her while she did, flattering her with appropriate comments whenever he could edge in a word. Finally, she paused, asking if he were staying the night.

"Nay, it's working I am, as well. I've a delivery for Collin. Is he near?" He took his eyes off her, casting a quick glance about, seeing neither Collin nor Mrs. Ross.

"I haven't seen him in a while. I believe he's out back." She took his arm. "I'll escort you; it's becoming rather dull in here."

The gardens were striking, despite it being the end of the season. Elisabeth would enjoy them. Rhee could tell her of them, if she'd seen them. Where the hell was she?

"There's Shad now, Liam. Do you see him?" She indicated a group standing by a fountain, Rhee not among them. Shad was a big man and stood out, his hands waving and his voice booming as he told a tale of his time in France. Somewhat jowly at a mere five and twenty, the abundance of drink and lack of work was telling.

"Aye." He needed to find Rhee first, before he used up his excuse for being here. "Listen Susan, how's the whisky? Long as I'm here, mayhap there's no rush?"

"Heavens, I don't know. You know I don't touch the stuff."

"I'm guessing a glass of wine wouldna come amiss, though, aye?" he asked, smiling. He squeezed her arm, then dropped it as he turned to go back inside. "I'll fetch ye something."

He walked back through the hall, thinking he'd step into each room as he went, starting with the kitchen. There was a chance she'd seek refuge in the comfort of a kitchen. *If* she needed refuge, and he shouldn't be so sure she did.

Because there was also a chance she'd seek comfort in one of the rooms upstairs; that this was nothing but a fool's errand. She was a grown woman, for Pete's sake, and a married one at that. More than capable of taking care of herself and none of his concern.

The room under the stairs—thank God—was empty. He sneezed, the dust he'd raised making its way to his nose. He looked in the room he'd first found Susan. More had come, but not Rhee. There were only two rooms left. What then? Was he truly going up those stairs?

Memories of the night he'd come with Tory threatened to work their way from where he'd stashed them, and he shook his head hard before they could break free.

He opened the door to the study, interrupting a couple in the midst of an embrace. Startled, they broke apart, and he recognized the man. He had a distinctive hawk-like nose, and his face was marked well by pox. He wore his fair hair short, untied, and a slick lock fell forward as he bent his head to check the state of his clothing and smooth out his breeks.

The man clerked for one of the merchants Liam often labored for on the wharves. Stephen . . . something. Hell, he couldn't remember.

"Stephen! Long time and all that, man." He walked to the desk, reaching for the decanter. Taking the top off, he held the crystal up to his nose, sniffing. "Ahh, here's where he keeps it. Can I pour ye one as well, mate?" he asked, pouring himself a glass.

"Liam, perhaps another—"

"This must be your lovely wife," he said, interrupting as he handed a whisky to Stephen, knowing full well Stephen's wife was anything but lovely. She was so huge they'd have had difficulty finding a horse strong enough to cart her here. "What's your pleasure, lass? Would ye care to top off that wine ye have? I hear tell Shad has—"

He missed the woman's reply as he spotted Rhiannon, standing aside a man not more than five feet outside the study door.

19

"WHO'S THAT MAN, Stephen?" he asked, indicating Rhiannon's partner with the hand that held his glass. "He looks familiar."

She stood at the foot of the staircase with a man he didn't recognize, her back to him. Nonetheless, he knew it was her. The man with her looked like a peacock, and his hands continually moved as they fluttered from smoothing his yellow neckcloth, to his blue lapels, to straightening his white cuffs and back again. He had small, beady eyes set back in a wide face, and they darted up and down her form as he kept up his chatter. Pompous arse.

He assessed her bearing. She wasn't at ease. Any fool could discern that, what with her shoulders squared tight, her arms crossed rigidly in front of her. Except that fool. The cove wasn't minding her space; he left nary a foot between them as he talked himself silly.

"Declan Rawls. I shouldn't be surprised he looks familiar. He's here from Pittsburgh, full of talk about the land he's been acquiring. Donaldson handles a lot of land transactions, doesn't he? You might have seen him there. Listen, Liam, could we do this another time? I don't mean to be rude, but . . ."

"Aye, mate. Sorry I interrupted. Give my best to your wife, aye?"

He walked out, shutting the door softly behind him. The

cove didn't look the least bit familiar, but Stephen had given him his opening.

"Mr. Rawls, it is, isn't it? Good to see ye, man." He extended a hand and the man, surprised, took it. "Liam Brock. We met at the Coffee House. Ye likely don't remember; ye were up to your coattails in dealings. I work for an attorney in town," he said, pumping the man's hand. He turned, seeming to notice Rhiannon for the first time. "Why, and Mrs. Ross it is, as well. What a surprise, the two of ye together."

"Indeed it is, Mr. Brock." She reached out and clutched his hand in hers, leaving him no opportunity to wipe the damp of Mr. Rawls from it first. "You've come about Elisabeth, haven't you? I *knew* I shouldn't have left town. Her time is so near; it was extremely selfish of me."

"Aye, well, she's taken a wee fall. It's nothing to worry about, but ye know our Davey. She's asking for ye, and he's worried sick. I promised I'd fetch ye." He tucked away the flash of irritation at the surprise he thought he detected in her eyes. Surprise that maybe he wasn't near as dimwitted as she'd suspected.

"Then we must leave immediately. Good day, Mr. Rawls. It's been a pleasure," she said, nodding as she turned, pulling Liam by the arm down the hallway beside her. She kept the pressure on his arm until they stepped out the front door, merely nodding to one person and another on her way out.

"Wait!" He gulped down his whisky, then walked back through the door to find the butler.

"Here you go, mate," he said, depositing his glass on the man's tray. "Could I ask you, sir, to deliver a glass of wine to the chattering redhead in the white gown outside? And to tell her Liam Brock regrets he's been called away?"

He shrugged at Declan Rawls, still standing at the foot of the stairs, seeming puzzled at the rapid turn of events. "Women," he said, commiserating with the cove before he exited. He trotted down the front steps, joining Rhee at the bottom.

He watched her for a minute as she paced back and forth, wringing her hands.

"Jesus. And ye think I'm rude."

"May we go now?" she asked, stopping before him, her eyes not meeting his. She reached out a hand to pull on his arm again, tugging him toward the stables.

Standing firm, he deliberately ignored the frisson her touch had sent shooting down his spine. He pulled away, folding his arms across his chest, and leaned against the railing, watching her.

She sighed, the sound audible in the quiet of the front porch. "I never said you were rude, Mr. Brock." Still not meeting his eyes, her gaze sought the safety of the stables.

"Nay, but I'm thinking ye've implied it often enough."

He wasn't moving. Not until she looked at him, not until she saw him. Him. Not the dirty wharf rat she chose to see.

"You haven't the faintest idea what I think." She stepped away, heading toward the back, then she stopped, as if it occurred to her anew she would need him.

He wasn't moving.

"At the moment, since you choose to play dense, I will spell it out for you. I want to leave. I want to leave *now*," she said, her voice quavering, her back to him. Then again, so softly he had to strain to hear her. "I want to leave."

He sighed, knowing he'd lost. He'd go.

"Please," she added.

"Right, then." He'd come to bring her back, hadn't he? Ashamed, he pushed off the railing and grasped her elbow, hurrying her toward the back. "Ye have a horse?" he asked, motioning to the boy ahead to bring out his.

She shook her head, mute, her eyes downcast. Hell, if she started crying now . . .

"I'll walk aside ye. Ye ride." The boy gave her a hand up, and Liam watched as she fumbled with her skirts and tried to maintain a grip.

"D'ye mind if I ride with ye, then?" She shook her head, and he mounted behind her, gathering the reins with one hand while he steadied her with the other. Clicking his tongue, he urged the beast forward, and they started down the drive.

He struggled to pay heed to the forest . . . the road . . . the small game that darted across their path—anything other than the soft press of her body against his, as he fought the urge to draw her closer still. She smelled clean, like the forest, and he came to crave each dizzying whiff as the gait of the horse rocked her to and fro. It'd be so easy, so natural to draw her close to keep her warm. She likely wondered why he hadn't.

No, she didn't wonder. The rigid set of her shoulders spoke the words plain as day. He kept both his hands tight on the reins.

She didn't cry until they had gone more than a mile, he could credit her that. But hell, when she did, it was a storm of tears. He couldn't keep ahold of her, she shook so. He led the horse off the road, to a spot under a stand of trees. Dismounting, he looped the reins round a branch, then reached for her. She came easily enough, still crying when she reached the ground. Sobbing, she clung to him, her hands fisting in his waistcoat lest he think to release her.

He was at a loss. To touch, or not to touch? His hands hovered inches above her shoulders as he debated, then he set them round her back and pulled her close, her head to his chest in an effort to console her.

It had been the wrong choice. Her nearness clouded his judgment, no less than if he'd overstayed the tavern by hours.

Without forethought, he closed his eyes and buried his face in the soft warm curve of her neck, taking his fill of her scent as he skimmed a hand down the slope of her back, lingering at the base of her spine to steady her. He moved a knee between hers, edging closer still, and her fists uncurled as she laid her palms flat atop his chest, mayhap in warning.

God Almighty. At times it seemed he couldn't take a straight step forward.

20

"I AM SORRY, LASS," he said as he drew away, shaking his head in apology. "I shouldna . . . I didna mean to . . ."

Hell. He was no better than the cove they'd left standing at the bottom of the stairs. He didn't even know the why of it. An hour ago, and he'd have wagered his best knife there wasn't a lassie alive who could rouse him weeping like that. Nay, a storm like that was the surest way to send him walking. So why hadn't he?

He drew in a long gulp of air, readying for the recrimination that would surely follow. With a last, lingering sob, she looked up at him, her eyes searching his.

Sweet Jesus, she was easy to look at. Even crying. Framed by long black lashes that glistened, spiked with the residue of tears, her eyes were pools of green so deep he thought one might drown in them.

He reached up, his thumb wiping away the tear trailing down her cheek. "He's a lucky man, your Mr. Ross is."

Which was the wrong thing to say as it brought on a fresh round of sobs. She pulled from his grasp and dropped to the ground, burrowing her head between the arms she'd rested atop her knees.

Sighing, he dropped down beside her, one hand reaching beneath her hair to knead the back of her neck.

"He's no' in the right, ken, leaving ye on your own. I'm no' saying it's no' done. It's done all the time. But I'll wager you're no' one for it."

"I'm not," she said, raising her head, the sharp words slamming into him, so unexpected were they. She hadn't uttered a word in almost an hour.

"I'm not," she said again, quieter, softer.

Her fingers twirled round the band she wore, pulling it off and then on again, over and over. The ring held no jewel; it was a simple band of rose colored gold. He wondered if her husband had given it to her, and if she reached for it when she needed reminding. He dug out his handkerchief and handed it to her, to keep her from worrying the ring any longer.

"I was frightened. Once I realized . . . I'm rarely frightened, Mr. Brock."

"Aye, I believe that."

A humbling emotion, fright. Powerlessness. He could attest to that. He fisted his hand as the force of the memories rushed through him. Emotions he'd vowed never to forget . . . *never* to experience again.

"It's an awful thing, fright is," he said finally.

"It is awful. You couldn't begin to guess."

"But there were plenty of good people there, lass. People who would have seen ye home, should you have asked."

Aye, as he had offered to see her home. Might even stop along the road to comfort her, hoping, as he had, that the comfort would lead to more.

No, he hadn't planned that. It hadn't been deliberate. He had scruples. He slipped, and often, but he had scruples. He hadn't planned that.

"You're a man. You make your own choices, and no one thinks to question them. You could have simply ridden away." She blew her nose and tucked his linen up her sleeve. "If I had demanded to be taken home, there would have been questions, Liam. And much more talk than if I had quietly found a corner to hide and wait the time out."

He didn't answer, stuck on where she'd called him by name

and the startling wave of emotion it had triggered. But as the rest of her words began to sink in, it occurred to him he should respond.

A corner to hide?

He reached a hand toward her again, running it up and down her back. "It isn't fair, what the world does to those helpless."

"No. It isn't. However, it was of my own doing. I only wanted . . ." She sniffled, her voice catching on a sob. "Sometimes I watch Elisabeth and David, and it makes me want to drop to my knees, railing at the injustice of it. I think maybe he loves her more than life itself."

"Aye, I believe he does and has for years."

"I don't mean to say I begrudge her that. I don't."

"I know. It's only ye'd like it for yourself."

She turned toward him, surprise showing on her face. "Yes, that's it exactly." She dropped her gaze, intent on tearing blades of grass from the ground. "Have you always loved her as well?"

His hand stilled on her back as something in her tone told him her meaning. He felt the blood drain from his head in a whoosh, and he blinked, lightheaded, as his belly began to churn and he worked up a denial.

"I've seen the way you look at her, Mr. Brock. But I'm not implying . . ."

He felt her eyes on him, and her voice took on a softer, concerned tone. "I shouldn't have brought it up; it's none of my business. I'm sorry I said it. You needn't answer. She hasn't the faintest idea. Neither does David."

He dragged a hand down his face, rubbing it hard, and turned to watch the horse, suddenly wishing he were anywhere but here. The beast stood content, its tail lazily slapping a soothing rhythm as it munched clean the groundcover, not a care in the world.

This woman vexed him too many ways from Sunday, and he had neither the time nor the inclination for it. Women weren't to do that, not the women he spent time with. And she was *still* talking.

"I want a baby. I want a man who loves me. And I don't want to be reduced to finding that love on a dalliance at an anonymous country estate." The tears started afresh and she swiped at them angrily.

"Then ye should settle for no less. Mayhap ye'll be a widow soon, aye?" he said, offering the only consolation that came quick to mind. It wasn't much, but she had him rattled.

She made a choking sound. "Pitter-patter, be still my heart!" she said, making a show of patting her chest. "That's it? That's the sum of your wisdom? Hell's bells! I'd have thought you'd have a silver tongue for situations such as this, Mr. Brock, considering the number of women you have trailing after you."

He shrugged. "They dinna trail for long, case ye havena noticed." He reached for her hair, playing with the locks that had fallen from her pins, twirling the curls round and round in his fingers, liking their cool, satin texture. He might as well touch as much as his conscience would allow, long as he had the chance.

"I'd been under the impression that was more your decision than theirs."

"It'd eventually come to be theirs, given time."

Her brows drew together in puzzlement and her eyes searched his. "Why on earth would you say that?"

"I think I'm no' good at giving what a lass seems to need." He gave her a wolfish grin, letting his gaze slide slowly down, lingering on her breasts. "Aside from what comes natural, of course."

She snorted. "Of course." She turned away and busied herself with the grass again. "Why did you come?"

He'd been waiting for the question. He hadn't been sure of the answer himself.

He could tell her he'd been sent with a packet from Mr. Donaldson. That he'd come on business. The truth, in a fashion, and it would serve to reestablish the distance between them. He dropped the lock of hair he'd been toying with and rubbed his chin.

"Davey mentioned where ye'd be, and I worried some. Collin has a reputation, ken? I didna know if you were aware of it or not. I knew David wasna, else he wouldna have let ye go."

He felt the "and?," though she didn't say it. It hung, waiting, suspended in midair. He needed to say more, more on why he had come. He took one of her hands in his, rubbing it lightly between his palms, entwining his fingers with hers to ascertain the fit.

"Lisbeth would ne'er forgive, if you were hurt. If I knew and didn't come."

Her eyes shot to his, a flash of alarm crossing her features. "You told her?"

He shook his head, and she relaxed.

"I didn't know. In retrospect, I suppose I was naive, but I didn't know." She sighed, her shoulders sagging, and for an instant, he feared the tears might start again. "My judgment was lacking. I was bored, Mr. Brock. I was tired of tagging along after Beth and David, the odd one out. I needed—" She darted a quick glance his way, as if she suddenly realized how much she'd revealed, and quieted.

The thought that she had been lonely brought an ache. He sometimes felt it himself. Not often. Only sometimes.

"Tell me, did you truly know that odious man?" she asked, the subject changed, the confidence back in her voice.

He grinned, relieved, and shook his head, dropping her hand. "Ne'er have seen the cove before this day."

She laughed, the sound rich and vibrant as it echoed through the forest. She crossed an arm over her chest, rubbing her forearm in a shiver, then raked her hand through the leaves at her side, idly sorting through their colors.

He stood, reaching to help her up. "Are ye ready? There'll be talk, ye be seen riding in after dark with me."

She ignored his hand, content to stay and doodle in the dirt with her finger. "It's considerate of you to be concerned, but it seems likely my reputation is already in shreds."

"Nay. You'll be seen at kirk tomorrow, first thing, and none will realize ye'd gone. Make sure you attend, now. I'll tell Lisbeth ye'd asked they stop to collect you. See that ye look stunning as always, aye?" he warned. "No dressing as if ye've reason for shame."

"You think I always look stunning?"

He grunted. "Just like a woman, ye are, honing in on the only thing you want to hear." He reached for her, settling his hands under her armpits, and pulled her up. "I think ye know damn well I find ye desirable," he said, stepping back quickly, as soon as she was on her feet.

"No," she said, bestowing one of those brilliant smiles. "I don't think I did."

He chuckled, relieved it took so little to cheer her. It wasn't much to admit after all; there wasn't a man who didn't. Although he wished he had used the word 'beautiful' instead. He feared he'd handed her too much with the word "desirable." He took off his jacket and wrapped it round her shoulders.

"Up with ye. We'll dismount, once we near town. You tell whoever, whatever, and I'll back ye, aye?" He put his hands about her waist and swung her atop the horse, then untied the reins and mounted himself.

As he nudged the horse toward the road, she settled back against him, her hands pulling close the edges of his jacket, her curves nesting in every angle of his body, filling every cranny as if she were melting. He placed both reins in one hand, freeing an arm to hold her steady, and within moments her head sagged against his shoulder as she fell asleep.

She had reminded him of things, of memories he'd tried to box up. It was a maddening thing, powerlessness. He could care for himself well enough, but women and children, often they couldn't. Often they needed to rely on others.

His mother had needed care. He'd tried. God's truth, he'd tried. But he hadn't been enough. She had died. Cold, hungry, and disheartened, she'd died.

Mr. O might need care one day. It was hard to credit, but it might come to pass.

And one day he might have a woman like this to care for. Not this day, not soon, but one day.

Cushioning his arm under her breasts, he tightened his grip and kissed her forehead. Lightly, lest she wake.

Voices Whisper

IT WAS WELL past dusk when they reached the outskirts of Philly. He'd watched the moon change from a brilliant ball of orange to one of white, and he'd had the thought to wake her, to witness it, but in the end he'd let her sleep. He was more than content to watch it on his own with her warmth pressed up tight against him.

He stopped the horse and prodded her lightly, reluctant to have the ride end. "Ye need to wake, lass. We're almost there."

She woke slowly, stretching languidly as she did.

"We'll be stopping soon, aye?"

"I don't want to get down," she murmured, her voice faint amid the buzz and chirps of the night insects. "I'll be cold."

"Aye, but ye should."

She turned as best she could to face him. Her eyes met his as her lips parted, and she held his gaze in the moonlight for moments, her breath warm, mingling with his own. He shifted in his seat, suddenly uncomfortable.

"I think perhaps I misjudged you, Mr. Brock," she said finally, batting long black lashes, her eyes settling on his mouth. "You have my sincere apologies."

Jesus, if he kissed her now, after she'd been plastered up against him these past hours, her scent filling him so he could scarcely think a clear thought, she'd find herself beneath him afore she could blink. Mr. Ross or no Mr. Ross. What was she thinking, looking at him like that?

With no more than another slow sweep of those lashes and a slight twitch at the corner of her mouth, she swiveled back in her seat and squiggled close till she was tucked back against him. Just in the event he was too dense to catch on his own—she wasn't dismounting before entering town.

"Don't play with me, Rhee," he said, his thighs tightening about the horse as he urged it forward. "Ye'll find I don't play fair."

21 November 1790

"It's good to see you, Miss Liss," John said, placing the teacup in front of her.

"Can you sit a while?" Elisabeth asked, patting the bench. "I've missed you, John."

"Nothing to stop you from coming by more often. Missus Hale sure would appreciate it."

Her mouth quirked sideways at the soft reprimand. "I know. I intend to, now that I'm feeling better." John sat across from her, his old pewter mug filled with small ale. "Tell me, have you had a chance to visit with Mrs. Slate?" Leo Slate had been Polly's beau, and he had died in the same incident that had taken Polly last year, leaving his mother in even worse financial straits.

John grinned, nodding. "I gave her the basket like you said. Her new husband done had himself a fit when he saw that money under those spices. She's Missus Calley now."

"She remarried?"

"Last month. Good man, too, Miss Liss. You won't need to send no more baskets."

"Oh, I'm so happy for her." It seems she had let another obligation slide, handing it off to others. It must have been several months since she'd visited the woman, if she'd already been married a month. She hadn't even known she'd had a suitor.

Leo's mother kept a market stand, selling soups and breads. John had advised her spices would be the most useful item she could supply, but she knew money would be helpful as well, given the loss of Leo's earnings. She had been taking a basket to her each month and had come to look forward to the visits. The woman talked up a storm, filling her with all manner of gossip. As a result, she found she often knew things even Liam had no knowledge of, which pleased her to no end, given the man was so certain he knew everything.

"I'm afraid I let time slip by."

"It's all right, Miss. Yous be expecting and yous plenty on your mind." He rose and went to the fire, pulling back the warming bread, tapping its top with a practiced finger. "Eat, now, hear?" He pulled apart several pieces and set them before her, dousing them with a generous serving of honey and butter. She would have refused, had the aroma been any less tempting.

She took one small bite, then another. "This is delicious. One would think I hadn't eaten twice already this morning. So, what did she have to say? Did you find out anything I should know?"

"She done told me how young David was doing work for that Baylor gal. Now hows come I gots to hear that 'bout town, Miss Liss?"

"He only started last week, John." She frowned. "Now, why would she know that, I wonder?" Reaching for the butter, she slathered it atop the additional chunks John had set in front of her. She would end up as big as Mrs. Smith, the baker's wife, at this rate. Her husband had been known to commission specially made chairs for her, she was so heavy.

"That one's help done talk more than most. Gots more to talk about than most, I 'spect."

Alert now, she set down the bread. "Is that so?" She chewed on her bottom lip while she thought. "Such as?"

John shrugged, suddenly absorbed in his mug.

"Do you know, as well then, John, why he's working for her?"

"She's teaching him some note taking. That's what I heard.

Like she does for her Papa."

Elisabeth nodded. "He's been so worried, not knowing from one day to the next if he'll find work. If he becomes proficient at shorthand, he's likely to have steady employment. Once Congress starts up, that is."

Had she let her appearance slide these last two months as well? She reached a hand to her hair, finding it smooth, then straightened her shoulders and pulled her bodice down tight. She hadn't thought to question David about the woman, she'd been so excited that he was excited.

"What is Mrs. Baylor like, John? Is she young?" She had pictured her as a contemporary of her grandmother. But servants didn't gossip about Grandmother.

"Ain't never seen her."

"But you've heard talk."

"She's young to middling age. Dresses like she wished she weren't."

"How so?"

"You know, flaunting stuff she's no business flaunting any longer."

"And?"

"She wears paint," John said, as if that sealed the woman's reputation. "Obvious-like."

"Perhaps I should make an effort to meet this Mrs. Baylor."

"Yes." John nodded, satisfied. "Yous ain't got no worries with young David, miss. But never hurts to know what's about."

"You're right." She finished the last piece of bread John had set before her and stood. "You're absolutely right. Rhee should be awake by now, shouldn't she? Do you think you might spare Jane? To draw a bath? I'll have Rhee help me wash my hair, so I needn't bother Jane for long."

"Now, Miss Liss, this here be your home. You ask for a bath anytime you please.

"HERE, ELISABETH," Rhee said, handing her one of her own perfumed soaps.

"Oh, no, Rhee. I couldn't."

"Of course you could. I'm handing it to you, aren't I? If you don't use it, I'll have cause to think you're not impressed with my handiwork. I was on my knees for hours, harvesting that lavender. Now, why haven't you any of that in your garden?"

Elisabeth brought the soap to her nose, inhaling deeply. Rhee had an impressive collection of soaps, made with everything from rose petals, to lavender, to orange peels, to sage. She'd even mentioned gathering pine needles, though she wasn't certain why Rhee would want to smell like a forest. "I don't know why, to tell the truth. It's certainly one of my favorite scents." She ran the bar up one arm and down another. "I'll ask Grandmother if we can grow some next spring." Although, if she was to be in Baltimore, there wasn't much point in that.

She'd miss her garden.

"Hold still." Rhee poured the pitcher of water over her head. "I'm glad you've come, Beth. I was beginning to worry; you've spent so many mornings in bed." She reached for the soap, rubbing it between her hands to work up a lather, then began to scrub Elisabeth's head, humming as she did.

"Your spirits have certainly picked up, Rhee. The countryside must have done its task well."

"Hmm, perhaps. I think it's merely the fact that we've seen the last of the abominable heat, those blasted flies, and the cursed mosquitoes. At least for a few months. Although I have to say, John has this fire so hot, it seems summer is still here."

It was uncomfortably warm in the room. But Grandmother had put her foot down, once she'd seen Jane carrying up the water for the bath.

"It's worse in the islands, you know."

"Oh? Are you speaking from experience?"

Elisabeth laughed. "It's selfish, I know. But I don't want to lose you, even to your husband." She wiped the soapsuds from her brow before they reached her eyes. "This feels wonderful. I don't remember the last time . . ." She frowned, looking up at Rhee. "Rhee, tell me the truth, do I look as bad as I've been feeling?"

"Well, you've let yourself go. Only a tad, mind you. But

nonetheless, we must deal with it. No, don't talk. You'll get soap in your mouth."

She filled another pitcher, pouring it over Elisabeth's hair. "And, you've left me only your friend Mary to have fun with. She's nice enough, but really, how you've done without me all these years, I'm sure I don't know. That girl is quite scatterbrained. Stand up." Rhee draped the towel around her as she stepped out of the tub. "She has quite a crush on your Mr. Brock, you know. I tried to dissuade her, but she'd have none of it."

"Liam's done nothing to encourage her, Rhee."

"Oh, I'm sure he's completely blameless, paragon of virtue that he is."

"Well, he is. Blameless." Paragon of virtue might be going a bit too far. She reached for her shift and pulled it over her head. "And you've only distracted me momentarily, so, tell me, how awful have I looked?"

"I merely said you've let your appearance slide a 'tad bit.' I don't believe I used the word 'awful.'" She pushed Elisabeth into the chair and reached for a comb. "Your hair had begun to look grimy, and you've grown far too thin. I thought you were supposed to become plump. You obviously aren't eating enough."

Elisabeth grimaced, recalling how the mere scent of food had been enough to cause her to gag in the past weeks. Only recently had she begun to feel an interest in eating again.

"I think I shall become quite plump. I ate practically half the bread this morning, and it had butter and honey on it. I've started feeling much better." She leaned toward the looking glass as Rhee worked the tangles from her hair. Turning her head from side to side, she examined her complexion in the morning light. She did look a trifle wan.

"Do you think we might go out, Rhee? I'd like to take a gift to Mrs. Baylor. Remember, she's the one who's been helping David perfect his shorthand?"

"Of course. We'll ask Mrs. Hale what she thinks the woman would like. I hear she's been recently widowed?"

"No . . . no," Elisabeth said, shaking her head. "Where did you hear that? It's only that her husband is a ship captain, and gone quite a bit. It's my impression she's not the least bit elderly."

"Oh. Oh, my." Rhee set the brush down, pursing her lips as she looked at Elisabeth's reflection in the glass. "Well, we can't go out today, I'll be scolded for certain if I take you out while your hair is damp. We'll visit Eliza first thing tomorrow. She's had our new gowns waiting for several weeks now." She reached around, cupping Elisabeth's breasts in her hands, sighing as she shook her head.

"I declare, Beth, we're going to have to add some padding until you get your own back."

22

"ELIZA WOULD HAVE HAD these delivered, Rhee," Elisabeth said, struggling to keep her package secure and uncrushed as they climbed the front steps.

"We don't have time for that." Rhee opened the Hales' front door with her free hand, then followed Elisabeth in. "I'll ask her to deliver the others, once she makes those alterations, but in the meantime we have need of these. Now, let's eat dinner before we get ready."

"But, I'm not—"

"You must be hungry. You need only a whiff of John's kitchen to remind you of it."

"No!" Rhee had placed her hand on her back, pushing her toward the kitchen. "No, Rhee!" she whispered, protesting. "John is bound to notice the rouge."

"Pooh. I barely applied a smidgen, and it's virtually undetectable. Being out and about has given you enough of your own color. You let me handle John while you eat."

TWO HOURS later they stood outside Mr. Donaldson's office, dressed in their beautiful new gowns. Elisabeth held one of Rhee's rose soaps, specially gift wrapped and specially chosen by Rhee after she had thoroughly quizzed John on what he thought David's reaction might be to each of the scents in question.

Apparently she thought Elisabeth too addle-witted to know as well as John did that David didn't care for the scent of roses.

She followed Rhee up the steps and in through front door, then stood waiting at the empty reception table. She grimaced as she caught a glimpse of Liam in the back office, head bent to his books, and hoped he wouldn't look their way. A hope dashed as soon as Rhee picked up the bell resting on the desk, shaking it before Elisabeth could stop her.

Liam strode to the front, his gait easy, seeming completely at home in the well-appointed office. Goodness, it was no wonder Mary still carried about a crush on the man. Those mischievous, vivid blue eyes practically danced against his dark coloring. She often forgot, until she glimpsed him in an unfamiliar environment, that the man was extraordinarily handsome.

"Why it's Elisabeth. Fancy that. I see ye've brought Mrs. Ross as well. Have you come for Mr. Donaldson?" he asked, his eyes on Rhee, who merely nodded her greeting.

"I'm sorry, Liam, We certainly didn't intend to interrupt you. Rhee and I thought we'd drop off a gift for Mrs. Baylor while we were out this afternoon." She felt his eyes as they left Rhee and traveled over her, taking in the new gown. Rhee left her side and walked around the room, ostensibly studying the few pieces of artwork that Donaldson displayed.

"Did ye, now?" Liam perched on the desktop, his eyes alight with amusement.

"To show our . . . my . . . appreciation of her helping David. It's been very kind of her, don't you think?"

"Oh, aye," Liam said, nodding, swinging his leg to and fro as he watched her. "Ye look very nice, Lisbeth."

"Rhee looks nice too."

"Aye, she does as well," he answered, though he didn't take his eyes from her. "Is that a new gown you're wearing?"

"I've had it for some time." Well she had. For several hours, at least. More if one counted the days since she'd gone to the first fitting.

"Mmm. First I've seen it, then."

"Yes, well. I supposed our paths haven't crossed much."

"Oh, aye. Least not since this morning."

"Oh, for heaven's sake, Mr. Brock. Stop teasing her. Whose side are you on?"

Liam grinned. "Are we at war, Mrs. Ross?"

"Why don't you tell me? Should we leave the gift on the table with a note of thanks? Or should we make ourselves comfortable until Mrs. Baylor returns?" Rhee settled in one of the chairs, as if she were certain of his answer.

Liam laughed. He stood and bent over Elisabeth, kissing her cheek. "Make yourself comfortable with Mrs. Ross, lass. I expect Mrs. Baylor will be back momentarily."

"Thank you, Liam," she said faintly, sinking into the chair beside Rhee.

She was mortified. Liam would tell David, and David would think . . . well, who knew what he'd think. Except about the new gown. She was certain she knew what he'd think about the new gown.

Lord, why hadn't she stayed in bed?

"I THINK THAT'S enough for tonight, Mr. Graham," Mrs. Baylor said, coming up behind him as he drew a line through the last sentence, rewriting the notations to correct the errors she'd pointed out.

"Aye, I apologize, ma'am. I didna mean to take so much of your time; it's only I struggled with—"

"Enough, David, relax now. We've worked hard enough." She set a glass of whisky in front of him, then took the chair opposite him.

He looked up, surprised by the offer of whisky. She was a nice enough woman and younger than he'd expected. And, as Liam had warned, she was beautiful. Especially as she looked now, her red hair and white skin lit softly by candlelight. Her blue eyes seemed to carry a wistful expression, almost sad, and he wondered if she were lonely without her husband about.

"We've made considerable progress tonight. You're entitled to a break," she said, reaching for the notebook in his lap.

Holy hell. He steeled himself not to move, lest he embarrass her. Because, surely, that brush of her fingers had not been deliberate.

If they were done with the teaching, he needed to leave. Now.

But he didn't want to be rude. The woman obviously expected some social niceties before he left.

"Where's Captain Baylor off to now, ma'am?" he asked, standing. He moved in front of the fire, holding his hands near the flames, on the pretext his fingers had chilled while writing. "It must be exciting, hearing the man's stories when he returns."

"He's in Jamaica, as far as I know. Lord knows, I've already heard more of Jamaica than I care to know."

"Aye, but there's bound to be a new tale." He shifted from foot to foot, warmed as much as he could tolerate. "I'll finish with the roof, tomorrow, Mrs. Baylor. I hope ye consider it a fair trade. I'm meaning, I hope it hasn't been too much of a hardship. I know I havena taken to some of it so quick . . ." Jesus, it was hard to talk a fair sentence with someone looking at you like that. He needed to leave.

"I should go now. My wife, ken? I hate leaving her for long. She's been feeling poorly."

"Oh? I'm sorry to hear that. She looked well last we met. Give her my best, will you?"

"Elisabeth?"

"That's your wife's name, isn't it?"

"Aye, of course. I didna realize ye'd met, is all." He set the glass on the table. "Thanks for the whisky, ma'am. I'll be back in the morning. Will ye let the help know?"

"Yes, Mr. Graham." She rose, walking with him to the door. "And you've taken to the lessons quickly, so don't disparage yourself. A few more evenings, and I daresay you'll have mastered it. I'll have to be careful Papa doesn't replace me."

He laughed, comfortable again. He'd made more of an accidental touch than he should have.

23   November 1790

"SEE, LISTEN. On October first," Rhee read, "my husband, Albram Barnuckle, without just cause, eloped from my bed. This is to forewarn all persons from trusting him on my account. It is supposed he is gone to Mount Hollyocks Iron Works, with a woman named Alice Smith, who used to work about the fish market. I intend to make action to the Legislature of the State, for an Act to divorce me from Albram Barnuckle, my husband." Straightening, she turned to Elisabeth.

"My, if it's that easy, perhaps I should consider a divorce. I think I should compose my own advertisement, Beth, and have it posted in Bristol. So that others are aware Mr. Ross' and my decisions aren't made jointly. What do you think? Of course, our circumstances are somewhat different, but perhaps David could help with more appropriate wording."

Elisabeth merely smiled, shaking her head as she counted her stitches. Rhee said the most outrageous things at times, primarily to entertain Papa. She didn't mean a word of it. She'd no more advertise her marital problems than she would walk down Market Street with her hair uncombed.

"David could add that Ross is in debt to Mother for your room and board," Hale said, smiling as he took the paper from her and folded it.

"Don't be absurd, Edward," her grandmother said. "Rhiannon, your company has been a gift, and we're the ones who owe Mr. Ross."

"Rhiannon knows I'm only teasing. Now, show me the notice for the property you were speaking of."

"This is the one," Rhiannon said, pointing a finger at a small ad in the newspaper. "Would you go with me to look at it, Mr. Hale? It's nearby."

He read through the ad, frowning. "Why, that's an inn, Rhiannon. You told me your husband wanted land for investment."

"I know. But what if something happens to my husband? Fevers abound in the West Indies. Heavens, I could be a widow even now and not know it!"

"I'm not certain what that's to do with an inn, but if we find that's the case, I pray you practice a more appropriate portrayal of grief."

"Ha, ha, Mr. Hale. My point is, I need to plan for my future. I need a solid investment if I don't want to be forced to marry again. And I don't—want to be forced to marry."

She paced in front of Hale, her fingers twisting round the ring she wore. "I could run an inn; I know I could. Why, I practically did, growing up. My father had visitors from all over the world come to stay. There was scarcely a night our extra bedrooms were free."

"That's true, Papa. You remember, don't you? And here, within only a few blocks, I know of three taverns run by women. There's Mrs. Brint, at the sign of the Hen and Chickens, Mrs. Kalm, at the Golden Fleece's Head, and then Mrs. Noll runs the one at the sign of the Sorrel Horse, right next to the apothecary. The places always look busy. If they can do it, Rhee certainly can."

Her father nodded absently, reading through the ad again. "Is he prepared to spend this sum?"

Rhee nodded, her green eyes shining with excitement. "I am . . . I mean, he is. It won't take all my capital. I'll still have enough cash left for my daily necessities. He's left a lot at my disposal,

Mr. Hale."

"It seems he has. You'll need his signature, you know."

"I can obtain it through the post, surely. Well, Mr. Hale? Will you come?"

"Yes. But I want Donaldson to look it over as well. I've no experience appraising the value of a going concern. He'll make the offer, if you're still interested."

Rhiannon threw out her arms and spun around, and Elisabeth laughed, glad to see her happy. She worried Rhee might be finding her visit too dull, and that she'd leave soon. Why, if she purchased an inn, she'd stay indefinitely!

"Now, I've a meeting to attend, so I must leave you ladies to your own devices. Will you be joining us for dinner later, Elisabeth?" he asked as he walked to the doorway.

"I'm not sure, Papa, but maybe." She detected a flash of disappointment and amended her answer. "Yes, probably." He left, his mouth curved in a trace of a smile.

She was so grateful for the timing of Rhiannon's visit. Having a guest eased the tension she might otherwise feel in her father's presence, and Rhee was adept at keeping him smiling.

Her grandmother stood, gripping the sides of her chair for support. "I must speak to John about the accounts now. I do hope we'll see you at dinner, Elisabeth."

"All right, Grandmother. I'll try."

"What should we do this morning, Elisabeth?" Rhee asked once they were alone. "The paper noted that Sitgreaves received a shipment from Europe. We could look as his assortment of flannel and start sewing for the baby."

"That's perfect. That's where my credit is, and I've been negligent in using it." Several of the women in her class had traded produce to Mr. Sitgreaves over the summer, instructing him to give her credit in exchange the next time she came in.

THE MOMENT they stepped outside, Rhee pushed her back in, shutting the door soundly. "Hell's bells, Beth. You didn't mention it was colder than cold! That wind will find its way straight to my godchild. Wait!"

Rhee ran upstairs, gathering shawls, scarves, and muffs. "There now, that's better," she said, piling the items on.

"I suppose David's been giving you an earful."

"Well, he's right, you know. You must take every precaution you can." She looked at her, frowning, and adjusted her scarf so that no part of her neck was left uncovered. "Keep your hands in those mitts, now."

It *was* bitterly cold. She was grateful David had inside work today. And soon, Congress would be meeting, and he would be spending the better part of each day inside, writing his notes.

"What are you thinking of purchasing with your credit?"

"I've been trying to decide for a month now. I think I'll use it on pewterware. The men are so hard on things. Glass doesn't last long."

"Elisabeth! That's your money! How will those women feel, knowing you aren't using it for yourself?" Rhee shivered as they turned the corner and confronted the frigid blast of air gusting up the Delaware. She hadn't taken the precaution of covering her own neck. "Gracious, I would have to pick Front Street, wouldn't I?" She held open the door to Sitgreaves' store, motioning impatiently for Elisabeth to go in first as their skirts lifted, each tangling about the other in the wind.

"Don't forget, it's the use of Mr. Oliver's rooms that makes those classes possible. The women won't begrudge me that." She groped behind her shoulder for her scarf, righting it before it fell completely away.

"I suppose not, especially knowing Mr. Brock will be one of the recipients."

Elisabeth laughed as she helped Rhee adjust the tilt of her hat. Though lately Rhee appeared to be making an effort to be cordial to Liam, it never failed to irritate her when women made a fuss over him. And women *always* made a fuss over the man. "No, I expect you're right. I'll have to make sure he thanks them."

Rhee rolled her eyes and turned her attention to the fabric. "Do you like this color, Beth?" She ran a length of cloth through her fingers, her expert touch assessing the quality. "It's good, and it will last. I think blue is perfect."

"David's eyes are brown, as will our baby's be. Blue is Liam's color."

"Pooh. Your eyes are blue. But this shade isn't even close to the color of that man's eyes. His eyes are a much darker blue, like that," she said, pointing to the table under the front window.

Elisabeth looked at the stack of cobalt blue duffil Rhee had indicated and saw that indeed they were . . . exactly. She looked back at Rhee, speculating.

"Don't you look at me like that, Mrs. Graham. I'm merely observant. And if you're searching for a gift, the man could certainly use a duffil coat. He manages to quaff more than enough ale with his dented pewter."

"Hmm." Elisabeth ducked her head as she sorted through the fabric, biting back a smile. "How about this one?" she asked, pulling out a length of copper-dyed flannel.

Rhee frowned, tilting her head. "It will do, I suppose. Mind, if this baby is a girl, I'm to choose her gowns, and she won't be wearing brown."

"It's copper. Besides, brown is a lovely color. It's warm and welcoming, like home. And the baby is a boy."

Rhee snorted and walked away from the fabric. "Oh, Elisabeth, look! We need this, and I'm buying it." She held up a pure white swanskin. "I'll make a powder puff for each of us and we'll have enough remaining for the baby to lay on. She'll love it." Rhee held the skin to her cheek, closing her eyes as she fondled the fur, stroking it down the side of her face.

"Here's the pewter, Rhee."

"I'll be with you in a minute, dear. I want to ask the shopkeeper how much this is."

She had a wide variety of cups and mugs to choose from. Mr. Oliver preferred the mugs with the handles, so she pulled four aside, checking them carefully for dents. Plates, no, they didn't need plates. Bowls, yes. They were forever running short of bowls. She and Liam both tended to prepare soup, and the men had only three bowls. Perhaps Jane, Rob's wife, had shared Rob's bowl when they lived here, as she had been doing with

David in the times the four of them sat to eat together. She made her selection and met Rhee at the counter.

Rhee had added a length of the blue flannel to her purchase, as well as a small striped blanket and a felt hat.

"For your papa," she explained, holding the hat up for Elisabeth to examine. "I think he should look a little less formal, from time to time, don't you? Especially when he's trooping off to look at land."

"That's generous of you, Rhiannon."

"Oh, no. Now I'm Rhiannon." She turned back to the store clerk to settle her bill, then waited for Elisabeth to work out her credit.

"Am I supposed to be angry with him as well?" she asked, as soon as the clerk had his instructions for delivery. "For heaven's sake, you haven't even told me why you're angry yourself."

"No, you're not." Elisabeth sighed. She expected she wanted Papa to suffer some, and that was childish. "Would you like to get some tea?"

"All right."

Huddled together, they walked to the inn at the corner, then hurried to settle in the tiny tea room, welcoming the rush of warmth the room offered. She loved this place. She and David had spent their wedding night upstairs.

Sipping her tea slowly, Rhee nodded toward the door. "Don't turn now, but a devastatingly handsome man just walked through the entrance. He looks simply mouthwatering in those breeches, and I daresay he knows it, given his swagger." She set her cup down. "Oh, my, he's coming this way."

Strong arms surrounded Elisabeth, and she caught a whiff of leather and ink as David planted a kiss on her cheek.

"David!"

"Bess, I didna know you'd be out today." He sat next to her, taking her hand in his. "Good afternoon, Rhee. Ye did well bundling her," he said, nodding toward the scarves and mitts they had set on the window seat.

"I take instruction well. What are you doing here?"

Elisabeth winced as his grip on her hand tightened, and she watched as he turned his eyes from Rhee to the saucers on the table. "I was to meet Mrs. Baylor here and take her to the Dry Goods. She wanted me to go over the roofing material bill with the clerk. She thinks the cove may have overcharged her, though I think it's likely more the high cost of the cedar shingles. She told me she wanted something long lasting, else I would have chosen other. I figured no sense redoing the roof now, only to have to redo it two years hence. Not me, I mean, but for someone to have to redo it." He looked at her, as if he were suddenly uncertain if he should have agreed to meet the woman. "She knew I was anxious to get home after the session yesterday, Bess, so she suggested today to handle the task."

My, that was a lot of chatting for David. He was uncomfortable.

Elisabeth set down her tea and reached to smooth his hair. "That's considerate of her. I would have missed you last night were you any later." She squeezed his knee in a quick caress, gratified to see the flash of heat darken his eyes.

"Well, well. Mr. and Mrs. Graham. Allow me to offer my belated congratulations."

David stood, hand on her shoulder, as Rory Smith filled the doorway.

"Rory! Thank you. It's so good to see you," Elisabeth said.

The two men exchanged nods, and David introduced Rhiannon.

"My goodness, it's been ages. The mill must be keeping you very busy," Elisabeth said.

"Yes. You look well, Elisabeth. Better than well. I can see marriage agrees with you."

She reached a hand to her shoulder and placed it over David's, smiling up at him as she answered Rory. "It does, very much so."

"Are you in town on business, Mr. Smith?" Rhee asked.

"Pardon?" Rory shifted his hat from one hand to the other and looked toward Rhee.

"Are you in Philadelphia on business? Elisabeth had

mentioned your mill was a good distance from town."

"Less than two hours ride, ma'am. And yes, I'm in town to meet with my attorney. I expect to ride back early tomorrow." He looked again at David. "David, might I reach Liam at the same address?"

"Aye, he's still there."

"If you happen to see him, would you tell him I'd like to meet with him next time I'm in town? I'll send a note to suggest a date and time."

Elisabeth held her breath as Rhee caught her eye, both of them waiting to see if David would mention they lived with Liam. The whole arrangement had been a blow to his pride, and being reminded of it by a man he regarded as a former rival would not sit easy.

"Aye," David said shortly. "I see my party waiting in the hall, so please excuse me." He bent over Elisabeth, murmuring in her ear that he loved her, then left.

Rory's eyes followed him, his gaze narrowing speculatively once he saw David's "party," then he took the seat David had vacated, apparently deciding his own business could wait a while longer.

"Are you enjoying your stay in Philadelphia, Mrs. Ross?"

"Quite, Mr. Smith. Elisabeth and David are wonderful hosts."

She would not turn. She would not. Rhee could see into the entry hall and watched, in spite of her stream of small talk with Rory, and Rhee would give her a full accounting.

"Elisabeth?"

"Pardon me?"

"Mr. Smith inquired after Becca, Beth."

She smiled, grateful for the diversion. "Becca made it through all of September without digging up a single bush. Grandmother had put her on probation, you see. I declare I had to watch her day and night, but she did it! And now I have Rhee to help entertain her. But honestly, I think she is becoming quite mellow, and Grandmother wouldn't turn her out for all the tea in China."

"Mellow, my eye." Rhee sniffed. "We must go, Elisabeth, if we don't want to disappoint your father for dinner. I enjoyed meeting you, Mr. Smith, and I trust we'll see each other again." She paused as she turned to reach for her bag. "Perhaps next time you're in town, you'll stop in for tea?"

The words were coming, Rhee needn't have kicked her. "Of course you must, Rory. I'll ask Liam as well. He'll advise us of the day you're expected."

"I'd be delighted," he said. "Good day, ladies."

"Rhee, why did you rush us out? Rory would have chatted another thirty minutes."

"That woman was well aware I was watching, Elisabeth. I think perhaps she might have staged a gesture or two, purely for my benefit, and your husband was uncomfortable. It's best you show you're not the least bit worried, leaving him alone with her."

"But I am worried!"

"No. You're not. That man adores you."

She tightened her lips, not willing to argue in public. Anyway, perhaps Rhee was right.

"Why do you think Mr. Smith wanted to see Mr. Brock?"

"Oh, probably some legal business to do with the mill. Rory has more lawyers than I can keep track of. I expect he would know Liam works for Mr. Donaldson."

"Hmm. Oh, my goodness, do hurry," Rhee said, reaching a hand to hold her hat in place as she hunched forward against the wind.

"You should have purchased enough flannel for a petticoat."

"Bite your tongue. I will never wear a flannel petticoat."

24 November 1790

"THE PEOPLE OF THE COURT fell silent as Mr. Thomas stepped to the podium. He cleared his throat and began, enumerating all the reasons his proposal should be considered." Elisabeth yawned, covering her mouth with the back of her hand as the book fell closed. "I think that's enough for tonight, don't you, David? You've been up since before dawn." She went to him, her hands caressing the back of his neck. "How'd you do?" she asked, leaning over his shoulder to peer at the notations he'd made. She watched as he slid his finger down the lines, his lips moving as he did.

Reaching for the book, he handed it back to her. "Five more minutes, Bess? I'll read it back to ye. Ye note where I miss?"

She kissed the top of his head and went back to the chair, doing as he asked. When he finished, she looked up. "Well, it's not word for word, but it's very close. It's quite perfect, I think."

He grinned at her as he rose. "Ye always name it perfect," he said, looking over her shoulder at the two marks she'd made. "It's no' perfect, but I think I did fine." Grabbing her, he swung her in a slow circle as he kissed her. "I'll ask Mrs. Baylor to look it over tomorrow. If she can read it through as well, there'll be no need to bother her further."

Elisabeth kept quiet. Nora Baylor was sure not to mind him

"bothering" her further.

One of the women in her class stayed on after the lesson last night, pulling Elisabeth aside as the others filed out. It seemed everyone knew of Mrs. Baylor, and her student had thought to relay a story of a "friend of a friend of a friend." She had finished in embarrassment, telling Elisabeth she was sorry she had said anything, and she probably never should have, given Mr. Graham's obvious devotion. She truly didn't want to cause her undue worry and had been debating talking to her about it for weeks. But Elisabeth had been so wonderful to all of them, and she had finally decided that, as a wife herself, well, she only thought Elisabeth should know of Nora Baylor's reputation. And Elisabeth wasn't to think *anyone* had heard a word of Mr. Graham doing *anything* improper. Elisabeth had hugged and thanked her before sending her on her way with the admonition not to worry.

David had taken such pains to ask her opinion of the arrangement. Had he heard of the woman's reputation as well, then? Had he had cause to know it was well-earned?

She actually had no complaint against her, she reminded herself. In fact, she owed Mrs. Baylor a great deal, given the skill she'd taught David. He didn't worry so any more, and his eyes shone with hope and ambition. And, once again, he walked across a room as if he owned it.

That regained confidence was due to a new skill, right? Not to a new conquest?

Of course it was. She knew he loved her, despite the way her emotions ricocheted from one extreme to the other, despite the way there were times she could barely keep her eyes open to talk to him, and despite the way her cooking still left much to be desired.

She had absolutely nothing to fret over.

"Would you mind if I took it to her tomorrow afternoon, David? If she pronounces your study complete, you won't be taking another of her evenings."

"Course I dinna mind," he said, his mouth nuzzling her neck. She arched back, giving him better access, a soft moan escaping her lips before she remembered Mr. Oliver could overhear from his room.

"Tomorrow morning," she whispered, her hands traveling down his body with a promise. He groaned, tightening his hold.

ELISABETH READ the passage out loud, then shut the book softly, looking at Nora Baylor. John's assessment had been a bit unkind. Tall and buxom, with luxurious auburn hair, she was lovely enough to flaunt anything she cared to. Looking at her, one could easily see why she was gossiped about so. She was sensual in a unabashed way, from the way she carried herself across the room, to the way her hands moved as she talked, to the way she dressed and the colors she chose to do so in.

As was Rhee, come to think of it. And she didn't mistrust Rhee for it.

"Well?"

"Did he send you, Mrs. Graham?"

"What? Oh. No. No, he didn't. I offered, you see, as he's to be working all day on the wharves. He'll be exhausted by day's end, and I have plenty of time."

"Hmm. That's not what I hear, between your charitable endeavors and your little school, you're quite the busy woman. Did you know one of my servants attended your class?"

"No, I didn't. Who is she?"

"Mrs. Angel. She's fairly short, walks with a limp, speaks with a lisp, one of her eyes—"

"Oh yes, yes, I know Mrs. Angel," Elisabeth interrupted before she was treated to a full list of the woman's physical imperfections. "She was one of my first students. She actually came further along than any in that original group, truth be. She loves to read."

"Well, I have to admit, having her read a few words has certainly made the marketing easier. She no longer forgets things, now that I can make a short list she'll understand."

Gracious, Mrs. Angel could certainly read more than a marketing list. "Yes, well," she said, pointing to the paper Mrs. Baylor held. "Are his notations accurate?"

"It's perfect, Mrs. Graham. He captured it perfectly."

Elisabeth clapped her hands. "Oh, he'll be thrilled!"

"As will you," Mrs. Baylor said, "to have him out of my clutches, I suppose."

Elisabeth's eyes widened, and she was unable to stop the flush that spread quickly over her face. "I . . . I'm sorry. I'm not certain what to say."

The woman laughed. "Nothing, you needn't say a word. You were right to be suspicious. A woman should worry if her husband spends long evenings with another woman, no matter what the reason." She stood, placing a hand on Elisabeth's shoulder. "But I'm going to give you some advice, my dear, as I know you're newly married. It's best to give a man some room to breathe. Once they start to suffocate, they do begin to look for an escape route."

"SHE SAID THAT?" Rhee paced, her hands fisting. "You should have slapped her, Elisabeth." She pointed a finger in Elisabeth's direction, stabbing the air. "The *only* reason she said that was due to her own husband taking an escape route. My word, of all the arrogance, of all the—"

"Rhee, stop! It's all right. Calm down. I wasn't angry, or even hurt by the remark. I only wondered if you thought it could be true. Eventually, I mean, not necessarily now." She chastised herself for bringing it up, for forgetting the subject might be painful for Rhiannon.

"Rhee, child, sit down," her grandmother said. Rhee sat, though it appeared as if she were poised for flight at any moment.

"Now, listen to me carefully. It's not my place to say this, but I'll say it anyway. Your Mr. Ross must be quite out of his mind. So you need to stop holding yourself accountable for his lack of perception because no amount of reasoning or second guessing is going to explain the workings of an unbalanced mind. Good heavens, when I see the way it eats at you, I want to strangle the man."

Rhee's mouth tightened rebelliously. "Thank you, Mrs. Hale, but this isn't about—"

"There's no need for Elisabeth to worry. You know that." She held up two skeins, frowning as she examined them, presumably worrying over selecting just the right shade of red. "You need to come to terms with your situation. Have you thought about joining him?"

Elisabeth looked from Rhee to her grandmother, frowning. "No, Grandmother. She can't!"

"Why ever not? He's her husband."

She reached for Becca, picking the spaniel up, hugging her so tight she squirmed. "Because . . . because . . . it's winter for heaven's sake."

"Stop talking about me as if I weren't in the room. Why do you suggest that, Mrs. Hale?" Rhee asked, leaning forward, her elbows propped on her knees.

"Well, if you want to start a family with your husband, you'll find it next to impossible to accomplish from this distance. Secondly, I sense you would like some resolution to the matter."

"You're right, of course. Don't look at me that way, Elisabeth. I married the man, and I failed at the marriage. I don't like to fail."

"Bloody hell!" Elisabeth stood, her hands flying in agitation, and Becca fell from her lap. With the air of one injured, the spaniel trotted to the comfort of her basket. "You did not fail, Rhiannon. Don't you dare say that you did!"

"Elisabeth Anne! Your language, young lady!"

"Pardon me, Grandmother."

Rhee smiled, winking at Elisabeth.

"Now, Rhiannon, it takes more than one to fail at a marriage, child."

"I know it does, Mrs. Hale. But I'm beginning to believe I might have been content to let it fail." She stood and walked to the window, looking down the street. "It's more than possible I helped it along."

"Oh, Rhee. Please don't go. Not yet anyway. It isn't safe. What would you accomplish?"

"Assess my competition? See a bit more of the world? See if I could nurture a tiny seed of affection into love? I don't know,

Elisabeth, but I'll aver it's certainly more than I'm doing now."

She wanted to beg Rhee to stay, at least until the baby was born, but that was selfish, and she had made a vow not to be selfish, hadn't she? Elisabeth looked at her grandmother, who shook her head slightly.

"I understand, Rhee. I suppose I'd likely do the same. But you must wait until after the worst of winter is over. Please?"

Rhee sighed, rubbing her hands across her face. "I expect you're right. It would be miserably cold onboard." She left the window and walked back to her seat, picking up her embroidery.

"I'm sorry, Elisabeth, if anything I said gave you needless cause to worry about David. I think perhaps Mrs. Hale is right. I was simply taking out my own frustation on poor Mrs. Baylor."

"Oh, she's not so poor as all that," her grandmother said, sniffing as her needle flew across the cloth. "There's no doubt she has her eye on your husband, Elisabeth."

25 December 1790

"I'M NO' SURE I can help, Rory," Liam said. "I've no credentials, ken?"

"Attorneys with credentials have me at a standstill. You're in the process; that's good enough for me."

"Aye, well, that's no' quite the case."

"I'm not asking in hopes to save a dollar, Liam," Rory answered, ignoring the disavowal. "I'm asking because I need someone with fresh insight. I'll pay you." He dropped his cigar to the floor and ground the stub with his boot, then tapped the papers again, impatient. The man bordering his paper mill was making trouble with the water rights, and Rory'd been fighting it since his Pa died and he inherited the business. "He can shut me down the way it stands. I need that water. He's got me by the balls."

Maybe he did, maybe he didn't.

"Well?"

"Leave off, man, I'm thinking," Liam answered, chewing the inside of his cheek. He could see the shape of a possibility. Maybe not a likely one, but one nonetheless.

"Can ye leave these with me? Maybe there is something I can do."

Rory grinned, seeming more certain of the outcome than he was himself, and pushed the papers across the table. "I'll be back in town the fifteenth."

"I'll see to it before then. I'll ride out next Sunday and talk it over with you, aye?" He'd like to wait until the following Monday. The stable fees would be less on Monday for one thing. Plus he'd told Molly he'd spend Sunday with her. Her sister was marrying, and the lass was insisting he come to the family gathering. He hated turning down free food and drink.

But Donaldson was insistent as well—insistent he spend each and every day but Sunday tied to that desk. It chafed, the loss of freedom to move about as he pleased, as Mr. O had always allowed.

He tucked the papers inside his waistcoat and stood, looking toward the doorway. His eyes watered as another blast of wind shifted the smoke of the fire, sending it about the tavern instead of up the chimney. He had expected to meet Mr. O here for coffee before he met with Smith; now he worried the man had headed home instead. He wasn't to do that; Davey wasn't expecting him. "I'm off now. I need to find—ah, here he is." Mr. Oliver strode toward him, one large hand attached to little Tommy Nailor's ear.

"What d'ye catch there, Mr. O?"

"Take this damned rascal to his mother, will you, Liam? I'm late," he said with a huff as he pushed the boy toward him, then turned and hurried out the door.

"DO YOU THINK he's planning on telling her, Mr. Brock?" Tommy Nailor looked at him, his face scrunched with fear at his mother's anticipated reaction.

Mr. Oliver had caught the lad scaling the boom of one of the ships resting in the harbor, a dangerous prospect with the wharves as full as they were.

"I expect that's up to you, lad."

"What do you mean?"

"The way round Mr. O is through his books, ken?"

"So?"

"Well, if I'd been caught climbing that boom, 'stead of you, I'd be all o'er the man, clamoring for him to explain this or that. Take his mind off the other, like."

He watched as the boy calculated, weighing his dislike of book learning against the prospect of his mother's switch.

"It was dangerous, lad, what you were up to. You lose your grip, fall betwixt those ships . . ." Liam paused for effect, then clapped his hands together hard and fast. "Bam! Your head will look like that watermelon ye dropped from my window last summer."

"For true? Just like that, you think?"

"If ye're curious, Mr. O's got books he can show you, with drawings and such."

The boy considered the possibility as he scratched his cheek, then shook his head. "No, books don't show that."

"Have ye never heard of a physician operating, then, lad? Where d'ye think the man learns it from?" He opened the door to the townhouse and ushered the boy in. "Best ye be taking your whipping, then. Ye willna have to waste time thinking o'er that."

"Wait, Mr. Brock," he said, grabbing the tail of his coat as he started back out. "If I do it, are you *sure* he won't tell?"

Liam shrugged. "If ye dinna, I'm sure he will." He walked out, and right into Rhiannon Ross.

"Good morning, Mr. Brock." Rhiannon nodded at him as she pushed past at the door, starting up the stairs. "Enjoy your day."

He grabbed her elbow, pulling her back before she reached the second step. "Join me for coffee, ma'am?"

"Another time, perhaps. Elisabeth is expecting me."

He steered her off the step and out the door, closing it behind him. "No' at the moment, she's no'. If ye tread up those stairs, I'll forfeit my take." He held up a coin. "Davey gave it to me, so as I'd make myself scarce for the next hour or so enjoying a cup at the Coffee House. Come, I'll share my good fortune."

Rhee frowned, yanking her arm from his grasp as she looked up at the townhouse window. He knew immediately when she came to understanding, for a faint flush spread across that lush display of bosom and crept up her slender neck, and a smile replaced the frown, an impish gleam shining in her clear green eyes. "Perhaps I could obtain another coin, and we could enjoy something sweet with our coffee?"

"Now, lass, dinna be greedy. He's my mate, ken?" He took her elbow and started walking. Though the Coffee House would no longer do, Mrs. Grayton's parlor certainly would. She stocked it afresh each morning with the best the markets had to offer. While she catered primarily to her lodgers, she never hesitated to welcome him as well once she found he could match her store of rumor tit for tat.

"I'll buy ye something sweet myself, seeing as how ye're no longer sniping at me."

"I never sniped at you, Mr. Brock."

"Oh, aye, ye did. And often it was, as well." He gave a brief knock on the door, then held it open for Rhee to follow through.

"Liam, my boy!" Mrs. Grayton bustled to the entry, her hands flying to his face as she patted him about, kissing him soundly. "Who is it we have here?"

"This is Mrs. Ross, Mrs. Grayton. She's a good friend of Elisabeth's. I thought I'd treat her to the best coffee in Philly whilst she's waiting on the lass."

Mrs. Grayton greeted her, then aimed a conspiratorial smile his way. "Saw the boy head home, I did," she whispered, for his ears alone.

He smiled back, not doubting it for a minute. She knew everything that happened on this street. Wonder she got anything done, lingering at the window the way she did. He'd have to ask her later about Mr. Oliver and Mrs. Holmes, and what he might do about it.

Rhee had wandered away to peek in the parlor, and he followed her. There were some guests in the room; however, the table by the entry was empty. He took the wrap off her shoulders, taking care his fingers grazed her neck as his did. Jesus, her skin was soft, her scent intoxicating. It was different today, her scent, and he inhaled deeply while he was close, wondering why she changed it often.

"Let's have a seat. Ye drink it black? She keeps a cow. Should you want milk, ye'll find it's fresh."

"I don't drink coffee."

"Yes, ye do. Ye're jus' being contrary." He ordered two coffees and a plate of sugary buns. "What did you and the lass have planned for the day?"

"Oh, this and that." She reached for a bun, breaking off a piece.

He watched her as she chewed the pastry, tensing as she licked the sugar from her fingers. This was the first time they had been alone together since that ride back into town several weeks ago.

Other than the times they had met in his dreams.

"Is your coffee good?"

"Mmm," she said, nodding, taking another sip. "It's been frightfully cold, hasn't it?"

"Aye, it has. I find I'm happy the trade is slowing, and I needn't be riverside."

She didn't change expression at his mention of laboring the wharves; she merely nodded and reached for another piece of the bun. Perhaps if he broke off the next piece and placed it in her mouth, she'd lick the sugar from his fingers as well. Perhaps . . .

He shifted in his seat and took a long swallow of his coffee, grateful for the distraction of the burn as it traveled down his throat.

"It seems Mrs. Hale willna be joining me for Judge Wilson's lecture next week."

The wicked turn in the weather had hit Mrs. Hale hard, and her doctor thought it best she stay inside, out of the wind's reach. He'd planned on taking Molly to the lecture, once Mrs. Hale had pleaded her case, dismissing Mrs. Hale's suggestion out of hand when she'd mentioned Rhee. But now it occurred to him Rhee might be the better choice. When Mr. Donaldson had offered the tickets, he had subtly hinted Liam begin paying heed to whom he carted on his arm.

It couldn't hurt to ask. No more than his pride, anyway. What could she say but "no, thank you?"

She could say "you forget yourself, Mr. Brock, if you think I'd allow you to escort me anywhere," or "my heavens, have you completely lost your mind?" or "that's quite a presumptuous request," or . . . Good God, the possibilities were endless. And all of them more likely than the one, "yes, I'd like to."

He'd never lacked confidence with a woman before; he'd never been unsure of one's response. It was unsettling, and suddenly he regretted past mockeries of his mates who had agonized over the same.

"Yes, she told me. I know she's not comfortable; it's painful to watch her walk."

"Aye. Most times it's easy to forget her age. Winter, though, she's no' so spry." He sipped his coffee, watching her carefully. "Would ye like to go?"

"Go? I don't think you've spent your allotted time away. At least I hope not, for Elisabeth's sake."

He blinked as the implication sank in, then adjusted his neckcloth, loosening it a bit. All save two of Mrs. Grayton's guests were women, and she had the parlor toasty warm.

He cleared his throat and forged ahead, knowing if he didn't, he'd be treating himself to a tongue-lashing for days. "Mr. Wilson's Introduction to his Law Lectures, Mrs. Ross. Would you like to go? Pay attention, aye?"

The college trustees had passed a motion to establish a law professorship, and James Wilson had been elected to be the professor. One of his duties was to deliver a series of lectures on law. The first would be held before the public.

It had been the final push, these lectures. The final push he'd needed to commit to more schooling.

James Wilson. God Almighty. He'd be a damned fool to pass that chance up. The man was one of his heroes. If Wilson was to be teaching, he'd be one of the first listening.

Alert now, Rhee sat up straight, her green eyes sparkling. "You're asking *me*?" She held out a hand, dainty white palm facing him. "No, no, of course you are—don't dare reconsider."

"Ye might find it dull, he—"

"My word, do you know who is to be present, Liam?" she interrupted, counting off the attendees on her upheld fingers. "I hear tell it's President and Mrs. Washington, Mr. and Mrs.

Adams, Robert Morris and his wife, Dr. Rush and his wife . . . and I think perhaps Mr. Jefferson and Mr. Hamilton. Mr. Hamilton is married, isn't he? Are all the Supreme Court Justices in town? Virtually all your members of Congress will be there, and then there's the Shippens, and the—"

"Enough, lass, you're past out of fingers. And, ye're having coffee with Jefferson this morning; he's the cove o'er against the far wall, the one reading."

Her eyes widened, then narrowed as she glared at him. "*Thomas Jefferson?* Why didn't you say so before now?" she hissed in a whisper. With a quick, nearly imperceptible motion, she flicked her handkerchief to the floor and then slowly bent to retrieve it, her gaze on Jefferson as she rose with the cloth in hand.

"You snake," she said mildly, looking back at him, apparently forgiving his lapse as she continued on with her discourse. "I'm quite interested to hear what the man has to say. You're aware, aren't you, that the whole world is watching these new United States and how well the union will handle its newfound liberty? There's been much speculation over how the new Constitution will be put into practice. Do you think Wilson will advocate simply assuming the British system of law? I wonder if he favors Blackstone. He sits on your Supreme Court, correct? I imagine he'll have a great deal of influence in the coming years. Although there are more than a few of them, so perhaps not an undue amount."

He listened, daunted, as she prattled on, speculating on Judge Wilson's political views.

He should steer clear of this woman. He knew it sure as he was sitting here, befuddled and wound up tight just from watching her.

Finally, she slowed, and he asked, "Am I to understand you're accepting my invitation, Mrs. Ross?"

"Don't be dense, Mr. Brock. Yes, I'm accepting your kind invitation. Now, what do you think I should wear?"

26 December 1790

"Who owns this land to the north, Rory?" Liam asked, tapping his finger on the map he'd spread over the tabletop.

"Bob Jenkins. He's got the eighty acres from here," Rory answered, pointing out the boundaries, "to here. None of it includes my stream."

"Are you on good terms with the man?"

"I suppose." Rory's hand went to his mustache, his fingers stroking the black hairs smooth while he considered. "We haven't talked since my father passed. I've heard rumors he's having financial difficulty. This is only one of his holdings. It's my guess he's overextended."

"Is he on good terms with Carlton?" Carlton was Rory's disagreeable neighbor—the one talking of damming up the stream that ran through his property before it reached Rory's.

"Carlton's on good terms with no one."

"Hmm." He walked to the doorway and looked at the sky. He had time for a ride north before he headed back. It'd be best to do it today while the ground was clear. Though, if it turned out his idea was sound, nothing could be done about it until spring. Nothing except the paperwork, that is.

And the paperwork and the talk often took longer than the deed. Those tasks should get started while Jenkins was feeling a pinch.

"While you're thinking, Liam, I'll show you around. You haven't seen the new drying house."

They walked outside, Rory's four spaniels leading the way. One of them looked to be the age of Becca, Elisabeth's spaniel. Like as not from the same litter. It ran roughshod over the other three, cavorting and tumbling about as they crossed the yard to the stone mill building.

He hadn't seen the development of the last four years. When he'd come with David the last time, Rory had been a mill hand working for his father.

In addition to the new drying house, Rory had expanded the mill building to accommodate another papermaking machine as well as built a dormitory for the workers.

"I've had a second vat installed," Rory said, pointing out the new tub used for boiling the linen rags. "But I've been shy of rags as well as water; so it hasn't been put to much use as yet."

Rory ended the tour back at the barn. The man had a cozy operation set on a nice tract of land. He was smart about it, as well; it was apparent his own abode remained modest and unchanged. No wonder the man chafed Davey so. Elisabeth *would* have done well to marry him.

And he himself would do well to cultivate the man as a future client.

If he wanted clients, which he hadn't decided as yet.

But . . . if he did . . . would Donaldson let him handle the account? Or would he be pushed aside, once he'd set it in motion and made the introduction. He could handle it, he was sure of it. Donaldson would need to sign off and would likely have his own suggestions. But he could do the bulk of it.

"Did Ian stop by?" He'd told Ian that he'd heard Rory's mill was expanding, and that he might find steady work if he took the time to ride out and ask. The lad hadn't shown much interest, but Liam thought perhaps some spark of initiative lay deep.

"Were you the one who sent him?" Rory snorted, tossing his cigar and grinding it underfoot. "It's true I need workers, but I'd as soon their first inquiries weren't of the number of days free and the pay. He seemed to think he could live in the city and ride out for day labor whenever the notion took him."

"My apologies." That spark must be buried deeper than he'd guessed. "Do you have time for a ride to the creek on Jenkins' land?"

"I reckon so. Why?"

"It's fed from Frankfort Creek as well, near as I can tell from that map. Ye might find you're better off negotiating with him than with Carlton. I'm thinking if the land's easy, like this I see here, it shouldn't be too costly to lay a pipe."

Rory smiled slowly, his black eyes sparking, his hands going to his hips as he looked to the north.

"If Jenkins needs funds, he might be open to negotiating a lease. If nothing else, the possibility should give ye more leverage with Carlton."

"Damn, I knew I liked the way you think. Let's go. We've got less than six hours of daylight."

27 December 1790

IT WAS TO BE a boy. David was sure of it. A son.

He had felt the lad move last week. Least he thought he had. Liam had wagered it was only her insides processing the three bowls of stew she had had for supper.

Thank God she was eating again. Thank God she was healthy.

He was lying in bed, curled round Elisabeth's backside, his hand cradling her stomach. She wasn't showing much; one couldn't discern she was carrying at all, once she was dressed. Maybe it wouldn't hurt to allow her to continue her class for the next two months. She was so set on it, the disappointment might harm the bairn.

She had taken on two more women last week. He hadn't recognized them coming up the stairs and he'd pulled her aside to question her.

"Lass, you'll be closing up in three weeks, what's the point?"

She'd looked puzzled at the question. "The point? They're eager, David. How could I possibly refuse them? Now, you mustn't worry. I sit practically the whole time, as Rhee does all the moving around, and besides, it's probable no one realizes I'm expecting—it doesn't show." She had tiptoed up, her arm pulling his head forward as she reached to kiss his ear, whispering,

"Please, David. Please? It makes me feel useful. And I love it."

It wasn't true, except maybe the part about the new women being eager. She scurried to and fro round the room, helping this one and that. He thought most must know she was expecting, else why would they have brought something in for the bairn? They couldn't pay, but they could sew.

He heard Liam and Mr. Oliver talking as they climbed the steps. He nuzzled her neck. "Time to wake, lass," he whispered.

"NAP TIME, EH, Davey?"

David grunted in answer, gesturing at the pitcher Liam washed from. "Ye need more? I'll refill it," he said, kneeling as he tended the fire. The public pump at the end of the street had been out of commission for a week now. It was a burden to walk the extra distance for water; he felt of some use if he were the one who did.

"Nay, it's near full. That stew smells good. She's getting better at it, aye?"

He grunted again, sure Lisbeth would overhear if he admitted one of her women had made it. Mrs. Marks had waylaid him coming home earlier, insisting she'd made too much supper for her small family and that he should take the stew back to Elisabeth, along with her instructions on how long to let it simmer. Lisbeth might get her back up if he commented. Generally he found it safer to say nothing.

Mr. Oliver poured himself some ale and settled in his chair by the fire, book in his lap. "How was the day, lad?"

"Aye, how was it? It's like having ye working at the *Gazette* again, Davey, having news firsthand."

The legislators had all straggled in from New York and Congress finally had its quorum. Earlier in the week, both houses had sat in the Senate, so they could jointly hear Washington's address. He hadn't been permitted there. But in the days following, the House alone considered Washington's address, and he had sat, pen and notebook in hand, listening.

It was faster than he'd expected, the speaking. Faster than he'd practiced. But he thought he'd been recording it accurately.

The session today, however, had had him reeling. He found it wasn't enough to simply record it. He'd like to understand the implications of what they were debating. It would help to talk it out.

"Ye gentlemen have plans for the evening? It'll take an hour or two."

Liam had filled the bowls and set them on the table, alert. "None until later. Give o'er man; I'm all ears."

"Was it Hamilton's report, David?"

"Nay, Mr. Oliver. I think that's not expected until Monday." Elisabeth joined them, sitting beside him, and Liam added another bowl to those on the table.

"Tastes good, lass," Liam said.

"Be sure to thank Mrs. Marks, Liam. She claims she made too much for her table."

"It's your biscuits, I'll wager."

She smiled. "Yes."

"Your husband's going to treat us to a report on what our duly elected have been up to. Have ye heard already?"

She laid her hand on David's knee. "Not yet. He told me I had to wait."

"The floor's yours, David."

He stood and brought his notebook to the table. "First, Philadelphia offers up the county courthouse; that's easy enough. Then Jackson," he said, pausing as he looked up. "Georgia, ken?" He looked back at his notes. "Jackson sympathizes with Ohio and their Indian trouble but balks at helping, wondering what happened to our treaty. Kentucky wants admission to the union, and they need help with the Indians as well. Then who is it to carry our trade if we decide we're to rid ourselves of foreign dependence? We haven't enough of our own ships, that's for certain. Then, what—"

"Whoa, mate. Back up to Jackson's request. Read the whole thing."

Elisabeth stood, clearing the dishes and cleaning the table of the meal, saying little. Mr. Oliver took her place beside David and the three of them talked, David's pencil flying as he listened to Mr. O and Liam argue a point. He glanced at her from time to time, relieved to find she looked content with her mending and not out of sorts at his distraction.

Mr. Oliver nodded when David finally closed his notebook. "Good. That's good, David." He took off his spectacles and rubbed his eyes, yawning. "And you've given me a few ideas as well for my lecture on Monday." He picked a fresh candle from a box and stooped at the fire to light it, then grabbed the book he'd left on his rocker and walked to his bedroom. "Good night, gentlemen."

"Good night, Mr. Oliver." David stood as he heard the watch call out the hour, and nudged the fire, setting the embers to glowing. He needed to get Elisabeth back to bed, where she'd be warm. "Sorry, Liam. I've kept ye hours."

Liam let out a long breath and stood, stretching. "Just as well. Molly had about had it with me anyway," he said, grinning as he added, "Dinna fash. It makes it easier, ken?"

David nodded toward Elisabeth, asleep in her chair, her mending on the floor beside her, and said softly, "She worried some when she heard ye were taking Rhee to the lecture next week."

"Oh?" Liam answered, a hard edge to his voice, the grin gone.

"Eijit." He trotted down the steps and out the door, heading back to the privy, Liam following. Lad could get his back up quicker than a porcupine. "Don't make it into something it's not. Don't make Lisbeth into something she's not."

"Tis women always making it into something. Mrs. Hale backed out and suggested Mrs. Ross. There's no more to it than that."

"She's only worried for Rhee's sake, Liam. That the lass will like ye too much, ken?"

"Remind her the woman's married, David," Liam answered from behind the privy door. "Does she think so little of me, then?"

Hell. Quarters were tight enough without him thinking the worst of Bess. "Nay. You know that's not the case. Forget I said anything; I shouldn't have."

Liam stepped out, the door slamming behind him. "Jesus, it's cold. It's forgotten. Now hurry."

"I'm done."

"Hmmph. Ye havena been on the receiving end of one of Mrs. Nailor's lectures 'bout those shrubs, then, have ye?"

28 December 1790

"All ye be needing now is some powder and a bag queue."

Liam turned from the looking glass to scowl at David. Elisabeth had cropped the man's hair short yesterday, and Liam still had to look twice to make sure it was him. He looked more like the David of eight years past than the David of last week.

"Don't tease him, David. He looks very handsome. I'll duck him in the river myself should he take to covering that head of hair with powder. No one does that anymore."

"See, Davey, ye're out of touch." He held still while Elisabeth straightened his neckcloth. If he looked at the floor and not in her eyes . . . and if he didn't breathe . . . "No one does that anymore," he said, his eyes trained on the charred spot outside the hearth where a log had rolled, years back. "'Cept for Mr. Blythe. Oh, and Mr. Saunders."

"And Mr. Daniels," David added, grinning, "and Mr. Sawyer and Mr.—"

"Stop. No one under thirty years of age does that anymore." Elisabeth stood back, assessing him, then nodded her head. "That black coat with your black hair, my word, you look simply dashing."

"Careful, wife. Dinna give me cause to plant my fist in the lad's pretty face."

Aye, careful—David's wife. Funny thing was, the nearness

of her was no longer the worry it had been.

"Oh, stuff. And I daresay Rhee and I did well, matching the color of your eyes, Liam," she said, fingering the new blue waistcoat she'd given him, one he didn't much care for as it barely reached his waist, but one he thought he ought to wear as she'd gone to the trouble. "And according to her, it's not too short, so stop pulling at it, or you'll rip a seam."

David came up behind Elisabeth, pulling her to rest against him. "We'll see ye in an hour, Liam, aye?"

They were to meet him at the Hales', from where they'd escort both Rhee and Elisabeth to the lecture. Davey planned to stand aside and take notes of the proceeding.

He looked at Elisabeth, still in her day dress, David's arms wrapped tight around her, his hands sliding up her forearms. The odds were against seeing them in any less than two hours. "Ye're late, I'll be leaving without ye, aye?"

"We won't be late, Liam. As a matter of fact, we're leaving in a few moments, so we'll arrive before you. Rhee is going to help me with my hair."

Liam laughed at the look that crossed David's face as he realized he'd be spending the next hour making small talk with Mr. Hale instead of trouncing his wife.

"In that case, ye want to come with me, Davey? After we drop Lisbeth off?"

"Aye. I'm ready enough. Ye dinna mind, do ye, lass?"

She pulled herself free and headed to their room. "No, I'll grab my bag. And don't eat anything, you two, understand? Grandmother has been planning this supper for a week now."

LIAM KNOCKED ON Donaldson's door, rolling up off the balls of his feet as he waited. Maybe he *should* have asked Molly to the lecture instead. He didn't know what had possessed him to ask Mrs. Ross. He'd spend the evening so tied up in knots being near the lass, he wouldn't be able to concentrate on Wilson. Plus it had riled Lisbeth. No matter how David'd tried to take the words back, he'd heard the truth in them.

It had surprised him, Molly's anger, when she'd asked about coming, as he hadn't realized she would place value on attending. Hadn't realized she'd assume he'd take her. Losing his touch, he was.

It was just as well she'd told him not to come around again. This time, he'd pay heed.

Donaldson's daughter answered the door in full dress. "Why, it's Mr. Brock and Mr. Graham. I didn't expect you as well, David. What a treat. Let me get my bag."

David looked at him, alarmed, and he shrugged. "Mayhap the tickets are in her bag," he whispered.

She returned a moment later, handing Liam the tickets and taking David's arm. "You won't mind taking me, will you? My escort had some difficulty at home, and he can't attend."

David shot him a look over her head, his eyes wide with something akin to panic.

"Course we won't, Mrs. Baylor," Liam answered, taking the woman's free arm. "Now, we're to pick up Mrs. Graham and Mrs. Ross in an hour, but we've more than enough time to get ye settled while we go back for them."

"I've a better idea. Why don't I treat the both of you to a refreshment at the Bunch of Grapes?"

He glanced at David who raised a corner of his mouth in defeat. They could manage it, *if* the service were fast. But if it wasn't, and if they ran so short of time they were forced to bring Nora with them to the Hales' . . . that would not go well.

AS LUCK would have it, the tavern was filled to bursting. Most of the better establishments were busy of late, what with Congress now in session, but this seemed extraordinary. Course he didn't frequent the place, so maybe it wasn't. Maybe it was only the anxiety bouncing off Davey that made it seem so. David shouldered his way in, and he followed behind with Nora, sheltering her as best he could from the crowd.

Mrs. Ross was not going to like this. Not one bit.

29

"YOU GIRLS ARE a sight to behold. Look at them, Mother."

"I am, Edward." Her grandmother stood at the foot of the stairs, shaking her head in awe. "Oh, my, I can't wait to see the look on those boys' faces when they see the two of you. Rhee, what talent you have."

The gowns were those Grandmother had gifted as wedding gifts to her and to Rhee, but Rhee had designed them, and she was very clever about it. "She does, doesn't she, Grandmother? I declare, I feel like a princess."

"And so you are, princess," her father said. "Now come on down and join us for a drink before you leave. You still have some time. Tom," he asked, "would you be so kind as to bring up a bottle of father's French wine. You'll find it on the north side, second shelf. Be careful not to choose one from Spain."

"Yes sir, Mr. Hale."

"Oh, I do love a good glass of wine. Thank you, Mr. Hale," Rhee said as he held out a chair for her. "And thank you, again, Mrs. Hale, for the gift."

"It was my pleasure. I only wish I had put an order in as well while you were about it."

"Oh, I have something in mind for you. Beth and I came across the perfect fabric, didn't we, Beth?"

"We did, and Rhee has shown me her sketch. You'll love it.

And you're to wear your amethysts when you wear it."

Her grandmother's eyes lit up. Grandmother could spend all afternoon in a shop, assessing the quality and color of different cloths and not be bored one wit. Perhaps in the summer, once the trade had resumed, and if she were up to it, they could plan a week filled with shop visits to see the new stock. That is, if Rhee were still here. And if she and David were still here.

"I saw Wilson in the land office yesterday."

"You did, Papa? Do you know him?"

"We chatted some, but no, we haven't been formally introduced. He's very keen on settling the West."

"Are you buying in the same vicinity, Mr. Hale?"

"Ahh, here's Tom back from the dungeon." He inspected the bottle Tom handed him and nodded, handing it back for Tom to pour. "Some, yes, Rhiannon. Although Wilson and his partners have much bigger ambitions than my own small group. We're primarily interested in western Pennsylvania."

"Is it far? Do you plan to see any of your investment first-hand? I'd love to go. It would be fun, wouldn't it Elisabeth? To see the West?"

"I don't think Elisabeth will be in the condition to travel, dear."

"But Papa could take you, Rhee, if he goes in the spring. Couldn't you, Papa?" It was selfish, she knew, but she prayed every night that Rhee would decide to stay in America. She prayed even harder her Mr. Ross would join her here, so she would have no reason to ever leave.

"I don't know, pudding. There's so much talk of Indian trouble now. But we can consider it once winter clears. Speaking of which, don't forget an umbrella tonight. I don't like the look of those clouds, and the wind is coming from the north." He stood and went to the window seat, retrieving a blanket. "Here, Mother, put this across your lap."

"Thank you, Edward. They won't need an umbrella."

Grandmother was their personal barometer, and if her bones promised no rain, there would be no rain. Tom handed them each a glass, then went to the fire, stirring it as he added another log. Elisabeth looked out the window. David should be here by now. She hoped there hadn't been a problem with the tickets. She'd be in full dress for nothing.

"We've plenty of time, Beth, don't fret," Rhee said, noticing her glance.

"I'm glad you were able to take my place, Rhiannon," her grandmother said. "Edward wasn't interested in attending, and I thought you might be. It's to be quite the occasion."

Elisabeth bit back a smile at the thought of her father attending with Liam. Granted, he was making a sincere effort, but that would be well above and beyond any effort she might expect of him.

"I'm sorry you needed someone to take your place, Mrs. Hale, but I'm thrilled to be attending. Simply everybody will be there. Do you remember my brother, Mr. Hale? He was studying law when you left England."

"Yes, I do. How is he?"

"Successful, I daresay. I'll have something to write him now, something that will actually interest him."

The knocker sounded at the door, loud, fast, and impatient. Tom frowned, leaving his post as he went to answer. Seconds later Liam entered the room, out of breath and somewhat disheveled, as if he'd been running.

David, something had happened to David. She clutched her stomach, fighting back the nausea.

"Good evening, ladies. Mr. Hale," he said, his words hurried, his eyes on her father, "might I have a private word with you, sir?"

"Liam, what's wrong? Is David hurt?"

"What? Oh, no, lass, he's fine. He'll be along. I didna mean to cause alarm. Mr. Hale?" he asked again, canting his head toward the hall.

Her father was too surprised to do otherwise, she supposed, and he followed Liam into the hall. She shared glances with Rhee and her grandmother, both of whom looked as perplexed as she felt, before she stood and walked to the doorway.

"Elisabeth!" her grandmother said sharply.

Elisabeth put a finger to her lips as she strained to listen. She couldn't make out the words, but it seemed as if Liam was trying to persuade Papa to do something he didn't want to do. Why on earth? She hurried back to her seat as the discussion ended, whispering to Rhee and her grandmother that she couldn't make anything of what had been said. The front door slammed, and Papa walked back into the room, his earlier good humor gone.

"It seems I'm to join you, and I have ten minutes to dress for the occasion," he said, gulping the last of his wine in two large swallows, then slamming the glass down on the table. He hurried out, calling from the stairs as he ascended. "Mother, have Tom set another place at the table. A Mrs. Baylor will be joining us for supper later."

Elisabeth turned to Rhee, her thoughts too jumbled to form words.

"Close your mouth, Beth. It's not becoming, hanging open like that." Rhee's own mouth had set in an unattractive hard line as she stood, vigorously slapping her skirt free of imagined bits of soot and dust.

Only Grandmother did not appear distressed. With a small cough that sounded suspiciously close to a laugh, she bent to retrieve her mending basket, gently scolding Becca as she coaxed a sock from her mouth.

30   December 1790

LIAM SPOTTED THEM as they exited the tavern and answered David's unspoken question with a curt nod, before the lad could take flight. Not that he could get far, given the way the woman clutched at him, lest he shoved her aside by force.

Was she being deliberately obtuse, playing him because she could? If so, he could well understand the temptation, as baiting Davey was entertaining. But not like this, not if it threatened Lisbeth.

"Why, there he is, David. Where did you go, Mr. Brock? My word, have you been running? In your evening clothes? I suppose that's one way to keep warm." She looked up at David, cuddling even closer. "There's certainly more gratifying ways."

"Nay, Mrs. Baylor, only taking care of something I'd forgotten." He took her free arm. "Mind if I share what ye're offering? It's a wicked wind tonight."

"You gentlemen really ought to have overcoats. A bachelor, perhaps I can understand, but you, David?" She left the implication unstated, having at least one ounce of good sense.

"Mrs. Baylor, would ye mind a favor?" David asked. "My wife's father, ken, he doesn't have an escort for tonight. I'm thinking if ye wouldn't mind an introduction, well, perhaps—"

"Ha! Good try there, Davey. Mrs. Baylor will have her choice of every free man in the place. They'll be dropping like flies at her feet, once they reckon she's alone." They were nearing the Hales', so he pulled her close, away from Davey. He ran his hand down her side, lingering appreciatively at her curves, then jostled her a bit in a display of camaraderie.

"Davey's jus' tryin' to heal a breach with the man, lass. There's been a rough patch or two since he swept his daughter from under the man's thumb. He likely figures the attention of a woman as beautiful as you could go a long way toward smoothing o'er those patches. Mr. Hale's been a widower for years, ken? And hasn't had much luck attracting women on his own. I think he's jus' too shy and forgot how to go about it."

David sighed. "Ne'er mind. Just a thought. Cove's too wrapped up in his business to appreciate what's before him anyway. Always has been."

Nice touch, Davey. Throw down the glove. "We're here. Now, ye've met Mrs. Graham and Mrs. Ross before, havena ye, lass?"

Nora pulled herself free, straightening her clothes and patting her hands about her hair. "Oh, yes. They came to the office one afternoon, together, and I've met Mrs. Graham several times. She keeps her husband on a short leash." With a final tug on her jacket, she added, "David, I'd be delighted to take Mr. Hale. He's one of Papa's clients, you know. I've met him a time or two on a professional basis."

"Hmmph. Ye'll owe her well, Davey," Liam said, sidestepping the kick David aimed at his shin as he followed Nora through the front door.

IT WAS A cold, blustery walk to Fourth and Arch, and the woman aside him was colder still. She hadn't deigned to take his arm until after the second time she suffered a near fall on the icy footpath, and by then, he knew well enough it wasn't by choice. Ahead were Mr. Hale and Mrs. Baylor, and it seemed Mr. Hale had risen to the occasion as both were chatting and laughing. Lisbeth and David were paces behind, and the man had her wrapped up so tight he practically carried her, their heads close as they whispered whatever nonsense couples like that whispered. He'd never know.

Just as he'd never know why this situation should be his fault. It'd worked out well, and besides, it had been his thinking that had seen the solution. Course Davey had helped, once it was on its way to being solved, but he hadn't been able to see his way to solving it. And where was he now, when he could use Lisbeth's help in melting this lass? Distracting Lisbeth with his canoodling.

There was a bright side, he thought, grinning. With Rhee set up tighter than mortar, she'd not be a distraction.

"Pleased with yourself, are you, Mr. Brock?"

Hell, maybe not quite as tight as all that.

"Aye, and why not? I've the most beautiful woman in all of Philadelphia on my arm."

"You idiot. Do you have any idea what you've done, inviting that woman along? We could see the three of you through the window. Her hands were all over David."

Now, that just wasn't true. He'd planned well enough for when they passed by that window. Did she think him an eijit?

Course she did. She'd just said so. In no uncertain terms.

"I'm thinking by the time we reached the Hales' window, her hands were all over me, not Davey."

"And you didn't mind that a bit, did you?"

"Jealous, are ye, then?"

"Don't flatter yourself."

He didn't answer, though he tightened his grip on her as she picked up the pace.

"And then, as if you haven't done enough already, you have the gall to invite her to dinner? In the event you haven't noticed, Elisabeth's emotions are unsettled of late. Now she must sit across the table from a woman who as much as told her she'd like David warming her bed?"

"Did she now? That's bold. Even for Nora."

"Hmmph. Stands to rights you'd know exactly how bold she is."

He sighed, defeated. This woman was irritating as all hell. What in God's name had possessed him to ask her along?

"Shouldn't ye be treating me with silence? As retribution for my sins?"

"Oh, do be quiet. Can't you see? We're late."

The entrance to the Hall swarmed with people milling about, waiting to get in. Hell, he hated to be late. They'd have a time of it, finding a free spot in the gallery. He took her hand, nodding back at David and pointing to the rear entrance as he pulled Rhee along. Davey could worry over gaining Mr. Hale's attention. He wasn't planning on missing a minute of this lecture.

There was a guard stationed at the back door. Course there was, way things were going. But as he got closer, he realized he knew him. He was one of John's mates.

"Good even'n, Mr. Liam," the man said.

"Evening, Frank," Liam answered. "We've tickets, ken?" He held them up and indicated the four coming behind. "So do they. Can ye see your way clear, man, to let us inside? The ladies are cold, and ye know Lisbeth—" Rhee kicked him, hard, reminding him that in polite society women didn't actually carry babies, it was the stork that brought them. Jesus. Women. "The lass hasn't been feeling well, as John likely told ye. He'll have my arse if I leave her waiting out here in the cold."

The man grinned as Liam reached out to shake his hand, depositing several coins. "Sure thing, Mr. Liam." Liam hurried through the door, pulling Rhee behind him, not waiting as Frank greeted David and Elisabeth.

"Up here." Rhee didn't protest; he'd give her that. Molly would be in a full blown pout by now if he thought to hurry her along in a pretty gown. He called down the hallway to David, letting him know the way, then trotted up the stairs. Only one of the lamps was lit, but he'd been up these steps before. He didn't need much light to take them two at a time. He opened the doorway at the top and grinned, finding the gallery still half empty. Turning to Rhee, reckoning he should apologize for dragging her in his haste, he was surprised to find a trace of a smile on her lips.

"Well done, Mr. Brock." She pointed to the only spot remaining empty in the front. "Do you mind if we take that spot and let the others fend for themselves?"

Well, then. Appears he was back in favor. Or at least out of disfavor. He led her to the front.

"No' at all." He turned to make certain David and the others had settled in behind them, then he leaned over the rail to see those on the floor.

"Look! There's the President! Is that his wife with him?" Rhee asked.

"Aye, and Adams as well."

"Who's that?" she asked, pointing at one of the younger men, one surrounded by women.

"Not sure. One of the congressmen I'm guessing. Davey will know. That's Rush to his right, though, and his wife. And there's Mr. O, see? Wave." Mr. Oliver was in the midst of one of his long-winded discussions, however, and didn't look up to see them.

"Is that him? Judge Wilson?"

She pointed to a tall man, somewhat stout, wearing a white wig and spectacles. "Aye, it is," he answered as Wilson made his way to the podium, his manner stilted.

"He looks rather full of himself."

"Nay. I've talked to him on campus a few times. He's only shy."

Rhee looked at him, her expression skeptical, and he shrugged. "He is. I'll introduce ye one day, and ye'll see for yourself."

"Shh," she said, placing a finger on her lips as Wilson stepped up, facing the crowd.

"Ladies and Gentlemen." He cleared his throat and fumbled with his spectacles, pushing them higher up the line of his nose. He waited for the crowd to quiet, then spoke out again. "Though I am not unaccustomed to speak in public, yet, on this occasion, I rise with much diffidence to address you. The character, in which I appear, is both important and new. Anxiety and self-distrust are natural on my first appearance. These feelings are . . ."

"I can't understand a word of what he's saying. Can't the

man speak proper English?" Rhee whispered.

True, the man carried a pronounced Scots burr, but she understood his own words well enough, didn't she? Often enough to throw them back. Proper English, his arse. He tore his eyes from Wilson to glare at her, and she smiled.

"I'm teasing, Mr. Brock."

He supposed his transgressions had been forgiven in full, then. "Hmmph," he grunted, fidgeting in his seat against the sensations her smile had wrought. Couldn't she have waited until Wilson finished up? God Almighty, she was tantalizing.

"WILL YE BE heading back home, Liam?" David asked, his eyes watching Mr. O on the floor, his hands encircling Lisbeth's waist as she chatted with Rhee.

"No, and neither will you. Have ye forgotten supper?"

David grimaced, his face contorting in all manner of irritation.

"Ye did."

"I did. Listen, do ye think—"

"No, I don't. Mrs. Hale is expecting us. You rob Elisabeth, she'll be disappointed."

David sighed as if accepting defeat. "Do ye know, then, what we're to be eating?"

"That's not a polite question, David," Elisabeth said, turning as she and Rhee finished with their gossip. "And what does it matter? You love everything."

"Only like to warn my stomach of what's coming, lass. Shall we go, then?"

"Where's Papa?"

Rhee laughed, taking Elisabeth by the arm. "I think he's old enough to watch after himself, Beth. He knows his way home, and he knows he's expected for supper."

"But—"

"Truly, Lisbeth, dinna embarrass the man, aye? When's the last time ye saw him stepping out with a lass?"

"May we play cards after supper?" Rhee asked, her eyes alight at the prospect of a foursome. Or mayhap she thought to distract Lisbeth, who still searched out her Papa in the crowd.

"Sure we can, lass. I'll take ye to coffee after, with my winnings, if it's not too late," he added with a wink aimed at David. Though he couldn't promise Mr. O's whereabouts.

"Don't put the cart before the horse, Mr. Brock."

"Been practicing, have ye?" They were downstairs now, and he watched as David and Elisabeth walked toward the exit, Lisbeth's worries about her father forgotten as she chatted away with some woman about children. The woman looked vaguely familiar, he thought, puzzled until he placed her.

"Well, I'll be damned," he mumbled, looking after her. Little Amy Steward, one of the first students in Lisbeth's class six years back. With a bairn, no less. He turned to mention it to Rhee and found she wasn't there. Stepping to the side of the crowd, he looked ahead, thinking maybe she was with David and he'd missed it, distracted as he was by Amy. She should be easy to spot; she was tall and held herself so, not the least bit shy about it.

"Are you looking for me, Mr. Brock?"

His gut clenched tight, keeping time with his loins. He knew that voice.

And he had hoped not to hear it again.

31

"I NOTICED YOU FROM a distance earlier. I wasn't sure if you had seen me."

"Miss Billings," he said, turning slowly. "Fancy that. It's a far ways from Kentucky, aye?"

"It is. Papa had business with Congress, and he thought it not safe to leave me waiting there."

He stared at her, disgruntled she'd come back, uneasy she'd sought to speak to him here, and angry his body had the temerity to act outside his will. None—and all—of which were her fault.

A year back, he had thought her the most beautiful woman he'd ever seen. It had blinded him to anything other than the fact that she had looked back. Not only had she deigned to look back, she had sought to share his bed. She knew things he didn't and had done things he hadn't, yet she was soft, she was clean and she smelled wonderful. It was an intoxicating combination, and he'd been at her beck and call since. In spite of the others she consorted with, in spite of her disdain for his life outside her clutches, and in spite of his self-contempt each time he returned to her side.

He didn't understand it, he didn't care for it, but he didn't know how to walk away from it. She was part of the reason he'd escaped to Charleston with Mrs. Hale.

"Are you settled then?" he asked while his eyes still

searched out Rhee. "In Kentucky?"

"Of course not, though Papa has selected his land," she answered, placing a gloved hand on his arm. "Did you miss me?"

"I've been busy, lass, but aye, of course I've thought of you," he said, his voice barely above a whisper as he looked at her fingers.

"You look well," she said, her hand trailing down the inside his forearm, her eyes roving over him in that way she had, that way that had had him trailing after her like a hound dog. Mind, he was only one in a long line of hounds. Her scent triggered memories his body remembered well, memories stronger than his reason, and he took a step closer, his hand reaching for hers.

"How long are ye staying, Tory?"

"I apologize for interrupting, but I thought I should tell you I'm walking back with Mr. Hale. In the event you wondered later. Where I was, that is."

Rhee's words flowed over him like a bucket of water straight from the Schuylkill, so icy they were.

"Nay," he said, stepping back from Tory and grasping Rhee's elbow. "Ye're not. Mrs. Ross, this is Miss Billings. Her father is a friend of mine."

"Mmm, so I see. Delighted, Miss Billings."

"Mrs. Ross," Tory murmured. He stood watching as their eyes met, wishing he knew the language well enough to assess the meaning of the silent exchange.

"I apologize for rushing off, but we've a prior engagement, Miss Billings," Liam said. "It was good to see you again, and I wish your father well in his negotiations."

"You may tell him yourself when you stop by later," she answered.

"DID YOU ENJOY the lecture, Mr. Brock?"

"Aye."

"Do you agree he hopes to be the one to codify American law?"

"Aye."

"I thought I recognized some of John Locke's input. What

do you think?"

"Hmm."

"But he seemed quite sure that American law must be different than that of England's. He thinks quite highly of the average American's intelligence, doesn't he? Did I hear correctly? I thought he implied the revolution principle resides in all Americans, so that they may modify the constitution and government as they see fit. My word . . ."

He glanced at her and saw that she had raised her brows and was shaking her head, her lips pursed as if in thought. Then she motioned for him to wait as she moved off the footpath and placed a hand against the building while she fumbled with her slipper, emptying it of a pebble. Rhiannon looked some like Tory, he realized as he waited; they shared the same coloring. But Tory was dark inside as well, where Rhiannon was not.

"Honestly, though, it was difficult to understand some of it. Whether it was the acoustics in the hall or his brogue, I don't know," she said, taking his arm and walking again. "I had hoped for a more lucid discussion from my escort for the evening."

"My apologies."

She huffed and stopped short.

"Oh, for God's sake, Mr. Brock," she said, crossing her arms and slamming them tight against her chest. "Just go. Please. I will explain the situation to Mrs. Hale, and you can make it up to her later."

Go? What? No. He didn't want to go. He didn't, not truly. It occurred to him he'd let an opportunity pass to catch a glimpse of Rhee's ankle, so caught up was he with seeing Tory.

Damn that woman to hell and back. She had only to crook a finger, and he found himself following behind, panting like a puppy. A stray one at that, all the heed she paid once she had what she wanted.

Rhee was worth ten of her.

"Listen, would ye mind if we stopped?" he asked. "To talk some?" They were standing near a frozen pond stacked full of families skating. The tavern adjacent would be busy later, serving up hot mugs of cider, but for now, they might easily find a quiet table.

"Yes, I do. I won't be late for supper. It's rude."

"I know. Only for a short while, afore we join the others."

A fireside table was free in the far corner of the room, and he led her there, requesting two hot ciders from the woman who greeted them as they passed.

"I smell chocolate," Rhee said, as he held out her chair and she settled in. "You don't suppose . . .?"

He sought out the barmaid to request a cup of chocolate, then took the seat opposite Rhiannon, studying her as he puzzled out his attraction. She looked particularly fetching tonight; he'd been more than remiss in not mentioning it before now. That wasn't like him.

He thought the gown new, and its design served well to set off the green in her eyes and the curves to her hips. He'd wager that wasn't entirely Eliza's doing, or she'd been hiding a store of talent all these years, waiting for this beauty to come to town. The blustery weather had tinted her skin a pale rose, and his gaze followed the color from her cheeks, down the graceful line of her neck, to the smooth, lovely swells that hinted at the full breasts beneath her gown.

A beauty, aye, but she wasn't soft, she wasn't pliable, and she sure as hell wasn't sweet. Unflinching, she returned his study, seeming content to sit quietly, waiting for him to say whatever it was he'd intended to say.

"Where's your husband, Mrs. Ross?" he asked finally.

The muscles of her face tightened with displeasure at the question. "What?" she asked unnecessarily, her eyes narrowing as she tilted forward in her seat, poised for flight.

"Mr. Ross. Where is the man?"

"He's in the Caribbean—not that it's any of your concern."

Maybe she was right. Maybe it was none of his concern. But it was something he wondered often. "And why is it ye're not there as well?"

"Good night, Mr. Brock. I can see myself home; it's but a few steps more," she said, rising.

"Stay." He reached for her hand before she walked away,

though he didn't rise himself. "Please? Just sit with me. I won't ask of him."

Perhaps she sensed his unrest because she didn't seek to be contrary, she just sat slowly, her eyes locked on his. The barmaid brought their mugs and set them on the table, and perhaps she as well sensed his unrest, for out of the corner of his eye, he saw her open her mouth, presumably to chatter about the chocolate, then shut it, choosing to simply set the cups down and scurry away.

"Your eyes are lovely, lass." A man could truly drown in them, and he felt the danger, though he couldn't seem to look away.

"Thank you."

"They match your gown."

"I know. I selected the fabric," she said, a faint smile on her lips. She began fussing with her ring, turning it round and round on her finger. He found himself wishing she'd not wear the band, that she'd leave it on the washstand, or perhaps lose it in the privy.

He wasn't sure why he'd brought her here, what he had thought to explain. He only knew he'd felt uneasy over her seeing him with Tory, unclean even, and he didn't want it to harm the fragile peace they'd found.

"I come from nothing, Rhee."

"I know that."

"Mr. O is the closest to a father I've ever known."

"It seems you were fortunate in that. He's a wonderful man."

"I mean to say, I've never known who my father was. My mother . . . she did what she could to put food on the table."

"A mother's love is remarkable, isn't it?"

"I never blamed her for it," he hastened to add, the challenge unstated.

"Gracious, I should hope not."

He wanted her to understand who he was. He couldn't say why, but that's what he wanted. At times he forgot, at times he put it behind him. But it was who he was, and seeing Tory had reminded him of it. He'd never measure up to the men Rhiannon grew up with, and he'd never measure up to a man like David. For whatever reason, he thought it important she grasp that.

"I don't always make the best choices."

"That makes you no different than the rest of us, Mr. Brock."

"Do ye think? I'm no' so sure." He drank from the mug, grateful for the warmth as the liquid slid through to his center, though he wished for something stronger. "I find I want a lot. Some of what I want, I shouldn't."

"But you don't always take, do you?"

She was meaning Elisabeth. He was meaning Tory.

"No, but it's a sin, regardless, aye?"

"Oh, pooh."

He grunted, having no answer, and searched her eyes, wondering if the disdain were sincere.

"Is Miss Billings among the things you want?"

He shook his head and dropped his gaze, watching her hands again as they worried the ring. "No," he answered. Not in the way she was meaning.

"She's very beautiful."

"Hmmph. So is the copperhead, in its way."

"How gallant," she said, laughing. "Why does she make you so wary?"

His eyes shot to hers. "What?"

"Miss Billings. Why does she make you wary?"

"Have you met her before?"

"Of course not. But I have heard of her through Elisabeth. Meeting her tonight, I'd say Beth's assessment was spot on." Her green eyes were dark with concern. "You're nothing like her, Mr. Brock."

The barmaid was making a clatter now, lining up a string of mugs along the countertop as she prepared for an onslaught of skaters. He watched her as she plied her trade, not knowing how to answer Rhee. Because he was very much like her. He mostly took what he wanted, with nary a backward glance. He always had. Just as Tory did.

"You're beautiful as well," he said, finally. "Inside and out."

"I'm not sure you know me well enough to determine that. But I'm happy I don't remind you of a snake."

"Nay," he said softly, looking at her, fascinated as the firelight danced over the clean, strong lines of her features. "Ye remind me of the forest." And she did. He sensed the refuge her arms might offer and wondered again at the absent Mr. Ross.

That brought forth another smile. "And that's good?"

"Oh, aye. The forest is all things. Things full of life and things full of death. Clean things, honest things."

"Well, that's one perspective." A lad came in with an armful of wood and dumped it on the floor behind Rhee. She started some, but kept her eyes on him.

"Anyway, I was thoughtless earlier, in not telling ye how fetching ye looked." He slid a hand over the tabletop to where she'd set her hands, stopping when he was close enough to feel the warmth of hers.

"You're forgiven. I didn't leave you much opportunity, as I recall." She stared at his hand, and for a moment, he thought she might take it in hers, but instead, she turned away to watch the lad replenish the fire, flinching as it popped and snapped with new life.

A crowd of children burst through the tavern door, and all of them swarmed toward the fire beside them, chattering loudly about this skater and that, breaking the spell she'd cast. He blinked, then reached for his mug.

"We should go," Rhee whispered.

"Aye." He didn't want to go. He wanted her to move aside him and place her head on his shoulder. He wanted to hold her as they quietly watched the fire dance and the children play. He wanted to wait with her as the adults followed their broods in, then spend time idly matching a set of parents with a set of children and devising stories on their family life.

He wanted to stay with her until the hollow ache he'd felt since seeing that woman was filled full with this one's warmth and laughter.

"Mrs. Hale is expecting us."

"Aye, I know."

"Please?" she asked, hesitant, as if his gaze had bound her in truth.

He'd seen the lass in many moods. Hesitant and pleading was not one he cared for. "Of course," he said, lifting his mug to finish the last few swallows. "Thank you for accompanying me tonight, Mrs. Ross. I enjoyed your company a great deal."

"I'm afraid I did 'snipe' at you earlier. I apologize."

He stood, helping her up.

"Did ye, now? See, I didna notice, so used to it I've become."

32   December 1790

FINISHED WITH THE morning chores, Elisabeth walked to the window and studied the steel gray sky. She had at least an hour before Rhee would come, so she could read, or she could mend. She poured herself a cup of coffee, not because she liked coffee, but because there was always coffee on hand in this household and never enough tea.

Which was naturally her fault, as she was the only one who drank tea regularly. She went to the fire, added another log to the dying embers, and picked up her book. She could take her basket and mend when she visited.

Later, lost in the words, she jumped at the sound behind her. Snapping the book shut, she stuffed it under her skirts.

"Sorry lass, didna mean to startle ye. Good book?"

"Good gracious, Liam. I thought you were long gone. I didn't save you anything from breakfast. Are you hungry? Would you like me to make you some eggs?"

He shook his head, yawning. She rose to pour him a cup of the coffee.

"You're not ill, are you? You were so quiet last night." Not only had he and Rhee shown up late, Liam had added barely a word to the conversation once he'd arrived. Then he hadn't come home with her and David.

"Hmmph. *A General History of the Robberies and Murders of the*

Most Notorious Pirates."

She spun around. He held her book, grinning as he thumbed through the pages.

"Where'd ye get this, Lisbeth? Escapades of pirates hardly sound like suitable reading for the soon-to-be mother of my nephew. Davey ken ye have this?"

"Put that down!" Snatching the book from his hands, she stored it under one of Mr. O's books. "The library had it. I thought it looked interesting." Cringing as she caught the defensive tone in her voice, she added nastily that she wasn't aware David needed to approve the household reading material.

"Here." She slammed the cup on the table, liquid sloshing over the rim. "Now, answer me. Are you ill?"

"Just having a lie in, tha's all," he said, rubbing his hands down his face. "Davey at the courthouse?"

"Yes, he left awhile ago. I'm going as well, as soon as Rhee gets here." She sat across the table from him. "Papa seems to have enjoyed Mrs. Baylor's company, don't you think?"

"Aye," he said, grinning, an impish gleam lighting his blue eyes.

Gracious, it was impossible to stay irritated at this man. "I can scarcely believe you were able to get his consent," she said. "He abhors crowds like that."

"Dinna forget your da is a man as well as your father, Lisbeth. And ne'er underestimate the lure of a beautiful woman. Though mayhap I overstated her allure a wee bit, so as he'd go."

"I doubt that's possible. She is very beautiful." It had surprised her, seeing him laugh with Mrs. Baylor. She had spent a good portion of the evening watching them. She doubted she could recount with accuracy any of what Judge Wilson had said.

Mrs. Baylor was married, and nothing would come of it. But there were many other women who weren't.

"I wonder that it never occurred to me to question his staying single after Mother passed. He may have been happier had he remarried."

"He's no' dead yet. He may still remarry."

"Perhaps." Papa did seem happier than she'd remembered.

Perhaps he had a woman in New York he cared for. Had he thought she would resent his remarrying, or even his keeping company with a woman? Goodness, she hoped not. She did want him to be happy.

"Liam, do you have a few minutes to explain Papa's land business to me?"

"I canna share that, lass."

"Mr. Donaldson handles many transactions, doesn't he, other than Papa's? I'm only asking for generalities. I don't expect you to violate any confidences."

"Well, all right, I expect I can do that. Then I need to wash and shave. I think I'll take tea with Mrs. Hale this afternoon. We missed yesterday. D'ye know if she has plans?"

"No. She expects me to visit. But, I believe she enjoys you more."

"Get on with ye. Ready?"

She nodded, alert.

"Right then." He reached into the candle box and pulled out three stubs. "We've three gents, ken? Each with money and an interest in land. They form themselves a venture, each of them with a separate task. Let's say this one," he said, pulling aside the shortest stub, "he only has five thousand pounds while the others have ten thousand. Well then, he must do more if he wants to play with the others. Mayhap he's the one to scout the land, or mayhap he's the one to keep the books and write out the deeds. So as the load is even."

She nodded, and he reached into her mending basket, pulling out two stockings, one brown and one blue. He set the brown one in a clump at the end of the table, naming it western Pennsylvania, and arranged the blue one in a curving line, naming it a river.

"Yon scout," he said, picking up the shortest candle stub, "he finds three choice parcels he thinks they'd do well to own." He set three chestnuts on the stocking, close to the "river," to indicate the parcels.

"Now, short gent, he trots back into Philadelphia, brimming with happiness, 'cause clear as day, he's gonna make himself a fortune. He tells his partners they can get each parcel for one thousand pounds today and then sell each for two thousand the next year. Why the way land's appreciating, mayhap even three thousand! Excited, they agree, and they each pony up their share of the down payment so short gent can scurry on over to the land office and get them three preliminary warrants."

She knew of the land office. Papa talked of it often.

"Now comes the tricky part. Now that they've secured the preliminary warrants, they've permission to survey, ken?" He looked at her for confirmation she understood, and she nodded. "Let's say I'm the surveyor, aye?" He stopped abruptly. "Tha's it. Holy hell, ye're a genius, lass," he said, jumping from his seat, reaching across the table to kiss her. "Tha's it."

"That's what? What are you talking about, Liam?"

"Surveying. I can live off the land well enough. I'd be happy, living on the frontier, no' answering to anyone but myself, moving about as I wished. Alone . . . time to think."

"Don't be absurd, Liam. You *like* people. I can't imagine you with no one to talk to but yourself. I also can't imagine you working for the government."

"I can get a hound dog for company. I'd enjoy a dog."

"What's gotten into you? I thought you liked studying law. Rory couldn't say enough about you yesterday."

"Some." He sat down again, sighing. "No, a lot. I do. And your grandmother is counting on it."

"She is not. She only wants you to be happy with whatever it is you decide to do. If it's not law, so be it." She hesitated to ask, but she did so anyway. "Did you and Rhee have words?"

"No. Where did we get these?" he asked, rummaging through a bushel of apples, discarding one after another until he found one that suited. Polishing it on his shirtfront, he took a bite, quiet while he chewed.

"Grandmother's larder. She asked David to bring them over."

She gnawed on her bottom lip, watching him. One never knew what Liam was thinking. She knew she should be accustomed to it, nonetheless it was frustrating. How could he possibly consider not pursuing law? Was he serious? The man was born to argue.

"Let's finish this, aye?" he asked, glancing at her. She nodded. "So these gents need an honest surveyor, one who knows his business, one who willna sell them out. Because if Mr. Short here sends the surveyor to yon plots," he said, indicating the chestnuts, "what's to stop Mr. Surveyor from taking the fee, surveying a rocky plot in the same general area for Mr. Short and saving the one along the creek bed for himself—or mayhap even another speculator, one who'll double his fee? And Mr. Short's paying all his expenses, to boot."

She looked at him, shocked. "And that's what you want to do? That's who you want to become?"

"Course not. Plenty of the Deputy Surveyors do, though, to supplement their income. That's why I'm thinking a top-notch surveyor who's honest might be worth his weight in gold."

"How does Papa know who's honest?"

"He doesna. Tha's the risk," he said. "So the surveyor comes back with his plats all nice and tidy-like, and Mr. Short takes the balance they owe in to the land office. Now they have right to the patent, on land they bought for a thousand and can likely sell in a year for two to three thousand."

"And what does the patent do?"

"It's a deed from the Commonwealth. It grants them full title to the land."

"Well, that doesn't sound so awful. As long as the surveyor has one's interest in mind."

"No, long as," he agreed, taking a bite of the fruit.

"Is that all there is to it?"

"Well," he said, "Mr. Short's got the bug now. That wasn't so awful, as ye say. Especially as they stand to make up to a three hundred percent profit. Gets the coves to thinking. Let's do more, they say. 'Fore you know it, they've got themselves a bucket full of preliminary warrants and not enough cash to redeem them 'fore they expire. The plan was to sell these," he said, indicating the first three acorns as he chewed, "to cover the price to redeem the new warrants, but what if they can't do it fast enough? They lose the money paid for the new preliminary warrants as well as what they paid the surveyor. Or, what if someone's squatting on the land they have a warrant for and have paid to survey, and yon squatter runs off the surveyor with a shotgun? Same result."

"But if you did it all in an orderly fashion? If you didn't commit to a parcel before you sold the last one, or only if you had the cash ready for it?"

"Aye, then it would work. But men, ye see, they dream. Land prices are skyrocketing. They know if they hesitate they may lose the big money."

"And if they can keep up a steady pace of buying and selling without using any of their own money, other than for the preliminary warrants, they can become very, very rich."

"Aye."

"And if they can't keep up the pace, they stand the chance of bankruptcy."

"Aye."

"And Papa?"

Liam held up his hands, palms facing her, refusing to say more.

"Thank you, Liam, for taking the time to explain."

Papa would not like to be bankrupt. She was sure of that. The shame alone might kill him, if he were to land in debtor's prison. Certainly the risk would cause him to behave prudently.

"I've heard rumors about Judge Wilson and his acquisitions. Do you think they're true?"

"I hope not, Lisbeth. I hope not." He stood, tossing his apple core in the fire. "I'm washing up now. Would ye like anything from the market on my way back in tonight?"

"No, I'll be out. I can get what I need."

"The ladies are coming?"

"Yes, at seven."

"Dinna bother with supper, aye? Mr. O is eating o'er at Mrs. Holmes again, and I'll take Davey off your hands."

"Mr. Oliver likes that woman, doesn't he? He's so rarely here anymore." At least she hoped that was why he wasn't here.

She'd hate to think it was her and David being underfoot.

"'Pears so," he said, a hard edge to his voice.

She laughed. "Oh, Liam," she said, kissing his cheek, "you're so protective when it comes to Mr. Oliver. I could give you the same advice you gave me regarding Papa."

"He's still sleeping here, ken?"

33

"I THINK WE OUGHT to stay in, Beth. I nearly slipped on the way over here. There's ice covering the footpath, and I'm not sure it will warm enough to melt it."

"I promise I'll walk very slow and test each step." The thought of lying in bed or sitting by the fire for the next four months frightened her more than childbirth. There was simply no way she could do it. "This winter will be my last opportunity to sit in on sessions. David and I will be in Baltimore next year. He thinks they might discuss the militia bill today."

"So? You could hear of it later this evening when he returns."

"Rhee! David could be drafted into a militia. I want to understand the requirements." Certainly, David would tell her. But he would also gloss over any information he thought might distress her, and she'd likely end up knowing no more than what was printed in the paper. She'd found it best to hear firsthand of anything that might concern her.

One of her students had told her the current draft of the bill included no exemptions. Another had told her it exempted university students. Another had said the government could draft any man under the age of fifty. Fifty! That would include her father. No, she wanted to hear the debate firsthand.

Rhee pursed her lips, disgruntled, and walked to the

window, examining the overcast sky as if assessing the chance of the sun breaking through.

"Besides, Rhee, we must stop by the stationery and purchase more slate pencils before the evening. Mine are down to mere nubs. I also promised Grandmother I'd come by."

"That's a lot for a day, lass. Especially as you have your women coming by later," Liam said.

Elisabeth opened her mouth to protest, then closed it, stopped short by the look in his eyes. Eyes he had trained on Rhee. Good Lord, his gaze carried that same heat David's did when . . . when he wanted . . . well, it wasn't any way to look at a woman who wasn't one's wife. She swung back toward Rhee and was relieved to see her only now turn from the window.

"Good morning, Mrs. Ross."

"Good morning, Mr. Brock."

"I'll stop for the slate pencils, Lisbeth, so don't head in to Market. And remember, I'm seeing Mrs. Hale for tea, so she's likely to be resting when you're finished with the courthouse. It willna hurt if ye save your visit till the morrow." He started down the stairs. "I'm off. Good luck with her, Mrs. Ross."

She noticed Rhee's eyes followed him as he exited, and she also noticed he hadn't taken any of the notebooks he usually carried to Mr. Donaldson's office.

"What happened last night, Rhee? With Liam?" she asked, going to the window to watch as Liam walked off, her heart sinking as she realized it was in the direction opposite Donaldson's. Oh, no, Liam. Why? Mr. Donaldson wasn't one to forgive any sort of misconduct.

Rhee turned toward her, her brow furrowed. "I'm not quite sure. We stopped for a warm drink on the way home, and he talked some, about his mother and such, then he brought me home. Oh! I met Miss Billings, the woman you'd told me about."

Astonished, she could only stare at Rhee.

"That's odd. That woman seemed to have the same effect on him."

"No." She shook her head. "No, Rhee, that's not it. I've never even met her. But Rhiannon, do you realize he's never spoken of his mother, not once in all these years?" At least she didn't think he had. It wasn't something David would volunteer, and she'd only asked him the one time.

"Oh." Rhee looked thoughtful, as if that hadn't occurred to her previously.

"Oh? That's all you have to say? *Oh?*" She picked up the chestnuts Liam had left lying and tossed them into the bin. Sweeping a hand across the table top, she pushed the stockings back to the mending basket with a force that had them landing in the ashes.

"Good Lord, Rhee. When he first walked into this room, he looked at you as if you were his next meal."

"Did he?" Rhee asked, smiling, her eyes still carrying a faraway look as she stooped to rescue the stockings. "He did pay me an inordinate number of compliments. An inordinate number for him, anyway." She picked up Elisabeth's overcoat and scarf and set them beside her, indicating she should put them on.

"Don't worry, Beth. It seems he's in the midst of some confusion. And, he's only mildly infatuated, as I'm beginning to believe he is at one time or another, with every attractive woman he meets. Some men are just that way. It will pass. Not too many months ago, he looked at you the same way."

"He most certainly did not!" She wrapped the scarf about her neck, throwing an end over her shoulder with a vigor that sent the whole scarf flying. There had only been that one time, at her wedding, that she'd sensed something amiss. She'd most likely imagined whatever it was as it'd been fleeting and had never reoccurred.

"Oh, yes, he most certainly did," Rhee answered mildly, picking up the scarf and setting it about her shoulders, securing it with a loose knot. She patted her cheek. "Don't worry, dear, he'll come to his senses. I'm certain Miss Billings will see to it."

"I'm not worried over him. It's you. Liam always walks away smiling. *Always*, Rhee."

"Honestly, Elisabeth, I do have some experience with men." Rhee took the poker and rearranged the embers, banking the fire. "I've no intention of forgetting I'm married, nor, I expect, does he. I've had enough heartache as a result of my husband's desertion, wouldn't you agree?"

"Yes, I would," she said quietly, donning her hat. "Which is precisely why I don't want Liam adding more. I won't forgive him. I tell you, I won't."

"Well then." Rhee swiped her hands together to rid them of ash as she turned to smile at her. "If nothing else, it's become quite clear which one of us is your dearest friend, hasn't it?"

34

"I TOLD LISBETH I'D see ye fed," Liam said, meeting David at the doorstep. He took his arm and steered him back out onto the street and into the rain.

"Why? It's Friday. Where is she?"

"She's sleeping."

"It's raining," David complained, looking disgruntled. He'd likely looked forward to a cozy meal by a warm fire with his wife at hand. But Elisabeth had seemed unusually tired, so Liam had sent her to bed with the promise to see to David's meal.

"So it is. But we won't eat in the rain."

"Is she all right?"

"Aye. She's only resting."

"This is close. It'll do," David said, gesturing at The Swan, the tavern four doors down from the house. A favorite tippling house of those who labored at the nearby tannery, the food was fair, the portions large, and the room warm. David shook his curls loose of the raindrops as they sat at the counter.

"Hey, mate! Watch it. Ye need to shake yourself like a hound, do so at the door."

"Why are ye finished so early? Are things slowing at Donaldson's?"

"I didn't go in."

"I thought—"

"I'm no' on a leash. I'll come and go as I please, ken?"

"Right. Ye know what's best. Did Rory Smith ever stop by to see ye?"

"Aye, several weeks back. He needs some research done on the mill's water rights. The land owner upriver is giving him some trouble."

David grinned. "Your first client? Is that legal? You're no' even out of school, nor have ye finished your trial with Donaldson." He gestured to the barmaid and ordered stew and ale for the both of them.

It was all moving too slow, this business of holding off life while he studied and then studied more. Classes, especially, were making his feet itch, though the prospect of sitting in on Judge Wilson's new lectures held hope.

There had to be other ways to get where he was going. Faster ways.

"There's so much I could be doing, Davey. I feel as if I'm doing nothing, as if I'm standing still. I'm no' saying I know it all. But how much more do I need to start, ken? Before I lose my chance at actually *doing*? I'll be an old man, 'fore I'm free."

David didn't answer, though his mouth quirked in wry acknowledgement as he toyed with his mug.

"Ye've a reason for your waiting. A good reason. Ye've a family in the making."

"Doesna make it any less frustrating, Liam."

"I reckon not." He shouldn't be complaining. He knew that. But he was restless as hell. "Researching the mill's water rights? I don't need to be an attorney to do that."

"Nay. But ye'd need to be an attorney to do something about it, once ye finished your researching."

"Maybe I don't care about water rights."

"Maybe you don't."

He did care, and the man knew it well.

"I got to thinking about surveying. I'd need to work under someone for a month or two, but I think I could be on my own quick enough. I've enough knowledge of the math and theory. "

"Surveying, huh? Sounds exciting."

No, it didn't.

"The warrant holders in this state could use an independent man to verify the deputy's marks, ken?"

"Ye could get someone to take notes for ye, while ye're gone, on the lectures ye miss of Wilson's."

He'd need to wait until Wilson's lectures were over, of course. He should be arguing with Lisbeth, not David. David didn't push back.

"I could be out and about each day. On the frontier, like I always wanted." Alone. Not that he minded being alone. But for months? Elisabeth was right. It likely wouldn't suit.

"Aye, ye could. All sorts of time to think and plan, aye?"

Think on what? The things he'd given up?

They were quiet for awhile, absorbed in their own thoughts while they ate. A surveyor's wage was not the size of an attorney's. But it'd be enough he'd not have to worry so.

Except during the winter months when snow prevented travel.

The work was not as stimulating, granted. However he'd be free a year or two faster.

He'd have more influence and respect as an attorney. He could be of some use to those he loved, should they need help. He likely could have kept Davey out of the gaol.

"How's Mrs. Hale doing on finding ye a wife?" David asked, breaking the silence as he pushed away his empty bowl.

Cove thought to tie him down, as well? "She hasna mentioned it lately, come to think of it. She's her aches and pains on her mind."

"I'll have to remind her, next I see her."

"No need for that. Forget the wife and tell me what you think of this. Donaldson has a fair share of clients purchasing land. What if his services included the task of the survey?"

"I'd say he'd be way ahead of others."

"I could sign on with others to assist, to start with. Sean could lead me about the area if I stuck with western Pennsylvania. You'd come as well. It'd be fodder for your paper."

David sat straighter in his seat, his eyes far away with the dreaming of it. He liked the idea, Liam could tell. They had talked often of visiting Sean. They hadn't seen him since they had reached Philadelphia some seven years past. Sean had headed to Pittsburgh to join his brother. Though he wrote occasionally, he hadn't visited Philadelphia.

"I love the law, Davey. I can admit that. But I canna imagine sitting in that office, day after day."

"Donaldson doesn't, Liam. I see him out and about, meeting and greeting. Ye have to earn it, 'fore ye do the same."

"Hmmph." He knew it to be true. He didn't plan on being a clerk. He'd have others to clerk for him.

"It's a good idea, though, Liam. The surveying coupled with Donaldson's business. It might suit. Did you talk to Donaldson?"

He hadn't thought of it in those terms—Donaldson'd likely still be his superior. On those terms, his own position wouldn't differ much from his current one. He didn't care for that. Donaldson was a hard taskmaster; it was best he sever that relationship now. Though it was likely there wasn't one left to sever. Why didn't he just go ahead and tell David that?

"No' yet. I need more of a plan."

"Ye talk to Mr. O?"

"No." He shifted in his seat, uncomfortable just thinking of the conversation. He'd not go easy with this.

"How 'bout we go before the baby is due?"

David set his jaw, working out his own plan of attack. Eventually he nodded. "Aye. Congress will be packing their bags come March. I can be absent for a few weeks. Come June, though, I'm headed to Baltimore."

Course he was. He'd have waited most of a year. Jesus, Mary, and Joseph, he'd miss them.

"Right, then. I'll see how Mr. O feels about it." The attorney didn't need to be Donaldson. There were plenty others who handled land. "You talk to Lisbeth."

A corner of David's mouth lifted in a grimace. "I think I'll wait till ye've worked out the details."

Liam grunted his agreement. Harmony was good, especially as they shared a table and fireside. Lisbeth wouldn't like the idea.

"Rhee will stay until after the baby comes. Lisbeth will be fine with the plan, long as she has Rhee by her side," David said, reading his thoughts as he motioned the barkeep for whisky.

He wondered if David believed that any more than he did. Or if, like him, he'd tell himself anything to be out and about.

"Tha's good of her," he responded noncommittally. He readied for the question about why he'd shown up late with Rhee that night. David had a right to ask, given Lisbeth would be after him about it, worrying as she did over her friend.

But he himself had a right to keeping his reasons private, especially as he wasn't sure of the reason he'd wanted the time. Other than that he found her company soothing, and he'd be damned if he'd tell David that.

"Ye showed an hour later than the rest of us that night after the lecture."

"Aye."

"I'm supposed to ask why."

"Consider it asked."

David chuckled, unconcerned. The thing about Davey was, he never thought the worst of him, even when warranted.

"Are ye done? I'd like to get back."

"Aye." The wind gusting up Carter's Alley hit them square on as they exited, and they hunched their shoulders and dropped their heads in defense. The rain had frozen to sleet in the time it took to eat, and the slush oozed up round the soles of their boots, its grimy ice splashing their stockings

"Listen, Liam," David said, practically shouting the words over the wind's howl. "I'd like to keep the lass around. Truth be, I'm no' sure I'd leave Bess for those weeks if she didn't have Rhee. And I want to, ken?"

"Course ye do. Ye've the time and the opportunity."

"Aye, well."

"Spit it out, David. Ye warning me? Keep my hands off? Stay away from her? What?"

"Huh?" David brows met in puzzlement as he looked at

him, his dark eyes showing surprise as he opened the door to the townhouse. "Hell, what are you talking about? I was thinking on asking if ye could see your way to being more agreeable round her. I dinna want her bored and leaving town. Hurry and get in here, will, ye?"

"Oh." Liam followed him in, his eyes sweeping the room as David latched tight the door. Little Danny Nailor, as it seemed he was four days out of seven, had been banished to the corner once again. Liam winked, getting a big grin in reply. The crime must have been worth it then, if the lad was still living it. He turned his head before Mrs. Nailor could catch his own grin.

"She's good company, if ye'd let her be. But she's not content sitting still much."

"Ye want me spending time with her?" He rearranged his features into his best leer, but it was too dark for David to appreciate it. "Unchaperoned? That's what ye ask of me?"

"Sure," David answered, shrugging. He started up the steps. "Rhee's no simpering lass. She has a husband to answer to. Sides, I hear Miss Billings is back in town, needs be."

That she was. Though he hadn't gone to her yet. It took a bit of will, but he hadn't. Not with Rhee's scent still stirring his senses.

"Nay. It's too much, Davey." He heaved a heavy sigh. "I can't see my way to spending time with Mrs. Ross, even for ye. Ye ask too much."

David fumbled in the candlebox at the top of the stairs, then felt his way to the hearth. "Eijit," he mumbled, stirring the embers back to life and adding a log. "So ye will?"

He shouldn't take up with Rhiannon Ross. She was too tempting by half. He stepped too far in her direction, he'd have all of Mr. Oliver, Mrs. Hale, Davey, John, and Elisabeth to contend with. He had enough trouble on his hands without adding the distraction of Rhiannon Ross.

"I'm thinking it's no' a good idea, but I'll see what I can do." Sometimes the crime was worth the punishment.

35

"LOOK WHO'S HERE, Papa. You remember Mr. Brock, don't you?" Tory gestured a graceful hand his way as he walked into the inn. Her rose gown was a shade darker than the jewels that glittered round her neck and beneath her ears. He hadn't seen her wear it before; somehow, it rendered her sweet and innocent, though that was likely wishful thinking on his part.

"Of course I do. Good evening, son. Have a seat." Billings stood to greet him, and Liam noted he'd exchanged his silk breeks and waistcoat for deerskin. The man hadn't gone so far as to don a ratty hunting shirt, but, unlike his daughter, he looked as if he might actually hail from Kentucky.

"Am I interrupting?"

"Not at all."

"I saw Miss Billings at Wilson's lecture, sir. I hadn't expected to see you back in Philadelphia so quickly."

"It was a short, exploratory trip. I wanted to see the land for myself before entering the warrants."

"Aye, that's prudent."

"It's magnificent, Mr. Brock, a paradise. It's bordered on two sides by streams rife with fish. Even Tory managed to catch several, didn't you, sweetheart? And the abundance of game—you'd have to see it to believe it."

"How long will the survey take?"

"I believe they'll be finished by summer. We'll head back in the spring with provisions. I'm telling you again, sir, you're missing an opportunity of a lifetime."

Billings had been after him for months to join him. The more settlers, the less danger from the Indians. He'd considered it some.

"I plan to make my way there, someday," he answered.

"One has to be careful of 'somedays,' right, sweetheart?" Billings said to Tory. "Tory found herself a sweetheart out there, Mr. Brock. A fine, strapping, young buck, first one she's had that I'd be proud to claim as a son. Fine family, even finer prospects. But he's with the militia. I told her I wouldn't condone betrothal to a soldier. With all the trouble in the Northwest Territory, one can never rely on 'someday.'" He patted her knee in a conciliatory gesture. "We'll see after the campaign is over. When he comes back."

A faint flush matching her jewels spread across her chest, but she smiled pleasantly at her father. "Yes, Papa."

Hmm. Seems he hadn't been considered a potential suitor. Not that he was. But seems she'd never even mentioned to her father they had been keeping company.

And if she *had* mentioned it, and if he *had* shown serious interest, guess Billings would have shown him to the door with his boot on his backside. No one could accuse him of coming from a fine family with even finer prospects.

"The militia?" he asked. "Was he involved in the campaign just past?" The army had suffered a crushing defeat against the Miami Indians, though they had managed to slay a hundred or more warriors and burn over three hundred wigwams and loghouses as well as thousands of barrels of corn and vegetables. But rumors were circulating, rumors questioning the bravery of the federal officer in charge.

"Yes, I believe so." Billings tapped his hat against the table, a sign he was soon to be on his way and Liam would be left alone with Tory. "I think I spotted your friend, Mr. Graham, at the courthouse today. His hair was much shorter, but otherwise, he looked the same."

"Aye, that would be him. He's been recording the sessions of the House."

"That's one reason we're here. I've been talking to congressmen all week long, stressing the importance of passing the bill for statehood."

The Virginia Assembly had passed an Act almost a year ago, allowing the area that had been Kentucky County to break off from Virginia and apply for statehood on its own. Admitting the district as a state had been one of the tasks President Washington had set before Congress last week.

"David mentioned they're speaking of it." He looked at Tory. "How are you finding Kentucky, miss?" Looking at her now—prim, proper and soft—it was difficult to picture her coping with deprivation. Then again, looking at her now, it was difficult to picture her as the woman he'd come to know—insatiable, scheming, and promiscuous.

Before he'd met her, he'd had himself a system that worked just fine. Philadelphia was spread thick with agreeable lassies, and he'd made it his mission to taste as many as he could. A taste was all he took, as the city was spread thick with harlots as well, and the cost wasn't out of his reach. Least not when compared to the cost of getting tied to a woman carrying one's bairn.

Tory had turned that system upside down. She was the one who took and then left, and she took more than a taste. He didn't fault her for it, not any longer. She'd never made any assertions of loyalty or fidelity. Perhaps he'd assumed them, but that wasn't her responsibility; she'd never made them. What troubled him now, above all else, was it seemed he hadn't the will to resist. He'd never been at a woman's beck and call before.

But at least with her, he'd only his own conscience to contend with. She wasn't surrounded by a protective clan of family and friends, and best of all, she had no husband.

"So you see, the frontier is full of opportunity, Mr. Brock," Tory was saying. "As long as Papa consents to returning to Philadelphia every few months for supplies, I'm sure I'll stay content."

Mr. Billings chuckled. "You'll have to settle for once a year, pet, or our entire time will be spent in travel." He set his napkin aside and stood. "Forgive me, but I have a prior appointment. You let me know if you change your mind, now."

"Of course, sir." He watched as Billings left the room, thinking he should follow.

"You look positively dejected, Mr. Brock. Why have you come? Did you quarrel with your lady friend?"

"Just came in for a drink. We can have a civil conversation, aye?" They hadn't often, the last time around, not toward the end. But there was no reason they couldn't. He could try harder.

"Maybe."

"Did ye find Kentucky rough?"

"Not so much."

"And Indians? Did ye run afoul of any?"

She shook her head.

"Tell me about your sweetheart."

"Actually, I'd rather not."

"Ye have an understanding with the man?"

"I prefer not discuss it with you, Mr. Brock. I trust you'll understand." From across the table, a small, slippered foot came to travel up between his legs, softening the words.

"Right, then." No sense wasting time. She was tolerating him for one thing and one thing only. There was no reason to mind that, right? Not a reason in the world, his loins piped up in response. He stood and helped her from her chair. "May I see ye safely to your door, Miss Billings?"

"Please."

HE WATCHED HER face closely as she wiggled out from under his arm. That is, until she raised her arms high in a languid stretch, diverting his eyes to her lovely breasts. As she'd intended, no doubt, preferring admiration to scrutiny.

"Keep looking at me that way, Liam, and I might be tempted to forgive you."

Last time he'd left her bed, he hadn't waked her. Nor had he told her he'd be sailing to Charleston the next morning. He'd offered himself to Mrs. Hale as a companion on a whim, near running from Tory in the interest of self-preservation.

He grinned. "I heard ye asked all over town after me." Not true. Though she had asked Davey.

"Don't flatter yourself."

He trailed a finger from her lips to her navel, watching as her nipples hardened and her hips shifted in anticipation of his touch. "Right then. I expect ye forgot me 'fore the sloop rounded the Capes."

Scooting to a sitting position, she sniffed, her pretty nose aimed high. With the dignity of a queen, she crossed the room nude to the dressing table, swept the clothing that littered it to the floor, and quickly penned a note. Sealing it, she slipped it under the door.

Ah, hell. She expected another. He sat and reached for his shirt, tugging it over his head, jerking at the linen when it refused to fall where it should.

"You have it on backwards. Here, let me help you." She straddled him, pulling the shirt off and tossing it to the floor, wrapping her arms about his neck. "You don't have to leave yet, Liam."

"Jesus, Tory. What are ye thinking? Ye think I should stay and welcome the cove? Who is it tha's coming? Your 'sweetheart' is marching out with St. Clair, aye? Or is he? Did ye even care to read the names of those killed?"

"Shh," she said covering his mouth with hers, tracing his lips with her tongue, whispering, "We'll have no company. You've made your preferences quite clear on that matter. I've left word I'm feeling a bit feverish." Looping her legs round him, she caressed him, sliding on the condom he'd discarded earlier, extinguishing the last of his resolve as she slipped over him, then tightened her grip. He groaned, pulling her hips closer.

"Now, don't be peeved, love," she whispered, moving in a slow rhythm while her teeth played at his earlobe. "How was I to know you'd come by tonight?"

True. He'd had every intention of staying away.

He held her close as he laid back and rolled her beneath him. "I expect you didn't," he answered softly, his conscience no longer troubled he'd replaced her face with another's more than once in the last hour.

36 December 1790

DAVID'S DINNER BEGAN dancing in his belly as he watched Liam watch Mr. O. He'd never witnessed Oliver raise a voice to the lad, much less a hand—but suddenly Liam was still as granite, as if he were expecting both. He'd finished his explaining over a minute ago, and the only sounds since were from the fireplace, logs shifting and sliding as they burned. Even the steady patter of the rain had silenced, the drops softening to snow as the night iced over.

Finally, Mr. Oliver raised one hand to remove his spectacles while another rubbed his eyes closed, as if they were causing him pain. Dropping his hands to his knees, he slowly drew himself up from the bench.

"Liam," he said, reaching for his scarf and wrapping it round his neck. "You've been the fortunate recipient of two opportunities. Ones you could scarcely have hoped for, ones you'd have gone down on your knees for ten years ago. You're your own man now. But if you take off, before realizing the full benefit of each, well, you're not the man I thought you were."

"And you," he said, turning to David, his watery blue eyes glinting steel, "You entered into a contract of your own not more than six months ago. Have you forgotten so quickly? To follow this rascal while he traipses round the countryside?"

"Now hold on, Mr. Oliver, you know that I—"

"Enough!" He shrugged into his coat and started down the stairs, muttering, "I've heard more than enough."

David stared after him until he heard the front door shut. "Jesus. He's worse than Uncle John."

"He forgot the third," Liam muttered, kicking over the empty ale bottles that stood in his way.

The third. Mr. Oliver taking him on.

"He didna mean it, David. No' as far as you're concerned. He knows damn well you're no' abandoning Lisbeth. It was me he was angry with." He donned his hat and started down the stairs. "I likely willna be back tonight. Keep Lisbeth from fretting, aye?" he turned to call before the front door slammed shut.

Ah, hell. That meant he was heading toward that Billings chit. And *that* meant he'd be out of sorts for the next week, kicking himself for going. He banked the fire, grabbed the game he'd set by the window, and left to fetch Elisabeth.

"HEY, JOHN," David said, wrestling with the wind as he pulled the door shut behind him. Warmth and the scents of a simmering beef stew, warm bread, and hot coffee surrounded him. He held up the two rabbits. "Cove is paying me on account. I'll set them in the larder."

"Shake off your boots, boy, or they'll be soaking wet in no time. You hungry?"

"A little."

John filled a large bowl with stew and heaped full a plate with bread. Pouring two steaming mugs of coffee, he added a helping of whisky, then sat.

"Where's Liam? My girls were expecting the both of yous. Mrs. Ross been planning for a card game."

"He's out of sorts o'er a disagreement with Mr. Oliver. I expect it'll be a day or two 'fore we see him again."

"Them Billings are back in town. Saw her father at the dry goods, talking himself up a storm about Kentucky. Would think gold was a crop, iffin I didn't know no better."

Reaching for another piece of bread, David nodded, his

mouth busy with the stew. The black community had the best information network in town, by far.

John knew far more of Victoria Billings than he did. Probably far more than Liam did. He was the one who'd made it known that David might want to let on to Liam that the lass warmed the bed of several lads about town, all during the spell he was courting her.

"She was with that no good scum, Bartle, last night. That man up and pulled himself out of a New Jersey jail, not two weeks past. Liam's better than that. Trouble is, the boy don't know it."

"Oh, I think maybe he does. He just can't help it. She's a comely lass."

John snorted. "Trouble follows. He needs to watch himself."

"I'll agree with ye there. How 'bout you be the one to go round him up and bring him on back here?" David said, grinning as he pictured the scene.

John didn't return the smile. "Mrs. Ross is gonna be disappointed he ain't here," he said, watching him.

"Mr. Hale can stand in."

"He's out." John stood, clearing the table. "Maybe it's for the best. You need to be getting my girl home, 'fore the snow piles up."

"There's time." He frowned, guessing he wouldn't be offered seconds. The man was obviously nettled about something. And it seemed it had to do with Rhee and with Liam. "Listen, John, I'm no' so quick about these things, ken? Are ye saying there's something between Rhee and Liam?"

John didn't answer, just jerked his head toward the rustle of skirts.

"David. I might have known I'd find you in here," Elisabeth said from the doorway. Rhee followed, and he watched her face carefully as her eyes swept the kitchen. The flash of disappointment was quick, but it was there. Hell, John might be right. He wondered if Bess suspected.

He stood and wrapped his arms round his wife, kissing the

top of her head. "Ye finished with your visit? If Mrs. Hale is still downstairs, I'd like to see her 'fore we go. Hello, Rhee."

"Hello, David. My, it's nice and cozy in here, John."

"Grandmother went to bed. We were hoping Liam had come with you. It's early still."

"It is early. John, ye have your dice, aye? Let's teach these ladies something 'sides those highbrow games they cotton to." Maybe he'd even have a chance on winning.

37 January 1791

"Did she speak to you about it, Elisabeth? You're aware this is twice now?"

Mrs. Habers had come to class late again last night, her face covered with bruises only partially faded. She'd insisted to Elisabeth that her own clumsiness was at fault, but Elisabeth knew from the others that Mr. Habers often raised a hand to her.

She had started the class with a small group of black women. Most of them had been Polly's friends, and it was her way to honor Polly's memory. But the class had quickly grown in size, and now included as many white women as black. But black or white, free or not, the women who came had so few resources. If she could help them learn to read, even if only a little, they would have one more tool for survival at their disposal. Maybe more than one, if one could count the friendships they'd formed.

Her heart ached for Mrs. Habers. She had so few options. Both of her parents had died on the crossing when she was but five. As she had no one in this country to care for her, she'd been sold into servitude. Then once she'd worked her way free, she'd exchanged one master for another by marrying.

It was hard to fathom. A husband who didn't love. A husband who didn't protect. But it wasn't uncommon; she wasn't naive enough to believe it uncommon.

"Of course I'm aware, Rhee. And no, she didn't. Well, I should say she didn't speak to me truthfully about it."

"I wonder if he's touched the child."

"No. I asked John to look into that for me."

"She needs to divorce him. There is no reason whatsoever for her to stay with that man. Why hasn't he been arrested yet? Everyone can see what he's done."

Sometimes Rhee . . . well, people thought *she* was naive. Sometime it seemed Rhee was much more so in her refusal to acknowledge how things were. Mr. Habers had the legal right to correct his wife, and until his violence passed that point, no arrest could be made. Besides, where was Mrs. Habers to go? She had no family; she had no employment. Her friends had no more resources than she did, and most had their own husbands—husbands who likely wouldn't countenance sheltering a runaway wife.

"Rhee, I think the only thing you and I can do is see to her instruction. Perhaps she'll gain confidence in the process. She knows how to cipher well enough; she could obtain employment as a store clerk, don't you think?"

"Of course. She has no reason to rely on that man."

"I agree. But she needs to agree as well. And until she does, there is nothing that can be done." Except to plan for the occasion when she did. Because it would eventually come, of that Elisabeth was certain.

Rhee sniffed to indicate her disagreement, but didn't comment.

They needed to do something fun today. The inclement weather of the past month had finally given way to a clear day; it would be a shame to waste it.

"The weather has warmed some. Do you think we might stop to see Mr. Bowen's exhibit this afternoon?"

"No, I'm to bring you straight home."

"It's four steps out of our way. You've been wanting to look at the wax works. I hear there are some items for sale as well. Perhaps you could find something for your inn. Wax fruit . . . or something."

"Or something." Rhee laughed. "It's not my inn. Not yet." She looked out at the cloudless blue sky. "It is a pretty day. Cold as the dickens, but at least it's not gray. You won't tattle if we go?"

"Of course not."

"Very well, then. As long as you're bundled up, I suppose we could enjoy an outing."

"THERE'S A miniature artist working here, right, Elisabeth?"

"Yes. Do you think you might sit for one?"

"Perhaps. My husband might need reminding, now and again, that he has a wife. Is this it?"

Elisabeth nodded, and they walked in, setting the shop bell to tinkling. "My, we have the place to ourselves." She wrinkled her nose at the heavy scent of wax and paint, then smiled as a woman walked in from the back room to greet them.

"Are you here for Mr. Bryson? He'll be out in a few moments; he's finishing with a client."

"Oh, no, ma'am. We're here to see the exhibit." Elisabeth handed her a dollar for the two of them.

"Call me Mary. Please, walk around and enjoy yourselves, and I'll return with your change."

"Look, Elisabeth. Here's one of Dr. Franklin. Oh, and an Indian! My word, what's that on his waist?"

Elisabeth peered over her shoulder, then wrinkled her nose in distaste. The clerk came back with her change and answered, "Why, that's a scalp, ladies. An authentic one, I'm told. See?" She reached out to turn it over, so they could ascertain its authenticity for themselves. Elisabeth covered her mouth and swallowed, pushing Rhee forward to the next figure.

"When you ladies are finished, be sure to look over the items we have for sale. You'll find them in boxes in the front where you started. Call out if you need anything."

"Yes, ma'am."

"THAT WAS entertaining, Elisabeth. I'm glad you suggested it." Rhee laughed as she rummaged through the boxes of wax flowers held for sale. "Good God, I'll never sit through a sermon on John the Baptist again without recalling this day and the sight of his head on a charger."

"I like this bowl of fruit, Rhee. What do you think about it for an entry hall?"

"Hmm. Maybe. I wonder what the sunlight would do to the colors?"

"They'll hold up properly, ma'am. For years," Mary replied, stepping from the back room. As, of course, she would say. It was her job to sell them. But perhaps Rhee had a point. They might do better in a room without a window.

"I could get it for Grandmother," she said, fingering the wax apple. It did look realistic, almost good enough to eat, and the table she envisioned it on received no direct light. She turned as a woman came from same room Mary had. A young woman who looked vaguely familiar.

"Good afternoon, ladies. It's Mrs. Ross, isn't it?"

"Miss Billings," Rhee said, nodding.

Gracious, Rhee had a sour look on her face. Elisabeth smiled at the woman, introducing herself in an effort to be cordial. Rhee didn't look about to.

"Oh, Mrs. Graham, it's so nice to finally meet you. I've known your husband for years. Look at this, and tell me what you think. I simply can't wait to show Mr. Brock." She unwrapped her package, then held up her completed miniature for them to examine.

"It's a very nice likeness, Miss Billings," Elisabeth said. She should invite her for tea. Heavens, Liam had known her a year, and she had never once called on her. "Did you have to sit long for it?"

"Oh no, Mr. Bryson finished in a matter of three afternoons. Or maybe it was four. I've been wanting to do it since last summer, after Mr. Brock and I'd seen some of Bryson's work when we attended a masquerade ball. I tried to get him to sit with me, but you know him. He's much too busy helping Papa with our plans for Kentucky, and he says the only portrait he's interested in is mine. Men!" She shook her head and smiled, rewrapping the painting carefully. "I suppose I'll have to give him this one to carry."

My word. She wasn't quite sure how to respond. Liam had never been one to wear his heart on his sleeve. Which begged the question—did this woman have his heart? And Kentucky? Where on earth did Liam find time to help Mr. Billings with that?

"I expect he would like that very much, Miss Billings," she answered politely.

"Oh, please. Call me Victoria." She stuffed the package in her bag, then turned to Rhee. "Shad Collin's keeps a slew of miniatures lined up along a table on his landing. Did you notice them when you were there, Mrs. Ross? It's an impressive collection."

"I'm afraid I didn't notice, Miss Billings."

Rhee had turned white as a ghost, and tiny beads of perspiration were visible above her lip. Elisabeth reached for her hand, startled as Rhee returned her grasp with bone-cracking strength.

"Oh, pity. Well, good day, ladies."

Drat, she had forgotten to extend an invitation for tea. She was surprised Rhee hadn't stepped in and done so. Maybe David could. He said he saw her in town occasionally. She turned to Rhee as soon as the door closed.

"Rhee, are you feeling unwell?"

"I think . . . perhaps the fish . . . earlier . . . take me home, Elisabeth."

38 December 1790

COLD.

Liam groped for his blanket while pushing back at the edges of the dream. When he couldn't find it, he opened an eye, wincing at what he saw. He was outside? He was lucky he was alive. He flexed his fingers and wiggled his toes. No frostbite.

He lay still and thought, retracing his steps. Whisky entered those steps at some point, judging by the ache in his head and the sour taste working its way up from his gut.

He had left Tory shortly after midnight. They had had words, over what he couldn't quite remember. Something significant, no doubt, such as why he hadn't shaved prior to sharing her bed.

Then the Man Full of Trouble Tavern. Ian had been at the Man, celebrating his joining the militia. He'd felt he ought to do his part in giving the lad a memorable sendoff. Maybe women after? He seemed to recall there were women after.

No wonder he felt like hell. Payment for company kept.

Well, it was daylight now, and his mouth felt as if it were stuffed with cotton. He extended a hand, groping for his pack. He had had it at Tory's; he remembered thinking he'd leave her bed at dawn. He'd planned to walk to Smith's first thing. Borrow a horse. Reassess the terrain between the mill and the stream running along the north border. They'd encountered only rock when they'd walked it the time before.

His pack would have water and hardtack, if he hadn't lost it between here and the Man. Though it seemed he had—his hand found nothing save pinecones. There was water near; he could hear it. If he just lay here moaning and groaning, he'd likely freeze to death.

He rose slowly and pressed his hands against his head, pushing back at the pounding. He'd chosen a good spot to lie, nestled well under an outcropping of rock, hidden behind a thicket of bramble. The site was familiar; he wasn't far from Smith's Mill. Matter of fact, he thought he heard the clang of the millworks in the distance. Though that could be his head.

Not bad, over six miles traveled, in the dark and lushy. He followed the sound of rushing water until he found the creek, then slid down the bank and dunked his head in the icy cold water, slurping greedily. When he'd had his fill, he rinsed and topped off his flask.

Coffee would be good. Strong, hot, coffee. But he hadn't brought coffee. Or a pot. He'd come with nothing more than he used to carry as a boy. Actually, less, as he hadn't come across his pack.

It was peaceful this morn. Cold, but not bitterly so. No wind, no rain, no snow. A week ago, he might well have died overnight. A feeling of calm enveloped him as he watched the water tumble over its path, its rhythm steady and soothing, mingling with the music of the morning birds, and he realized why he'd come.

Not to visit Rory Smith.

And not on a lushy lark.

The forest was his refuge. This one may be a thousand miles from his woodland of boyhood, but he'd wager it offered the same.

Closing his eyes, he paid homage to the God of his own choosing.

HE SAT STILL as stone, watching as the doe took water, until a shift in the breeze alerted her to his presence. She didn't run, not immediately; she just raised her head and watched him back. He fancied her big brown eyes locked on his, sharing brief snippets of age-old wisdom, before she bounded off, her hind hoofs kicking up small tufts of dirt.

His third day out, and tonight would be a cozy one. He'd found a discarded bear skin in his wanderings today, left behind unwittingly, no doubt, and he had occupied his mind for hours on the circumstances that might have led to such. He was finding no end of useful leavings in this forest.

JUST A LITTLE closer, now. Come lad, come . . . that's it, that's it . . . aye! He yanked on the line, closing the net, and brought the fish up dancing. Dinner.

Yesterday had been a good day. He'd snared a rabbit first thing. The meat had kept him filled that day and most of this. The satisfaction of this trout would likely last past noon tomorrow.

It was his fifth day out, and he'd need to begin thinking. Starting tonight, while his belly was full and his mind was at peace.

SEVEN DAYS. The weather was turning; he could feel the change in his bones, just like Mrs. Hale. Seems one only need slow long enough to hear the voices whisper. The aged slowed, willingly or not, and they listened.

He could smell the change as well. The hint of snow in the breeze. He didn't have the gear to survive this turn. He'd head in to see Rory this morning; walk back to Philly tonight.

"IT'LL WORK, Rory. There's easy terrain this stretch here, and the flow is heavy." He glided a finger down the map, linking the neighbor's stream with Smith's mill. "And if, like ye say, he's no' on agreeable terms with this one here," he said, stabbing the point east, "he'll have the satisfaction of helping ye out."

Rory stroked his mustache while he thought, his dark eyes gleaming as he considered. "I wonder if he'd sell, rather than lease."

Liam grinned. "Aye, I think he would. I looked up his

holdings at the land office. He's three warrants coming due in February, for land outside Pittsburgh. The clerk also told me he had to let another expire in November, as he didn't have the cash."

"How much did that cost you?" Rory asked, laughing.

"Nothing. He's a mate of mine. Dinna let it be known ye know, though."

"Of course." Rory rose from the bench and stooped by the fire to light his cigar. He walked to the window, and looked out, surveying his holdings, no doubt. The window was situated to give him full view of the mill and the barn. "I rode in from town last night. Did you know they're looking for you, the Grahams?"

He sighed, not answering. That was his business.

"Did you leave word with Donaldson?" Rory turned to look at him.

"No."

He knew well enough he should have left word. He didn't need this man reminding him.

"I'd like you to handle the negotiations, Liam. I think I might like you to handle all my transactions, eventually. I admire your resourcefulness and your initiative. The only reason I'm asking is I'd prefer a practicing attorney to oversee this one. It's too important." He walked to the fire and picked up the coffee brewing, refilling their mugs.

"Donaldson would be the one preparing the paperwork." Of course he couldn't promise that.

"I've no qualms with how you spend your time, none whatsoever. But I won't jeopardize this mill. I need someone I can rely on."

"Of course ye do, Rory. I'd not think otherwise. Let me talk it over with Donaldson, to see if he sees any missing pieces, and I'll get back to you, aye?"

Easier said than done. He knew well that man had no patience with "shenanigans." He'd told him that time and time again. And last time, he'd made it clear it would be *the* last time.

39

"You've no shortage of audacity, Mr. Brock, showing your face in this office. I'll give you that. Get out." Donaldson had kept him waiting in the hall for over an hour afore he'd granted him an audience. Now, granting him no more than ten seconds worth of words, the man dropped his gaze back to his paperwork, dismissing him.

He'd made it back into town late last night, relieved all were sleeping as he crept up the stairs and into bed. He hadn't wanted to explain himself just yet. He needed to settle with Donaldson before he explained. He needed to have his future sorted, so as they wouldn't worry along with him. Struggling to lie quietly, he'd spent the night sleepless, filled with impatience. Impatience for morning to come, now that he'd decided.

And chagrin as well, chagrin that it had taken so long to decide.

And excitement, excitement now that he finally had a plan.

He'd told himself it was the bondage that had had him fretting. But it wasn't. He'd enjoyed the time spent bound to Mr. O, helping him set up his academy. He knew he'd helped a great deal; the school had been successful. No, what had him fretting was the possibility of a bondage that led to nothing, a future he couldn't quite envision.

But now he could, so this bondage to come was anything

but. He could serve it. He would serve it.

"I'd like to talk to you sir. To explain. And to apologize."

"Are you hard of hearing? I said, get out."

"It was irresponsible, my leaving without word. It wasn't planned, but I could have rectified it earlier, had I made the effort. I didn't, and I apologize. It was rude, ungrateful, reckless, rash, and foolish." Donaldson peeked at him above his spectacles, so he took a chance and sat in front of him, his hands clasped still on his lap.

"Thoughtless also comes to mind. It was thoughtless as well." No response from the man, so he continued. "I needed to consider things, sir. That's the only explanation I can offer."

"Fine. I've heard it. *Now* get out."

"I aim to become an attorney, sir. It took me some time to come to that conclusion. But that's what I aim to do. I'd like to study under you. If you won't have me, I'll ask Richardson or Baker."

"Fine. Don't expect a recommendation."

"I don't."

"Well? Why are you still in my office?"

"Ye haven't answered me, sir. You're the best, to my mind. I want to study under the best; I want to study under you. Will you take me on? No trial basis. I'll sign papers this morning."

"No." Donaldson stood and walked to the door of his office, sweeping it open with a quick yank of his hand. "I don't know how I can be any clearer, Mr. Brock. No."

Somehow he found his feet and rose. He walked silently past the man, not having the wits to say anything in parting. Nora said something as he passed; what, he didn't know. The roar filling his head drowned out her words.

Jesus, what was he going to tell Mrs. Hale?

As his senses had predicted, the weather had taken a bitter turn for the worse this morning. He near lost his footing as he descended the steps; the snow had iced over the marble while he'd awaited his dismissal. The wind hit him in the face as he turned east, his gait slow and hesitant, and he dropped his head against its attack.

What was he to tell David?

Others pushed past him, anxious to reach their destination, irritated at his aimlessness. It wasn't the weather for aimlessness. Yet he had nowhere to go. He was back to a future he couldn't envision.

He'd miscalculated. Without a doubt, he'd miscalculated.

What was he to tell Mr. O?

40 February 1791

"You've a good eye for opportunity, young lady. It's a good location. My assistant reviewed the ledgers and we know it's operated at a profit for the last three years. Will your husband be returning to run the place?" Donaldson asked.

"Of course," Rhee murmured, her eyes downcast. Elisabeth bit the side of her cheek to keep her expression neutral. Mr. Donaldson was so old-fashioned; she wouldn't put it past him to decline helping Rhee if he thought she were acting on her own.

"Would you like more tea, Mr. Donaldson?" she asked, refilling his plate with another teacake.

"Yes, please. Now, has Mr. Ross authorized you to offer the full asking price?"

"Oh, no. He would never do that. He's a very frugal business man. He told me to offer eighty percent of the price to start, then to counter with no more than ninety. Do you think that's reasonable, sir?"

Of course he'd done nothing of the sort. Rhee hadn't heard from the man in well over a month.

Donaldson nodded as he chewed and scribbled numbers on his pad. "Now, I'm in court for the next three weeks. Shall we say the Monday following? I'll draw up the offer in the meantime."

"Three more weeks?" Rhee eyes flashed, her demure

posture forgotten. "That's simply unacceptable, Mr. Donaldson. It's been several months already. Someone is bound to make an offer and steal it right out from under me."

The pencil stopped, and he looked up at her, his mouth set in a frown.

"What I mean, sir, is my husband is expecting an answer before I sail. I simply can't afford to disappoint him." She withdrew her handkerchief from her sleeve, dabbing at the corners of her eyes.

"Perhaps an assistant would be willing to make the offer in my stead. I'll see about that."

"That would be perfect, Mr. Donaldson. I've met Mrs. Baylor several times now, and I know we can work well together. Thank you, sir. I'll write Mr. Ross immediately. He'll be so pleased with me."

"For God's sake, woman. I don't send my daughter out on these errands." He rose to signal an end to the conversation and turned to her grandmother, shaking his head with an expression of bemusement. She patted his hand, as if commiserating, and rang for Tom to escort him to the door.

"Good day, ladies."

"Good day," they answered in unison. Rhee excused herself as soon as the front door shut.

"It's wonderful, isn't it?"

"What is, Grandmother?" she asked, watching Rhee as she left the hall and hurried up the steps to her room.

"That he trusts Liam with such a task so soon. Why, he's only been in the office five months now. Mr. Donaldson told me last month he wouldn't be surprised to see him pass the bar this summer. But you're not to tell that to Liam." Her grandmother clapped her hands, her eyes alight. "I tell you, I'm so pleased with his progress!"

"Well, yes. Yes, it is wonderful. Liam has always been one to excel. I'm pleased as well." Grandmother had been quick to forgive Liam his disappearance. He must have explained it adequately to Grandmother; he hadn't bothered explaining it to her and David. Something was off with Liam; she wasn't certain exactly what, but something was. She wasn't convinced Liam was the assistant Mr. Donaldson spoke of.

It seemed Rhee also expected Liam to be the assistant to whom she'd be handed off. She was fuming.

She wished she knew what had happened between the two of them. She had worried over this very thing as soon as she had discerned his interest. She hoped he hadn't behaved inappropriately. Rhee flirted with everyone. Surely he knew better than to act on it. Surely he did.

"Elisabeth?"

"I'm sorry, Grandmother. What did you say?"

"Your father and David approached me yesterday."

"Together? The two of them?"

"Yes. They share their worry. They thought you might listen to me, as you hadn't listened to them."

"No." She shook her head as soon as she discerned the direction of the conversation. "No, Grandmother. I'm not moving back. Papa was awful to David. I won't subject him to that."

"David was the one who approached your father first. He bears no grudges. Your father said the same. They want you here, child. With your husband. Now, I know Mr. Oliver has gone out of his way to make you comfortable, and I'm very grateful for that. But child, you must admit those stairs are a risk in your condition."

"There are stairs here as well," she said, her foot tapping a quick rhythm while her hands twisted the stocking she was to mend. She was being stubborn; she knew that. The ones here weren't nearly as steep, and they had the advantage of a banister.

But, drat it all, she couldn't forgive so quickly.

Add to that, David still doubted her ability to keep house without servants, no small thanks to Liam. He always stepped in with the cooking, telling her it'd been his job for years, that he did it without thinking. If she moved back here, it would be even worse. She'd not be allowed to lift a finger. John or Tom or Jane would wait on her hand and foot. David would think her spoiled beyond redemption.

She liked it there. Though the men were out most of the day, Rhee always came, and Mrs. Nailor often came up to chat, dragging one or more of her boys. Sometimes Tommy came by himself to look through the pile of books Mr. Oliver had set aside for him. He'd ask her questions, and they'd end up chatting for an hour or more. She wasn't the least bit lonely there.

But her baby. Was she truly risking her baby's health by staying? Was she selfish to stay?

"I'll discuss it with David, Grandmother." When she found the time.

41

"YOUR DA IS likely to be at your door any minute now," Liam said softly, returning her caress. He'd roused some when she burrowed close, her hand seeking. Roused enough to note the weak gleam at the window was sunlight, not lamplight.

"He's come and gone," she mumbled sleepily, her face buried in the crook of his neck.

He closed his eyes, silently cursing as he realized he'd be reduced to skulking from her room in the light of day. But there was nothing to be done for it now. He rolled over, sinking into her yielding softness before his annoyance could grow into more, before he relived the sharp words she'd thrown about hours past—words that had led to the excess of whisky that had led to his still being here come daylight. More than likely, he deserved the sharp words. She hadn't been pleased to hear he'd decided to accompany them to Kentucky. She hadn't been pleased at all.

"THERE HE IS now, Papa. Mr. Brock, you're late." Tory's eyes held no softness as she looked his way, her hand resting on her father's elbow. It was difficult to reconcile her with the woman he'd lain with an hour earlier.

"I apologize, Mr. Billings. I stopped at the stable to check on the man's progress, and we got to talking." How easily the lies came these days, as if his tongue welcomed the comfort and familiarity of an old friend.

"Don't think twice about it, Mr. Brock. I meant to stop at the stables myself."

"Did the panes arrive?" he asked, changing the subject quickly, afore Billings could probe into a progress Liam knew nothing of.

Distracted, Billings proceeded with a rant on how slowly things moved on this continent, and no, the ship had not arrived. Liam nodded, listening half-heartedly while he watched Victoria, her black eyes darting every which way but his.

She had been the one taking the brunt of his frustration the last few days. He hadn't told her why. Hell, he doubted it'd even occurred to her to wonder why, or to wonder what he had done from day to day, before, and why he wasn't busy doing it now. She'd never asked, and he'd long ago wearied of watching her eyes glaze over when he thought to tell.

Yet, for some reason, he still had an open invitation to visit her room late each night after she and her Papa returned to the inn. Maybe she liked him better contrary.

Until last night, when he'd told her he'd spoken to her father about joining them.

She didn't care for the idea. It had no place in her plans; she'd made that clear enough. Life in Kentucky couldn't mix with life in Philadelphia. Kentucky would be the place of husband, children, and family. Philadelphia would be the place of fancy gowns, pretty trinkets, and diversions. And she had stuffed him in the cubbyhole labeled diversions.

"It is the middle of winter, sir. The delay gives you more time to talk to the congressmen, aye?"

"You're one to look at the bright side, are you, Mr. Brock?"

"I try, well enough. I'll travel to New Jersey this afternoon, if you like. They may have some of the items you require."

"No, no. You're right. There's no reason to rush."

ONCE HOME, he washed up and changed his clothes, removing all trace of anything that Donaldson might interpret as evidence of dissipation. He tucked the lease he'd drafted for

Rory Smith into his only clean waistcoat—the one Lisbeth had made that he rarely wore—as well as his memorandum on the negotiations he'd had with the neighbor on behalf of Smith. He'd taken the matter as far as he could. Perhaps Donaldson would take it from here. If not, he'd have to find another attorney.

Though he had another option. He wasn't certain he'd take it yet, but he had another. It could certainly appear as if Donaldson had prepared the paperwork. He knew where the man kept his seal.

"AHH, IT'S THE lovely Mrs. Baylor. Good afternoon to you, lass. My days have been dark indeed without ye."

"It's not me you have to convince, sweetheart. I'd have kept you in a heartbeat, if only to look at you." She came from behind her desk and embraced him, then patted his back as if consoling him. "What are you doing now?"

"This and that." He nodded toward the office door. "He in? I have some work he may be interested in."

She nodded, her eyes soft with compassion. "He never changes his mind, Liam."

"I know. Dinna fash, lass," he said, kissing her cheek. "Listen, my notebooks, do you—"

"Nora! Where the hell is that boy? You were to have him here a half hour ago," Donaldson bellowed from his office.

"No, Papa. You said tomorrow; I have it written right here."

"Damn it, I don't need him tomorrow. I need him today. I have to be in court in less than an hour."

She walked to the office door. "I can't possibly get him here. You know darn well you sent him to New Jersey for the day. He won't be back until late this evening. Would you like me to find a substitute? Or perhaps I could go in his stead."

"Don't be ridiculous, woman. Go to Marley's. See if his lad is available. Hurry! Now, damn it, don't just stand there."

"Mr. Donaldson, is there something I could be doing to help ye? No obligation, sir. Just for the day?" The man turned to face him, his color rising at the sound of his voice.

Nora glared at him, as if he were responsible for the state of the man's health. "Papa, Mr. Brock's only here to . . ." She looked at him, uncertain why he had come. "He's come about his notebooks. Sit down now and calm yourself," she said, pouring him a glass of the sherry he kept near. "I'll fetch Mr. Marley's—"

"Don't coddle me, woman. Where's my wig?" He slipped a file into his satchel, the one he used for going to court, and clasped it shut with a clang while Nora placed the wig on his head. "Take care of this today, Mr. Brock," he said, holding out a slip of paper. "The woman's a pushy one and claims her husband can't afford to wait. I'm sure you're able to handle it."

Liam looked at the address. "That inn?"

"Right. You've examined the ledgers. Perhaps it's just as well you meet with the parties, as you're the most familiar with it. Don't sign anything without my approval and don't mangle the negotiations. And don't expect compensation."

"Right. What's her offer?"

"Eighty percent to start, no more than ninety. Cash."

"Cash? Well, now. Mind if I start with sixty?"

Donaldson grunted short a laugh, albeit it seemed reluctant. "Have at it, lad. But don't forget, a portion of my fee is tied to the price paid. Now, Mrs. Applegate will open the place at one o'clock, to get it tidy and whatnot. It's been shut up since her husband passed. Give her time to do that, but make sure you arrive before Mrs. Ross does. She's expected at three."

His heart did a series of somersaults, landing somewhere near his gut. "Who?"

"My client, Mrs. Ross." Donaldson hauled his satchel off the desk with a groan. "Hell, this gets heavier each day."

He'd have to withdraw his offer to help. He couldn't spend the day with her; he hadn't told her yet. He hadn't told any as yet, of what he'd lost. He'd have to back out.

"Mrs. Ross is your client?"

"You turning daft on me, lad? Yes, she's my client. And she's a looker, so mind you remember your manners. I don't want to hear any complaints from the woman. No shenanigans."

"Yes, sir. It's only . . . well, I know Mrs. Ross. If you're meaning the woman lodging with the Hales."

He remembered this transaction well. The inn's location was good, and the ledgers indicated it had been profitable and well run. He had had some concerns though, given its age, and he wanted to make certain they were addressed. Especially now that he knew Rhiannon was the one interested. Marley's lad was an ineffectual eijit who wouldn't think to be concerned about his concerns. He would go.

"Oh. Right. I should have remembered. Well, there's no harm there." Donaldson stepped out the doorway, telling Nora to give him the paperwork, calling back, "Good luck, Mr. Brock."

He'd need all of that. The lass had been icier than the Delaware shallows of late. Could he do this without telling her he was merely standing in? Should he do this without telling her?

"I'll be back, Nora," he said, grabbing the paperwork. He still hadn't retrieved his notebooks.

"No," she said. "Come tomorrow. I'm locking up in an hour."

"Right, then." He rushed out the door to follow Donaldson, then reached to relieve him of the satchel.

"I'll carry that to court for ye, sir. I'd like to talk to you about another matter on the way, one ye may have an interest in."

There was a possibility he'd have no need of that seal.

42

"YE'RE NO' SUPPOSED to be here 'til three."

"Neither are you."

"Ye didna speak to her, did ye?"

"I've only just arrived, Mr. Brock. Please, do calm down. I know this is your first experience in the field without adequate supervision, but I've every faith you shant err so badly Mr. Donaldson can't mend it."

He treated her to his widest grin. "Why, thank ye, lass," he said, meaning it. Her sharp tongue kept his mind from wandering. "Let me do the talking from this point on, though, ken?"

Rolling her eyes in answer, she pushed past him to the door and dropped the iron knocker. He placed himself beside her, though an inch or two ahead.

"Hello, miss," he said, assessing the woman with a quick glance. In her middling years, she was likely the widow herself. Yet she'd dressed her hair in the current style, the jewels she wore played up the color of her eyes, and the lines about her face were from laughter, not discontent. She wasn't one who'd mind a bit of flattery. "Would you tell Mrs. Applegate that Liam Brock, Mr. Donaldson's associate, and my client, Mrs. Ross, are here to speak with her?"

"I'm Mrs. Applegate," she answered.

"My apologies, ma'am. I had expected someone older. It's a pleasure to meet you."

"You are an hour early, sir."

"I know, and I sincerely apologize for that. It's only Mrs. Ross decided, since we were out this way, we should try to fit in a visit to another property. We're hoping to do so afore nightfall."

"It's my fault, Mrs. Applegate; I apologize as well. It's so hard to find Mr. Brock free these days; I decided to take advantage of his time as soon as I heard of the other."

"I hadn't heard of another property out this way. Who's selling?"

"That's confidential ma'am. I'm afraid I can't tell you."

"Hmmph. Well, come in, as long as you're here. This is the best time of day to see it anyway." She opened wide the door and ushered them into the hallway. "You'll note we have full sunlight in this front room. That's very important for our winter guests. Mind, now, it's not as tidy as it should be. My Robert passed only a month ago, and I haven't been back since."

"Of course you haven't, Mrs. Applegate," Rhee said with sympathy, placing a hand on the woman's arm. "I imagine the sun casts quite a pretty sparkle when you have that lovely tea set in place," she said, gesturing to the china on the sideboard.

"Oh, it does indeed, Mrs.—I'm sorry, I've already forgotten your name, dear."

"Mrs. Ross. It's Spode, isn't it?" Rhee said, bending to examine it.

The widow nodded, appearing pleased. "Follow me upstairs, Mrs. Ross. I have a feeling you'll appreciate the washstands. We ordered them special from England, you know. I insisted we have one in each of the guest rooms . . ."

Liam let them wander alone upstairs as it seemed he was the one who should keep quiet, not Rhee. There were three rooms downstairs, and he walked through them all, examining the char in each of the fireplaces to assess the draw, and opening and shutting each of the windows and doors to assess the soundness of the carpentry. Ripping a sheet from his notebook, he rolled the paper into a makeshift torch, then took out his flint box, drew a spark, and lit it. Passing it round the windowpanes, he noted the flame held steady, even as a gust of wind scattered the trash heap outside the house.

Turning from the window, he tossed the torch into the empty fireplace and headed up the staircase in time to note Rhee watching him from one of the bedroom doorways. Holding his hands high to indicate he hadn't stolen the silver, he brushed past her and went through the rooms she and Mrs. Applegate had already visited, repeating his inspection.

"Do those fruit trees still produce, ma'am?" he asked when he reached the room where the women stood.

"They certainly do, sir. Didn't you read the advertisement? I told the gentleman to include that."

"I did read it. But it never hurts to ask again. If you ladies are finished up here, do you mind if I taste the water from the well?"

"It's a new well. My Robert had it dug last year. I can assure you, the water is good."

"My mouth's watering already, ma'am. I'll wager it's the sweetest water I've tasted since leaving Scotland."

She allowed him to inspect the well while she and Rhee visited the kitchen. The water tasted sweet enough. Picking up a stone, he stepped into the privy. Lighting a scrap again, he dropped the stone as he held up the flame, using his ears and eyes to assess the depth. He couldn't, so he concluded it deep enough to serve a few more years. Satisfied, he joined the women in the kitchen.

"Ye mind if we sit a minute, Mrs. Applegate?" He took out his notes and went over the few questions he'd raised with Donaldson after looking over the books, while Rhee wandered round the kitchen, ohhing and ahhing over knick-knacks and such.

"So, Mrs. Applegate, if you only kept a staff of three, were you working day and night, then?" he asked.

"Oh, no, dear. My Betsy and Robert Jr. helped out as well. And sometimes Betsy's husband, Earl, if we got to be real busy."

"I imagine so. Things are so tidy; I can tell caring hands had a place in things," Rhee said, joining them at the table.

"Their pay isn't reflected in the ledgers, is it ma'am?" he asked.

"Well, no. They're family, you see."

"I do see. But Mr. and Mrs. Ross, they don't have a family as yet to draw on. What they can't do themselves, they'll need to hire out."

"Well, yes, I suppose so."

He went through the motion of scrawling numbers on his paper, then wrote a figure on a fresh sheet and passed it to her. "We're prepared to offer this price, Mrs. Applegate."

She looked at it, frowning as she calculated the difference off her asking price. "Oh, no. No, Mr. Brock. I can't sell it for that."

"I understand. But we'll leave ye an hour or two to consider it, just the same, while we visit the other property."

Rhee reached for the paper and took the pencil from his hand, her touch setting him off balance. "Of course you can't, Mrs. Applegate. Really, Mr. Brock. She's a woman alone. We must offer a fair price," she admonished, scribbling her eighty percent on the paper and sliding it back. "I can pay you that. After all, you said you might include the china. But my husband has authorized not a penny more."

The woman looked at the increase and nodded, appeased. "Yes, that's fair, I suppose. You will have to hire more help. Mr. Brock was right about that."

"Then we have a deal?"

"If it's cash, as Mr. Donaldson promised. I can't afford the risk of lending it, dear. I'm sorry, but it must be cash."

Rhee nodded, and Liam sighed in defeat, filling in the amount on the papers Nora had given him.

"Sign right here then, ma'am, as to your intent." He pointed out the stipulation for cash. "I'll have Mrs. Ross sign after Mr. Donaldson's approved everything. Can you come by the office tomorrow for the balance of the paperwork and the down payment?"

"Yes, I'll be there." She looked at Rhee. "When will I get

the full amount, dear?"

"In about nine weeks, Mrs. Applegate. I need my husband's signature, you see, and he's presently out of the country."

"Title won't transfer until she pays you in full, Mrs. Applegate. In the meantime, we'd like you to bring your insurance contract into the office when you come for the down payment."

RHEE WAITED until they'd walked more than a block before she squealed her glee, spinning round and round in one of her merry twirls.

"Careful, lass. It's icy."

"Oh, I don't care. It's a wonderful place, don't you agree, Mr. Brock?"

"It's a fair deal. Ye could have had it at seventy, if ye'd held out. Then it'd be a good deal. Would ye join me for a cup of coffee?" He wanted to tell her of his disgrace. It would help to talk to her, he realized. It would help a great deal to talk to her.

"No," she said, sobering instantly, as if the mention of coffee reminded her she detested him. "Our business is complete. I thank you for your help. Good day." And with that she walked away, leaving him standing alone on the footpath.

What had he done to anger her so? His mouth quirked in resignation as he walked alone to the Coffee House. He spent a good portion of his days there now, whenever he wasn't at school. He could always find a quiet corner to read, write, and study. The City Tavern had become the place for men who did things, leaving the Coffee House a place for men who only thought about doing things.

And today he needed that quiet corner to write up the offer, given Donaldson's office would be locked up snug.

43 FEBRUARY 1791

"IT'S BEAUTIFUL, BETH. Oh, I wish you could have come to see it. The rooms face south, so even in the dead of winter it isn't dreary. And there's practically a full orchard in the back."

"What kind of fruit?"

"Well, I don't know. But it produces. Mr. Brock asked about it. And it comes fully furnished. The woman has good taste; I'll only change a few things."

Elisabeth laughed, knowing better. Rhee's passions included decorating, and it was likely she'd redesign the whole scheme of things before she finished. Her hand was already busy as she talked, sketching out ideas.

"Are you hungry, Rhee? Did you have tea?"

"No, but I'm fine, don't trouble yourself. On second thought, it is getting late, isn't it? I'll run down to the Market and bring back some food. The ladies will be here in a few hours."

She lowered herself into the rocker, her hand covering her belly. "I think I must tell them it is to be the last time. David's becoming quite unreasonable about it."

"Oh, Beth, I'm sorry. But you know, don't you, that he wouldn't be if you'd sit still like you promised? I don't blame the man. Look at you. Your ankles are as swollen as your belly."

"Thank you for reminding me."

"Do you think I could do it? I've watched you enough. You

could sit there and correct any errors I might make."

"Of course you could. But it's not only that. The doctor came by earlier. He scolded David a full half hour about the stairs."

"Why'd he send for the doctor, lass? Are ye going to tell her that as well?"

"Liam!" She rose and went to meet him, throwing her arms around his neck.

"Careful, lass. This soup is hot." He disengaged one of her arms and set the bucket on the table.

"My word, you're home early. I feel as if I haven't seen you in weeks. I've missed you so."

"I've missed ye too, lass," he said, hugging her tight and kissing her forehead. He stooped, throwing an arm under her knees to lift her. Carrying her to the chair, he deposited her with a thump. "Jesus," he said, his hand rubbing his lower back, "ye've grown heavy."

Rhee had stashed her sketch pad by Elisabeth's mending and was headed down the steps. "I'll be back after your supper, B—get your hands off me, sir!" she called from the stairwell. Liam had picked her up as well, depositing her, screeching, back on the bench.

"Ye're no' going anywhere, Mrs. Ross. Not until ye tell me why I'm suddenly of no more consequence than the scum at the bottom of a privy."

"Liam! Rhee doesn't think that!"

"Oh, aye, she does. Don't you, Mrs. Ross?" he asked, his hands on her shoulders as if he thought to hold her until she answered.

"She does not. She told me how helpful you were this afternoon." Rhee had said one nice thing about him. She was sure she had. Something about trees.

"She can speak for herself, well enough. While she thinks on it, how 'bout you answer my question."

"What question?"

"The doctor. Are ye telling Mrs. Ross why he was sent for?"

"It was nothing. David always worries about the littlest

thing."

"Davey's not one to throw coins at a doctor for the littlest thing. Ye're bleeding, aye?"

Rhee gasped, struggling in his grasp. "Mr. Brock! You're overstepping. Elisabeth, is that true?"

"Liam, stop!" she said, her hands covering her face.

"Hell, Lisbeth, I empty the chamber pot round here, less Davey gets to it first. You're family, for Christ's sake. Did the doctor say the stairs were a problem?"

"Yes, but—"

"Did the doctor say ye shouldn't be on your feet teaching a class?"

"Yes, but—"

"Did the doctor say ye should stay seated or better yet, in bed?"

"Yes, but—"

"Did he suggest ye move back home?"

"Bloody hell! There are stairs there as well, Liam. And worry isn't good for my baby either. You think I won't worry every time my father crosses paths with David in the hallway? Do you think I won't worry every time I leave the house, wondering if David will be there when I get back? Do you think I won't worry if my father will have finally found an insult he can't possibly tolerate, and he'll have left?"

"Elisabeth! Calm down, dear. For heaven's sake, it isn't like that. I've never heard Mr. Hale say a word against David."

"Davey wouldna leave ye, lass. No' e'er. Give the lad credit."

"I like it here, Liam." And she did. She truly enjoyed the evenings they'd all spent together.

"And I love having ye here. The both of you. But ye need to do what's best for the bairn. Now, Mr. Hale approached me at the Coffee House. He asked my help in moving things out of his study, so you and Davey could have a room downstairs."

"He did? His study?" Mercy. Papa had talked to David and Liam? Maybe he truly did want to make amends.

"Well, truth be, he asked my help in convincing ye to move

into the study. He's help enough with the labor."

"David and I've discussed this. No one needs to go through any of this trouble, not if I stay in bed when I am supposed to. I promised I would. I told him tonight would be my last class.

Liam left Rhee and went to kneel in front of her.

"See this here log?" he asked, indicating one that had been laying by the fireside for as long as she could remember. It hadn't been split, and the men claimed it would only smoke, not burn. They used it as a stool. "This here reminds me of Davey. Used to be, I'd win at cards, someone would decide I'd cheated, and I'd end the night bruised and broke. Now, with Davey at my back, not a man even thinks to try. He crosses his eyes, men run."

Perhaps that was the case five years ago. However, Liam was no longer the thin waif she'd first met at sea. Nearly as tall as David, though not as broad, he certainly was strong in his own right. She rolled her eyes and crossed her arms, waiting for him to get to the point.

"Now this here," he said, holding up one of the reeds she had stashed for making baskets, his blue eyes twinkling with devilment, "this is Davey in your hands." He bent the reed so that it resembled an upside down 'U.'

Oh, for heaven's sake.

"Make no mistake, Liam Brock. David is *nothing* like that in *my* hands!" She extended a finger, flicking loose an end so that the reed bounced straight. "There, that's more like it. Moreover, I think he'd be offended if he heard you say such a thing."

"Elisabeth Anne Hale!"

"See there, Mrs. Graham?" he said, laughing, rocking back on his heels. "You've shocked your dear friend with your forward behavior. Ye'll no' distract me from my mission, however. Will ye do as David asks, please?"

"Yes." She shivered as one of the Nailors opened the front door and a draft gusted up the stairs.

"Yes?"

"I said I would, didn't I?" she answered, too weary to fight it anymore. Next thing, David would be sending John to talk to her. It would be awful for David if all the men thought he were putty in her hands.

"Aye, well. I expect I had prepared for a bit more of a battle."

"You'll come to visit, won't you?"

"Of course I will." He stood, his hands swiping the ashes from his knees. "Well, then, that's settled. Now tonight Mrs. Ross and I are sharing in the teaching of your class." He glanced at Rhee, and she nodded, mute. "And ye'll sit, right there, calm and still. If we do a fair enough job, perhaps ye'll trust us to continue on with it. She and I can alternate, needs be. So as the ladies don't have to give it up."

"Liam, that's wonderful of you to make the offer. But you have so many commitments already, I couldn't ask—"

"Ye didna ask. I offered. I'm thinking Mrs. Ross doesna mind offering as well."

"No, of course not," Rhee murmured, her eyes on Liam.

"Now, David will be here shortly. He's helping Mr. Hale with one thing or another. Stay put," he said pointing a finger at her as he added a log to the fire. He rifled through the books, found the one he wanted, and brought it to her. She smiled at the sight of the cover. He'd brought her the book on pirates. Pulling the dish chest over, he set her feet atop it and covered her lap with a blanket.

"Now, dinna move till we get back. We'll have supper then. I mean it now. Mrs. Ross and I are going out for a talk."

"Liam, you can't push Rhee around as if she were me. I love you. She doesn't. She's not going with you unless she wants to."

"Mrs. Ross?"

Rhee nodded slowly and stood. "I'll see you shortly, Beth. Please don't get up. Do as he asks."

44

RHEE DIDN'T SAY a word as they walked the two doors down to Mrs. Grayton's, nor did she protest when he placed her hand on his arm. He looked at her, worried. She may not be crying yet, but her eyes were wet with tears, so it wouldn't be long. He opened the door and led her in, gratified to find the parlor empty of all save two.

"Sit here, aye?" he said, settling her at the table fireside. "I'll be right back." He found Mrs. Grayton in the kitchen, supervising supper preparations.

"Mary will be right out, Liam. Is anyone else waiting?"

"One group only, ma'am. Two ladies." She nodded and allowed him to carry back two mugs of coffee.

"Here," he said, handing Rhee a mug. "Drink this, it will warm ye. Dinna cry, aye?"

"I'm not crying. Could you get Mrs. Grayton to add whisky to this? I'm cold."

He left again, returning with a small pitcher of milk.

"That's milk."

"Is it now? I hadn't noticed. Do you have to be so contrary all the time?" He took a flask from inside his coat and poured a measure in each of their cups, then added milk and stirred. He slid her cup across the table, watching as she picked it up for a sip.

"It's very good." She nodded. "Thank you."

"You're welcome. Now, then. Why are your eyes wet with tears?"

"She didn't tell me. I had no idea. Her mother . . ." Tears fell freely now, and he cupped her face with his hand, moving his thumb across her cheek to stop the trail.

"She'll be all right, lass. She's no' her mother."

He couldn't promise she'd be all right. Rhee knew that well enough, just as she knew Elisabeth could die in childbirth as her mother had. He could promise nothing. Hell, he'd been so self-absorbed, he hadn't noticed the troubles Davey was having with Lisbeth, and them not more than three feet away. But he did know the bleeding had only started today. And he'd told Davey first thing, in case he thought the doctor warranted.

"Only a day it's been, lass. The bleeding. Only today."

"Can I have another?" she asked, pushing the empty cup toward him. He gave her his while he motioned to the girl now waiting tables for two more.

"Will you truly come? Even though I'm there?"

"Where?"

"To the Hales'. To visit Beth. She'll be confined to the house after this."

"She will no'."

"Oh, yes, she will. Doctors do that. Maybe it helps. I don't know."

"She willna like that."

"No, she won't. So, will you come?"

"Why'd ye ask that? Why wouldna I?"

She shook her head and pushed the empty cup toward the young girl as she brought two more. She held out her hand, beckoning for the flask. "Just one more, then stop me."

He grinned, thinking maybe he wouldn't, and emptied his flask into her cup. Mrs. Grayton would have more, needs be. "I'll keep two of these on hand, now on," he said, indicating the empty flask, "if tha's what it takes to make you sweet."

"Oh, do be quiet, will you?"

He laughed. "Right then. Glad it's no' so easy as that."

She sniffed. "You might find I hold my whisky as well as you do."

He might indeed, he thought, recalling her skill at cards. "So tell me, why wouldna I come? Did Mr. Hale say he'd no' allow it?"

She looked at him, her eyes round, then narrowed as she drew her brows together. "No! Why would you say that? Hell's bells, Mr. Hale's been nothing but cordial. To both you and David. He's a wonderful man."

He'd let that pass. "Why, then?"

She raked a hand through her hair, loosening several pins so as a lock fell loose round her face. It occurred to him his hand may have been too heavy dosing out the whisky, as she didn't raise a finger to mend it. He reached for the stray lock, placing it behind her ear.

"Don't touch me."

"Why?" She didn't mean it. He knew women well enough to know that. She leaned closer by the minute. "Why, Rhee. Why?"

"I don't need you to try to be nice to me. Am I that pitiful? The poor woman whose husband has abandoned her? David has to request men to be nice to me?"

His eyes widened as he listened. She couldn't be serious. Could she? There wasn't a man alive who wouldn't stand in line for the chance to be nice to this woman.

"Keep your voice down, lass. What are ye talking about?"

"You said you couldn't force yourself to be nice to me any longer. That you found it too difficult."

The words sounded vaguely familiar. He had said that. Something like that. To David, in jest. When? He closed his eyes, his mind racing back through the days, pinpointing when.

"I'm sorry if I'm embarrassing you, Mr. Brock. You insisted."

The Nailor lad. Damn him. Aye, he'd encouraged the lad to repeat what he'd heard on the street. But surely never to repeat what he'd heard *him* say. The lad ought to know better than that.

Sweet Jesus, what else had he said?

"You're not embarrassing me. I did insist," he said, shaking his head slowly while he thought. He recalled the evening, a wretched one. Wicked cold, icy wet.

He stared at the women at the next table, the ones who'd been watching since he'd poured her third drink, their mouths pursed in disapproval, ridiculous mock flowers atop their hats dancing each time one of them bent her head to whisper.

"A wise man once told me, Mrs. Ross," he said, loud enough so as they'd had have no trouble overhearing, "that no good comes from eavesdropping. 'Yous never know if yous be getting the truth of the whole story,' he said."

Rhee laughed at his mimicry. "That sounds like John."

"Aye, so it be. One of the wisest men I've the honor of knowing." Moving his chair to her side of the table, blocking the women's view, he placed an arm round her shoulder, drawing her close as he said softly, "I'm to tell ye the truth of the whole story now, and I want ye to remember, because I'm no' repeating it, ken?

"I told you, don't touch me."

"Shh. Listen, now." He took a hand to fix her hair again, letting his fingers linger on her cheek while he watched her eyes. "I said it in jest. Davey made the request, sure, but no' the way ye heard it told. He's more likely to think we're the ones too pitiful to keep ye here. See, he wants ye here. I want ye here as well."

Her gaze narrowed as she thought on his answer.

"There was some truth to the jest, Mrs. Ross; I'll admit that. I find ye distracting as hell. The more time I spend in your company, the worse it is. You're easily the most enticing woman I've ever met. But I've things I need to be doing. Things I canna do when I'm filled up with being distracted."

"You don't mind that woman distracting you."

He laughed. No mystery on the identity of "that woman," not given the venom in her tone. "Hell, Tory's not distracting. She merely scratches an itch."

Likely more than he should have said, but the comparison was absurd. Her and Tory? Good God.

"How gallant."

"Aye, well. She feels the same about me."

She stared at him, opened her mouth, then shut it, as if she thought the better of what she'd intended to say. Finally she clamped her lips tight and looked down at her hands, worrying her ring.

"Truly, lass. She and I . . . it's hard to explain. I canna even explain it to myself, most times."

"You told her. You told that witch about Mr. Collin's place. Did she find it amusing? Had you run short of things to laugh about together?"

The words slammed into him, and every muscle went limp with shock as he absorbed them. His arm dropped from her shoulders, and he stared at her, unable to respond.

"You told her I went there."

Numb, he could only shake his head.

"She asked me if I'd seen the miniatures when I was there."

"I never . . . Rhee . . . I never . . ."

"You're denying you took her there?" The lock of hair had fallen forward again, obscuring her face as she played with her cup, twirling her saucer beneath it.

"No. No, I'm no' denying that." He swallowed, concentrating, and anger slowly replaced shock. He reached for her chin, pulling her face toward his, and tucked the stray lock back once more, so he could see her eyes. "I've made no secret of it, Rhee, that I've done things I'm no' proud of."

She flinched, pulling away, but he held tight.

"Elisabeth heard."

He cringed, biting the inside of his cheek. David hadn't lambasted him, not yet.

"When was this?"

"Does it matter?"

"Aye. When?"

"Several weeks ago."

"Then Elisabeth didna know the implications. Dinna fash. She's filled with other. She didna think twice on it, or I'd have heard 'bout it thrice over." He stroked her cheek, keeping his eyes locked on hers. "I've never discussed you with her, Rhee.

I've never said your name in her presence." He shook his head slowly, giving weight to his words. "I'd never give her that power. She'd know I cared."

And he knew enough of women to know, whether she cared for him or not, Tory would not hold with him caring for this one. "She knows some of the women that were there, ken? When you were. She must have heard it from them. She said it to hurt you. I'm no' sure why, but I'm sorry for it."

She looked at him for the longest time, absorbing his words, then said simply, "We need to go. I think it's time."

"Aye." She had more to say. Somehow, somewhere, she'd had a conversation with Tory. There would be more to say, but he wouldn't press. He didn't think he could hear it just now. He hoped to God Tory hadn't spoken of Kentucky.

He'd hate it if David and the others heard of his decision to leave from the Billings, instead of from him. But if the conversation had been weeks ago, Tory couldn't have told of it. He had only just made the decision.

They stood and he secured the scarf round her neck. A small sigh escaped her lips as she closed her eyes briefly, a pained expression crossing her features. "A masquerade ball, Mr. Brock? Truly?"

He shrugged a shoulder in chagrin, giving her a lopsided grin.

"I'm puzzled why women tolerate you, Mr. Brock. I honestly am."

"Aye, as am I. I've told ye so afore."

"Right. And warned me as well."

"Aye. But seems ye dinna listen."

She tilted her head and looked at him, as if she were considering his worth. "You're fine enough to look at; I'll grant you that. But you can be quite vexing."

"I can say the same of you."

She quirked a corner of her mouth, then sighed. "As can my husband. I suppose that's why he left." She raised a hand, to forestall his protest. "So, will you come? If I stay upstairs while you're visiting?"

Her husband had to be the biggest arse this side of China to leave a woman like this untended, though it wouldn't do to say so. She'd likely see it as his questioning her judgment in choosing a mate, just to be contrary. He refocused on Elisabeth and Davey, and the question of them settling in at the Hales'.

"Nay, dinna stay hidden. I like being distracted. Much more than I like the things that need doing."

She smiled at him then, her green eyes sparkling. "Are you ever going to kiss me?" she asked.

Now *that* was the whisky talking. He grunted, taken off balance again. "I think your husband might object, aye?"

She shook her head. "No."

"Then I expect it's likely I will," he said, pulling at his neckcloth to loosen it some. "One day."

But not this day.

Distraction was one thing. Surrender was another entirely.

45

"MR. BROCK." Tory nodded her greeting. "Papa missed you last night."

"Aye, I spoke with him earlier." He ignored Tory's unstated question; he knew she wondered why he hadn't come to her. He could see the query in her eyes.

He had spent the night at home, at the table, burning one candle after another, rewriting the purchase contract for Rhee. He had set aside the standard one Donaldson had drafted. To his mind, the man hadn't protected the lass sufficiently. Her down payment was substantial. What if Mr. Ross didn't agree to sign? What if he demanded Rhee go back to England? What if the inn burnt to the ground between now and then, and the insurance contract didn't list her as a beneficiary as well? What if the well were poisoned between now and then, or pranksters filled the privy with brick? The place was vulnerable, abandoned as it was.

His "what ifs" had added two pages to the contract. He'd timed his delivery to Donaldson this morning so the man would have only enough time to read them, but not enough time to change them before the women were due to sign. And as far as he'd known, he hadn't. He'd taken them with no comment and not a word of thanks.

With an effort, he returned his thoughts to the woman before him. He'd learned earlier her father had business at the

City Tavern this afternoon, business that should last him well into the evening, so he had sought her out at tea time, knowing she'd likely be alone.

"Listen, Tory," he said quietly, for her ears only. "I've been ill mannered toward ye lately; I know that. I don't mean to be. Ye don't deserve it. Ye deserve better. I think it best if we don't . . . enjoy . . . each other the way we have been. Now that I'm accompanying you to Kentucky, ken? I think it will only cause ye complications, especially with your soldier."

Her eyes flashed hard, her expression unyielding, and he knew she was having none of it. "Do you now, Mr. Brock? Well, I think it best if you let me decide what might cause me complications." She poured tea from one of the two pots setting on the table and added two spoonfuls of sugar. She'd become persnickety about her brand of tea and had taken to requiring her very own pot at the table. Just one more prerogative of the wealthy.

"Ye'll have no pity for me then, lass? Ye'll break my heart without a care?"

"I've ordered supper for us later this evening," she said, her voice taking on a honeyed quality as her gaze spilled over him like a sheet of warm water, starting at his eyes and somehow reaching his lap as it lingered on the tabletop beneath his hands. "I've taken your favorites into consideration. You'll enjoy it; especially the dessert."

Shifting in his seat, he swallowed, then looked toward the window, hoping somehow he could dredge up an ounce of gumption from without, since it had become hopeless to find it from within.

"You may state your case then, Mr. Brock," she said before he could come up with a reply. "Right now, however, I fear you must abandon your seat to the gentleman waiting behind you. I had a prior engagement for tea."

Surprised, he looked behind him, and indeed, a man stood in the doorway, deep in conversation with another, though he kept glancing their way. He was an unkempt character, dressed in dirty buckskin, and he wore his lank, fair hair loose.

"Tory, what business do ye have with a man like that?"

"At the moment, we have a date for tea. Your presence isn't required."

He sighed, rising. He'd tried, hadn't he? Couldn't say he hadn't tried. "Until this evening, then, Miss Billings."

If nothing else, this left him with some hours to visit the land office and follow up on his questions about Kentucky. His mate had promised to send his queries on to the Virginia office; answers might have returned.

He wondered where he could visit to ask about becoming a eunuch.

46

"GOOD MORNING, JOHN."

"Miss Liss, it's good to have you back."

She sat, gratefully accepting the hot tea he'd set before her. There was a lot to be said for being spoiled beyond redemption. "Thank you. Has David been gone long?" She remembered him kissing her, but then she had fallen asleep again almost immediately, their room was so cozy and warm.

"Nah. He visited for a while 'fore he left. And ate some." John laughed, obviously pleased to be cooking for someone who wholeheartedly appreciated his efforts. "Here, he told me you're to eat this." He placed a bowl of porridge in front of her, topped with a generous helping of molasses. Her stomach growled, and John laughed.

"Boy's talking already."

"Mmm, what a luxury, John." She hated making porridge, but she loved eating it. "Thank you. Can I help you with anything this morning?"

"After you eat that. Then I got some potatoes you can chop for the stew, long as you stay right in that seat."

"All right." She would no longer argue. The attention and worry had frightened her. Her hand went to her stomach, cupping it protectively. She'd worked so hard on separating her experience from her mother's, perhaps she had taken her baby's health too lightly.

"What's Papa been up to? He came in very late last night. I declare, it was near morning."

"Now, Miss Liss, that be your Papa's business."

"No one minds interfering in my business. Does he come home late often?"

"Some."

"Do you want to know why?" Rhee asked, dropping down beside her, a smug smile lighting her face.

"You know?"

Rhee nodded. "I had dinner with Mrs. Baylor last week. I was doing some snooping, because as John says, he's been coming in late. I'd hate for it to be because of Mrs. Baylor. She is married, after all. I meant to tell you, but then I got so wrapped up in the inn, and you moving back in, that I forgot about it. She says she introduced Mr. Hale to a maiden aunt, on her husband's side—so the woman's a bit less staid than our estimable Mr. Donaldson, mind—and they got on quite well together. It's wonderful, don't you think?"

Elisabeth nodded, watching in fascination as Rhee rambled on, her moodiness of the past few weeks nowhere in evidence. It looked as if she had taken extra care with her toilet this morning. Her hair had been brushed to a fine sheen and arranged in a particularly flattering way, highlighting the lines of her face. Her cheeks and lips seemed to have more than their usual color, and her eyes were spectacular: wide and sparkling with merriment, the green even more vivid due to the emeralds she wore in her ears.

"Can you make me look this pretty, Rhee?" she asked, running her fingers down Rhee's smooth, milky white cheek.

"You already are. But I can pamper you some. I've some treats for you in mind."

"What did you and Liam do that night?"

"We stopped for a coffee. Or two. Maybe I had three."

"Hmm. Well, you've certainly been in agreeable spirits the last few days."

"Must have beens some real good coffee," John said, setting

a plate of biscuits before them. "You watch that Mr. Liam, Mrs. Ross. He don't need no more womenfolk tailing 'long on his coattails."

"Thank you for your worry, John. But he's been the perfect gentleman. And I know better than to hang on any man's coattails. Besides, Mr. Brock has those adorable sweet girls for that."

"And Miss Billings."

"Ain't his coattails that one be hanging on to, Miss Liss. Now you girls finish up and go on and do some visiting with Mrs. Hale, 'fore she ends up in this here kitchen out of loneliness. That bench there be way too hard on her bones.

"SO, GRANDMOTHER. What can you tell us about Mrs. Baylor's aunt?"

"What is it you'd like to know, dears?" Her grandmother frowned as she plucked away at her embroidery, removing stitches that had proved unsatisfactory.

"Does Papa care for her?"

"Well, you should ask him that question, but I expect he does. Or so Mrs. Salisbury tells me."

Elisabeth glanced at Rhee, triumphant that Grandmother knew more details.

"And who is that, Mrs. Hale? Her neighbor?"

"No, no, dear. Mrs. Salisbury works for Miss Allen."

"Who is Miss Allen?"

Her grandmother set down her embroidery and looked at Elisabeth. "Child, haven't those boys mentioned anything?"

David would certainly be doing some mentioning when he returned. "No, Grandmother."

"Well, Miss Allen is Mrs. Baylor's aunt. She's the woman your father has been seeing. Her servant, Mrs. Salisbury, has a husband who is a member of the PAS. She introduced herself to David and Liam several weeks ago. She holds both Miss Allen and your father in high regard. That bodes well—when the help approves, don't you think?"

"Look at her enjoying herself, Rhee. She can barely keep her smile contained. She loves it when she knows things I don't."

"What's PAS?" Rhee asked, laughing as her grandmother made a very unladylike snort and picked up her needle again.

"The Pennsylvania Abolition Society. David and Liam have attended the meetings for years. It's one of the organizations Grandmother supports."

"Well, I've never been told of it."

"That's my fault, Rhee. The meetings have been on the same night as our class." Mention of the class reminded her—she wondered if Liam had finished the paperwork for her project. "Rhee, did Mrs. Beekam come to the reading class this week?"

"No. She didn't, and when I asked after her, the others simply sidestepped my questions. They don't trust me yet, Elisabeth, not the way they did you. If she doesn't come this week, what do you suggest I do?"

The woman's husband didn't like her attending the class. He claimed it took time away from her "God-given duties" and made her sassy. Elisabeth suspected it was more. Mrs. Beekam was an intelligent woman. If she had more options, she might not opt to stay with a man who often used his fists on her.

Hence, her new endeavor. She had been making substantial headway obtaining contributions before the doctor decreed she stay off her feet. Grandmother had suggested that if Liam could devise something more structured, the project would attract even more funds.

Mrs. Beekam, and others like her, deserved sanctuary from an abusive husband, so they could focus on making a life on their own. And food and shelter took money.

"Don't do anything yet. You know what happened last time." Interfering only made things worse—she had learned that with Mr. and Mrs. Habers. They mustn't make the same mistake with Mrs. Beekam and her boy. Before they interfered, she must have a sanctuary set up. "Let me think some more about it, and then I'll need to ask your help."

"Hmm." Rhee had her own ideas about possible refuges, all of which involved using Rhee's money. Elisabeth had no intention of doing that. "Have you met Miss Allen, Mrs. Hale?"

"No, dear. Edward hasn't brought her to visit. I don't want to rush him." She set aside her needlework and rose slowly, clutching the arms of her chair for support as she did.

"Where are you going, Grandmother?"

"I have some things to take care of before tea, child. I hope he doesn't have to cancel again. He's been so busy lately."

"It's Wednesday, Beth, don't you know? Mr. Brock takes tea with her each Wednesday. I only hope when I'm your age, Mrs. Hale, that I have a standing date with one of the most sought-after bachelors in town."

Elisabeth choked on her tea, her hand flying to her lips to contain the mouthful. "My word, Rhee," she said after swallowing, "*What* did Liam put in that coffee?"

"Oh, hush. Let's go upstairs with your grandmother and make you even more beautiful, shall we?"

47

"Mercy, if the staid Mr. Donaldson could see you now!" Rhee laughed as she watched him, bouncing up off the balls of her feet with a shiver, her arms crossed tight in the afternoon chill. "You'd be out on your backside."

Liam extracted his pick from the keyhole and stood, opening the door with a flourish. "Your inn, madam."

"Thank you, kind sir," she said with a curtsy before hurrying in to the relative warmth of the hall.

"Ye'll need new locks before ye stay here. Any fool could wrangle this one open."

"I couldn't. May we start upstairs?"

She had asked him for a key to the place in order to start her planning, and he'd had to tell her no, it wouldn't be available until after ownership had transferred. On the off chance she'd accept, he'd offered an alternative method of entry in jest. She'd jumped at the chance.

And he'd jumped at the chance to have her to himself.

Billings could decide to pack up and leave at a moment's notice. If that were the case, he'd like the kiss she'd all but offered. Or more. She may have had more in mind. After all, he was here at her request.

Either way, however, he should tell her about the apprenticeship.

"Aye. But first, I need to be saying something."

"Oh no, don't. Please. When one begins with that, whatever follows is certain to be unpleasant." She turned from him and started up the stairs.

"I must Mrs. Ross; ye'll be hearing it from others soon enough." He reached for her, stopping her in her steps. "I *have* been thrown out on my backside, little o'er a fortnight back."

She turned to look at him, her brow in a wrinkle. "But . . ." Raising an arm, she indicated the room at large with a sweep of her hand.

"He had me follow it through as I was the one who examined the ledgers to begin with. Otherwise, he's finished with me."

"I'm sorry. I wouldn't have made that jest, had I known." She placed a hand on his arm, and the look in her eyes truly seemed to match her words. "But why, Mr. Brock? Why did he?"

"I deserved it, no doubt. I didna follow his rules."

"I don't understand. Deliberately? With forethought? It wasn't what you wanted?"

"Nay. It wasn't what I wanted." He took her elbow and nudged her forward. "No more of that now, aye? It's said; let's move on, afore your day is spoilt."

She hesitated. "Who else knows?"

"No one else. Only you. I'd like if ye'd keep it that way. Please, lass, can we let it lay?"

"Then you haven't told Mrs. Hale, have you? Oh, please, don't tell me this is why you've postponed your last two calls on her."

"Aye, it is," he said, dropping his gaze from her eyes to study the curves of the balusters.

"Look at me. You know Mr. Donaldson is certain to tell her?"

He nodded. He knew. He'd had every intention of calling on Mrs. Hale last week and telling her. Every intention. Right up to the time he'd donned a clean neckcloth and walked down the stairs. Except from there, he'd made the wrong turn at the foot of the steps. And, instead of heading out the door, as he'd intended, he'd headed left, into the Nailors' quarters, to ask Tommy to run over and give his regrets.

Rhiannon looked at him for the longest time. Her mouth twitched now and again as if she planned to speak, then thought the better of it. Finally she released his arm and grabbed hold of the banister. "Very well. We'll not discuss it now. But the conversation isn't over."

"Fair enough." He realized he'd spoiled his hopes for the afternoon. But it had had to be said.

"NO, WAIT. That can't be correct." She pointed at the space she planned to place a wardrobe. "If that was sixteen, how can this be only eighteen?"

Dropping the measuring string, he crossed the room to stand behind her. Peering over her shoulder to read her notes, he stood as close as he could without touching. She'd be a perfect fit in his arms if he pulled her back into them; her curves would cushion all the right places.

"Ye wrote that one down wrong," he said softly, as he wrapped an arm round her side to point out the error. "I called out six, not sixteen. It couldna be sixteen, now, aye?"

She stood still as a statue at his nearness and didn't respond, staring fixedly at her pad.

"Besides, it matters not." He flipped the page in her notebook to one further back and slid his finger over the notations. "We've measured the spaces in this room already, an hour back, ken?"

A flush crept up her neck, and she took a step back, hitting him square. He steadied her with a hand, and she jerked away, her eyes averted. She wore the scent that baffled him, the scent of forest floor, heavy with pine. It triggered memories of sharing a saddle, and he wrapped his arms round her waist and drew her near.

"Dinna run," he whispered, his lips touching her ear. Her hair was soft against his cheek, her body warm against his.

She *had* asked him to kiss her, in one manner or another, and more than once, hadn't she? So what he was thinking now . .

. what he was hoping now . . . it wasn't such a stretch.

He'd felt her eyes on him all afternoon. She might have been watching out of pity. Even curiosity. Curiosity as she puzzled reconciling the man with the eijit who couldn't face Mrs. Hale.

But she wasn't. She'd been watching the way she'd watched him in his dreams.

She wanted him. Him.

"I can't do this. I can't . . ."

"Oh aye, ye can." And very well, he'd wager. He'd wanted this woman for months. And now she was here—pliant, soft, and willing under his hands. She didn't mean the words.

She'd come here, hadn't she? Knowing they'd be alone? If he backed away now, he may never have another chance.

She'd worn her hair up today, and her neck waited inches from his mouth. He inhaled, drawing her scent in deep. Only a taste he'd take. The taste he had wanted from the moment he'd first seen her. If she still voiced protest after, he'd leave off.

He placed his lips in the curve her neck, groaning as her flavor filled his senses, shooting straight to his loins. He'd been a fool for waiting as long as he had. An utter fool.

She tasted of hope. He hadn't known what hope would taste like afore now, but she did. Hope and dreams and answers, laden with a heavy dose of lust.

Her pulse raced under his mouth, matching time with his, as he trailed kisses down the slope of her neck. The pad and pencil slipped from her fingers to the floor as her head lolled back against his shoulder, offering an tantalizing glimpse of the full curves hidden beneath the neckline of her gown.

He should stop now. He should stop while he still had the wits to stop.

Gliding his hands down her sides, his fingertips skimmed lightly over her breasts in a teasing caress, then followed the lines of her stays to her hips. She sagged against him, moaning softly, as he splayed his hands across her belly, pulling her back tight against his arousal.

As she tilted her head back to kiss him, her eyes met his.

Shimmering pools of deep green peeked at him beneath black lashes so heavy and lush they weighed down the lids. His hands stopped roaming, and he stared, unable to look away.

Eyes full of trust, eyes that believed he truly meant to stop at a kiss.

A memory rushed at him then, dizzying in its impact, and he faltered, suddenly unsure. So real . . .

"Liam?"

So right . . . a memory of her . . . here in his arms . . . in this room . . . a child asleep as they watched . . .

He shook his head and the memory faded, though the sensation of contentment remained.

"Liam?"

Not a memory. Not possibly a memory. He blinked, then touched her face. Not a dream either.

Her eyebrows arched in question as she covered his hand with her own.

"For a moment I thought . . . it seemed as if . . . never mind." He tightened his arms about her and kissed the top of her head, holding her snug. "Ahh, lass . . . ye're too tempting by half. You make a man forget what he's about. We should go downstairs."

She was married. As often as he tried to forget it, she wouldn't thank him for having her do the same.

"Are you feeling well?" She pulled away and looked at him, her eyes scrutinizing his face. "Did you hear me say someone's at the door?"

"What?"

"Someone is at the door." She said the words slowly, her enunciation precise, as if she were uncertain of his ability to understand. By the time she'd reached the last word, he'd heard the banging himself.

"Hell. Stay here." He hurried to the top of the stairs, calling back softly as he trotted down, "Will ye pick up? Make certain things appear undisturbed."

"HOLD ON THERE, lass," he said as the girl fell into his arms, gulping for air. He grabbed her shoulders and held her upright. "What is it, now?" He'd recognized her immediately. She was one of those who worked at the inn. Tory often used her as her maid.

"She . . . she . . . sent me to find you . . . she's bleeding . . . the baby . . ." Her words came in gasps as she struggled to catch her breath.

"Elisabeth? Oh, no!"

Rhee. He grit his teeth and counted to five. He'd told her to stay upstairs, hadn't he? Whatever this lass had to say, it concerned Tory, and he didn't care for her to be hearing it.

Or did it concern Tory? She had said "baby."

"What baby?" he asked the girl, stooping to face her.

"Her baby, sir; the one she didn't want. You must come now; she sent me for you."

Didn't want . . . the one she didn't want . . . the words rang in his ears, over and over.

"Tory?" he asked, confused.

"By all means, Mr. Brock. You must go immediately." For Rhee, the words had made sense at once. He stood, watching as she turned and headed back up the steps, then he turned to question the girl further.

"Miss Billings is with child, lass? Start o'er, will ye?"

"I don't think no more. No one was ever to know. She started bleeding this morning. It took me forever to find you, sir."

"Had she done something to harm herself?" He tilted the girl's chin with a finger, so her eyes met his, his tone hard. "You said she didn't want the baby."

Her eyes grew round, and she averted them, staring at the ground. "I don't know nothing about that. All I know is she said find you."

"Were you sent to find anyone else? Earlier this morning?" She shook her head, still looking at the ground. "Last night then, did she send for a midwife? A doctor? Or anyone?"

"She sent me to find you, sir. Now I found you. Will you come?"

He didn't want to. He could offer her no comfort if she'd deliberately harmed a child. But he would. Of course he would. "Go on back now, lass. You did well. You found me."

"What do I tell her?"

"Tell her you found me and told me. Go on, now. I'll be there soon." The girl backed up a step, then turned and took off running. Rhee appeared as he watched her go, handing him his coat.

"I picked up everything. No one will know it's been occupied." She walked out the door. "Will you lock the door again?"

"Aye. Wait for me." He wasn't sure she would, but she did. She even took his arm as they started walking.

"You must go, Mr. Brock."

He couldn't speak to her of this. He could scarcely conceive she thought to speak of it.

"You're planning to go, of course. Aren't you?"

From the moment she'd stepped in and overheard, he'd felt detached, as if he were another, looking on. He hadn't quite recovered from the uncanny experience he'd had upstairs. And now this? She'd had to overhear this? It was dream-like, to hear her speak of it. He answered with the first thing that came to mind.

"It's likely no' mine."

She sniffed.

"It's likely no'. She has . . . I've been . . ." He dragged a hand down his face and closed his eyes. "Jesus, I canna speak of this with ye."

"Does any of that signify?" she asked. "The woman's in trouble, and she's asked for you."

Something in her tone made him turn to her. Her lips were pursed, either in disapproval or anger, he didn't know. It didn't matter which, given he expected both. What mattered was she didn't seemed peeved that Tory might carry his child, but only that he might not go to her.

Yet another dizzying thought.

"She may have harmed the bairn on purpose. I think it

possible she did."

She yanked her hand from his arm and jammed it into her mitt. "I'll go, then," she said, her voice flat as if she were telling him she expected it to rain soon.

"The hell ye say. Ye will absolutely no' go. Is that clear? Ye will no' go."

"Nothing whatsoever can be done now about what she might or might not have done earlier, Mr. Brock. It's over. What's not over is the woman's own life. Do you understand she may very well be in mortal danger? Are you telling me that doesn't concern you at all? Given your relationship, forgive me if I find that somewhat distressing."

"Of course I'm going to her, Rhee. Jesus, Mary, and Joseph, give me leave, will ye?" He sighed, defeated. "I thought it not appropriate to say so outright. Not to ye, anyway."

"You forget yourself, sir. I've no claims on you. You may spend your time as you please."

He'd like her to. The thought surprised him, but he knew it to be true. He'd like her to care who he saw or didn't see. Maybe he'd even thought that she might.

"I know," he said quietly. He had no claims on her, either. However he suspected he'd care—he suspected he'd care deeply, if she left his side to return to her husband's.

Once again, it seemed he'd miscalculated.

48

"I DON'T NEED YOU anymore. Go away."

Tory scarcely managed to croak the words, her voice laden with defeat, but he heard them well enough. Her black eyes flared with anger and accusation, stark against pasty white skin. He schooled his reaction at her appearance, knowing full well she'd never let him see her like this willingly.

He poured a glass of water from the bedside pitcher and propped her up, placing the glass against her mouth. "Shh, lass. Drink." She gulped it in one long swallow, then swiped at his hand, pushing the glass away. She didn't bother to wipe the droplets that pooled about her chin.

"What happened, Tory?" He perched on the edge of the bed and blotted her face with a corner of the sheet, then began stroking her glossy black hair, his touch light and rhythmic overtop the tangles. "Tell me what happened."

"No." She spun away, turning from him as her eyes filled.

He waited her out, lengthening his caress to the base of her spine while his gaze roved the room. A pile of dirty linens sat stuffed in the corner, accounting for the odor. Otherwise no evidence of her ordeal remained. He wondered where her father had been.

"Where's your da?"

"Where were you?"

Where was he? She'd never cared enough to ask where he was. "I was showing a property to a client. Tell me what happened. Are ye with child?"

"No."

Her face still buried in the bed linens, he couldn't assess the veracity of her response. Although perhaps he hadn't asked the right question. "Were ye, then?"

"Why didn't you come? I needed you, and you didn't come. I needed you."

She started with the tears, then, and reached a hand back his way. The gesture ignited something unexpected within him. He picked her up, cradling her in his lap.

"Ahh, lass. I came. I'm here."

Rocking her gently, he kissed the top of her head and smoothed the tangled hair from her forehead. She wrapped an arm round his neck and sobbed into his shoulder, clinging tightly. "I came as soon as I heard. Shh, dinna cry, now."

She had asked for him. Out of all, she had asked for him.

"Has the bleeding stopped, lass? Are ye in pain?"

He wondered if a midwife or doctor of some sort had attended her. He wondered if she were now out of danger, or how he would know if she weren't. She didn't answer; she just tightened her grip on him as she cried out the day's sorrows.

He should have checked in on her last night. They had argued the day prior, once she'd realized he hadn't bought the cameo they had admired while walking the markets. It had made him angry: first, that she'd had no idea he hadn't the means to afford something like that; second, that she expected him to provide whatever she'd admired on a whim, mayhap as her due for favors rendered; and last, that she thought to wear and dangle a bracelet chock full of garnets before him, one he knew damn well had come from another lover. He'd stormed out, thinking— but not saying—a whore would be cheaper.

He hadn't the urge to see her after the argument, but he should have. She'd likely not be in this predicament if he'd cared for her properly. He hadn't known she was with child.

She had needed him.

"You could marry me, Liam."

His hand froze mid-stroke, and he forced up her chin so he could see her face. She was flushed now, though not overmuch. Her eyes were wide and glistened with unshed tears, filled with pleading. He held a hand to her forehead and found it warm.

"I wouldn't need to suffer this again if I were married. There'd be no reason to suffer through that awful concoction. A child would be expected."

He blinked, recalling her special brand of tea. She had harmed the child. A child that might have been his. Anger tore through him as he considered it.

"Papa would provide for a nanny, if that's what you're thinking. If I were married, I know he would. He'd shower his grandchild with care. You needn't be concerned about that. You wouldn't be expected to manage that; I know your means are limited. See? You thought I wasn't listening, but I was."

She hadn't asked; she hadn't consulted. She had simply taken it upon herself to harm the child. A child that might have been his. Tears stung his eyes as he stared at her.

"We're the same, you and I," she said, clutching his hand, her dark eyes beseeching him to see the truth.

"You know me, Liam. You understand. You wouldn't think to give me rules. You're not like the others; you don't raise a fuss when I come and go as I please. I'd promise not to raise a fuss if you did the same."

He carried fault in this as well. She thought he was the same. Good God, was he?

Maybe he was. He had entrusted the chance of a child to this woman. A child that might have been his.

"I could travel whenever I pleased if I were married. Papa wouldn't need to leave his property to escort me, not if I were married."

He thought of Davey. How he stood now, more often than not, with Elisabeth: close and snug behind, arms snaked round her and two large hands cupping her belly. Wasn't quite proper, you ask him, and he expected Mrs. Hale to take Lisbeth aside any day now and tell her so. Yet he understood Davey's need. To hold and protect what was his.

Tory squeezed his hand. "Say something."

If she had been another, empathy might have rolled alongside the anger. But this woman had choices. This woman had resources. This woman hadn't even asked for his help, not when it mattered, not afore she'd done what she did.

He stood, carefully laying her on bed. He pulled the covers up and tucked them round her shoulders, ignoring the question in her eyes. He left her side to summon a maid to remove the bloody linens and add fuel to the fire, then crossed the room to the window and pushed open the sash, heedless of the cold. The salty tang of the Delaware swept through the room, clearing it of the stench and his head of the cobwebs.

"An enticing offer, to be sure, lass."

He'd bring her supper and stay beside her the night, to see she made it through. Then, he'd bring her breakfast. But more than that, no.

He was done; it was finished.

"You're ill, however. I willna hold ye to it."

49

"THIS IS NICE," David said, as he laid back on the bed beside her, clasping his hands behind his head. His eyes roved round the room as if he were tallying the number of bookcases along the study wall. "Watch the shadows the firelight's throwing on yon books."

"I'd rather watch you," Elisabeth answered, her fingers tracing trails through the coarse brown hair on his chest. She loved this man with a completeness that frightened her when she dwelled on it. She loved everything about him, from his integrity, his resourcefulness, and his determination, to the way he made her feel: cherished and special. It didn't hurt that he looked simply magnificent, and every bit as strong as Liam had suggested. He was hers. She hugged that thought close every moment of every day.

"Ye're no' angry? Over being here?"

"No, I'm not angry. I'm sorry I've been so stubborn."

"Your da and I have made peace, Bess. Ye're no' to worry on that score."

"It seems you have. Joined forces for this campaign, anyway."

"I think it's for more than this. He talks to me now. When he sees me in town, he'll actually acknowledge me. Today, at the City Tavern, he invited me to the table with his mates. They had questions on what had happened during the morning House Session, with Mr. Hamilton's bank. Your da seemed . . . I don't know, proud maybe . . . that I could answer their queries. He even boasted he'd soon be a grandfather."

Her hand stilled, and she squeezed her eyes shut tight, thanking God silently and fervently. "That sounds like Papa before Mama died. That sounds like he used to be."

"I think mayhap he had to suffer through a very long grieving period, ken?"

"Ken," she answered, smiling. "I love you, David."

"I love you as well, lass," he answered, bringing her hand to his lips. He turned toward her then, propping himself on an elbow. "Will ye take off your shift?"

Nodding, she reached for the hem to pull it over her head, gratified by the flash of surprise in his eyes, knowing he had expected her to refuse. Her size had embarrassed her for weeks now, and she hadn't wanted him to see how huge she'd grown. But tonight she craved the feel of his skin against hers.

He lowered the sheet and goose bumps chased his calloused hand as he skimmed it lightly over her body. Looking at her, he swallowed, his eyes moist as a slow smile spread over his face.

"Do you know I still feel butterflies race through me each time you smile?" She traced each of his dimples in turn, then pressed his hand to the baby. "Feel? He loves it as well."

He held his hand still for a moment, cupping her belly, then jerked it back as if burnt. "Holy hell, Bess. What was that?"

She laughed. "He kicked you." She brought his hand back. "Can you feel his legs?"

His long fingers explored, singling out the baby's parts. "His rump, I think. Or mayhap tha's his head. Do you know? Tha's a leg, most definitely. Jesus, the bairn's strong."

"Like his Papa."

"My mother writes she's to be sending some things for the baby, soon as she can find someone traveling this way. You'll likely have it all by then, but she wanted the bairn to have something from her."

"Of course she did. This is her first grandchild. Do you

think we'll ever go back? To see your family?"

"Aye. It will be years. But aye."

His hand had wandered, and she reached for it, placing it firmly back on her belly. "The baby's not in that direction, David. Not yet, anyway."

"C'mere," he whispered, turning her effortlessly and cradling her back against him as he caressed her. "The doctor mentioned only one thing I wasna allowed to do, just the one."

"Perhaps he hadn't anticipated the scope of your imagination."

"I checked with my mother as well."

"You did not!" She struggled against his grip in a vain effort to face him. He only meant to tease, right? He couldn't have asked something like that of his mother. What would the woman think of her?

"Nay, I did not. Now, shush. Ye keep up that wiggling, I'll be forgetting doctor's orders."

50   February 1791

LIAM WAITED, CROUCHED aside a bush in the park opposite Donaldson's place; his thoughts patient, his limbs aching, from both cold and immobility. The faint light in the upstairs room had disappeared well over an hour ago, and the flame in the lamp outside Donaldson's place was near sputtering. Five more minutes, it'd be out; five and a half, he'd be in.

This wasn't stealing. With few exceptions, he'd honored Mr. O's request of years ago. And those few times were only because he'd forgotten the request, in the heat of the moment. Mr. O would have forgiven, had he known.

No, this wasn't stealing, not in truth. The notebooks were his, and most of the work had been done well outside of Donaldson's tutelage. Maybe not all, but most. The man had no right to hold them, and no reason to want to—outside of sheer meanness. Liam had no plans to ask again. He'd had enough groveling in these last days to last him a lifetime.

Breaking and entering? That was, of course, a crime. And not an easy one to pay for. But he had no intention of getting nabbed.

"Half past one on a starlit night!"

There. The watch had made the round. He had a good ten minutes to get in and out. He'd need less than five. He crept back from the footpath, following the cover of the foliage, until he'd reached the next street over. Then he circled the block with an easy saunter, just another lad strolling in late, while his eyes roved every which way.

He was well out of practice for this sort of thing; it'd be the final humiliation if he were caught. He slowed as he drew abreast Donaldson's door, his hands fumbling in his pocket, as if retrieving a key, then he bounded up the steps to the cover of the dark alcove.

He knew this lock well, though the last time he'd approached it he'd had a key at his disposal. But the lock wasn't one of the newer ones, and he'd picked many of its kind in the past. Thankfully, Donaldson was slow to change. He stooped before it with his pick and set to opening it, his fingers nimble and quick. Just one more—hell, what was that? He froze, his hands still round the doorknob, at the sounds of a door opening, the rustle of clothing, then whispers.

The noise came from the house aside, from Nora Baylor's. A man, and maybe a woman. He couldn't be certain; the second whisper was indistinct. Nora had had no light showing; he *was* certain of that. Why was she awake? A late night assignation?

Or was it Nora at all? Perhaps the whisperers were intruders. If so, they seemed in no hurry, lingering at the doorstep. Had they done her harm?

The notebooks forgotten, he removed the pick, a fraction at a time, then tucked it into his pocket, his fingers clutching it tight in the event he should he need a weapon. Shifting slightly, he eased into a position facing the street, inching his head round the alcove toward the whispers, then froze.

God Almighty. His heart raced as the blood rushed to his head, and he wondered they didn't turn at the sound of it. But they didn't. They saw only each other. Nora placed a hand on the man's cheek in farewell before he stepped away.

Liam sank to his seat, all fear of detection gone in his shock. He blinked, shook his head, then looked again as the man headed down the street with a carefree swagger. Aye, it was David.

David Graham, his mate. David Graham, staunch Presbyterian lad. David Graham, Elisabeth's husband of less than a year.

Had he been in her home that entire time? That hour he'd watched and thought the world still made some sense? Or had he come skulking in the back way, outside Liam's line of sight? Why? Why would he do it?

Because women were God's own temptation, that's why.

But David? Him, he was weak. But not David.

He couldn't take it in. He looked again, catching sight of the man as he turned the corner, his profile lit by the corner lamp. Aye, it was him.

God Almighty, women were a trial. David. David had succumbed.

There was no hope, then, for a man like himself.

51

TIME HAD RUN out. He'd need say something to Mrs. Hale and the others. If not tomorrow, then the next day.

He'd come to terms with the loss of his position; he had no reason to delay further in speaking of it. It had already been well over a fortnight. If he didn't do some talking soon, any talking he did from this point forward would be outright lies. He hadn't lied of it as yet, unless one counted omission as a lie. He didn't.

He walked through the room, making note of his possessions, deciding what he could take. There wasn't much; however he didn't need much. Back at the table, he reviewed the list again, this time placing a mark beside the things he had and writing an estimate of the price he'd pay for each he didn't. His savings could cover it, but only barely. He'd need to earn more for expenses, and fast.

Billings wanted to leave in late March. For whatever reason, he'd decided the trail would be free of snow by then, and they could travel safely. The wealthy were like that, oft as not. They wanted something, they simply thought to make the request, and it'd be granted. Even if the request was of nature herself. Though to be fair, there were others traveling at that time as well. One did well to travel those parts in numbers. There was safety in numbers.

Hell, he'd forgotten to list the rifle. He'd need the rifle, no doubt of that. He'd likely need that more than any other item on the list.

Sighing, he crumbled the paper and threw it into the fire, watching as its edges curled, glowing red hot before the whole piece caught fire and was consumed. Women could do that to one as well. Dance around one's edges, flirting until the flame caught and left one glowing, burning with desire, out of control . . . until there was nothing left but ash.

Jesus, Davey. What were you thinking?

He'd taken the brunt of Lisbeth's anger the last time, keeping Davey's secret. And it had been fierce. That time the man had done nothing wrong, save not telling her of Sarah Wallace's accusations firsthand. This time . . .

He crossed his arms on the table before him and dropped his head on their cushion, staring into the flames, too weary to make sense of something that would never make sense.

"Mr. Brock. Might I have a word?"

He jumped high, his legs crashing hard along the table edge. Turning toward the stairs, he blinked.

"Tom?" he asked, staring at the black man that stood at the top of the steps. He would think he was dreaming, if not for the throbbing pain in his thighs. He rubbed absently at one with the heel of his hand.

"I apologize for startling you. I knocked below. No one answered."

"Aye, it's the butler's night out." What in God's name was this man doing here? They shared nothing save concern for Mrs. Hale. "Has something happened to Mrs. Hale?"

Tom shook his head, and Liam motioned for him to take a seat while he went to the corner and grabbed the jug of whisky and two glasses.

"Thank you. I'm here on a personal matter. I need help. Or rather, Sabrina, my daughter, needs help."

"You have a daughter? How long have ye had a daughter?" He regretted the question as soon as it'd left his lips.

"I'm a man, Mr. Brock. Same as the next man. I had a woman. I have a daughter. Does that surprise you so much?"

It did.

"Nay." Tom couldn't have a family. Tom's place was at the Hales', watching over Mrs. Hale, keeping the household free from riffraff like himself. The man had no time to have a family. "Your daughter, is she . . . is she free?"

Tom turned his gaze toward his glass. Liam watched as he turned it round and round on the table and was struck by the tidiness of the man's nails. He tucked his own hands out of sight.

"Yes. Yes, she is. Her mother was white. She's my stepdaughter, but I've had a hand in raising her since birth. A month ago, she left the city to follow her man south to Chester. She carried his child. The child was born dead. She's been charged with infanticide."

Man got to the point quick, he'd give him that. "Tom . . . well . . . that's a very serious offense." She could hang for infanticide, same as murder.

It was murder. Killing an infant was murder. The state should just call it that.

"I wouldn't be here otherwise. Her trial is this week."

What did he expect of him? Why was he here, telling him this? "I'm no' an attorney, Tom. I canna help ye. Even if I were, I've no' studied criminal law."

"You're known to be resourceful, Mr. Brock. The child was stillborn."

Tom didn't know that. Sure, his daughter might be claiming that, and sure, many children were dead at birth. But Tom didn't know if her claim were true.

"Have you talked to Mr. Richardson? He handles criminal cases."

Tom studied him for a long time before standing. "Thank you for your time," he said finally, tossing a wad of paper toward the fire on his way out.

Liam went to the top of the stairs, calling down as Tom reached the door, "I'd help ye if I could, Tom."

The man gave a short nod before he disappeared. He didn't bother banging shut the door; it closed with a gentle click.

Liam slammed his palm against the wall, welcoming the

sting it brought, then punched it, watching as pieces of the plaster crumbled and fell to the floor. He kicked at the plaster, raising a fine dust that settled atop the empty jugs standing near the stairwell, awaiting return. He stopped short of kicking the jugs themselves. Mrs. Nailor would be all over him, he woke little Georgie. Never mind the brat had awakened him once or twice a night, each and every night of the past week, with his wretched coughing fits.

Damn that man. He had no right. No right to piss on him for months, then expect him to drop everything simply because a bastard of his got herself in a jam.

He flung himself into Mr. O's rocker, setting it to a jerking motion, his foot pressed against the mantle. Richardson would not take on a black man, least not without a handful of money up front. Tom knew that, of course. Even then, the amount of energy he'd expend on the woman's behalf would be questionable.

His thumb scraped at the loose dry skin covering his lips, drawing blood. He sucked on the taste as he rocked, his rhythm erratic. He'd told Tom no less than the truth. He'd had no experience with criminal law. None. He'd studied it, sure. But he wouldn't even know where to begin, not in a practical manner. He had no experience with any sort of law, truth be. There was not a damn thing he could do, save go to Mrs. Hale for money and clout. And if Tom hadn't done that by now, he'd had his own reasons for not.

He dropped his foot and kicked aimlessly at the wad of paper Tom had thrown. Richardson was only the first who'd come to mind. There were others out there, others with less skill and greater heart. Maybe he'd find one for Tom tomorrow. Though likely not. The son of a bitch could go do his own crawling.

He stood and readied for bed, banking the fire, dousing all candles save one. As he stooped to retrieve the paper he'd booted, he opened it, curious in spite of himself. It was a drawing, a drawing of a woman. He went back the table, smoothing out the wad on a flat surface, and held the candle over it. If the illustration were accurate, it was his daughter, and daughter by blood. Tom was lying when he said otherwise. Mayhap he'd reason for it, given it appeared she could easily pass as white. But she had Tom's eyes, wide set and somber, and his nose, long and thin, a nose that hinted of ancestry other than African.

He shared that with Tom, the not knowing. He wondered if Tom thought much of his ancestors, or if he'd simply come to accept that which he could not change—to live with what he knew and to leave lying those who came before. This woman, Sabrina, would be important to Tom, the flesh and blood he knew and could claim as his own.

Grunting, he stretched his hands high, then rubbed the nape of his neck. For all he knew, the man could have a passel of parents, grandparents, and great-grandparents, all stashed two blocks south.

He traced outside the lines of her face, careful not to smudge it any more than had already been done, and stared into the woman's eyes. Did she love the man she'd set off to find? Had he fled, not wanting the child? Had she killed her babe, perhaps in the hopes of keeping her man?

The artist had caught a lot in the sketch, but not enough to answer those questions. A memory teased its way free, and he realized he'd seen work similar. In Mrs. Hale's hall. The portrait she'd kept of Davey and Lisbeth. Good God, had Tom drawn this?

He flipped the paper, looking for a signature, and found another drawing, smaller, not as well executed, as though it'd been completed hurriedly. It was of a man, one with broad shoulders and even features, dark hair and dark eyes. The artist had shaded the skin using light strokes. Not Negro, but perhaps mulatto? Was this Sabrina's man?

Georgie started in with one his attacks, a deep barking cough that reminded him of a seal. The lad's throat must be as raw as a back newly lashed by now. Maybe Rhee could help. She'd soothed him often enough. He'd have Tommy Nailor ask David to ask her, given he'd likely never have the chance himself.

He took the sketch to his room and placed it carefully between the pages of a book. Laying back on the bed, hands behind his head, he watched as the candlelight danced about the shadows. Why had Tom lied about being her father? Had he thought he'd refuse to help if the girl had Negro blood? And what made him so certain her claim was true?

Blowing out the candle, he pulled up his blanket and rolled over to sleep. He'd need be content not knowing the answer to any of those questions. It wasn't as if he hadn't enough of his own to answer first.

Had Tom known he'd refuse to help at all?

52

"Uh-oh. You caught me." Seeming startled, she raised her eyes from the sweetbread she held.

"Mrs. Ross," Liam said, slowly nodding a greeting. "Good afternoon."

He had entered through the kitchen door, telling himself he wanted to visit with John afore he took tea with Mrs. Hale, though, in truth, it was because the front door meant Tom. He'd half-hoped the kitchen would be empty as he wasn't keen to squirm under John's knowing eyes either.

He hadn't expected to encounter Rhee in the kitchen. He hadn't seen her alone since that day at the inn. Yet, here she was, sweet as pie, addressing him as if they were still friends. Maybe they were.

Uncertain, he asked, "Are we to be friends, then?"

Her laugh filled the kitchen, melodic and genuine. She nodded as she took a bite and indicated the food with a wave of her hand. "I think these are meant for your tea tray," she mumbled around a mouth stuffed with bread.

"Then it's good I've only recently finished dinner." He sat, placing his hat on the bench beside him.

"Oh, no, you don't, Mr. Brock." She tugged on his elbow. "You mustn't delay. She's expecting you."

"Will ye join us, then? She willna mind. Ye can eat all the

rest of the sweets if ye join us. I'll forfeit my share."

"Coward. Find me after, if you've the heart for it. I think I spied the sun breaking through that gray. I'd planned to take a walk, and I wouldn't mind some company."

With him? She'd like to walk with him? Christ, women were a puzzle. He'd wager even John didn't have this particular one reasoned out.

"I'd like that." He stood, picking up his hat and starting toward the hall. "I'll hold ye to it, so mind ye wait."

SHE KNEW. He could see it in her eyes, first thing. Of course, Donaldson would have told her in due time. He was an eijit for not expecting it sooner.

"I'm sorry, Mrs. Hale. I know you tried to help. I should have told ye of it immediately."

"Don't be, Liam. I'm sure you gave it a fair trial. I shouldn't have pushed. It wasn't for you."

"Hmmph," he answered shortly, his eyes on the floor as Tom set down the tea tray. He'd swear the cove took his time pouring the tea, stretching out his service simply to make him uncomfortable.

"Thank you, Tom," Mrs. Hale said, finally. "Well, Liam, what are your plans? Will you continue with another attorney, perhaps? I wish I had selected someone younger. Mr. Donaldson is too set in his ways; I can see that now."

"I'm traveling to Kentucky, ma'am."

Her hand paused midair, her grip unsteady on her cup. He reached for it as tea sloshed over the side and set it back on its saucer. "I've an opportunity to travel with others settling the same area. You know it's something I've always considered, ma'am."

"Of course, dear. Of course," she said, her voice so faint he had to strain to hear.

"I've brought the papers for your women's sanctuary," he said, hoping to take her mind from his disappointment. She'd been speaking to him for months now, on the plight of women abused by their men. Elisabeth had told her stories of one or two of the women who attended the reading class, and it had set the both of them to thinking. "Would ye like me to go over them with ye?"

She glanced toward the hall. "Not now, Liam. Edward is home. I don't want to disturb him. Tell me instead about Kentucky."

Huh. Mr. Hale didn't know about the sanctuary then. Well, Mr. Hale'd likely not be one to interfere with a man's rule over his own wife.

He filled the next minutes with chatter on Kentucky until she was laughing again, then poised the question that had been on his own mind for days now.

"How are David and Elisabeth settling in? Has it been a rough transition for Davey? What with him and Mr. Hale . . .?"

"Oh, no. Edward's so relieved to have her back. David has been the perfect son. He's taken care of so much while he's been here. Edward hasn't had to think twice when something breaks. David has it fixed within hours. I daresay Edward will grow to miss him as much as he'll miss Elisabeth when they leave."

She switched to prattling over the baby, and he let his thoughts wander some. If things were as she said, why had David strayed? Least he could do was have had a good excuse. He might forgive if the man had good reason for it.

"But, of course, it won't do to hope for the baby early, right? Early babies have such a time of it."

"Right."

"Oh, Liam." Her eyes glistened as they filled with tears. Real tears that fell, one by one, down her cheek as she reached for his hand, gripping it hard. "I know I shouldn't. But I do worry so over you."

"Mrs. Hale, please don't cry." He bit his cheek and dropped his gaze. Her hand was cold in his, so he wrapped his other around it to warm it. Paper-thin skin she had, as fragile as butterflies' wings. He could see the blue-gray vessels that crisscrossed beneath it. "You're no' to worry o'er me, aye? Please? I'll get by."

"I'll try." But her small smile quivered as she looked at him.

"You deserve so much more. I only wish—"

"Don't, Mrs. Hale, please don't," he said before she could speak further. "I'll get it sorted, aye?" He turned his head as his own eyes filled. "Things have a way of sorting; ye'll see."

But he knew as well as she that it wasn't always so.

His chatter, her prattle—it had fooled neither of them.

53

"KENTUCKY, LIAM?"

David barged into the room, brushing past Liam, deliberately knocking him aside with his bulk. He should knock the lad on his arse. Pete's sake, he had to hear this from Mrs. Hale? "Answer me, damn you."

"I didna hear a question."

"Ye're leaving for Kentucky? What the hell's the matter with you?"

"Aye, well, ye're going to Baltimore."

The inane response startled him as much it seemed to startle Liam. David stared at him, and Liam gave his head a quick shake.

"Sorry, Davey. Dinna ken where those words came from. I hadn't thought them."

Dodging the books that lay scattered across the room in piles, David crossed the room and sat in Mr. O's chair, placing his feet on the nearby bench. "Sit, will ye? Talk to me. What were ye doing just now? Organizing Mr. O's library?" he asked, waving a hand at the floor.

David knew he'd been looking out the window, doing nothing. He'd seen him from the street. Odd that Liam hadn't noticed him coming.

"What? Oh, the books. No. It's only things have been piling

up, I expect."

"Talk to me."

"Donaldson tossed me out, so I decided to join Billings. I've been considering it for a year or so, ken?"

David schooled his reaction in spite of the bile that rose, making him feel slightly ill. He wished now he hadn't eaten the third helping of pepper pot soup. It roiled about his gut, riding atop a wave of worry.

He also wished he had taken the time to hear the whole story from Mrs. Hale before bolting out. He hadn't heard more than the word Kentucky before he'd dashed over here.

He swallowed, stalling for time. What he said now would matter; he knew that. What he didn't know was *what* he should say. He should have thought this out. Maybe even talked to Elisabeth about it.

"Donaldson tossed ye out?"

"Aye."

"I hadn't heard that part. I'm sorry for that, mate."

"No need for that. It's no' your fault. It's my own."

Didn't mean he couldn't help but be sorry for it. Liam had worked years toward that. Years. Whether he realized it or not. The disappointment had to be huge. He pushed at the bench with his foot, setting the rocker in motion.

But what he'd chosen to replace it? Kentucky? David had nothing against Kentucky. He knew the frontier had also been a part of the man's dreams. In truth, it'd been a part of his dreams for longer than the law. But Kentucky meant the Billings; at least he thought it did. The Billings meant Victoria Billings. A man-eating, rapacious, mean-spirited tramp.

He didn't think Liam knew the half of it. The things that were whispered about her. But maybe he did. Or maybe the whispers weren't true. Who knew?

"Right, but I'm sorry nonetheless. And ye and Tory? Is that part of the Kentucky package?"

"Good God, I hope not," Liam answered, raking a hand back through his hair, loosening the leather thong that held it. David felt a wave of relief rush over him, and might even have laughed if it weren't for the man's expression. He seemed deeply troubled.

"When will you leave, Liam?"

"In a few weeks, I'm thinking."

So soon. Would he have left without notice? Would he have come the night before to say his farewells? "Hmmph. Well, maybe ye would have found time to write. To stop me from wondering where ye'd got off to."

Liam still hadn't looked directly at him. Was he truly angry at him about Baltimore? Hell, he'd miss the man too. But they'd always talked of this—practically from the time they'd first met. "Have ye considered joining us in Baltimore, Liam? We havena spoken of it lately, but ye know I've always wanted ye to join me. Lisbeth would be thrilled if ye'd consider it."

"Lisbeth," he answered flatly.

"Right, Lisbeth. My wife. Remember her?"

Why had he said her name that way? All irritation gone now, it was only the worry that was left. Liam was near listless. Did he not want to go to Kentucky? Did he feel he'd run out of options here? Restless, David stood and paced, careful to avoid the piles of books. He ought to build Mr. Oliver a bookcase. He ought to have Liam help him. "Do ye have anything to eat?"

"Nay." Liam looked at him then, his eyes a vivid blue up against the black strands that hung loose round his face. "David, what were ye doing there?"

"Huh? Here, ye mean? I'm here to see you, Liam. Are ye feeling peaked?" He crouched before him, examining his face. His cheeks weren't flushed, and his eyes weren't bright with fever, though they did seem hard with anger as they returned his scrutiny. Anger? At him? What the hell!

He backed away and rose before Liam thought to take advantage of his position. "Tell me what ye're thinking, Liam. Tell me now."

"I saw you at Nora Baylor's this sen'night past. Well after midnight. What were you doing there, David? No' inspecting her roof, I'll wager."

"Mr. Graham!" They both turned toward the stairs as

Tommy Nailor burst into the room. "Me and Danny, we thought we heard your voice. Can you—"

"Not now, lad. Go on back downstairs. I'll speak with ye later, aye?" Tommy didn't move, his eyes wide as if he sensed the tension in the room. "Downstairs. Now!"

The boy took a step back, his hands outstretched for the wall behind him, then turned and fled down the steps.

"You think . . ." David whispered, taking another step back. "You think . . . Jesus, Mary, and Joseph." How could Liam think that of him? How could he even begin to think that of him?

"Answer me, David."

"I ought to beat the hell out of ye is what I ought to do." His hands fisted at his side as he considered the prospect and discarded it.

Liam just sat there, his forearms resting on his thighs, his hands clasping and unclasping between his knees. "Answer me."

"I thought ye knew."

"Knew what? Elisabeth gives ye leave for that sort of thing? Given her condition?"

"Ye say that one more time, ye'll have cause to regret it. I'll no' warn ye again. Ye were anyone else, ye'd be on the floor senseless by now. Mrs. Beekam . . . Mrs. Habers . . . remember them?" They were the two women in Lisbeth's class whose husbands didn't take kindly to their attendance. Nor to how they kept the house, prepared the meals, and raised the children. "Jesus, Liam. I thought ye were the one set the thing up for Mrs. Hale."

"Get to the point, David.'

"Mrs. Beekam's man had a hard day, took it out on his Missus. Her boy came for Elisabeth. It was prearranged. She'd promised to help, she and Mrs. Hale. The Safety Net, ken? I fetched the woman and took her and her boy to Mrs. Baylor's. Lisbeth had enlisted her aid ahead of time, just in the event it'd be needed. Because Mr. Beekam had no knowledge of her, ken?"

David had to grin at the last. His wife was canny as hell reaching out to Nora like that. "Mrs. Baylor and some others have agreed to provide a place for any of the women who need it. To give them a few weeks of safety to make plans afore they go on their own."

He wasn't certain it was a good idea. What were the women to do after the few weeks were finished? What if they couldn't care for themselves and their children on their own? What if the interference made it worse for the missus?

But his opinion hadn't been asked. All that had been asked was that he escort the women when and where needed. The women had named the organization Safety Net.

Liam's eyes lit up as he looked at him. David imagined he could see the workings of his mind as he swiftly sifted through the pieces, verifying their fit and thence their veracity. "Aye?"

"Aye." He kicked the lad's booted foot. "Eijit."

"I only planned the money part of that Safety Net, David. I didna know the players."

Which was odd. He would have expected Liam to have his finger in every step of the process, especially if he were involved in the actual planning of it. "Tha's no' like ye, Liam. Tha's no' like ye at all."

Liam nodded, agreeing. "I expect I wanted to get in and out, 'fore Mrs. Hale took to asking too many questions about the apprenticeship. I'm sorry I thought the worse of ye, Davey."

A thought occurred to him as he watched Liam relax in his seat, one worry gone. "You weren't readying to speak with Lisbeth, were you? Without talking to me first?" Liam glanced toward the empty fireplace and his feet took to shuffling in the stray embers that had scattered the night before.

"Damn ye, Liam! Ye were!"

"I didna know what to do. The last time, it got to be all my fault, 'stead of yours."

His anger evaporated. The last time. The time with Sarah Wallace. The time that also hadn't happened. She had been angry for months at Liam for keeping it from her. He'd only done so at David's request; Liam had wanted to tell her all along. He'd been right; it would have eased things some if he had.

"Ye've the right to say anything ye please to her, of course. She's your friend, much as she's my wife. But this, Liam? It would devastate her. If it's something like this, I ask ye speak to me first, aye?"

Liam nodded, silent.

"What is it? Why is it we so rarely see ye? Is there something else ye think I've done?"

"Nay. It's only the things I've done myself." He stood, going for his hat. "Can we go for supper? D'ye have plans?"

He did. He needed to ride to Chester in the morning, and he might be gone overnight. He'd like to spend this evening with Elisabeth. "Nay, none. Where d'ye have in mind?"

Liam shrugged, and David sighed. He stood and grabbed his hat, pausing as the door downstairs slammed with a bang. Alex Mannus appeared a moment later, out of breath, dancing from foot to foot as if he had no time to spare.

"Hey."

"Hey, yourself. I'd been wondering of your whereabouts," Liam said. "Ye're overdue, aren't ye?"

Alex nodded. "Some. Will it be all right if we stay a few nights, Liam? It's only me and five others."

"Aye. Mind ye keep them quiet coming in. Mrs. Nailor bent Mr. O's ear a good thirty minutes the last time."

David remembered the last time. The crew had awakened the whole household with their drunken revelry. "Where ye off to, Alex? Liam and I were going for supper if ye'd care to join us."

"The Man. First, though, I brought Mr. O something." He brought out the bottle he'd held stashed behind his back and handed it to Liam. Liam uncorked it and sniffed, his eyes widening and his mouth settling in a grin. He took a sip and passed the bottle to David.

David sniffed as well, then closed his eyes as he inhaled a longer whiff. Heaven and home.

"We were waylaid in Islay, due to the weather. Did I do good? There's two more waiting, if so."

Liam laughed and slapped his back, sending him forward a step. "Ye did better than good, lad. Let's have a wee dram, 'fore we head out, aye?"

54

"SABRINA? I'M DAVID GRAHAM. I know your pa through Mrs. Hale." The woman sat on the floor of a cell in the Chester gaol, her head and shoulder propped against the cold stone wall. She slowly turned her gaze his way, but moved not a muscle more. She looked near death and well past caring.

Tom had told him she wasn't his daughter by blood. Mrs. Hale had for some reason thought she was, and looking at her, he'd have to agree. Though he couldn't detect an ounce of African blood in the lass, it was Tom's eyes that stared back at him from beneath the grimy tangled ropes of dark hair. Dark, somber eyes that hid all thoughts from the viewer.

"Elisabeth Hale's my wife, ken? She says she's met ye. She sent some things for ye." He sank down beside her and took a blanket from the bag he'd brought. Laying it atop her, he tucked it round her shoulders, then down over her bare feet, averting his eyes from the streaks of blood caked along her arms and legs as he did. It looked as if she'd been scratching herself raw, as he'd be scratching his own self raw if he sat in this vermin-infested hell-hole for long.

The jailhouse was cold; fuel was at a premium this time of year and not to be squandered on the likes of prisoners. He handed her the stockings Lisbeth had packed. "Hold these, lass. Ye'll need put them on yourself. I'll stay while ye do, so they end up on ye instead of others."

As he held up the flask of water he'd brought, he detected the first spark of interest in her eyes. "Thirsty?" She didn't reach for it, so he held it to her lips and she drank greedily, emptying it. She displayed no notice of the food he'd brought, nor the tobacco. "Use them as coin then, for barter, aye?" He tucked them behind her.

She blinked, seeming too tired to nod. "Is Daddy all right?" Her voice was gravelly, as if it hadn't been used in days.

"As right as he can be, ken? It's hard, knowing ye're here." He held her hand and sat close, hoping his own heat would warm her some.

"The man your da drew the picture of, Sabrina. Was he the baby's father?" When he got no response, he asked, "Was he the one who helped ye, then?" She nodded and he tried again. "Did he say where he was headed, where he'd come from?"

"Running from trouble, seemed like. But he stopped to help me when he saw the baby coming. He stopped to help me. He stayed."

"A good man, then." He wondered how the man knew how to help. He'd never been allowed near a woman giving birth. He wouldn't have a clue how to help Elisabeth. Not unless it was the same as a sheep. "Was he a doctor, then?"

"Just a good man," she said, turning her eyes from him wearily.

"He saw the baby die?" A dog had sniffed out the corpse. It had been stashed under a bush along the road linking Philly and Chester, several hundred yards from where Sabrina was found sleeping. She claimed she'd gone to sleep with the babe in her arms.

She shook her head, and his heart sank. There were no witnesses then, none other than herself. The man would be no help, even if they were to find him. Matter of fact, he'd likely do more harm than good. If he hadn't seen the baby die, he couldn't say Sabrina hadn't done it.

Defeated, he propped himself against the wall and put an arm around her, pulling her close in an effort to still the shivers.

"Was it a boy or a girl, Sabrina, the bairn?"

She froze for a moment at his touch, then convulsed as the memory of her baby flooded back, spilling over the walls she'd erected.

"My boy . . ." she wailed, clutching his shirt. She wept hysterically through spasms of grief, until all the water he'd given her had been sobbed out on his chest. He held her tight and rocked her, having no other comfort to offer, until, finally, the crying slowed.

"How long did the lad live, lass?" he asked. He wasn't asking merely to fill the silence. Over the years he'd learned it helped to talk of one's loss, so that others might share in the grief as well. "Did ye have a chance to cuddle him, afore he passed?"

"My boy was born dead." She shook her head and tears fell again. "I don't know where they buried him. I don't even know if they did."

Born dead. Stillborn. The man would know then, the man would know that.

"Did the man tell you his name, lass?" She'd withdrawn again, and he received no answer or acknowledgement he'd asked. "Your boy, lass. Who were ye thinking on naming him after?"

"Samuel. Samuel, after his daddy." She pulled away and looked up at him. "The man's name was Samuel, too; he told me so. I remember. I remember I laughed." Her face fell, and she collapsed against him again, reminded nothing was funny, not anymore.

"Where is your man, your boy's daddy? Does he know?"

"He's done gone to sea. He'll never know. He'll never know his boy looked just like him."

HE'D HATED walking away. The accusation in her eyes as he made his exit, he understood it well.

He'd made her aware of her surroundings again, he'd made her feel. She'd suffer unspeakable hours before she could close off the feeling again, before she could retreat deep within her own mind. He deserved no thanks for the warmth and the sustenance. He'd only made it worse.

It had been over a month since the incident. It was unlikely Sabrina's mystery man was anywhere near town, especially if he had been running from trouble, as Sabrina had said. But still, he'd ask around, as Tom had requested. Maybe someone would recognize the man from the drawing he had. Tom had had no luck, but perhaps a white man could come up with more answers.

But truly, there wasn't much he could do except what Mrs. Hale had asked him to do, and that was to gather information and to print a broadside commemorating Sabrina's life. Something sympathetic, something that would counteract the inevitable hell and brimstone broadsides that would follow her hanging.

"Hey."

David jumped at the greeting. Liam. Liam was waiting outside the jailhouse door. How had he known he was here?

The man didn't chatter; he didn't say a word, not after he studied him. He just jerked his head toward the road, and they started walking.

"Why are ye here?" David asked finally, after they had walked an aimless mile.

"I didna have anything else to do. Besides, ye ne'er know the right questions to ask."

"Hmmph." David fought to keep his expression neutral. Mrs. Hale had told him of Liam's refusal to help Tom. Or Tom's side of it, anyway. He'd had difficulty believing it, that is until he confronted Liam about Kentucky. The man he saw last night might easily have refused Tom.

"I've been in the Stag, chatting up the barmaid. The baby's father is Samuel Perkins. He's a sailor, and left a month ago for Ireland. He's expected back next month. He'd told the barmaid he was to be a father soon."

"So he wasna running from it, then. What about the man who helped Sabrina?"

Liam shook his head. "Nay, she didn't know of him. I

showed the picture to the others in the place. No one recognized him. We'll go back in a few hours, once the crowd has changed."

Fine with him. For if he slept, he might roll into Liam's arms when the dreaming started. The stench of the gaol had revived his own unpleasant memories.

He wanted Elisabeth.

55

"THE BABY WAS BORN too early, Davey," Liam said, throwing off his blanket. "Tha's what was said, aye? Both by Sabrina and the barmaid?"

"Aye. So? Why aren't ye sleeping?"

"Same reason ye're no'. Ye've been lying here for two hours now, staring at yon window." He stood and paced, from the bed to the window and back again. They were fortunate; they shared a room above the tavern with no others. Tomorrow night this room would be filled to bursting with those in town to witness the hanging. It was to be a double. He'd found that out today, while he was waiting for David. Nothing like a double to draw in the crowds.

"Thing is, Davey, babies born too early aren't likely to live. So how long is long enough?"

"Eight months?"

"I thought it longer. Count, eijit. Count. Let's say Lisbeth conceived the night ye married and no earlier." He was grateful for the dark, as he was unable to stop the flush that spread as he considered the proposition. "Her doctor says it will likely be April, 'fore the bairn is born."

"Over nine months, then. Mayhap a week or so more."

"And if Sabrina had only carried for seven or eight months?"

"The babe likely wouldna survive if it was only seven months, I'm thinking. Dinna ken about eight. But how does that help? Who knows when Sabrina conceived, Liam? Who could even guess? She's no' newly married. And she's been keeping company with the man for years now."

"A doctor might know. If they had a doctor pronounce the bairn dead, he might know."

"The doctor was one of those gave testimony against her."

"Are ye sure? What did Sabrina say, exactly?"

David lit the candle and fumbled through the bag at his side, drawing out his ream of notes. "She didn't. Maybe the jailor told me. I didna write it down."

"Ye need to ask." He was itching to do the asking himself. A seed of doubt about the verdict had been planted, as well as a seed of remorse. David had traveled to Chester for Tom and Mrs. Hale, where he himself had not. David had a wife who needed him home; David had a job he needed to perform. He had neither.

"I'd as soon it was ye who did the asking, Liam. I'd like to use my time to see her again tomorrow."

"Hmmph. Well enough, then." He had questions aplenty. He'd heard rumors the bairn was found with his head bashed in. Did the doctor agree? Who's to say his head wasn't misshapen due to the birth?

"I dinna think she did it, Liam. The way she cried . . . "

"Aye, well. Lassies are free enough with the tears."

"I'm thinking an animal dragged the body from her whilst she slept that night."

Liam grimaced, picturing the possibility. He'd need to ask the doctor if the body had any tooth marks, or signs it'd been dragged over rocky soil. "Mayhap. I'll ask. Listen, she might have gone to the Guardians of the Poor, aye? Afore she traveled to Chester?"

"She might have, aye. But she didna say she did. She said she went to Tom. He's the one gave her money."

"But she *might* have gone for public help first. Mayhap her da was the last resort, ken?" Liam tapped David's notes with a finger. "We don't know that she didna seek help. Ye didna ask that, did ye? There may be someone in Philadelphia, someone other than herself or a barmaid, who *can* pinpoint how close she was to birthing the child. Did ye get her pack from the jailor? Is that it?"

David nodded as he pointed to the cotton sack on the floor beside his own. "I didna open it. It's hers, then Tom's."

"Hmmph." Liam grabbed it and dumped the contents on the floor. "Will ye look at this?" he asked softly, holding up an infant's gown.

"Aye. So?"

He took the candle to the table underneath the window. Rummaging through his own pack, he cursed, then brought out a pencil and notebook. Her attorney should have argued the benefit of linen. Why hadn't he? "Get out of bed. We've work to do."

"Are ye saying ye'll help?" David didn't grumble, he did as Liam asked.

"Aye." She had a gown for the bairn. She wouldn't carry a gown for a child she planned to murder, would she?

His mother had kept the first gown she'd dressed him in. She'd draw it from the chest some nights, when she was feeling herself, and tell him how she'd come by the fabric. It had once been a fine white linen, she'd told him, not the gray it had become. The edges were trimmed in a blue the hue of a robin's egg, in small, precise stitches that had held up over time. She'd said she'd sat by the fire an hour a night for weeks, carefully crafting the gown so that it would be perfect, dreaming of a son as she did. Not just any son, but "a son as perfect" as him.

So she said, anyway. Mothers didn't know their sons, not inside and out, not like they thought they might.

"Put on your boots, will ye, Davey? Go find me two blocks to carve, about so big." He made a quick blocking motion with his hands. "I dinna care for the woodcut you're using for Sabrina's broadside."

He needed to think, and fast. Carving always helped him to think.

SLUMPED AGAINST the outside wall of the tavern, David closed his eyes and turned his face to the stars, offering up a long, fervent prayer of thanks. He knew just where to find what Liam had requested; he'd seen scraps earlier when he had ridden in.

He pushed away from the wall and grinned as he headed toward the stables, thinking he might break into one of Rhiannon's silly twirls of joy himself. He'd been glad enough to see Liam, glad the lad still thought enough of their friendship to offer his companionship.

But this was more than he'd hoped for. Much more.

This just might be Liam at his best.

56

"I'VE NEVER SEEN a woodcut like that. Christ, you'll use up my whole damn stock of ink."

"Nay, Mr. McAllister. I'm only showing ye his work. It's likely the sheet won't be printed." He hoped, anyway. Liam had been cagey, but he was on to something. Having given David his marching orders, he'd left the room as soon as day broke. David hadn't seen him since.

The woodcut was unusual and would indeed fill a good quarter of a broadsheet. Impressive as hell, as were all the man's carvings.

"Who did it? One from her family?"

"Nay, my mate did. He's never met her."

"Hmmph." He looked at him, his eyes gleaming as if he were calculating his share of the profits. "If you decide it's to be printed, I think we best print a few hundred more than you'd contracted for."

Liam had forgone the usual depiction of the accused hanging from the gallows. Instead he'd fashioned a woman with her baby at breast. Somehow he'd managed to convey love, adoration, and devotion with a few deft swipes of his knife. David knew what McAllister was thinking. Readers would go wild over the contradiction—a mother's love up against the charge of infanticide.

He dug out the other woodcut, a smaller one. "I hear there's a second execution scheduled as well?"

"Right. James Brand. Sheriff's right proud of that one. Brand's been passing counterfeit bills all over this state for months now."

"Would ye like to print that one?

"You and your friend in the business of chasing executions, Mr. Graham?"

"Nay. Only hoping to recover some of our expenses on coming down here."

The man fingered the second woodcut. Liam hadn't spent as much time on it, but nonetheless it caught one's eye. He'd used the typical depiction of the unfortunate sinner swinging on a rope, but he'd bordered it with currency symbols as an indication of the man's crime. Though not heartrending, as was the one intended for Sabrina's broadside, it still managed to provoke reflection on the accused's transgressions.

McAllister shook his head, smiling a small smile as he turned the piece round and round in his hand. "I can handle it. Dorsey's shop usually handles this type of thing. I don't have the appetite for it. But I don't mind giving the man a poke now and then."

They bargained through the terms of the broadside while David looked over the press. He declined the names of the pressmen McAllister suggested, telling him he planned to press it himself. The machine looked to be in decent repair; he should be able to handle it in a smooth enough fashion.

"D'ye have a companion lad I might use, though?" He'd thought briefly of recruiting Liam. But Liam had no experience whatsoever at the press. They wouldn't sell a thing if the copy were unreadable. "And might I see the type?"

He was worried some about the type. If it had been stored dirty, or set aside because the letters were worn . . . well, he had enough to worry over today without that.

"You'll find them all there and in good shape."

He nodded as he riffled his finger through the boxed letters, glad to see none were baked. They tumbled freely under his fingertips, so evidently the compositor before had cleaned them properly. He examined a few, finding them only slightly worn and stored in their proper box. He'd like to look at them all, but he was lacking the time. He'd take the man's avowal on faith.

"Right then. I'll be back tomorrow to set the copy."

He shook McAllister's hand, then hurried to the gaol. Tom had communicated the bones of Sabrina's family background, but he wanted more. He wanted to know of her hopes and dreams, where she'd met her man, and about the future they'd planned and hoped for. God willing, she'd talk to him of it.

And God willing, he wouldn't need it, though he couldn't hope on that now.

After he saw her, he planned to visit with Brand, the counterfeiter, to find out his story. Liam had listed two pages of questions for him to ask. He'd write down the man's answers, but that's all he had the time for.

That broadside was Liam's idea. A good one, to be sure, but time was flying. So whether his story be "good family, boy gone bad" or "bad family, boy hadn't a chance," he would count on Liam to fill it in and make the copy cry.

His own focus must remain on Sabrina. He'd promised Mrs. Hale she'd be remembered for the woman she was, not for what she may or may not have done.

He was lucky, however. If his copy fell short, the woodcut would more than compensate.

57

LIAM SPOTTED DAVID tucked alone in a corner, head bent down and pencil in hand. He must have been at it awhile to have snagged a table. Shouldering his way through the crowd, he stopped at the bar and grabbed two of the mugs just poured, winking at the barmaid and tossing her a coin before she could voice protest.

David looked up as he sat, his eyes alight at the sight of the full mugs Liam carried. "I've been waiting a good quarter of an hour for that," he said, reaching for one.

"Aye, it's busy. Nothing like a double hanging to draw in the crowds." He watched as the man's face fell, disappointment replacing appreciation.

"It's still to be a double, then?" he asked, after he'd appeased his thirst.

Liam shrugged. "No' sure."

"It's well past dusk. Where've ye been all day?"

"Philadelphia," he answered, grinning.

"Eijit," David said, aiming a kick at his shin. "Tell me, aye?"

"Aye. I looked up the good doctor first. No one had thought to ask him if he'd thought the bairn strong enough to survive delivery. When I asked him, he said most likely not; it was evident the birth had been premature." He had stopped his questions about the birth there. He hadn't wanted to know if

Sabrina could have somehow forced the baby's early delivery.

"And the injury to the bairn's head?"

"Likely from birth, he said. Though it also could have happened if he were dragged. The bairn's back was scrapped some. But there were no puncture wounds, so he couldn't say for sure what might have dragged the body."

The man couldn't say much of anything for sure, but he swore he hadn't testified one way or another about anything other than the fact the bairn was dead.

They must have lured the incompetent cove out of retirement. Same as her counsel who had somehow managed to get himself laid up from a riding accident two days past. The attorney's wife wouldn't let him near the man to question him, though she didn't hesitate to tell him at length that Sabrina deserved the sentence handed down. Furthermore, if there were any justice in the world, all wanton women would suffer the same fate.

He'd sought out the justice then, first thing after he'd been turned from her counsel's door. He'd found the court was no longer sitting in Chester; it had moved on to Philly. So he'd ridden hard, only to be told he'd need to wait until one. He'd kept busy enough, writing and rewriting his arguments. He'd brought coffee to the clerk and set the man to talking of the justice: what he favored, what he didn't.

It had been coin well spent, and he'd scratched an argument from his pad after. The justice didn't care for the "busybodies in Philadelphia," those who had gone soft on crime and hadn't handed down a single death sentence in two years. He'd made note to be sure to sympathize with the law-abiding counties that had to deal with Philadelphia's reprobates once they'd served their meager sentence and then took their lives of crime on the road.

With that, along with the hint of the possible involvement of "those busybodies, the Guardians of the Poor," the man had agreed to listen further. Then he had agreed to accompany Liam to the State House, to seek out the governor and argue for a pardon.

At that news, Davey's jaw dropped near to the floor.

"Ye got her pardoned? Jesus, Mary, and Joseph, Liam. Ye got her a pardon?"

"Shh!" Several heads turned their way in interest, and he lowered his voice. "Dinna be stealing the sheriff's thunder. Nay, no' a pardon. A stay." But it would be a pardon. He knew sure as he was sitting here, the stay of execution would turn into a pardon.

"And the doctor will testify to it?"

"Dinna think we need him. Thing is, Davey, the jury shouldna have found her guilty. The state didna do a thing to prove she'd murdered the bairn, plus she had the benefit of linen. Did anyone look in her pack to see if she had prepared for the babe? Sabrina's counsel must no' have even tried. Or cared enough to try."

"But the child was dead."

"D'ye remember the Wilson case?"

David nodded. Of course he would. It had been a sensational case, occurring shortly after they'd settled in Philly. The woman had been convicted of killing her infant twin girls and had been sentenced to hang for it. Her brother had obtained a stay of execution from the Council at the last possible moment and had ridden hell-fire from Philadelphia to deliver it. But he'd arrived at the hanging moments too late, the woman had already been turned off. Attempts to revive her were unsuccessful.

"And d'ye remember the act shortly thereafter? The one that dealt with the penal reforms?"

"I remember helping Robert with the copy. I dinna recall the details."

"Aye, well, there're many. No reason ye should, 'cept it was the act that gave us the wheelbarrow men. But see, before that act, in order to hand down a capital punishment in a case like this, the prosecution only had to establish a baby was dead and the mother didn't report it. The state didna have to establish the baby was born alive, nor did it have to establish criminal intent. It is much easier to prove concealment than intent to murder, aye?"

"If ye say so. But Sabrina's baby *is* dead. Worse, she has no one to say she didna have a hand in it."

"Aye, but no one can say she did. And that's what the reforms were meant to do. Concealment's no longer a capital offense. The prosecution must establish that she killed her bairn, ken? She doesna have to establish that she didna. They had nothing to prove she had the intent to murder. Nothing. So, if they canna prove the babe was born alive, they havena an inkling of a case. Her attorney dinna even argue it right. And for whatever reason, the jury was quick to judge."

"Sabrina's mother used to be Quaker 'fore she set up with Tom. The jury was sure to be filled with Quakers, aye? Maybe there were some hard feelings, leftover from when she left the faith."

Liam shrugged. It could be that; it could be because Sabina was a black man's daughter. It could be both. No telling what a jury was thinking. The attorney, though. There ought to be telling what an attorney planned to accomplish.

Tom likely hadn't found someone who'd help for what he could pay.

"So we don't want to find the cull who helped her, do we?"

See that, Davey wasn't so slow. He nodded. "Aye, we most definitely wish the man to remain hidden." Just in the event he'd say the bairn *was* born alive.

"So now what?"

"The sheriff has the stay. The governor will look over the case in the next thirty days, then she'll likely be freed."

"Will ye follow it through?"

"I'll have Mrs. Hale speak to Donaldson. I'll likely be gone 'fore it runs its course. I might set you to a task, though. I'm no' so sure Sabrina's a free woman. Her father wasn't, no' at the time she was born, and we know nothing of her mother's status. If for some reason she's no' free, mayhap there's something that can be done to make it so."

"Tom said he met her mother when Sabrina was days old, that she's no' actually his."

"Hmmph. Aye, well. It's curious she shares his features. I'll no' be the first to notice."

"All right. I'll look into it. Did ye stop at the Hales'? Does Elisabeth know?"

"Nay. Something could still go wrong."

"Ye're the one was so sure she should know everything."

"That was of your failings, mate; no' mine." He reached a hand out for a piece of the hardtack David munched on. It was beginning to look as if they'd never receive service. "Are those your notes on Brand?"

"Aye." David pushed them his way.

"They've still another to hang. All these people in town, tragedy to disappoint them, aye?" He scanned the page quickly. "Jesus, what have ye got here? Four clergymen? He met with *four* clergymen?"

"Aye." David grinned, always one to gloat when religion was pushed front and center. "He found the path to God here at the end. He related all they taught him these last few days. I've only jotted a few of the good points."

"Good points, my arse. I had hoped for salacious escapades. This is dull."

"Then get to work."

"Right." The faster they got it on the street, the faster they'd make a profit. David also planned to print another batch in Philly. "Will ye see if ye can locate Tom whilst I do? To let him know there might be some hope? He ought to be in town somewhere." He didn't think he could face the man's gratitude, that is assuming he had any.

"Aye."

"Are we the ones to be hawking this, David?"

"Nay, I'll hire it out. I need to return to Lisbeth soon as I can."

"Mind if I stay and do it?" He could hawk the broadside as well as any other. He had nothing else to do, and he could use the extra coin for his Kentucky provisions.

David studied him as if assessing his state of mind. He didn't blame the man. His state of mind had concerned him for months now.

"I'll stay as well, then. Lisbeth has Mrs. Hale and Rhee. She willna even notice I'm gone.

"Nay, Davey. Lisbeth needs ye. I'll get along without ye. I've been practicing, ken?" He had been practicing, though he hadn't done so well. He could though, and he would.

David dropped his head and reached back to rub his neck, but not before Liam caught the look in his eyes. Cove better not go soft on him.

"If ye'd like," David said, finally. "I'll tally up what we'll owe McAllister—ye'll need to be the one settling with him then. Finish up that copy. After I find Tom, I'll work on rustling us up some supper."

"Aye." He drew a fresh sheet of paper from his pack. He could do better than regurgitating four sermons from sanctimonious preachers. Deep down, the man would appreciate it.

No one wanted to go to his grave with a story too boring to tell.

58

BONNY DAY FOR a hanging. Didn't seem right, somehow.

All attending must have sensed it as well, for the last few minutes—once Brand had said his prayers and been turned off—had been strangely quiet.

The deputy on horseback circled the gallows, his horse mincing its steps as if one or the other of them were uneasy. As well they should be, given Brand's body was still twitching on the rope, the acrid odor of his fear permeating the nostrils of those close enough to smell it.

David stood aside Liam and Tom at the forefront of the crowd, waiting and watching without words.

Tom knew of the stay. He stood, tall, straight, and unmoving, his eyes trained on Sabrina. But out of the corner of his eye, David could see that the man's gaze darted to and from Liam. As did his own.

Neither of them dared voice a question to the lad. Liam was clearly shutting them out, along with the crowd, as he directed the full might of his attention in the direction of Sabrina and Sheriff Wagner. David imagined the force of his thoughts as a visible thing, crossing the full distance. As might Wagner, who backed up half a step upon glancing their way.

Two deputies mounted the wagon bed, their added weight setting the weathered wood to creaking. They lifted Sabrina to her feet, then handed her down to the two waiting on the ground. Good thing they had manned up as they had. A slight lass like that, shaking in fear with her hands tightly bound behind her? Why, there was no telling what trouble she could stir.

The deputies stood beside her as they faced the spectators, supporting her as Reverend Blake approached them, his bible in hand. She cowed before him, her gaze fixed on his feet. A breeze kicked up and all four of them flinched as the branch holding Brand's swinging body gave a loud, crackling groan in response.

Was the stay still in place? How far would the sheriff carry this farce? David glanced toward Liam again, but his rigid stance offered no answers.

The throng of thousands behind him, did they know of the stay? Was that the reason for the number of armed militiamen keeping them all at a safe distance? The tide of public opinion had changed some over the last decade. Citizens were no longer so quick to accept the state's harsh rule of punishment by death.

Some in this crowd may have witnessed Elizabeth Wilson's execution. It may have been on this very hill. He looked up the road in the direction of Philadelphia and imagined he could see the lookouts that had been staged some five years back, white flags in hand, ready to signal at the first sight of Wilson's brother riding south with the notice of a stay.

But her brother had arrived moments too late and was greeted by the sight of his sister's body swaying at the end of a rope.

Sheriff Wagner had Sabrina's stay in hand.

The reverend's voice carried across the crowd, ringing with his promises of retribution and salvation, impressing on those watching that they were sinners all, even if some of them had yet to be caught. A turkey buzzard, drawn in by the scent of death, soared overhead, signaling his agreement. Tears streaming down her face, Sabrina hunched her shoulders and glanced up when the buzzard's shadow traveled over her, as if she feared it would mistake her for the corpse swinging behind.

An almost silent keening escaped from Tom's lips as he stood watching. David studied him covertly. Sweat dripped from his forehead, even as cold as it was atop the hill, yet he moved not a muscle to wipe the sting from his eyes. Was this Tom's only child? Had Mrs. Hale always known of his family, or had it been a surprise to her as well? Tom had been a slave up until a few years ago. How had he managed a family?

Sabrina dropped to her knees at Reverend Blake's request. Well, that and a push from the deputies flanking her. Racked with tremors, she bowed her head in prayer, her voice near inaudible as she followed along with the prayer.

Now would be the time, sheriff. Now would be the time. Before the lass suffered the further humiliation of wetting herself before thousands.

David understood the need for the state to flaunt its power. Wouldn't do to have the rabble forget who was in charge. But hadn't it done that already? By hanging Brand an hour before?

Four gun-toting militiamen had been placed in charge of keeping the crowd back, and they paced the line relentlessly. Two more were added as a deputy moved forward to speak.

"Sabrina Abernathy, you have been brought here under sentence of death . . ."

One of the militia men, a tall, beefy man whose belly peeked from beneath a tear in his shirt every time he took a step forward, slowed as he passed by the three of them, spitting his wad of tobacco at Tom's feet, narrowly missing his boots. Cradling his rifle in the crook of his right arm, barrel pointed their way, he fumbled to button his waistcoat. Shifting his eyes to the right, David noted Tom remained the picture of passivity. Liam, however, had a steady twitch building behind clenched jaws.

" . . . the murder of your . . ."

David edged a small step in Liam's direction, readying to stop the lad should he take a step forward

". . . have you any words . . ."

The soldier uprighted his gun and moved on. A woman behind them shouted out, "Whore." Another started sobbing, leading to another and then another.

Sabrina shook her head violently from side to side. She had

no words. She likely couldn't recount her own name. The deputies handed her up to the two waiting in the wagon. One man placed a white coned hood over her head while the other dropped the rope round her neck.

Wagoner was abusing his power for the sake of a show. It had gone too far now. Enough was enough.

David shifted from foot to foot as the crowd grew silent, and Liam's hand touched his as he jutted his chin toward the wagon. Sheriff Wagner was climbing up with a paper in hand. But Sabrina couldn't see. She couldn't see the sheriff.

The roaring in his ears was so loud now that he didn't hear more than a word or two of what Wagner uttered. Some nonsense about mercy and forgiveness. Seems Sabrina did, however. Her legs gave way and she dropped, that is until the rope snagged her tight, just before she reached her knees. A deputy helped her to her feet, the same one who had draped the rope about her neck.

The multitude behind them stirred restlessly while Sheriff Wagoner read the stay—some in support, some in disappointment. He noted Tom had placed a hand on Liam's shoulder and was squeezing it, though both were too pigheaded to do other than look straight ahead at the wagon.

"Tom will need your help, Davey. I'll catch up with ye in Philly." Aiming a wad of spittle two feet forward, Liam turned from them.

"State's mercy, my arse," he muttered, walking away.

59 March 1791

"I'VE NEWS TO SHARE, Mr. Billings."

"Sit down, Mr. Brock; sit down." The man leaned so far back that his chair balanced precariously on two legs, and he propped an ankle atop a knee while he looked up at him, his dark eyes attentive. "I haven't seen you in a while. I reckoned you were up to something."

"I was out of town. But I stopped by the land office first thing yesterday, soon as I got back. Charley heard from Mrs. Taylor and, aye, she was willing to sell a portion."

"Indeed? Well I'm glad to hear it, son. It's a prime piece of property, but unsuitable for a woman alone. Like I told you before, I'd buy it myself if I didn't already have more than I can handle. I assume you were able to come to terms?"

He nodded. "I rode out to meet her yesterday."

The widow Taylor owned a thousand acres adjoining Billings' tract. Billings had mentioned it weeks ago, telling him he ought to look into it before someone else took it off her hands. The man thought it best to surround himself with those he knew—so much so that he'd even offered to carry the note if need be. Given his tumultuous relationship with the man's daughter, Liam had thought it best to decline the generous offer.

He hadn't the means to purchase it all, but he'd thought he might manage a hundred acres if she would sell on terms. So

Billings had sketched out a rough survey, advising him which hundred he should try for. And indeed, it was a prime piece, bordered by watercourses on two sides.

Mrs. Taylor had generously agreed to a ten year note, claiming he reminded her of her nephew. She'd also promised she'd let him know if and when she sought to sell the remaining nine hundred acres. A good day, all in all.

Maybe David would consider buying, if he found his Baltimore paper didn't suit.

"Then we'll be neighbors, won't we?" Billings grinned, obviously pleased with the turn of events.

"Sooner or later, aye."

"Do you happen to have the sketch with you?"

"I do." He withdrew the paper from his pocket and handed it over. The man loved nothing more than to recount his adventures on each coordinate of a map. Liam settled in his chair, knowing from past experience he was in for several hours of "here's where I shot the . . ." and "there's a pool on this stretch where I caught . . ." or "we encountered six Cherokee braves right about here."

Not that he minded. Envisioning the acreage roused a zeal he hadn't felt in months. He could spend days listening to and questioning the man about his adventures. Days without pause.

As it was, though, Billings had plans elsewhere. They were only two hours into the stories when he reached for his hat.

"We'll be heading out in three weeks' time, Mr. Brock. Will you be ready?"

"I believe so." With the exception of a rifle. He was fast coming to the conclusion he'd need to sell some of his books in order to purchase one. But it wasn't as if he planned to cart a load of books over the trail anyway. "D'ye think ye can spare the time to go over my provision list, sir?"

"Glad to. McKinney and I are meeting at City Tavern at sunset tomorrow. Join us, why don't you? Oh . . . forget that. Let's try for the day after. I think Tory has you tied up escorting her to some function or another tomorrow night."

Which brought him to the second reason he had come to

the inn.

"D'ye know if she's in?"

"It's the damnedest thing. She's been feeling under the weather for days now. She won't thank me for saying it, but normally, she has the constitution of an ox. It might cheer her up, though, having your company for supper."

He doubted that. He'd left for Chester without a word, not long after she'd lost the bairn.

"I can't, sir. I've a class to teach tonight. But I will look in on her."

"Tory mentioned you were a teacher. Funny, I have a hard time picturing it. But hell, teaching may be your ticket. I don't think there's a school within a hundred miles of the settlement."

"MISS BILLINGS?" he called, nudging halfheartedly at the door left ajar. Tory sat at her dressing table, and a maid stood behind her busily rearranging a stray curl or two.

"Look who's shown up at last, Maribel," she said, shooting him a sideways glance without moving a muscle. Her tone wasn't as harsh as he'd expected, not given the circumstances.

"Hello, Miss Billings. Ye're looking well."

"Thank you, Mr. Brock. You may go, Maribel. Remember I'll need you shortly after sunrise tomorrow. Be a good girl and tell the innkeeper, will you?"

The girl nodded, her head bent low, and scurried from the room, closing the door behind her. Wasn't easy to cater to a woman of Tory's temperament. He knew the staff often gossiped over it when the manager wasn't within earshot.

Tory crossed the room to embrace him. "Well, well, well. My wayward fiancé." She draped an arm round him and leaned close to nuzzle his neck before she waltzed back to her looking glass.

"I know I gave you leave to do as you wished, Liam," she said sweetly as she fiddled with her earring clasp. "However, I'm not sure even *I* would disappear for a week without a word."

"I was called out of town without notice. I hadn't planned it. Listen, Tory, about—"

"Have you seen Papa? He was asking after you."

"Aye. I've just left him."

"He's been so busy, now that the time is drawing near. I'm certain he told you we're to leave in only a few weeks." Her earrings in place, she turned her head from side to side, assessing the view in the glass. Seeming satisfied, she sat to put on her slippers.

"He won't be able to accompany me to the Messingers' ball tomorrow. I'm so glad you've returned from your trip. Is your good suit laundered?"

"Tory, please lass, listen—"

"Have you eaten? They brought supper in only moments ago. I'm sure it's still hot." She came to him and fussed with untying his neckcloth, setting his heart to hammering. "It's turtle soup, but not much more. I can order something else if you'd like. I'll ring down for some bread," she said softly, her delicate palms sliding down his waistcoat as she unbuttoned it. "You smell like dust. Have you only just returned?"

He grabbed her hands, stopping their journey short. He couldn't do this anymore.

"Tory. Stop. I dinna have the time for supper. I've only come to see if ye were well."

She wrenched free from his grasp, all sweet humor gone. Scowling, she flounced off to the dinner service and ladled out her serving, the soup spilling over the side of the tureen as she did.

She knew, then, that he had refused her offer. Fever or not, she knew. She'd merely chosen to ignore it. Mayhap in the event he'd reconsidered.

He hadn't.

"I'm no' a marrying man, Tory."

"Oh, please. Rid yourself of any notion I'd stoop low enough to marry you. You could be the last man on earth, and I'd not."

"And ye'd be in the right of it. Ye'll do much better than me. I'm penniless and likely to remain such."

"You certainly don't have to convince me, Mr. Brock. Why

are you here? What can I do for you?"

"When I left . . . before . . . I wasna sure if ye'd heard what I—" He realized his error seconds too late as the tureen came flying, its contents splashing. He jumped back, recoiling as the soup covered him and burned a trail down the neck of his shirt.

"Jesus, Tory!"

"Out! I want you out! I never had any intention of marrying you. Do you hear me? I never had any intention. I want you out."

"I hear ye." As could every other guest on the hall and the floor below. "I'm out." Slamming the door shut behind him, he winced as he pulled at his shirt and more of the soup trickled down to his belly.

EIJIT. SHE'D already renounced him—why hadn't he left it at that? Why had he thought it necessary to recount the decision as his?

He sponged gingerly at his skin, the rough cloth chafing, over and over until he'd removed the last of the bits of soup that clung to him.

It wasn't until he'd thrown aside the rag and pulled a clean shirt over his head that he felt her presence. Rhiannon. He closed his eyes, gritting his teeth against the visceral wave of yearning that uncoiled in his chest.

It had begun yesterday, the yearning, when he'd ridden in from Chester. The closer he got to Philadelphia, the stronger it grew. He had wanted nothing more than to see her. Simply to see her and to talk to her. The longing was so sharp he'd deliberately turned the other way, seeking the distraction of the land office.

He'd given over wishing things had ended differently that afternoon at the inn, that he had lain with her. It did no good to tell himself that if he had, he'd be free of his obsession, that the root of his obsession was simply that she was forbidden.

It did no good because he was beginning to suspect it wasn't true. He was beginning to suspect he was in uncharted territory. Men often lost all in uncharted territory, and he couldn't afford the loss.

He turned toward the staircase. "Good evening, Mrs. Ross. I hadn't expected ye."

She flushed at his words, then stepped into the room, her manner seeming uncertain. He wondered how long she had been standing there and what he had done this time to have her behave so.

"I did knock, but the boys are noisier than usual tonight, aren't they? What happened?" She reached out to touch him, then dropped her hand as if she thought the better of it. "Your neck . . . it looks as if you've scalded yourself."

"I stepped in the path of a flying tureen."

"Is that what I smell?" She reached for the shirt he'd discarded and sniffed. "Gardenia spiced with curry," she said, wrinkling her nose. "Not a complementary combination, is it? I'm surprised you haven't learned to move faster, Mr. Brock."

"Aye, well. I've found it's often best if the anger doesna fester. I'm willing to pay the small price of a laundress."

"I encountered the girl who came to the inn. She was in the Market on Saturday. She said Miss Billings has fully recovered."

"Well enough." He wasn't certain he should speak to her of Tory. It struck him as disloyal. Not to Tory, but to her. He knew she didn't care one way or another what he did or who he saw. But nonetheless, it struck him as disloyal.

"I'm glad to see ye, lass. I'm always glad. But why have ye come?"

"I know it's not my turn to take the class, but I thought I'd offer. You've been so busy. What you did for Tom was—"

"Let's no' speak of it, aye?"

She frowned, seeming puzzled by his shortness. "Very well. Would you like me to leave?"

"Nay. Nay, of course not. I'd like it very much if ye'd stay. I could use your help with the lassies. Seems I'm a bit off with women this night. Ye can save me from further misjudgments, aye?"

"Honestly, Mr. Brock," she answered with a playful smirk as

she plucked a bit of parsley from his chin, holding it up for view. "You give me far too much credit. I'm not sure how you arrived at the notion I can perform miracles."

60

"IT'S STRAIGHTFORWARD, Beth, once you reason it out. Each dollar has a hundred pennies. So instead of writing this as one dollar, thirty pennies, I would write one point thirty dollars."

Sprawled belly down on the parlor floor in front of the fireplace, her legs bent at the knee and her ankles crossed and swinging, Rhee clutched a slate pencil and scribbled figures as she worked on making sense of the decimal system and the proposed United States currency. Grandmother had retired, otherwise even Rhee wouldn't have dared assume so unladylike a position. Her own position would likely bring a frown, given her feet were resting in David's lap.

"I understand that, Rhee. But how does that help you decide how many dollars the tariff should be per night?"

Rhee frowned, then yawned as she reached for Becca and ruffled her ears. "It doesn't." She glanced at David, slumped in his seat, eyes closed and harmonica forgotten in his lap as he half-heartedly rubbed Elisabeth's feet. "He's no help."

"I can hear ye, Rhee."

"Well, do you know?"

"Nay."

"See? No help."

"Ye give the coves too much credit. The rate of exchange's no' near to being decided. What's your hurry?"

"I told Rhee you wouldn't mind printing her rate sheets for her. She wanted to write them out for you before she set sail. You don't mind, do you?"

"Course not. But ye're not leaving for a while. Not before the baby comes, aye?"

"Whether I do or not, I expect you'll be very busy at that time, and I don't want to impose," Rhee answered.

"Write it out in Pennsylvania's currency, lass. The bill is still in Congress, and even once it's out, it's likely to be a year 'fore anything comes of it. They'll no' be printing money next month."

"Well, then, all right."

"I'll show you the ornaments tomorrow, and ye can choose which you'd like for the border. If ye find your rates differ in May, I'll make the change."

Rhee's face lit in anticipation, and she switched from her slate to her paper, swiftly sketching the design of her broadsheet. Elisabeth was worried sick about her sailing to the Caribbean, but she dared not voice her concerns. She knew she needed to settle the purchase of the inn with Mr. Ross and to clarify the status of her marriage as well. Rhee anticipated he'd be so intrigued with her venture he'd accompany her on her return to Philadelphia. Elisabeth wasn't so sure.

"Mr. Hale said he'd book my passage today. I might be sailing next month," she said, her features fixed in concentration as she worked out the design of a corner.

"Next month!"

"I want to be back before you leave for Baltimore."

"But you might not have heard back from Mr. Ross before then."

She shrugged, tossing the pencil aside as she sat, crossing her legs before her and pulling Becca into her lap. "I've no reason to wait. I am the man's wife after all, so I needn't have an invitation. The sooner I leave, the sooner I can return and get started."

"She'll avoid the summer storms, Bess. As well as island fever."

"Well, yes, but . . . never mind. It's only you took me by

surprise. Of course, the sooner you return, the better." Next month?

Rhee reached for her glass, taking a slow swallow of Papa's best whisky before she passed it to David. David would never pour it on his own, but he didn't mind sharing. "Perhaps you could tell your wife, David, how a woman might entice her husband from his mistress's bed to her own."

David's eyes widened and a flush crept up his neck. He didn't comment.

"She's teasing, David. Papa's whisky is strong."

"Oh, no, I'm not. I intend to make the most of this trip. You see, I'd like to have a child. I'd rather you tell me, Beth, than search out advice elsewhere."

Elisabeth wondered whom she meant by "elsewhere." Rhee had asked her not to share confidences about her marriage outside the family. Did Rhee now consider Liam family? Surely not.

"I'll see what I can do," she said, tickling David with her stockinged feet. He stilled them with one big hand, glaring at her, this apparently being one of the times his strict Presbyterian upbringing chose to rear its head. She smiled sweetly, and his expression softened.

Becca cocked her head, alert to a noise only she had heard, then raced to the front door. Papa was home. Rhee jumped up, took the glass from David's hand, and settled herself demurely on the settee beside Elisabeth. David placed Elisabeth's feet on the floor and rose from his chair to greet her Papa.

"Did ye enjoy the theatre, sir?" he asked, as Hale entered the room, his hat in hand.

"I did. Thank you, David."

"Would you like a drink, Mr. Hale?"

"Yes, Rhiannon, if I've any left," he said, with a pointed glance at the glass by her side.

"Oh, you've heaps left. I've been to the cellar to check."

He laughed, taking the chair by the fire, the seat David had vacated. "Of course you have."

"How were your seats?"

Voices Whisper

Rhee had seen *The Widow of Malabar* in London last May. She had attended the American version this season, escorted by one of the endless gentlemen that came calling. As soon as she had come home, she'd drawn a map of the interior of the playhouse, indicating the best spots to sit with an 'x'.

"Honestly, Elisabeth," she'd said as she pointed out three marks, "the best seats are most likely on the front bench of the gallery. But naturally, your father can't sit there with Miss Allen. Now, Mr. Murdock and I sat in countless spots once the play finished, and we determined these three had an unobstructed view. He's a very agreeable escort, my Mr. Murdock." So agreeable Rhee could tolerate his company no more than once a sen'night. Any more, she said, and he would bore her silly with his obsequiousness.

So, with Grandmother's blessing, Rhee had insisted Tom go to Southwark Theatre early this afternoon with instructions on exactly where to sit to reserve a spot for Papa and Miss Allen. He was not even to use the privy until Papa showed to retrieve the seats. It was the first time she had ever seen Tom flustered, though the only indication he'd given was a slight flaring of his nostrils. The second time was when he'd returned and pointed out on Rhee's drawing the seats he'd secured. She had thrown her arms around him, thrilled, declaring he'd obtained the very best seats in the house. That time, the man's black skin had colored a most unbecoming shade of rust.

"The seats were perfect, Rhiannon," Papa was saying. "Thank you for your thoughtfulness. Miss Allen certainly appreciated your effort."

"What did she think of the play?"

Papa shrugged. "I expect she enjoyed it."

Rhee shook her head, her mouth slanted in an expression of amusement. Elisabeth knew she thought the story wildly romantic. It told of a recent widow condemned by a priest to throw herself atop her late husband's funeral pyre. Only she didn't mourn her husband, an older Indian man; it had been an arranged marriage. She had had an earlier love, an officer in the army, and by happy coincidence, that officer was the one to enter the city and stop the *sati* ritual.

Papa dismissed any notion of sentimentality, maintaining he would attend the melodrama merely to witness the pyrotechnics Mr. Hallam had promised for the funeral pyre.

"I'll call on her tomorrow and ask her myself. So, were you able to book my passage? Will I be sailing with Captain Baylor?"

He reached inside his coat pocket and pulled out a sheaf of papers, handing them to Rhee. "Yes, and no. Here's the paperwork. She's set to sail the middle of next month. Captain Baylor isn't due back in port for eight more weeks. I assumed you wouldn't want to wait. You won't be taking much, will you?"

Elisabeth's heart sank. Rhee would be gone within weeks.

Rhee shook her head as she looked through the papers. "No, only one trunk. Do you think I should request another copy of the papers pertaining to the inn purchase? The packet may not have reached him."

"Absolutely. I'll speak to Donaldson about it. He's also promised to give me a name of an associate you may contact in the event you experience any difficulty while you're there. I've told you before, Rhiannon; I don't envy you this trip. There's been unrest in the West Indies."

"There's trouble all over the world just now. Russia's in revolt; France and Spain will be soon; and, the Barbary States are in a constant state of turmoil. I can't possibly sit in a parlor waiting for events to right themselves. And besides, Mr. Ross writes that everything is in order on his estate."

"Yes, so you've said. I still recommend you send a proxy in your stead for his signature. You don't need to go."

Elisabeth exchanged glances with Rhee. Rhee intended to put her marriage to rights. She *did* need to be the one to go.

"Rhee's promised to return almost as soon as she disembarks. Right, Rhee?"

"I'll stay not a moment longer than I must."

Elisabeth looked at David and he nodded, acknowledging he remembered. Alex had promised to sign on with the crew of the ship Rhee sailed if the timing worked. Rhee liked him, and he adored her. It would be a set of friendly eyes watching over her.

61 MARCH 1791

DAVID HID A YAWN behind his fist as he gingerly stretched his legs in the small space allotted him. He should come up with a quick notation for "the report (bill, or message) was read for the first (second, or third) time and ordered to lie on the table." It seemed most days that would cover all that was done in this House.

Think of the time it would save, not having to write the words out, over and over.

The gallery had cleared for a short time an hour ago, so as the gents could conduct "secret business." Now they were back, and David settled in his seat, ready to listen to more hemming and hawing and delaying. The orphaned children of the late Lieutenant Harris would likely grow to majority before this committee would decide to allow compensation.

Though Vermont had been admitted as a state last week. Can't say progress was *never* made. He sighed and sat up straight, tightening his grip on the pencil. Mr. Boudinot was speaking again. Best pay heed.

"David," Liam whispered, sidling up the bench beside him a short while later. "Can ye come now?"

The session was near to ending so he nodded, following Liam silently out the courthouse door.

"It's colder in there than it is out here."

"Keeps me awake. How did it turn out?"

"I haven't seen it yet. Lad was fair to bursting, but said I had to wait. Anything new?"

Liam had been anxious for any news on Kentucky's statehood. David shook his head.

"They'll surely finish by recess, aye?"

"I would think so. Else they won't finish half of what Washington charged them with in December."

Danny Nailor ran out from behind Mr. Oliver's townhouse, his arm outstretched, beckoning them with quick shakes of his hand. The lad was a copy of his older brother, Tommy, right down to the lock of lank brown hair that hung across one brown eye and pockmarked forehead. At first he'd thought they were twins, but Tommy had quickly set him right, asserting he was the elder by thirteen months, and five years older than the smallest of the bunch, Georgie. It was no wonder Mrs. Nailor always seemed weary.

He didn't want to see Elisabeth weary like that, day after day.

She couldn't have another baby next year. She didn't have the strength for it. Question was, did he have the strength to see to it she didn't?

"Mr. Graham, hurry!"

"I'm coming, lad, I'm coming. Give me leave now; I've just finished a full day's work. I'm tired."

"You were only sitting. Ain't no one gets tired from only sitting. Me and Tommy, we're the ones been working." He took David's hand and pulled, and David obediently trotted with him round the house to the yard and their project.

The sedan chair set unevenly on blocks, some of which had sunk halfway into the mud. He eyed it critically. Perhaps if it were righted . . .

He walked around the thing, his hand cupping his chin. Liam stood off to the side, his head cocked as he assessed it from different angles. He ignored the boys as they clamored at him, jumping this way and that, demanding his opinion. Moving closer, he inspected the joints he'd had them reinforce, pleased to see they'd followed his instructions meticulously. He tried the door and found it opened without a fuss, though it fought back some as he shut it. Finally, he stepped back.

"Looks sound, lads."

The boys shouted and jumped about, falling all over themselves as they rolled and wrestled in the icy mud at his judgment. Mrs. Nailor would likely be taking *him* to task for that.

There was a lot of laundry with a passel of young ones. A never-ending task to hear Mrs. Nailor tell it. He sighed, adding another worry to his list.

"Course there's only one way to tell for sure. Aye, Davey?"

"How's that, Mr. Brock?" the boys asked in a plaintive chorus. Tommy disentangled himself and stood, holding a hand out to his brother.

"Well, ye've got to test it," David said. "I canna allow Mrs. Hale to ride in it if I'm no' sure it's right, now, can I? I'll volunteer to be the first ye carry."

Their eyes grew round and large in their still, white faces as they stared at him. Finally, Danny spoke up. "I think Mr. Brock should be the one, sir."

"Nay," Liam answered. "Needs to be David, here. He's the closest we have to the size of Dr. Franklin." Dr. Franklin, corpulent to excess in his final years, had been a prominent user of a chair.

David shot him a glare, then turned to the boys. If they wanted to cart for a fare, they needed to be prepared. "Right then." He opened the door and climbed inside. "Careful, now. Take me to Front Street and back."

"Up the hill, Mr. Graham? We can't do that," Danny said, his thin voice veering awfully close to a whine. His brother kicked him.

"Course we can," Tommy said. "We'll have you there and back 'fore you know it."

David closed the door behind him, steeling himself against the brief flash of panic that flowed through him. He did hate tight, closed spots, for sure. "Hurry on now, lads," he called out, his voice rigid from behind clenched jaws.

Liam reached through the opening, wordlessly drawing back the curtain to let in the tiny shred of light left over from the setting sun. He nodded toward the other side, indicating a curtained window he could open as well. Then he slapped his palm twice against the side of the chair, and the boys lifted the poles and took off toward the harbor.

If the ride down was a rollicking jumble, the ride up was worse. He was jostled violently from side to side as they struggled with the climb as well as the load. Maybe this was why Mrs. Hale had refused the chair. It was like riding a ship in a storm, least the way these lads carted it. The dark, airless interior brought forth memories of being locked below in a ship's hold. He bolted free as soon as they set it down in front of Mr. O's.

"What do you think, Mr. O? Wanna try it?" Tommy asked. Mr. Oliver had joined Liam at the front stoop, waiting for them under the lamp. David gave a slight shake of his head when Mr. O looked his way.

"I'll wait until daytime, boys. I need to speak to Mr. Brock right now."

David quirked a side of his mouth in sympathy at Liam as Mr. Oliver placed a hand on his shoulder and led him inside. Mr. Oliver had not been happy with Liam's decisions of late. Wait until he heard about the whisky still David and Liam were designing.

"Tommy, Danny," he said, calling the boys back from where they'd run. "Ye canna leave this sitting here, now."

He gave the boys instructions on what he'd like them to work on, including adding an opening to the front wall of the chair, comparable to those on the sides. "Mayhap a wee bit smaller. Aye, like this," he said, nodding as he traced the outline with his finger. "Ye did good, lads. I'm impressed. Take it on back now, and I'll look in on you in a few days."

He had one more stop to make before he headed home. Now was as good a time as any. He'd get no peace until he'd talked to the man.

Trouble was, he feared he'd never again have peace *after* talking to the man.

"MR. GRAHAM?" Reverend Ewing peered at him from inside the darkened doorway, clearly surprised to see him.

"Good evening, Reverend Ewing. Might I have a word?" He took off his hat as the man motioned him in.

"What can I do for you, son?" he asked, after they had sat and prattled the requisite nonsense for a while.

"It's my wife. She's to deliver soon."

"Yes, I know."

"She's tiny, ken? And her own ma didna survive her second child."

"I'm sorry to hear that. It doesn't mean your wife won't survive this birth."

"Nay, it doesna." He twirled his hat round and round in his fingertips. "I've two things, sir."

The man merely nodded, waiting.

"Well, she's worried. She willna discuss it, but I know she is. Would ye mind overmuch, if I asked Father Bard to visit her?" Elisabeth had attended the Presbyterian service with him since they'd married. She'd promised she'd allow the child to be raised in the faith. But it couldn't hurt much, could it? If she found solace in her own faith on occasion? As Liam was fond of saying, it was the same God, right?

The Reverend's eyes glistened in the candlelight, and he placed a hand gently on David's knee. "No, I wouldn't mind. I expect maybe I should, but I don't."

"Thank you, sir." He wasn't sure he'd have been given the same answer by his Uncle John. "Thank you," he said again.

"And your second concern?"

David fidgeted in his seat, not certain how to word his request. He looked down at his hands and set his hat on his knee while he scraped at the ink that had dried round the cuticles of his right fingers. "I'm guessing she shouldna have a second child."

The man stayed silent, waiting, not helping him out. Or maybe he truly didn't know the question. Maybe he didn't yearn for the comfort of his wife the way David yearned for Elisabeth.

"I'm wondering . . . since we're married . . . and the risk . . ." He stood and paced, mindful of the man's watchful eyes.

"You're wondering if the Church might condone the prevention of conception?"

"Aye. Aye, that's it." He sat again.

"No. Marital relations are for the purpose of procreation."

"Oh. Given the circumstances, I thought perhaps—"

"No, David."

"Hmmph. Well, then . . . I shouldna take more of your time. Thank you, sir, for seeing me."

"Of course. I'll include you and Mrs. Graham in my prayers this evening." His eyes searched David's as they stood in the entryway, until he was certain the man could see deep into his soul. Deep down to the black part, the part that had no intent of keeping hands off Bess.

"I think you may want to speak to a midwife about the significance of periodic abstinence, David," he said as he shut the door.

62

"Sir? I've come by to thank ye again, for everything ye've done for me. I'm also to deliver this for Mrs. Hale." And to get his notebooks back, by God. "May I come in?"

Donaldson looked up from his paperwork, struggled with his focus a moment or two, then put aside his pen. "Mr. Brock. Have a seat. I hear you're planning to go to Kentucky."

"Aye, sir. We're to leave by the fifteenth. Afore I left though, I wanted you to know I truly am grateful for everything ye've taught me. I've been told I'm a trial, at times."

The man snorted, then asked, "Will you be continuing on with law in Kentucky?"

"No, sir. Likely not." Since Edmund Taylor's widow had agreed to sell him that acreage on terms, he'd need some occupation to keep the payments up, but it wouldn't be the law. Not given the remote location of the land. Who would he counsel?

The remote location would be advantageous, however, for the activity he had in mind—making whisky. He had talked to David about it. If he still wanted to pursue it after he visited the Kentucky property, David was anxious to help.

Baltimore wasn't in another world, after all. It wasn't even across thousands of miles of water.

"I'm headed for a remote location, sir. I'm no' sure the law will be of much use."

Donaldson reached a hand across his desk for the papers concerning the women's Safety Net, then quickly scanned the first page before he focused on the second, nodding his head as he did. "She's pleased, I imagine?"

"With the concept. She asked that I bring it to you, for review."

"I see nothing missing. It will serve to accomplish what she wants. She's a remarkable woman, isn't she? Just when I thought she was slowing down, having had her hand in one too many pies, so to speak, she decides to champion another cause."

"Aye, sir." Was this man actually chatting with him?

"She and her daughter have raised more money in a month than my club has in a year."

Interesting. He'd had no idea they'd done so well. Though he knew Elisabeth had peddled the cause to every woman who'd come to visit during her confinement, he had supposed they responded with mere token contributions. Shame on him. He knew firsthand of both those women's powers of persuasion. "Granddaughter, sir."

"What? Oh, right."

Donaldson reached behind his desk for the inkpot and carefully began to refill the ink. A task for a clerk, a task Liam used to undertake. A task that didn't need doing as the thing stood more than half full.

"I had a visit from Justice Blake. He stopped by solely to make inquiries of you, I believe." He took a piece of cloth from his drawer and carefully blotted up the drop that had spilled onto the tray. "Mifflin granted the pardon. That gal owes her life to your efforts, son."

"Her life shouldn't have been forfeit to start with, aye?" He wished people would stop speaking of it. If he'd done as Tom had asked, Sabrina likely wouldn't have been sentenced at all. Now, because of his apathy, she was destined to relive that noose round her neck each time she closed her eyes, from now until the day she died.

"Nevertheless, it was." His duty with the ink complete, he

leaned back in his chair and studied him. Liam couldn't assess the expression in his eyes as the sun streaming in the window behind the man hampered his own. "Mr. Smith and Mr. Jenkins signed the water lease yesterday. Construction should begin in early May."

Donaldson had agreed to act as attorney for Rory in the matter. He'd never told Rory the truth of the situation. He probably should do that, afore he left town.

"Truly? Did Jenkins' attorney change much?"

"He tried, but Mr. Jenkins had no interest in the fight. He needs the cash. Not a word was changed." He stood, gathering the books that were opened across his desk. "I wager you've done more since you've left my service than you did in all the months here."

Likely because the man had him tied to that chair in yon corner.

Donaldson pointed across the room to the clerk's desk. "Your notebooks are in there."

He stood as well and crossed the room to gather them.

"I read through them, Mr. Brock, after Justice Blake came to see me. I was impressed. Impressed enough to believe I might have made a mistake regarding you. That's years of work there," he said, indicating the notebooks with a flick of his hand. "And on your own, from what I can discern. That takes discipline. So it's there. Somewhere. God knows I didn't see it."

Donaldson walked to the bookcase and began reshelving the books he held. Another task for his clerk.

"I recommend you pursue law in Kentucky, Mr. Brock," he said. "It would be a waste of talent otherwise. If for some reason your plans change, consider talking to me again. We can work something out."

Liam froze, glad his back was to the man as he knelt to clear the notebooks from the desk. "Aye? What might ye have in mind?"

"Six months. Monday through Saturday, dawn to dusk."

"Dawn to noon on Saturday."

"Dawn to dusk, all six days. Until you pass the bar. From

that point forward, your time is your own."

"Do ye have the indenture drafted?"

"I do. It's in the top left drawer, right below your hand."

Liam pulled out the contract and carried it to Donaldson's desk, holding it with one hand as he read it, while reaching for the inkstand with his other. Donaldson swatted his hand away, thinking, no doubt, to remind him he must always read carefully before signing.

"I read fast, sir." He read through the last page, then signed his name with a flourish.

He studied fast as well. No telling how soon he could pass the bar.

63

"LIAM," MR. OLIVER SAID as he reached the top step, his bushy eyebrows raised high. He trudged across the room and dropped heavily into his rocker, sprawling like a sack of flour. "To what do I owe this honor?"

Liam glanced out the window, confirming it was just now twilight. To the best of his knowledge, Mr. O visited that woman well into the evening on Sundays.

"I didna expect to see ye, Mr. O."

"Ahh, that explains it."

"Explains what? Are you feeling well, sir?"

"I'm fine. Don't let me detain you; go on about your way."

"I'm here for the evening, sir. I helped the lads build a shed for the sedan chair like ye requested. They were all o'er it." Now that the Nailor lads had worked the chair into fine enough shape, they might earn a coin or two, carting those unwilling to walk the streets. Mrs. Ross had told them she wouldn't ride in it until they'd kept it clean and out of the weather. Now that they had, she was in for a heap of pestering.

"Good. I'm glad you found the time."

Right, then. That was twice now. The man was vexed. He stood and went to the wine jugs lined up under the window, lifting five before he found one full. He should have carted the empties back to market long before now; he hadn't realized they'd piled up so. He sniffed the cheese that lay under the cloth, found it fresh enough, and brought it back to the table with the wine. Before he sat, he rummaged through the crate for the cups Elisabeth had left.

"Will ye eat with me? And, as long as you're here, sir, I'd like to have ye read o'er my indenture contract. I copied it out for ye." He reached into his satchel, pulled it out, and pushed it over the tabletop in Mr. Oliver's direction.

"I heard you'd signed it."

"Aye, I did," he answered, puzzled at the aggrieved note in the man's voice. "I thought it what ye wanted."

Mr. Oliver shut his eyes and sighed. "No, son."

"Mr. O! Ye said—"

"I believe I said you should follow through on the opportunities given. The semester. The trial. In your impatience, you ignored the advantages the trial offered." He reached for the papers and adjusted his spectacles, then looked up again. "Had you even given the matter due thought before you signed? One minute you're running from it to follow another half-formed dream, the next you're embracing it."

Jesus, Mary, and Joseph. Was there no pleasing the man, then?

Liam rose to add another log to the fire. He *had* given thought to the matter. For two years now, he'd given thought to the matter. He refilled his wine while the man read, nursing the wrong as he did.

It wasn't a lark, if that's what Mr. O thought. Liam knew well enough what he was committing to afore he signed. It's what had had him in knots all last fall. He kept his eyes on Mr. O until he'd finished the last page and set the papers back with no more comment than a grunt.

"Is it ye think it a waste of my time, then?"

"Why would I think that, Liam?"

"Do ye think I canna do it? That I no' have it in me?" He drummed his fingers on the contract, keeping time with an agitated rhythm only he could hear. "Ye think someone like me will no' draw the clients needed? The trust needed? Is that it, then?" Mr. Oliver only stared at him, his mouth agape, his pale blue eyes glistening. "Well, sir?"

"Why did you sign?"

"What do you mean, why? I needed to do something, aye? Jesus, the years ye've invested. I needed to do something."

"The years I've invested?"

Liam winced. It wasn't often the man shouted, and it never failed to take him by surprise.

"Good God Almighty! The years I've invested?" Oliver closed his eyes and shook his head. He rose slowly, as if he were in pain, and headed toward the window. Finishing his wine in a swallow, he reached for his whisky bottle. He turned to Liam, his eyebrows raised and bottle held high. Liam nodded, and he brought it to the table, sitting across from him.

"The years I've invested . . ." he said again, his voice near a whisper as he rubbed his eyes and sighed.

Something was wrong. Granted, he accounted for some of Mr. Oliver's vexation. It was only last week he'd told him of the whisky venture.

But that had been before. Before, when he'd run out of options.

Though he had to admit the idea intrigued him even now. Maybe he would do it still. One day. He did plan to continue making payments on the property.

But for now, he'd abide by Donaldson's rules. For now, he'd work toward passing the bar. And, by God, he'd pass it before the year was out. He could understand Mr. O's reluctance to accept that on faith, but there seemed to be more to the man's melancholy than his own behavior.

"Why is it ye're here this afternoon, Mr. O? Dinna ye usually spend Sundays with Mrs. Holmes?"

"What could I have done differently, Liam? How is it you . . ."

"Sir?"

"It's apparent you don't know how I . . . you're a son to me, Liam. For God's sake, you're not an investment. How is it you don't know that?" He took a long draw on his drink, then turned his head toward the stairs and sighed at the clamor of the Nailor lads straggling in, armed with plaintive cries of starvation for their ma.

"Mrs. Holmes didn't know she was important either. Or maybe she did and didn't care. I don't know. But she's leaving. She's to be married next week."

Shame washed over him as he recalled his glee when he and Mrs. Grayton had speculated Mrs. Holmes might leave town to marry a widower. Mrs. Grayton had told him the woman's sister had passed, leaving a grieving husband with a passel of bairns he couldn't care for on his own.

"I'm sorry for that, Mr. O." The man sniffed, a grimace turning up a side of his mouth. "No, sir, I am. I know you're not one to give your affections lightly."

He shook his head again, then swiveled to face the fire, his chin cradled in the hand. "You're wrong, lad. You had my affection from the moment I first caught glimpse of you. Always running this way and that you were, to keep things up for your mother. I wasn't sure, not until she approached me first that is, that you'd sit still long enough to learn from a book."

"Ma came to you?"

"She did. To plead your case for a spot in the new school. She came to me not too long after I arrived."

"Did she offer a way to pay?" Liam asked, his belly churning in dread at the answer. Or mayhap in protest at the mix of wine and whisky.

Oliver shook his head. "Of course not. I accepted no payment from those unable to give. You know that. I was glad to have you. You were bright, quick, and eager to learn. A schoolmaster's dream." His mouth closed as he looked at him, his lips twitching as if he were deciding how much to say.

"Liam, when she passed . . . I'm ashamed to say I wasn't completely sorry. Very ashamed, as I know how much you loved her. I told myself I was thankful she was finally at peace. But in truth, it opened up the possibility I could . . . keep you. As my own son." He let loose a long breath and aimed a foot at the fire, sending the small flame flying high.

"With you and Rob both . . . well, I felt I finally had a purpose. Don't misunderstand. I enjoyed my school. However, the prospect of raising the both of you, well, it made me completely happy. There're not many married men with sons as fine as you two." He paused to sip his whisky, then slumped forward as he shook his head yet again. "Good God. An investment."

Liam swallowed with difficulty, his throat tight.

"How is it you don't know your value, Liam? I fear I've failed miserably on that account. Because, God knows, everything conspires to tell you of it. You've two brothers in David and Rob, good men who would do anything for you. Elisabeth loves you dearly as well, and there's not many young women of her caliber. And Mrs. Hale . . ." He paused, seemingly at a loss. "And what about all those women so eager to step out with you?"

The last charge he could easily answer. "I mean nothing to those lassies, Mr. O. To them, I could be any of a number of lads. Most dinna care much if I'm coming or going. We're just passing time." He was surprised Mr. O knew of them, though; he'd never brought anyone home.

"I think perhaps you shouldn't speak for them. But you now, have you considered you chose them precisely for that reason?" He snorted. "Never mind. Who am I to give advice on matters of the heart?" He took off his spectacles and dragged his hands down his face, lingering to rub round his eyes.

"I can tell you, however, that there are many men in this town who will be eager to sign on as a client of yours, Liam. Your background be damned. You mustn't forget, we're in America now. There are different rules for those canny enough to seize opportunity. And you, you're nothing if not canny. And, for God's sake, Liam, think of what you did for that Abernathy gal. Seems that's all anyone can speak of now."

If Mr. O thought he could do it . . . well, Mr. O was one to consider his words carefully; he wasn't one for pretty platitudes. A feeling of relief washed over him, tempered by shame at the thought of Sabrina. Mr. O didn't know the whole of that story.

"So why then, sir, if ye've the confidence I can do it, why is it ye're angry with me?"

"I'm not sure the decision was something you wanted, or only something you thought you should want. Because you knew Mrs. Hale and I wanted it. It's too important to take lightly, Liam. It seems to me you forgoing the trial is just that. It was only last week you planned to follow the Billings to Kentucky."

"But I do want it, sir." He hadn't had a second of hesitation when Mr. Donaldson had hinted he'd reconsider. And not for a single second since, not once, had he regretted the commitment. "And I want to make ye proud; that's true as well. It's no' a crime, aye? Aspiring to make a father proud? And, if I find years from now I no longer care for it, well then, I'll do something else. Ye're not to worry, ken? Ye've prepared me well for anything I might tackle. I'm grateful for that, just as I'm grateful ye took me in." He stood and went to the window, watching those on the street before he turned back to look at Mr. Oliver.

"I couldna ask for a better father, Mr. O. Not if I'd made a list of my requirements and sent it high—I couldna have landed with a better father."

Mr. Oliver's eyes glistened as he turned away. Liam saw him fumble for his handkerchief, give up, then dab a sleeve about his face.

"And I know ye care for me as well, Mr. Oliver. I shouldn't have phrased it as I did. Before. I know better." Well, he did now. If he'd allowed himself to dwell on it over the years, he likely would have come to the same conclusion earlier. "You, Rob, and I are a family. He's said as much to me, if he hasn't yet to you."

Liam left the window and went to Mr. Oliver, placing his hand on the man's shoulder. "I am sorry o'er Mrs. Holmes causing ye pain, sir; I am. Ye might consider . . . well, I find it best to replace a lassie quick, afore ye get to missing the last one too much. It averts all sorts of trouble."

The man's mouth twitched, as if he fought a grin, before it settled back in a morose line.

"I'll keep that advice in mind, Liam. But tell me, is that how you plan to handle matters when Mrs. Ross leaves town?"

The question took him by surprise. That was different, he thought, his grip tightening on Mr. O's shoulder. Completely different. Rhee wasn't just another lassie. She was his friend. Plus she was another man's wife. Had Mr. O forgotten that part?

"Aye, and why no'?"

"Why not, indeed," he answered, reaching back to cover Liam's hand with his own. "We'll see, son, we'll see."

64 April 1791

"DAVID, YOU KNOW YOU can't go in there." Mrs. Hale stood in front of the study door, her gray eyes soft with compassion.

"The hell I can't." He leaned forward, a hand propped on the wall as he struggled to catch his breath, then dragged an arm across his face, mopping the sweat so he could focus. "Pardon, ma'am. I apologize. Please . . . I'm meaning no disrespect. I only aim to see her, to let her know I'm here. Please, step aside," he said, his eyes on the floor.

He couldn't look again. Something in her eyes had shot straight through to his core, grabbing hold of his gut and twisting it in a death grip. If he looked again, he'd heave his dinner right here in the hall.

"Please, Mrs. Hale. I willna show her the worry."

She sighed, placing a hand on his arm, then opened the door and whispered a few words to the midwife who sat aside Bess. The woman rose and moved across the room. He sat, taking Elisabeth's hand in his.

"David, you've come," she said, opening her eyes at his touch, the corners of her mouth trembling as she tried for a smile. "You shouldn't have left work. I hear babies take a long time to be born."

"Aye, well, work had about finished for the day. How are ye

feeling? Can I get ye anything?"

"Will you make Grandmother rest? She's been sitting here for hours. She's going to ache so."

"Aye, I'll ask Rhee to see to it. John says she'll be here shortly. He sent Jane to the inn to round her up." Rhee had been spending hours at that inn, making lists and decisions. She should have been here. But Elisabeth had given them no clue this morning that today was to be the day.

"Rhee . . ."

"She'll be peeved, not being here for ye."

"My hair . . . I'm hot. Would you ask her to braid it?"

Jesus, had she been abed all day? "Aye, Rhee will fix it."

Her grip tightened, and she drew up her knees, her face contorting in a grimace as she squeezed her eyes shut.

"Don't push, miss," the woman said, her hands on Elisabeth's knees. "You must try not to push."

This was his fault. She was too small to carry a child of his. He looked at the midwife. "Where the hell is the doctor?"

"It's not time for the doctor, sir. He knows when to come."

"Hot, David."

"Aye, it is, some." He pulled the sheet covering her, off, finding she was covered in perspiration.

"Cold," she said several minutes later, her teeth clenched tight. He covered her and turned again to the midwife.

"Wha's your name, ma'am?"

"Anna."

"Anna, fetch Mrs. Hale."

"I don't know—"

"Find her." He brushed the damp strands of hair back from Elisabeth's forehead.

"David?"

"I'm right here," he answered, squeezing her hand. Mrs. Hale came in the room, and he whispered, "How long?"

"Since shortly before noon. The doctor has checked in twice already, but he thinks it won't be for some time."

"Can ye have someone fetch fresh linens? Her bed's damp. It's making her shiver." Mrs. Hale left to do as he asked as the sound of Rhee's voice drifted through the doorway.

"Elisabeth Anne! You were to tell me if I needed to stay home. I'd never, ever have forgiven you if I missed seeing this baby born. Oh, look at your hair. David, where's her brush?"

David shrugged.

"It's in that top drawer on the left, Rhee," Elisabeth said with a small smile. "And there's no hurry, not according to the doctor. Will you see that Grandmother lies down?"

"Of course. But let's take care of your hair before you have a rat's nest. You know, by this time tomorrow you aren't going to have a moment to call your own. Are you excited?"

"Mmm."

Lisbeth's grip slackened as Rhee combed and fixed her hair. Mrs. Hale and Anna came in carrying a stack of linens.

"Lift her, David." He did, cradling her, and she looped an arm behind his head, her lips warming him as she nuzzled his neck.

"You feel good. Hold me until the next pain comes." Mrs. Hale caught his eye, shaking her head vehemently.

"The bairn's too heavy for my back, lass. I'll hold ye while ye lie."

"Grandmother said you couldn't, didn't she?'

He grinned. "Aye, she did. I expect she knows what's best." He set her down against a fresh pile of pillows as Mrs. Hale shook out a clean white shift, then he turned while they changed her.

"It smells like sunlight," Elisabeth murmured as they tugged the garment over her.

"That's because it's fresh off the line," Rhee said. "Baby David chose a beautiful day to join us."

"Do you really think it will be today, Rhee?"

"I think so, Beth. But Lord, I don't know."

It had to be today. She was so weak, and it'd been five or six hours already.

"What do you think, ma'am?" he asked, looking over his shoulder at the woman the doctor had left behind. Anna shook her head, no, mute, her face drawn.

"She thinks possibly, lass. Is that better, then?" he asked, as she scooted back against the pillows, settling.

"Yes. My back doesn't ache so when I'm propped up."

"Should I start a fire?" he asked, not sure who to direct the question to.

Anna spoke up. "That might be a good idea, sir. She'll be cold again as the pain changes."

"How far apart?" Mrs. Hale asked.

"Long. Maybe an hour, ma'am." Mrs. Hale nodded and left the room, Elisabeth's damp shift in her hand.

"I'll stay with her, David," Rhee said. "You go have some supper."

Bess shot a glance his way, her eyes wide with panic. "I'm no' hungry. And I'm no' leaving until I must." He reached for Elisabeth's hand. He wondered about the hour apart. Did it mean five hours more or twenty? Did the pain come harder as it came faster? Placing his free hand on her belly, he idly traced a finger round and round the lad's rump.

"Nice," she whispered. "Feels nice."

It might be a girl. Mothers didn't always know. They were wrong, often as not. Bess could be wrong.

"Bess, if she's a lass . . . what will we name her?"

"Boy, David. He's a boy, and we'll name him David."

"Right, then."

"Do you remember the first time you kissed me?"

Aboard the *Industry*. "Oh, aye. I remember it well. You kissed me, first."

"Did not."

"Oh, aye, ye did."

"Well, you were slow." He had to strain to hear her voice. "Tell me."

"It was a bonny day on deck. Cold as a witch's teat, but sunny."

"Mmm."

"I couldn't do much, but I could sit and listen."

"You had been ill . . . so worried."

"Ye told me of home until the sun neared the horizon."

"And you slept through half my words."

He grinned, then leaned over to kiss her cheek. "I liked that ye didna mind."

"Well, you'd been . . .ill . . . I hadn't realized . . . I'd need to become accustomed . . ."

He snorted. "I've heard every word ye've said since."

"You never said much. I wonder how I knew . . . that I loved you."

"It was no' my mind that drew you, I'm thinking."

"Ha." A grimace quickly replaced her smile, as if she were feeling pain, and her knees drew up some as her hand tightened on his. "David, if I don't—"

"Ye'd nursed me," he said, interrupting her quickly, before she could go further down that path. "I felt your hands on me."

"Fever. You can't possibly remember."

"Ye saying I dreamt it? I know I felt small, soft hands, traveling everywhere." He drew the last word out, suggestively, and was rewarded with a faint smile.

"Liar. That would have been your uncle. My hands never . . ."

Her words died out as she fell into a fitful sleep. "Canna blame a lad for dreaming," he whispered, his eyes wet with unshed tears. He ducked his head as Rhee caressed his shoulder.

"I'll be back, David," Rhee said. She left, taking Anna with her. He waited until he heard the soft click of the door closing, then he dropped to his knees and started praying, one hand still gripping his wife's as he held on for dear life.

65

"COCKY SON OF A BITCH, isn't he?"

"Wily son of a whore is more the way of it."

"You're only tetchy he out-argued you."

"The hell he did. The bastard cheated. He had to have had Donaldson coach him."

"I wonder how he merited Donaldson. Lucky break that . . ."

Kneeling beneath the table to retrieve his pencil, Liam froze. His pencil snapped within his rigid grip as the words drifted off, and he realized the lads were speaking of him. He knew the voices, of course; he had just sat aside them in Judge Wilson's moot legislature, arguing over whether property should be represented in Pennsylvania. Though he wouldn't have named them friends, given their status as sons of Philadelphia's elite, he'd never before suspected the depth of animosity.

But he couldn't stir enough of an answering anger to respond. Another day, he'd have wiped the floor with their faces or have gone down trying. He'd have never let the insults pass.

But this day, he would. Aye. This day, he would. Their slander paled in comparison to the worry he had this day.

"STILL? IT CANNA be still, John. Does it always take this long? Something's wrong, aye? Is that why it's so long?"

John only shook his head, mute, his eyes heavy with worry as he bent to stir his kettle. The smell wafting about the kitchen set his stomach to roaring, and if it wasn't enough to break Davey free to eat, something *was* wrong. The lad sat rooted to the floor outside the study, still as a statue, stubbornly refusing to leave.

Liam had slept in the kitchen all night, waiting. He'd gone to school first thing this morning, and then on to Donaldson's, knowing Elisabeth would be peeved if she knew he was here, instead of there, though his mind was here, instead of there. And now, there was still no news. Except for her cries, which were coming faster than they had been before.

He didn't know how David could take it, hearing her cries.

Or Mr. Hale, come to think of it. Was he waiting this out alone?

Mrs. Hale entered the kitchen. "John, please go for the doctor." She turned, leaving the room before he could get a word out to question her, and John hurried from the kitchen, calling back to ask him to watch the kettle.

Maybe he should heat some water. It might be useful.

He wished Rhiannon would come in. She'd tell him the truth. She'd tell him if there were cause for worry. And if there were not, she'd distract him. Ask of his day, ask about the moot legislative session, argue the point opposite his . . . she'd distract him.

He knelt and stirred the kettle.

"MR. HALE. COME in the kitchen, sir, aye? It's warmer, and John's got supper on."

Hale looked up, his light blue eyes glistening, seeming puzzled by the request. He'd been sitting in the dark, staring fixedly into the empty fireplace. Liam set the candle on the table and crossed the room to kneel at his side.

"John's got a fire going. It'd be a comfort if ye'd come. The doctor's on his way. You could greet him." How that might help, he hadn't a clue. But Rhee wouldn't like that he'd left the man sitting in here alone, and Liam didn't want to sit in here with him. He wanted the comfort of John's kitchen.

"Mrs. Ross thinks it better if you eat." She hadn't said so; Liam hadn't seen her in days. But it's likely she would say so, if she were here to see. And Hale would likely listen if he brought her name into it.

And he did. He stood, seemingly with an effort, and walked out of the room. Liam retrieved the candle and followed him into the hall, reaching the kitchen as John arrived back with the doctor. Hale rose to the occasion, greeting the doctor and accompanying him to Lisbeth.

David was ousted from the hall. He may boss about the lassies, but the doctor would have none of it.

John set bowls full of stew in front of each of them, admonishing them to take care, it was hot. They ate the meal in silence, save for Elisabeth's cries.

IT WAS THREE more hours before they heard the bairn's cry. David had long since left the kitchen to pace before the study door. Jane hurried in to fetch more water, and Liam followed her out, in time to hear Mrs. Hale tell David he had a son.

"Lisbeth, Mrs. Hale? How is she? Can I see her now?"

"In a few minutes, David. Not yet."

"Why? She's all right, aye? Now that it's o'er?"

"She's very weak. But yes, it's over."

Mrs. Hale looked ready to drop. "And you, ma'am?" Liam asked.

She turned, a faint smile on her face. "Why, Liam, I didn't know you were here."

"Come with me, ma'am. Her ladies can see to her for a bit." He took her elbow and led her to the parlor, pleased to see Tom had started the fire.

"Sit a spell, aye? I'll ask Tom to bring ye some supper."

She sighed, taking a seat at her table. "I expect I should eat something, though I'm not hungry."

"Ye've a great-grandson to watch o'er. Ye do need to eat." Tom appeared, laying out the meal as he spoke, so efficient was the cove. Maybe he could see to it that Lisbeth recovered as well.

66

"HE WANTS HIS MAMA, I'm thinking. He was getting all wiggly out there."

David balanced their child inches from his body, clearly uncomfortable with the responsibility of minding him on his own. Though he was hardly on his own "out there." Jane and John were awake, and her nose told her Jane had changed him.

Elisabeth smiled, reaching for him. "Of course he does. He's always hungry, just like his father."

She brought the baby to her breast, smiling as his tiny face rooted frantically for her nipple. She didn't care what that doctor told David and Grandmother. There would be no wet nurse. No one would nurse this child except her.

It seemed to be the only thing she was capable of anymore. Plus, it was satisfying; little Davey grew as she watched.

She remembered when Elsie, one of the daily women who came to help Jane with the housework, had had her baby last year. Or rather, she scarcely remembered, as the woman had been back at the house, ready to work, one day after the fact.

One day. She herself struggled to reach the kitchen after five. She felt the force of David's scrutiny as she fondled their baby, his eyes alert for any change in her health, and she wished, yet again, he wouldn't worry so.

She knew she had almost died. She knew the doctor had

thought she would die. But she hadn't, and she wouldn't. Not yet anyway. Not until she nursed this child through infancy, not until he no longer needed her.

But what if she couldn't? What then? "David, we must talk—"

"Nay, we mustn't. I'll be late. Here's Rhee coming now." He kissed her and quickly exited, holding the door ajar for Rhee as he left.

"Drink this, Beth. John made it from the blackberries you and David picked last summer. I added an extra spoonful of sugar for good measure, to give you more energy."

She sipped from the cup Rhee held to her mouth, pleased to find the berries still retained a hint of tartness underneath the sugar. "Umm. It is good. Set it there, will you, and I'll finish it this morning."

"I'm not leaving until you drink it all." Rhee sat, spreading her skirts with a flourish, and made a show of settling in as she picked up Papa's paper.

"You must. Otherwise, you'll be late to meet that carpenter."

"Mmm. Shh, now, I'm reading. Did you know there's talk of harvesting maple sugar in the interest of replacing our sugar imports from the West Indies? My, that would eliminate a lot of misery and hardship, wouldn't it? I wonder how Mr. Ross would feel about that. Ha! This gentleman is likening the women who are boiling the sugar to 'woodland nymphs.' Well, I never . . ." She lowered the paper and reached to stroke the back of the baby's head, shaking her own at the writer's words.

"Leave it to a man to portray a woman at work as poetic and picturesque," Elisabeth said. She put her finger in Davey's mouth, loosening his grip on her breast so she could shift him to the other. He was such a beautiful child. She fondled him as he latched on greedily, stroking back the soft wispy curls of dark hair. She discerned little of herself in him; he was all David, complete with doe-brown eyes and strong, sturdy limbs. It was too soon to tell, but she wouldn't be surprised if those sweet chubby cheeks hid dimples.

"I wonder what words the man would use to describe you now. You look the very picture of motherhood, home, and all things good," Rhee said, her voice sounding soft and dreamy, her eyes bright.

"Rhee, if something happens to me—"

"Stop. Nothing will happen to you. It takes time to recover from childbirth. You mustn't be impatient."

"But if something does, I want you to ask David for the baby. You'd be a wonderful mother, and I know David couldn't care for him. Not unless he remarries promptly, and he won't discuss that."

"Of course he won't discuss it. I won't either." She lifted the paper, hiding her face behind it.

She wished she had thought to settle this before Davey had been born. Perhaps she should simply write her wishes on paper. She sighed and asked Rhee about the man and his maple sugar.

"Do you think he might be right? That our own crop of sugar could replace our imports?"

"I don't know. I find it hard to credit, but perhaps. I think it more likely he has abolitionist tendencies and is merely grasping at hope wherever he can find it."

"Maybe." Rhee started on another article, one about the new national bank. She seemed inclined to sit there and read the entire paper aloud, simply to keep her company. Elisabeth knew she had a busy day planned—she needed to get out and start it. "Rhee, I'm fine," she interrupted. "You needn't worry so. There are more than enough people in this house to look after me."

"The bank news bores you, does it? How about this, then? This gentleman is advertising his nursery now that the risk of frost appears to be over. Would you consider an apple tree? He also has pear and cherry trees, if you'd prefer. You did mention you'd like another tree. Oh, he'll take grain in lieu of credit. Hmm, I wonder if he'd take cash in lieu of grain?"

Elisabeth stretched an arm across the baby's head and picked up her drink. She finished the shrub in several long swallows, then held out the empty cup. "There. Go, now. You don't want to be late. Liam said the man is one of the most sought-after carpenters in town. You'll want to secure him. The *Hope* could sail any day, you know."

Davey had fallen asleep at the breast. She stuck a finger in his mouth, teasing loose his hold, then settled him beside her. Rhee helped her adjust her clothing.

"He's only coming for an estimate, dear; you're not to worry about anything on my account. Did I tell you Mrs. Beekam stopped by while you were napping yesterday?"

"No! How is she?"

"Very well, by all accounts. She and Mr. Beekam are speaking again. It seems he appreciates her worth now that she's gone. She plans to stay on with Eliza, however, at least for a while."

"Oh, thank the Lord." She and Rhee had immediately recognized Mrs. Beekam's skill with a needle, once she had gifted Elisabeth a gown for the baby. Rhee had convinced Eliza, their dressmaker, to take her in on a potentially permanent basis, once she left Mrs. Baylor's. Safety Net would pay Mrs. Beekam's lodging and wages for a month while the women decided if the arrangement suited.

She couldn't be more delighted that now it seemed as if it would. Mrs. Beekam had volunteered to contribute to Safety Net as well, once she got on her feet. It wouldn't be much, Elisabeth knew, but she had wholeheartedly welcomed the offer, knowing it'd be important to the woman's self-respect.

She had understood David's reluctance for her to get involved in another venture. Especially one such as this. The arrangement could so easily have gone awry. But she had had to try. She had had to do something.

"Well, good morning, Mr. Hale," Rhee said, rising to surrender her seat.

"Good morning, Rhiannon." He put his hand on Elisabeth's forehead, checking for fever.

"Did you find out, Papa?"

"Yes, pudding. The *Hope* should sail Friday, God willing."

"How long was the return journey, Mr. Hale?"

"Nineteen days."

"See, Elisabeth? I'll return before June."

Perhaps if Mr. Ross met her on board the ship and she didn't need to disembark.

"Don't hurry on my account, Rhee. David has decided it best if he goes ahead and secures lodging first. I might be here most of the summer, waiting for him to return for us."

"We'll see. Nap after your Papa's visit, and I'll be back before you wake."

She nodded, and Rhee left.

"He looks like David, doesn't he? I don't think I've ever seen a more beautiful child."

"Would you like to hold him, Papa?" She shifted, handing her father the sleeping baby. Her eyes filled with tears as she watched him take him, and his own eyes filled with something resembling awe.

"Thank you, Beth." His voice shook slightly as he stroked the baby's head, his touch soft and slow.

Was he thanking her for the opportunity to hold Davey, or for the fact that she had given him a grandson? Either way, it seemed she had pleased him for the first time in years.

67

LIAM WHISTLED AS HE trotted up the steps leading to the Hales' front door, happy to have an excuse to visit the delightful Mrs. Ross.

"I've something to give Mrs. Ross, Tom. Who's traveling?" he asked, seeing the trunk stashed in the hall. Not that he expected an answer from the man, but merely to needle him with the familiarity. The cove still managed to make him feel fidgety with a glance, and damn it all it if he didn't now seem to enjoy it. Neither of them had spoken of Sabrina's pardon, and Liam was more than happy to keep it that way.

"It's not my place to say, sir. Will you be requiring confirmation of receipt of this package?" he asked, extending a hand for it.

"Hell yes, I will," Liam answered, hugging it close. "I'll deliver it myself. Is she here or no'?"

"I'll see if Mrs. Ross is expecting visitors. You may wait in the parlor by the fire."

Well, then. He'd moved up some, hadn't he—trusted in the parlor on his own. He walked into the room and wandered about picking up this and that, working to shake the uneasy feeling settling over him. It was likely Mr. Hale's trunk.

No, it wasn't. Hale was having supper with the Donaldsons and his Miss Allen this Saturday evening. Nora had been prattling about it all week, asking if he'd like to attend, and then if he'd like to bring someone. He'd finally politely declined, citing other obligations, knowing full well the invitation had been extended only out of politeness on Donaldson's part, after Nora had insisted. Donaldson wasn't one to welcome socializing with mere clerks. He wasn't one to welcome socializing at all, less there was business to be gained.

David and Elisabeth weren't traveling, and neither was Mrs. Hale; she would have mentioned it. Which meant the time had come. It was her trunk. Rhee's. He halted his pacing and sat, taken aback as a sensation of overwhelming loss flowed through him, swiping his knees out from under him. He didn't want her to go.

"Mr. Brock. It was good of you to deliver the paperwork. I presume those are the copies Mr. Hale requested pertaining to the purchase of the inn?"

"Aye." He stood, as courtesy demanded, watching her closely as she sashayed into the room, so as he'd recall each detail come nightfall. Her hair was dressed yet another way, and he feared he'd never remember her style, so often did she change it.

But her face, he'd have no trouble there. She was a vision that haunted him: skin like cream, a hint of peach along the line of her cheeks, eyes the green of the sea, at times calm, at others stormy, and lips the color of Mrs. Hale's most vibrant roses. She never feigned modesty when his gaze dropped to the milky expanse of skin displayed above her gown, the full hint of bosom. No, this lass wasn't shy of appreciating his appreciation.

"Have I dirt on my face?"

"Nay. Are ye going to him, Rhee?"

Her eyes flared at the intimacy his use of her name implied, and she shot a glance back toward the hall, as if she feared Tom would overhear and send word to Ross.

He'd spent over a month of Sundays in her company. Sometimes here, with David and Lisbeth, others, such as one they'd spent skating and the one walking through the forest after a light dusting of snow, with her alone. On each of those days, for self-preservation as much as for propriety, he'd never behaved other than a perfect gentleman.

And now, he had lost the chance.

He didn't want her to go.

"He's my husband, Mr. Brock." She sat, busily rearranging her gown with a graceful hand whilst she avoided his eyes. "And I require his signature," she added quietly.

"I will take it to him. I'll obtain it for ye." He would. Mr. Donaldson would postpone the apprenticeship for Mrs. Hale. She'd only to ask, and he would.

"Thank you for the offer. However, I think it best I go."

Of course she did. She was the man's wife. Of course she did. He couldn't answer.

"You've known for a while now that I planned to go."

"Aye." He watched the smoldering fire as he turned his hat round and round in his fingertips, thinking Tom would soon be in to replenish its fuel. "I expect I didna think it so near. I should get back to the office." He stood, depositing the packet on the table nearby.

"Will ye return?" he asked, his eyes trained on the tabletop as his fingertip traced the line of the grain, lingering round a knot. Return without her husband. As Rhiannon, his friend. Not as that man's wife.

She stood, coming up behind him, her scent enveloping him. "I don't know," she answered softly, and he knew she'd not mistaken his meaning.

He turned to her, suddenly angry. "Were ye leaving without word, then?"

"I only learned of the date several days ago. I thought you might deliver my papers, and I'd tell you then. If you hadn't come, I would have left a note."

He flinched as if she'd struck him.

"A note," he repeated, the words flat as he stared at her.

"Hell's bells, Liam! Would you have me visit her inn to find you?"

He swallowed, his anger gone as hers ignited. He had spent little time in Tory's company since he'd learned of her miscarriage. The only time they had been alone was the time he'd thought to confirm his rejection of her proposal of marriage.

He considered himself cured of his obsession, and Tory had been canny enough to sense it—though he had an inkling she'd expected he'd come sniffing back after time. And God help him, maybe he would have, given his weakness. But he'd been spared the possibility of capitulation, as she had since left for Kentucky.

He'd not tell Rhee she was gone, lest she think it the reason for his melancholy. It wasn't.

"Nay, lass. I apologize. A note would have been something to slip under my pillow whilst I dream." He placed a finger under her chin, tilting her face up so her eyes met his. "Will ye write it still? And add to it what I can be dreaming of? Dinna be sparing in the details, ken?"

"You're incorrigible." She batted his hand away, smiling. "I hear tell you may be able to handle my account on your own soon. I left instructions with Mrs. Hale to see to it, in the event you're able to do so before I return."

"Truly?"

"Of course. I get on much better with you than with Donaldson."

"What if I don't? Finish?"

"You will."

"You're certain?"

"I am. However, I've a bit of advice for you. You may find it easier to stay the course if the course isn't so furtive. At least that's what I've found."

"Hmmph." She was right, naturally. Now that Davey and Mr. O knew of his commitment, he was completely certain he'd follow through. He wasn't about to fail on a challenge before either of them. Not a chance in hell.

"I have another letter for you. Mrs. Hale's not happy with the contents, but I trust you to carry out my directives precisely. I've transferred the inn contract and my accounts to her name."

"Ye've done what? Ye canna do that. Why would ye?"

"Relax, Mr. Brock. It's simply a precaution. In the event I'm delayed and the closing must proceed. I chose Mrs. Hale as she can act on her own. She'll give them back when I return, don't you think?"

"Who wrote it out?"

"I did. Elisabeth witnessed our signatures."

"You did," he said, his voice filled with disbelief.

"I may not have used all the proper 'whereas' and 'wherefores,' but I've stated my wishes quite lucidly, if I do say so myself. Besides, chances are the document will never see the light of day. She'll tear it up as soon as I return."

"What if she marries? Whilst ye're gone? Or what if she passes, and Mr. Hale inherits?"

"Oh, for mercy's sake. Now you're spoiling the good-bye."

She took his arm and escorted him to the hall. Placing his hand on the door, he willed it to stay shut and turned to her.

"I don't want ye to go." The words had been on his tongue since he'd walked in and seen the trunk, and now, as he prepared to leave, they tumbled out before he could stop them. "I don't."

Her eyes widened, and she stepped back as his hand clasped her waist. Threading his other through the thick silk of curls draped about her neck, he drew her in close, reveling in the solid feel of her, so unlike his dreams. He kissed the top of her head, inhaling deeply as he held her, then dropped his mouth to kiss her forehead, lingering only briefly before he sought to taste the lips she'd parted.

"Liam."

She yanked back at the sound of David's voice, laden with caution as he stood outside the study, wee Davey cradled in his arms. As well she should. What the hell was he doing? Thinking to kiss her here in full view of all?

"Take care, Rhiannon," he whispered, walking out the door..

68

"YO! LIAM!"

Looking up, he spotted Alex, waving to him from high in the yards. And not on the *Hope*, the brig sailing to the West Indies, as he'd promised he'd be. The lad scurried down the mast, swift as a monkey, and sauntered over to meet him.

"Alex—"

"Just having some fun with me mates, Liam. I've signed on with the *Hope*."

"Captain Lee. Have ye gone to sea with him afore?"

"Aye, she'll have no worries there. His wife travels with him, oft as not."

"For you," he said, holding out a pouch full of silver. "And for Mrs. Ross. In case she needs ye, aye?"

Alex reached for the bag, whistling as he opened it to peer inside. He hefted its weight. "You rob a stagecoach, mate?"

"Lucky at cards last night." And so he had been, which made him somewhat uneasy. Not often he won that much cash. He'd gone into the game for the sole purpose of giving the money to Alex. Had he won so much because she'd need so much?

"Do ye think it'll be enough to keep you in port until she's ready to return? She may be delayed, ken?"

"That and more. You could have your Kentucky rifle for this." Alex looked at him, his kind, dark eyes thoughtful. "I'll watch over her best I can, Liam." He grinned, bouncing off the balls of his feet, backing up a few steps as he prepared to run off. "Mind she might come to like me more than you," he said.

Liam chuckled, nodding. "Fair enough. Just bring her back and keep her safe."

He crossed the street to the counting house and delivered Mr. Donaldson's paperwork, keeping an eye out for her as he did. He didn't have much time to spare; Mr. Donaldson kept a hand tight atop his collar. But he could afford one last glimpse of her before she sailed.

He saw David first. Saw him lean forward to say his good-byes, saw her place a hand on his cheek as she said hers, then watched her turn from David and walk toward the loading ramp. He stared after her as she boarded, watching as Alex stepped forward to greet her, accompanied by a chorus of wolf whistles from the waiting crew.

Hell. He ran, pushing his way past the milling crowd, mumbling pardons as he went. He brushed aside the cove collecting the tickets, telling him he was only delivering a message. He noted the first mate had signaled two of the brawniest crew members, no doubt to haul him off. They stopped short when they recognized him as the one who had provided a place to lay their heads the night before.

"Mrs. Ross," he called out.

She turned, surprise written across her lovely features when she spotted him.

"Mrs. Ross," he said again when he reached her.

"Mr. Brock? What is it? Did I forget a document?"

"Nay." He studied her, committing yet another image to memory.

"Well?"

"I didna care for the good-bye."

She smiled. "I think no one particularly cares for good-byes."

"If ye . . . when ye . . . when ye come back . . " He couldn't get the words out. He couldn't even recall the words, drowning as he was in her eyes.

"Yes?"

"Ye'll come back?"

"I plan to. You know that."

He felt the eijit now, with a ship full of eyes watching him. He should have brought a parting gift. He could have bought her something if he'd thought ahead. If he hadn't given Alex all those coins, he could have bought her something. Nothing like the jewels she wore . . . but something. Now he was stuck, and the back of his neck crawled with forty-odd pair of eyes watching and waiting. He clutched the token he'd taken to carrying in his pocket, his fingers turning it round and round.

He couldn't give her the token. For God's sake, the woman wore emeralds in her ears and round her neck. She had no need of a hastily carved woodcut.

"I meant to give ye something."

"Yes? What?"

"It's no' much. I had some time, ye see, whilst I was in Chester, ken? I had some time and . . ."

She placed a hand on his elbow and drew him the few paces to the stern, where now only twenty or so pair of eyes had view.

"I'd like to have it, whatever it is."

He should have kept it stashed until she returned, then worked it into bone once she did. As he'd planned. It was best to stick to one's plans. Why had he yet to learn that?

Truth be, he should have tossed it. Once she returned, she'd likely have her husband aside her.

He withdrew the token from his pocket and handed it to her. "It's no' much, like I said. I had planned to finish it in bone, once ye decided on the changes ye were making. I'd planned to give it to ye then, not now."

She studied it silently for a moment, her head bent. He couldn't see her features as she worked out a polite way to accept the grubby, hastily carved depiction of her inn. A polite way to ask him to hold it for her until it was finished, until she'd returned.

"But I never could decide, could I?" she said finally, her voice nearly inaudible above the cackle of gulls and the sailors shouting orders. She turned the disc round and round in her fingers. "You knew. You knew precisely. I don't think this portico was even one of my choices. It wasn't, was it?"

"Nay." He had watched her sketch out plan after plan of renovations to her inn. Each had been discarded not long after she had drawn it.

"You knew what I wanted before I did myself." She looked up at him then, her eyes glistening. "It's perfect."

"I'll rework it, then. Ye'll have it in bone once ye return." He reached to take it from her.

"You'll do no such thing," she said jerking her arms back, hugging her hands to her chest.

"Ye're saying ye'll carry it?"

Her lips quirked in an almost smile. "Honestly, Mr. Brock." She shook her head, and lush, black lashes swept low in an expression akin to exasperation.

"Liam!"

He turned at the shout. Alex canted his head, indicating he needed to return to shore. He nodded in acknowledgement just as Rhiannon called back, "A minute more, Mr. Mannus."

"I don't know how to thank you," she whispered for his ears alone. "It's lovely, and I'll keep it always. Do you think I might ask Alex to put a small hole in it? So that I might place a ribbon through it and wear it? Would you mind terribly?"

He shifted from foot to foot as the yearning he kept coiled inside snaked tentacles round his core, testing his will. Would he mind? Would he mind if she wore it against her skin? Night after night, day after day?

"Nay. It's yours to do with as ye will."

She closed the distance between them, and he caught a whiff of mint as her breath warmed his skin and she murmured, "Thank you." Her mouth touched his for the briefest of instants; a whisper of a kiss so fleeting he wasn't sure he hadn't conjured it up.

Jesus, Mrs. Hale had bestowed kisses with more substance. Yet the longing stopped its prancing and shot straight through him, filling him until he forgot how to breathe. She touched his face, running her thumb lightly over his lips.

"Good-bye, Mr. Brock," she said softly, her eyes meeting his. And for just a moment, just for one fleeting moment before she turned and walked away, he felt as if he were the only man in the universe of any consequence.

She would come back.

"YE HEADING to Donaldson's?"

Liam stared at the ship as it was towed out of the harbor, conjuring up all manner of mishaps. Would Alex be enough? Would he keep her safe?

"Liam? Did ye hear me?"

"Huh?" He wasn't surprised to hear David's voice. The lad had been keeping a close watch on him of late.

"Are ye heading back to Donaldson's? I'll walk with ye if so. I've work two doors down."

He nodded absently, then turned, placing a hand on David's shoulder as they started up the hill. "What are your views on uncharted territory, Davey? Men can lose all in uncharted territory, aye?"

"Aye. But I'm thinking it's more than likely they'll gain all. The dirt we're walking o'er was uncharted territory no' so long ago, ken?"

One of the best things about Davey was that he never pried. But mayhap the very best thing was that he was always there.

"Ken," he answered.

69 Caribbean Sea, May 1791

"Mrs. Ross? Did ye hear the Captain, ma'am?"

Rhiannon stood at the rail, her fingertips tracing her lips. Even now, weeks later, she could almost fancy the taste of his lips still lingered.

"Mrs. Ross? The captain gave orders, ma'am. Did ye hear?"

"What?" She started at the touch to her elbow, then turned to find Alex studying her. "What did you say, Mr. Mannus? I'm afraid I was lost in thought."

"You must go below now, ma'am. Captain's orders."

Hell's bells. Her mouth tightened rebelliously, for the weather was so lovely and the hold was so stuffy. She couldn't remember the last time she'd seen anything as beautiful as this sea. The sunlight sparkled and played over its rippled surface like glittering diamonds. What she wouldn't give for a length of satin just that shade of green. It would make a lovely petticoat.

But that was neither here nor there. And the orders weren't this poor boy's fault, after all; he was simply the messenger.

"Of course, Mr. Mannus. But why?"

Alex pointed to a sail some distance away. She squinted in the direction he indicated, but could see nothing that would cause concern. The sloop appeared to be flying Dutch colors.

"No worries, though, ma'am. Captain says we can outrun 'em."

"Outrun them? Why on earth should we want to?"

He looked at her quizzically as if he were assessing her sanity. "You didn't hear? They ordered us to back up the foretopsail and come under stern. Their guns are pointed this way."

"Oh. Oh, my." She looked again, giving the matter more attention. The deck of the other ship was full of men. Both white men and black men. Many, many, more men than the *Hope* carried. Pirates? From the uprisings?

"You must give me a moment alone, Mr. Mannus. I'll go down directly, I promise." He looked as if he were uncertain, so she added, "You have my permission to drag me if I don't. Be a dear, now. I only need a moment."

Good Lord. It was well past time she stopped dreaming of that scamp and paid heed to her surroundings. Pirates?

She withdrew a page from within her jacket and methodically ripped it into tiny pieces. If she were caught with such a letter in hand, she'd be deemed foolish indeed. Holding her palm face up, she watched as the scraps took flight and danced merrily in the breeze.

She suffered no urge to read the letter yet again. She could quote it word for word, having read it over a hundred times in the month since she'd received it.

"Under no circumstances should you proceed with your plans to journey southward. Your husband advises he will meet you in Bristol this July. You may entertain any discussion of investment then."

Bristol. She'd never return to Bristol. Never. She'd sooner be at the mercy of pirates than return to Bristol. Well . . . perhaps. She'd never been at the mercy of pirates before.

Albert had never been guilty of having any gumption, but for mercy's sake—tasking one's solicitor to write one's wife? Why, who's to say he even posted it?

She reached for her talisman, taking care her fingers didn't rub the image carved into the soft wood, and brought it to her lips. It had been an appalling lack of judgment on her part, kissing a man on the quay in full view of all, but she didn't regret it, not in the slightest. Life carried far too many unexpected twists and turns to leave room for regret.

Alex lingered nearby, his gaze darting from her to the masts above. It seemed she was keeping him from an important task. With a sigh, she picked up her skirts and turned from the rail.

"Don't forget you've stashed me now, Mr. Mannus. I want out the very moment it's safe."

She hoped the men were quick about it, whatever it was they intended to do. She had placed her future on hold for far too long; the time had come to take charge of her fate.

Now that Jamaica was in sight, nothing, not even pirates, would stop her.

GLOSSARY of Eighteenth-Century Vocabulary

baggage – an insulting term for a woman
bairn – a child
bawbee – a silver coin of minimal value (*cant*)
blunt – money (*cant*)
Caslon – an early typeface of English origin
chit – a dismissive term for a girl
close – an alley
cove – man (*cant*)
cull – man (*cant*)
duffil – (duffle) a coarse thick woolen material
eijit – idiot
fash – fret, worry
gaol – jail
masquerade – masquerade balls of the eighteenth century were an opportunity to engage freely in sexual commerce while maintaining anonymity.
moot – a hypothetical case argued by law students as an exercise
sati – Hindu custom of burning a wife with the body of her dead husband
sen'night – a week
skite – can mean a vain, frivolous girl, implying femininity
swiving – to have sexual intercourse
to skink – to wait on someone—stir the fire, snuff the candles, etc.
to take a flyer – to have sex with a woman while she is fully dressed
turned off – the moment when the cart or ladder is driven or pushed from beneath a prisoner, leaving the condemned to dangle and strangle from the hang rope.
wheelbarrow men – convicts compelled to work on public works (cleaning the streets, digging ditches, making roads, sawing firewood, etc.)
wherry – small boat

CAST of Characters

New to *Voices Whisper*:

The Nailors – Mrs. Nailor (widow), Tommy, Danny, and Georgie – family leasing Oliver's first floor

Mrs. Holmes – widow Mr. Oliver is seeing

Mr. Donaldson – Mrs. Hale's attorney

Rhiannon Wynn Ross – Elisabeth's childhood friend

Nora Baylor – Mr. Donaldson's daughter, married to Captain Baylor

Hannah – girl Liam is seeing

Amy – girl Liam is seeing

Molly – girl Liam is seeing

Shad Collin – client of Donaldson's, hosted the house party

Mrs. Grayton – owns boarding house on Carter's Alley

Mrs. Habers – Elisabeth's student, abused by husband

Mrs. Beekam – Elisabeth's student, abused by husband

Bob Jenkins – neighbor of Rory Smith, rights to alternative source of water

Mr. Carlton – neighbor of Rory Smith, threatened water rights

Mrs. Applegate – sells inn to Rhiannon

Sabrina – Tom's daughter

Mrs. Edmund Taylor – sells land in Kentucky to Liam

Sheriff Wagner – the sheriff in Chester

Miss Allen – Nora Baylor's maiden aunt

Richardson – an attorney in Philadelphia

Passengers who arrived on the *Industry* in 1784:

David Graham – of Scots Irish descent, David emigrated to America in 1783 to fulfill an apprenticeship to a Philadelphia printer

Elisabeth Hale – of English descent, accompanied her father to America after the loss of her mother

Liam Brock – an orphan of Scots descent, apprenticed to Mr. Oliver

Reverend John Wilson – David's maternal uncle, a Presbyterian minister

Edward Hale – English gentleman, father of Elisabeth

Mr. Oliver – a scholar, guardian to Liam and Rob

Rob – of Scots descent, apprenticed to Mr. Oliver, marries Jane, moves to Charleston in 1790

Sean – young boy under Mr. Oliver's care on the *Industry*, now in Pittsburgh

Sarah Wallace –Sarah had her eye on David

Mr. Wallace – Sarah's alcoholic father

Crew on the *Industry*:

Captain Honeywell – *Industry's* captain

Alex Mannus – young sailor who befriends David and Liam

Print Shop:

Mr. Hall – David's master

Mr. Sellers – Hall's partner

Robert Store – journeyman in print shop, David's superior

Ian – apprentice closest in tenure and age to David, reached journeyman status months earlier

Samuel – young apprentice

Hale household:

Mrs. Hale – Elisabeth's grandmother

John Black – cook

Polly – maidservant and friend to Elisabeth (deceased 1789)

Tom – butler

Jane – servant

Others:

Rory Smith – owns a paper mill outside Philadelphia

Victoria Billings – Liam's mistress

Mary – friend of Elisabeth's

Eliza – Elisabeth's dressmaker

Becca – Elisabeth's cocker spaniel

Made in the USA
San Bernardino, CA
14 February 2018